DARK RULE

Other Books in The COIL Series

Dark Edge, Prequel
Dark Liaison, Book One
Dark Hearted, Book Two
Dark Vessel, Book Four
Dark Zeal, Book Five

Books in The COIL Legacy Series

Distant Boundary, Prequel
Distant Contact, Book One
Distant Front, Book Two
Distant Harm, Book Three

Other Books by D.I. Telbat

Arabian Variable
Called To Gobi
God's Colonel
Jaguar Dusk
Primary Objective
Soldier of Hope
The Legend of Okeanos

Coming Soon

Fury in the Storm
Tears in the Wind
Steadfast: America's Last Days

DARK RULE

A CHRISTIAN SUSPENSE NOVEL

Book Three in The COIL Series

D.I. Telbat

In Season Publications

USA

Publisher's Note: This is a work of fiction. Names, characters, places, and incidents are a product of the author's imagination. Locales and public names are sometimes used for atmospheric purposes. Any resemblance to actual people, living or dead, or to ministries, businesses, companies, events, institutions, or locales is completely coincidental.

Printed in the United States of America

Dark Rule/D.I. Telbat. -- 1st ed.
The COIL Series, Book 3, Christian Suspense

ISBN 978-0-9864103-3-8

Book Layout ©2013 BookDesignTemplates.com
Cover Design by Streetlight Graphics

To Randy and Shawn,
for their years of
Christian dedication and commitment
to the people of Cameroon.

The Materia

Explorer Vessel - Deck Three
180' long

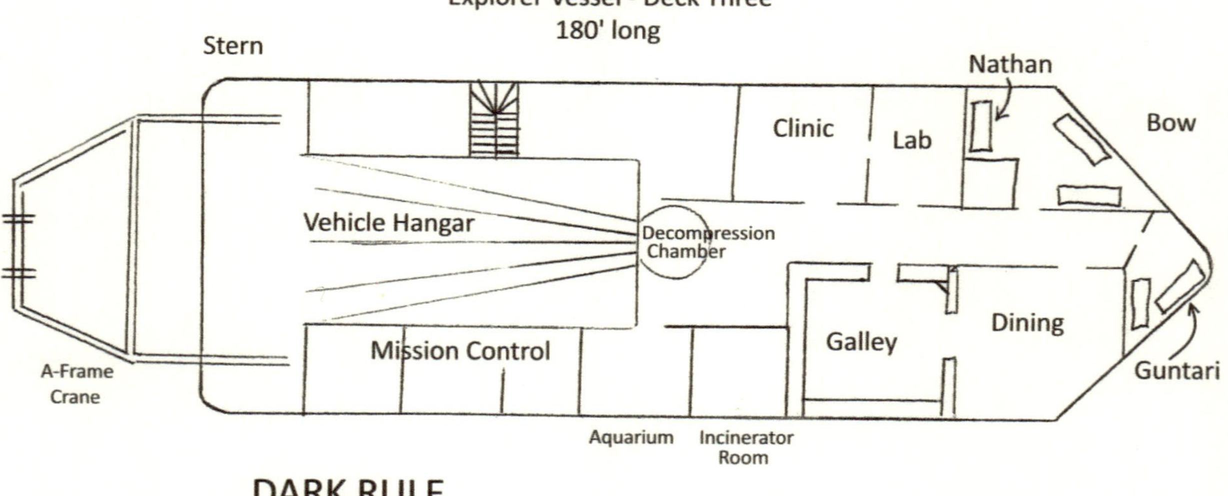

DARK RULE

D.I. Telbat

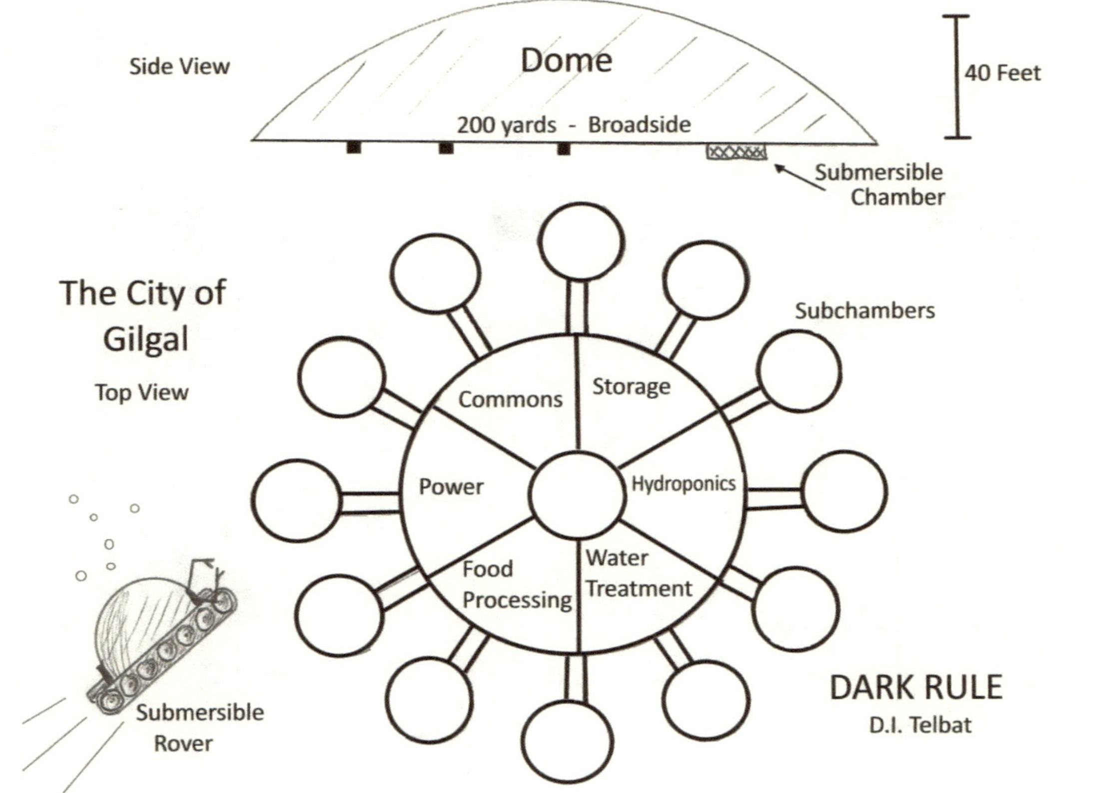

Side View
Dome
40 Feet
200 yards - Broadside
Submersible Chamber
The City of Gilgal
Top View
Subchambers
Commons
Storage
Power
Hydroponics
Food Processing
Water Treatment
Submersible Rover
DARK RULE
D.I. Telbat

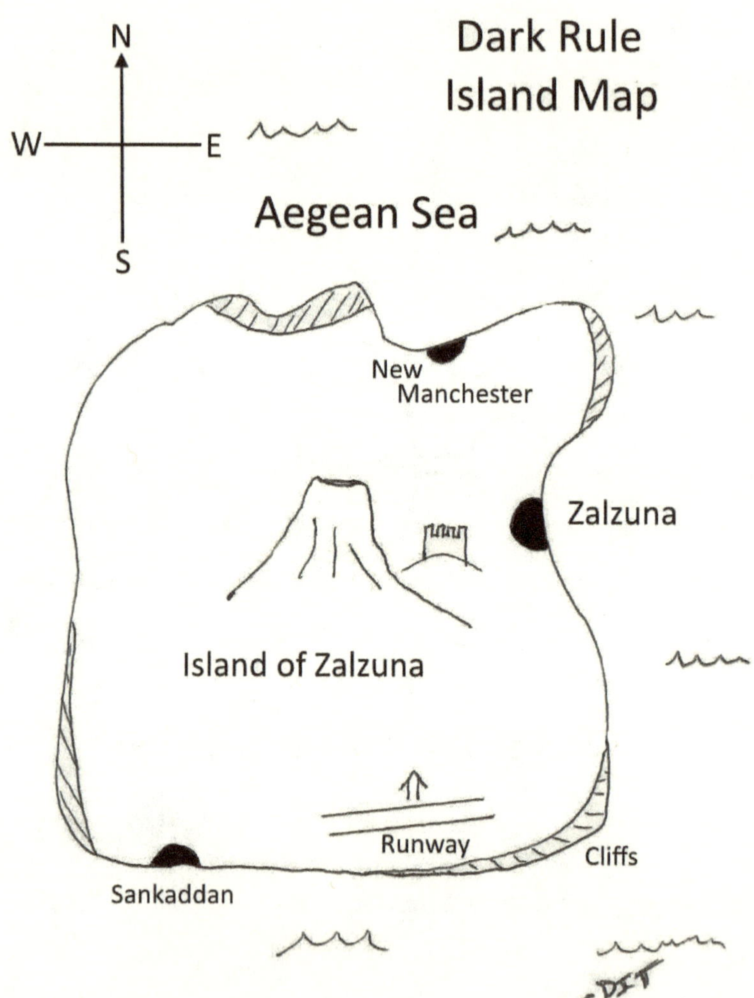

N
W
E
S
Dark Rule
Island Map
Aegean Sea
New
Manchester
Zalzuna
Island of Zalzuna
Runway
Cliffs
Sankaddan
-DST-

✝

Heather Kooper leaped off the roof and balanced on one foot atop a blazing neon sign in Mong Kok, Hong Kong. Two stories below, the narrow street bustled with gangsters-turned-businessmen hustling karaoke joints. If she fell now, she'd land on a car parked in front of a massage parlor. Another sign above the shop boasted in Chinese and bad English of the luxuries within.

Before she had a chance to fall, Heather reached out with a gloved hand and gripped the metal grating. When she stepped off the top of the neon sign, she hung for a moment by one hand above another sign that advertised noodles and a movie for tourists looking for an authentic Hong Kong experience.

"You have four minutes. Over."

The voice in Heather's ear reminded her she didn't have time to enjoy the view overlooking Mong Kok's nightlife for even a moment.

Like the spelunker she was, with practiced ease that would've impressed a gymnast, Heather swung her legs over a water pipe, hung by her legs, then clung to a vertical flange on which she could've slid down to the street. Instead, she applied rock climbing shoe soles to the side of another building and climbed straight up the steel like an island native might climb a coconut tree. One story higher, she reached a closed window. While holding herself with one hand and her two feet wedged against the metal flange, she fit a knife into the side of the window frame.

Click. The window slid open.

"Three minutes, Caver. Over."

"Got it," she said back to Bruce Lavers, a square-jawed Brit across the street. His job was to keep his binoculars trained on the office she was breaking into—to warn her if the security guard made his rounds ahead of schedule. "Almost there."

Hooking a leg inside the window, Heather drew herself inside the lit office where computer screens glowed and a pot of tea steamed in the corner. The office would open in two hours.

However, that first office was of no interest to Heather or Bruce, or Bruce's brother, Clifford, in the van below. Instead, Heather opened the office door to the hallway, checked the span of linoleum, then darted diagonally across to a second office door. After checking the knob, she knelt to pick the lock.

"Two minutes."

But the lock tumblers weren't cooperating. Heather preferred mapping a cave in Belarus over picking the locks of a criminal organization's headquarters.

"Sixty seconds, Caver. You better be inside!"

Stepping away from the door, Heather closed her eyes. She didn't have time to pray, but she prayed anyway. God knew what was happening and what lives depended on that very infiltration of the headquarters of—

She pulled off her gloves with her teeth and knelt again to

her task. In seconds, the tumblers slid upward, and she turned the doorknob as the tap-tap of the night guard's shoes echoed up the hallway from around a corner. Heather dove into the room and pivoted on her knees to softly close the door.

Seconds passed. A shadow moved across the crack under the door. Heather squeezed her eyes shut and pushed the door handle button-lock as the guard tested the door from outside. He jiggled it again.

His footsteps continued down the hall.

"I'm in," she whispered to her mic. "Count five until next rounds. Over."

"Roger that." There was relief in Bruce's voice, which made Heather bite her lip. He cared for her, and she had a thing for him. But now hardly seemed like the time to dream of what adventures they could have as a couple serving the Lord, and not just as teammates on a Christian Special Forces team.

Heather counted down a row of cubicles until she located the office space she'd visited two days earlier. The eighth cubicle was labeled in Chinese and English: *Materia International.*

She sat at the chair and inserted a flash drive into the USB jack. After holding down four keys simultaneously, the spyware wormed into the hard drive and parsed the data that was too dangerous to be caught stealing—and would certainly cause too much suspicion if asked for directly.

The screen streamed an allocation table and stopped suddenly. The photograph of a Chinese national blinked onto the screen, a short biography under the hardened face of the woman.

"I've got her." Heather took a breath of relief. "She's here, guys. She's going by the name of Chen Li. According to this, she's still alive. Over."

"Roger that, Caver, but where is she? Over."

"I have the coordinates. On my way out." Heather plucked out the flash drive and left the chair as she'd found it. When she looked back at the screen, it had returned to seemingly inconsequential sea level erosion and coral damage statistics along the Great Barrier Reef. "Hang on a little longer, girl. We're bringing you home."

PART I

CHAPTER ONE

Nathan Isaacson sat in the cockpit of the bright red floatplane he'd been told to procure in Cairns. From the outside, it looked like any other floatplane, but inside, Nathan admired fresh welds and a complete airbag deployment system recently installed into the control panel. An airbag in a plane? What was Corban Dowler up to now?

The dock to which the plane was tied in the small Australian harbor rocked unnaturally in the water. Glancing up, Nathan saw Corban in a white baseball cap, a black briefcase in his hand. Nathan hadn't seen the ex-CIA agent for months, but it comforted him to see that the aging man hadn't changed. Their world of international espionage was in a constant state of change, but God's people seemed to be in a state of changeless zeal.

"You don't exactly look like a tourist, Boss, at least not with that briefcase." Nathan hopped onto the dock and grinned as he shook Corban's hand. "I got your message. You sure I'm ready?"

"Ready or not, God's people need you." Corban crossed his legs and sat down, the briefcase on his lap. "How's the leg?"

Casually, Nathan studied the shoreline. A man with a dog. A woman jogging while pushing a stroller. A highway with little traffic beyond the parking lot where three vehicles were parked. Finally confident they weren't being watched, and certainly not being listened to, Nathan sat down as well, his left leg extended, a metal brace over his jeans.

"I'll wear this thing for the rest of my life, but it's a healthy reminder of how the Lord kept me alive in Germany."

"I like your attitude, Nathan. Always have. Any problems to share? Spiritual or otherwise?" Corban opened the briefcase and arranged his files, then looked at Nathan in the eyes. "Spending six months with Luigi is good for training, but how's your faith? Luigi isn't exactly a beacon of Christ's light."

"No, he isn't, but I like to think I rubbed off on him a little." They both chuckled, knowing well the stubborn Italian's view of Christians. "I'm good. A little lonely, I guess."

"Yeah, I understand. When God talks about counting the cost, serving alone is certainly part of that price, Nathan, and it won't get any easier." Corban opened a file. "This is a pretty rough mission for your first undercover. You've been an exemplary soldier, but you've been learning that espionage is a different game. Now it's all about being wise as a serpent and harmless as a dove—without the non-lethal weapons you were used to using. It takes more faith and less muscle, I'd say, though there's a place for muscle, too.

"One year ago, I sent this woman to infiltrate an ocean explorer group." Corban passed Nathan a photo of a brown-eyed Chinese woman in her thirties. "Two months ago, she stopped making weekly reports. She's going by the name of Chen Li."

"Does she have a personal transmitter or a beacon of any sort on her?"

"She had one, but we've received nothing for weeks.

Maybe she had to disable it if the company she's around began to suspect her." He gave Nathan a printout. "A freelance COIL team broke into a Hong Kong-based company called Materia International three nights ago. It's the group she joined for a six-month recon since they have communist ties in Europe and they've been publishing hostile propaganda against Christians. These are not nice people, and with all the instigation that arose from the IRO that Team Jaguar uncovered in Croatia, we can't be too careful."

"I read the reports you sent me. According to this data, Chen Li is a tropical ecologist currently on board the *Materia*, an explorer vessel."

"That's right. We think she's still alive, but that's for you to discover. If she's alive, I want you to bring her safely home."

"What's her COIL file say? Is she experienced?"

"Not so much, though she was trained well." Corban sighed as if a heavy weight were on his shoulders. "If you're asking if she could've changed sides, I can't answer that. All of our agents are tested to various degrees, as you know. Sending you in without more information is part of the danger. This is a secret group, Nathan. The few reports Chen Li did make before she went dark suggested they had guns aboard, and there was some rumor about taking over a settlement of Christians, but she hadn't confirmed anything specifically."

"Her silence may mean she's been exposed, Boss, in which case—"

"If she's still alive, get her out." Corban's firmness made Nathan remember how much the boss cared for each and every COIL operative he managed—over one hundred acting as teams or individual field agents. "This was supposed to be a basic in-and-out operation, maybe an evidence-gathering mission, before we contacted authorities. You know better than anyone how the most basic circumstances can escalate."

Corban took the photograph and printout back and closed his briefcase. Nathan looked down at his own hands. He'd known peace and war, but more often war. Whatever burden God asked him to carry now, he knew God would give him the strength to endure it.

"Just tell me what to do." He felt a chill of excitement crawl over his skin. "To tell you the truth, I'm tired of running mole exercises with Luigi. I need to get back in the field."

"You're still a Marine at heart." Corban smiled. "You can't help it, can you?"

Nathan shrugged and grinned, then became thoughtful a few seconds later.

"How're the boys?"

"Scooter's on a new team operating mostly in Colombia nowadays. Bruno's been in Africa."

Rising to their feet, Nathan felt a little unsettled that Corban hadn't given him more details about his old COIL teammates. Perhaps it was for the best since they all thought he'd died in Berlin the previous year.

"Glad to see you're getting used to life without your mustache, Nathan. It was one of your most identifying characteristics."

"Who said I was getting used to it?" Nathan touched his upper lip. "Luigi kept threatening to tranquilize me and shave it off if I didn't do it myself!"

"How'd our mechanics do?" Corban stepped past Nathan and onto the port side pontoon of the plane to look into the cockpit.

"Well, she flew up from Gladstone without incident, but if you're referring to the reinforced fuselage and the airbag, I have to tell you that's got me puzzled." Nathan tapped his foot against the pontoon as he waited for Corban to respond, but the aged spy continued to admire the cockpit. "Okay, Boss, I get it that she's built for a potential crash, but how does that get me close to these Materia International people?"

"You've got it halfway figured out already." Corban moved back onto the dock. "You're a bank robber. There's a gadget in the engine that'll start to smoke on cue. You need to crash within sight of the vessel known as the *Materia*. They'll pick you up."

"Just like that?"

"A brazen robbery will be reported tomorrow morning, and a plane theft an hour later. The rest is up to you. Make an impression and become part of the crew."

"You've been busy, Boss."

"Just survive the plane crash, will you? You're not exactly replaceable, Nathan."

"I'll do my best." Nathan smiled.

"And get Chen Li out alive."

Nathan's smile faded. His reunion with Corban Dowler, founder of the Commission of International Laborers, was over. God's people were in danger. It was time to get to work.

"I'll do everything I can, Boss."

"I know you will. Come up to the car. I've got the cash in a couple duffel bags."

"Cash? Duffel bags?" Nathan followed Corban up the dock. "Exactly what cash are you talking about, Corban ?"

"You're a bank robber, Nathan. I have half a million Aussie dollars in the trunk." Corban stopped and turned to Nathan. "Unless you'd rather be a bank robber with no props to show off to those on the *Materia*..."

"Half a million, you say?" Nathan swept his hand before Corban. "By all means, I'd rather be a successful bank robber than a failed one. Lead the way."

...✝...

At an altitude of two thousand feet, Nathan flew the floatplane toward the coordinates Corban had given him—near the 147-degree longitude, just east of the Reef, deep in the Coral Sea. As soon as the *Materia* explorer vessel came into sight, Nathan kicked a lever into the downward position, which triggered the recently installed engine mechanisms.

The plane's engine sputtered and the controls began to shake, but the plane reacted when he flew it in a broad arc around the obviously anchored *Materia*. Looking over his shoulder, he saw a trail of black smoke against the blue January sky. When it came to boarding the *Materia* as intended, a long list of problems now faced Nathan. But it all relied on him living through the crash first.

He checked his speed and descended in altitude. The surface of the water looked calm enough for the ocean, but he thought of all the other things that needed to go right as well. For one, the plane had to sink so it couldn't be inspected and her new alterations discovered. This put further pressure on Nathan to perform some sort of controlled crash—a stunt he'd never practiced, let alone attempted!

The crew was on the explorer vessel deck now. He had their attention. The engine continued to cough loudly, and Nathan eased her speed even more. The pontoons caught an ocean wave and the plane bounced back into the sky. Still too much speed. After decreasing a little more, he tested his seatbelt harness and steadied his breathing. The plane glided over the surface.

"This is gonna hurt," he mumbled, then pushed the controls forward.

The plane dove the last yard into the sea. The nose caught and immediately flipped the plane over on its top. The airbag deployed and slammed into Nathan's face with such a punch to his nose that he knew it broke on impact. The seatbelt held against his collarbone as he hung upside down. Though dazed, he shook his head and acknowledged the water flowing into the cabin through holes in the fuselage put there for the express purpose of sinking her.

Nathan released the seatbelt and fell onto the ceiling. He splashed around in the rapidly increasing water for the two bags of money strapped in the copilot seat. Without the money, his bank robber story carried no weight. Holding his breath, he fit through the cockpit door and dragged the money with him—the bags becoming more waterlogged by the second. But Nathan had already looked inside the bags at the bundles of money; they'd remain buoyant for a while before they sank like wet rags.

On the surface, he gasped and splashed wildly for effect, in case anyone were watching with binoculars. His leg brace had once been cumbersome, but not any more problematic than him treading water in the jeans he still wore. As he climbed halfway on top of the floating moneybags, he watched the tail section of the red floatplane slowly slip below the waves.

The *Materia* was a half-mile away. Even at that distance, she seemed to be a large vessel, like an oversized tugboat, or a battleship without guns. A blue and white helicopter sat on a helipad near the stern, and above the control tower, a cluster of modern communication equipment clung to a tall antenna. Off the stern was the *Materia's* most recognizable feature—a massive A-frame crane, which Nathan knew from several printouts was for lifting explorer submersibles in and out of the water.

An inflatable motorboat hydroplaned across the water toward Nathan. He waved one arm frantically, but in his heart, he prayed for safety from evil, not the elements. Helping God's people was Nathan's calling to serve God. When wickedness seemed to prevail, God chose to use His ambassadors to prove otherwise. Darkness would seem to win occasionally, Nathan accepted, but the safest place to be was still doing God's will.

The light outboard engine was cut and it drifted up to Nathan. Two men reached for him as another steered the boat. Instead, Nathan offered the straps of his bags to his rescuers—as he figured a bank robber would do, having already supposedly risked his life stealing the money. It took both men to drag each bag into the boat, then it was Nathan's turn. Though he was in the best shape of his life at thirty-two, he collapsed and gasped on the bottom of the tender as if he'd been in the water for hours.

"My plane . . ." He rolled over and looked over the edge of the boat. "My plane!"

"Your plane's gone, pal." One man scoffed and signaled the pilot. "You're lucky to be alive."

The man had an American accent rather than Australian. Nathan had been studious as a soldier for such details, but since being trained by Italian superspy Luigi Putelli, Nathan's senses were on extra alert—except for his olfactory sense with his nose now swollen and bleeding from both nostrils.

The outboard started up and the boat bounced back to the *Materia*. They approached the starboard side where an access door sat ajar in the hull, only a few feet above the surface. Above, a davit arm hung where two men operated the controls of the winch system. Others from the access door reached down as Nathan extended his arms to them. They hauled him into the ship's dive locker room where men and women gave him space after setting him on a bench.

Nathan panted and held up a hand as if he were still catching his breath. He asked God for cautious wisdom. Now that he was in the lion's den, he was all alone, though he knew God's grace wasn't absent.

"You guys . . . saved my life!" He put his hand on his chest for effect. "Thank you so much! Where are my bags?"

Instead of responding, the half-dozen people parted to allow a dark-haired man through. Nathan started to rise on supposedly shaky legs.

"No, don't stand." The newcomer had a European accent. "You're a little far out to sea for a plane like that. There's not a vessel or island around for kilometers."

"I guess . . . I got turned around." Nathan looked out the open access door. "Where are my bags?"

"My men will see to them. Look at me." The commanding

man crossed his arms as Nathan pretended to have trouble focusing. "Where did you take off from?"

"Um." Nathan glanced from face to face. Someone handed him a rag for his nose. "Townsville."

"You're a long way from Townsville. Where were you heading?"

"Lizard Island, I guess."

"You're an American?"

"Uh, yeah." Nathan grinned. He knew he was being tested. "Is that a problem?"

"What's your name?"

"Patrick. Patrick Gibson."

The commander looked at a broad-shouldered, stocky fellow against the wall and nodded at him. The stocky man left the room. Nathan knew, after so many missions with COIL, that his false identity would hold up under their scrutiny.

"Well, Patrick, you're aboard the *Materia* of Materia International, an underwater exploration team mapping the ocean side of the Great Barrier Reef. I'm Trevor Niles."

Two of the men who'd rescued Nathan from the water entered the room with the two bags of money, and one of them whispered in Trevor Niles' ear.

"Everyone out!" Niles ordered, but the two rescuers remained as the six others exited. A watertight door closed with a clang.

"Patrick Gibson, if that's your real name, you have some explaining to do." Niles reached down and unzipped both bags, exposing the soaked bundles of money. "Do you want to tell me about this?"

Nathan opened his mouth, then closed it and looked down at the floor.

"It's probably better I say nothing."

"We heard some news from the coast a few hours ago. A bank was robbed. Five hundred thousand was stolen. These two duffel bags look to be about that amount. What do you have to say to that?"

"Speak up!" one of his goons, a younger man, shouted and slapped Nathan on the side of his wet head. Nathan took the abuse, but if he was to become a part of the crew, he'd have to project himself in such a way as to gain respect from a crowd that respected only their own kind.

"Mr. Niles asked you a question!" the young goon yelled.

"I'm sorry. I don't think I should say anything. I want to see a lawyer."

"A lawyer?"

The goons laughed together, and Nathan knew if he didn't make his move soon, the sharks would think he was bait, and they'd tear him apart. In years past, Nathan had represented Christ as a soldier armed with non-lethal weaponry. But now, as an undercover operative, there was a line he needed to cross—a dotted line perhaps—to make a point and gain access to what he'd been sent to recover—the life or body of Chen Li.

When the young rescuer lifted his hand to slap Nathan again, Nathan was ready. He caught the man's wrist and stood from the bench. The crewmember was caught off-guard and flinched away as Nathan twisted his arm and shoved him into the second goon.

Reaching behind his back, Niles drew a semiautomatic handgun from a holster that Nathan had already glimpsed.

With his good leg, Nathan kicked the gun to the floor.

The goons recovered, and one charged for a tackle, his arms held wide. Nathan dropped a heavy elbow to the side of the man's head and he dropped to the floor. But the second goon now held a six-inch blade, drawn from his boot, the point aimed at Nathan's belly.

"You got me." Nathan seemed to concede. He raised his arms out wide instead of up, and stepped toward the knife. But suddenly his arms swept forward and clasped the man's wrist with both hands, then kicked him in the abdomen. The man went down, and Nathan shoved Niles into the wall as the commander reached for his scattered gun. Without hurry, Nathan picked up the gun and aimed it at the disheveled men. He'd never kill them, and he abhorred violence, but in this case, it was a means to an end.

"Look, I just want a ride to Lizard Island. That's all. A helicopter ride. I don't want any trouble."

"And what do you think Lizard Island will do for you?" Niles stood slowly, straightened his collared shirt, and combed his wavy hair with his fingers. The other two men remained in the background, scowling while rubbing various body parts. "You're a hunted man. The news said you put a bank manager in the hospital. After what you just did here, I believe it. You're a man who knows how to cause injury. There isn't a safe place for you within ten thousand kilometers, except right here on this boat."

Nathan frowned but his gun hand was steady.

"I'm not staying on this boat when I have a retirement to enjoy on some island."

"Patrick, you can't spend that money. Not yet. You need to

lay low for a while. Look at me. What if you were actually among friends right now?"

"Zip up my money! Kick my bags over here!"

"No! Listen to me!" Niles held his palms wide and seemed remarkably calm, like a man familiar with both the criminal mind as well as getting his way with them. "You're no fool, Patrick. You successfully stole thousands of dollars. You just bested two of my sharpest men. You obviously have skills few men alive can rival. Now, look around. What do you see?"

"What do you mean?" Nathan snarled. "Just take me to Lizard Island!"

"Look at me, Patrick! What's that in your hand? Go ahead. Think this out. You're not among enemies. Come on, what do you have in your hand?"

"A . . . gun." Nathan was willing to play along.

"Exactly. I carry a gun in Australian waters. You must know Australia's gun laws. I'm just an explorer—but with a gun? Look, one of my men carries a boot knife. You probably served in the military, didn't you?"

"Yeah. A long time ago."

"Exactly. See? We're not that different. We both write our own rules. I'm not mad at you. It's your money. You're among friends. Put my gun down."

"Australia does have steep gun laws." Nathan turned the gun sideways and acted like he was considering Niles' words. He couldn't seem too anxious to join them. After a moment, he ejected the gun clip. "How do I know you're telling me the truth? How do I know you won't throw me to the sharks as soon as I'm not looking?"

"Patrick, I don't care what you've done. I'm an adventurer

as well. Look, we're on an underwater expedition. Your plane sank. No one knows where you are, and I run this ship. I have nothing to gain by turning you in or . . . disposing of you. To tell you the truth, I need you."

"And my money?"

"That's yours. It's pennies compared to what I spend to keep this ship afloat."

Nathan seemed to consider the offer a moment longer, then ejected the bullet from the chamber. The round clattered on the metal floor. He tossed the gun and clip back to Niles, but remained ready to move if the man aimed it at him. However, Niles replaced the clip and stuffed his gun in the holster in the small of his back.

Just then, the inner door opened and the broad-shouldered man entered.

"Mr. Niles, the information you asked for . . ."

"Well?" Niles waved expectantly at the man. "Go ahead, Marlon. You can speak freely in front of Patrick here."

"Patrick Gibson was in the US Army. He served two tours in Afghanistan, specializing in close combat and tactics. He wears the leg brace from an IED attack."

"Specialized in close combat, huh?" Niles studied Nathan. "That information is about five minutes too late. Patrick, let me show you to your quarters. You and I have some talking to do."

†

CHAPTER TWO

The buzz about the newcomer on board the *Materia* reached Guntari's ears within minutes. As the captain's first mate and unofficial bodyguard, Guntari wasn't one to associate with the crew, at least not verbally. Though the *Materia* vessel was sixty-one meters long, the living quarters were close, and secrets were few since vents and corridors alike carried voices easily.

For this reason, the slender black man from Ghana waited until the plane crash victim was alone before he moved across the hallway and into the cabin where three bunks were mounted in a triangle. The newcomer emerged from the closet bathroom when Guntari signaled him. The man, tall and muscled, seemed to understand Guntari wished to speak out of hearing of the crewmembers in the hallway.

"I speak to you in confidence." Guntari nodded stiffly, questioning with his gesture whether the man understood his words through his Ghanan accent. "You are not safe on this ship. Captain Sardan and I live like hostages. I have heard you were a soldier. Is this true?"

"Yeah, years ago I was in the Middle East, but—"

"Listen carefully! Mr. Niles is a killer. This is not an expedition; this ship is a ship of death, regardless of first appearances. Do you hear me? If you must appease them to stay alive, so be it. But make an alliance with the captain and me now, or you'll be implicated in the deaths that are to come. My name is Guntari, and I wish you safety!"

The stranger frowned and scratched his head. Perhaps the Yankee wasn't very intelligent, only a soldier who'd by luck bested Niles and his two minions.

"Well, I'm not real sure what's happening on board. I'm just along for the ride."

Guntari recognized a look of amusement in the Yankee's brown eyes. This newcomer was no fool after all, even if he pretended to not understand or care about his predicament. Everyone on board was either a pawn or a piece in play.

"When it begins . . ." Guntari pointed to his eye. "You watch Guntari crush the enemy. Do not be on the wrong side. Remember that."

Before anyone could discover him talking to the new arrival, Guntari darted back to his own cabin, shared with one other man, a mechanic. Guntari made unnecessary noises with his locker space next to his bunk as several of Niles' men passed his cabin, glanced in, then moved on. But Guntari knew it was more than a glance. They were concerned he would talk to the Yankee, to inform him of the conflict on board—and the prize to be had under the water!

A pawn or a piece, Guntari mused. He left his cabin and walked up the gangway to deck four. The seed had been planted in the newcomer's ear—a potential ally. Captain Sardan would want to know a pawn was nearly in their grasp. The Yankee had to be a pawn, of course—since he and the captain were pieces in play!

On deck four, Guntari paused next to other crewmembers'

quarters to listen to the talk. The Yankee was on everyone's mind. Whose side would he take? The volcano was due to erupt in a matter of days—a ship full of greedy merchants and a city full of ignorant Christians to determine the winner. No one involved could remain neutral. Well, Chen Li and the others had chosen their loyalties, and had sealed their fates with the Christians. Hopefully, the Yankee wouldn't be so foolish!

Outside the captain's suite, Guntari knocked three times, then entered. Captain Sardan was seated at his desk, a gun in his hand, but when he saw it was Guntari, he slipped the gun into a shoulder holster under his jacket.

"I need good news, Guntari." The captain was a scowling man about Guntari's age, though he looked much older because of the multitude of wrinkles. "In three more days, we'll have drilled the last sub-chamber. You know what happens then?"

"The new man may be an asset. Two of Mr. Niles' men are complaining of injuries the Yankee gave them after only minutes on board."

"Really!" Captain Sardan rose from his chair and tucked a digital notepad under his arm. "The enemy of my enemy is my friend. Who is he?"

"Patrick Gibson. I restored an identity scan the crew did. He's an American war veteran, thirty-two years old."

"A child, and already so bold. The one-way news feed from the coast is true, then? He stole all the money and then crashed his plane?"

"Yes, it's true."

"Hmmm. That was reckless, but he could still be useful.

How certain are you of an alliance with him?"

"It's too early to know, but he's on deck two with two of Mr. Niles' men, who are certainly there to watch him. So, it may be awhile before I can speak to him again."

"You must! Who knows what kind of poison Mr. Niles will feed him about us. I know well your skills, Guntari, but to succeed, we need others to stand with us."

"I agree, and I will continue, Captain. Patrick Gibson will be ours by the time the last sub-chamber is drilled."

...✝...

Nathan Isaacson was still in his cabin, reviewing the words the black man named Guntari had spoken, when three of Niles' men entered the cabin. By their faces, Nathan guessed they were there to throw him overboard. One of them had been in the dive locker—the one with the knife. His wrist was wrapped as if sprained.

"Hope I haven't taken one of your bunks." He smiled broadly, intent on at least the illusion of ignorance to keep him from another brawl. The scuffle in the dive room had been to make a statement. Now, they knew he could fight. "Where can a fella find some grub around here?"

"Mr. Niles has asked to speak with you." One man hooked his thumb toward the corridor, and the other two men moved aside. "That way."

"Okay . . ." Nathan tucked in his shirt while assessing the situation. Three on one, and they wanted him to pass between them to exit the cabin? "Why don't you guys lead the way. I don't know where Mr. Niles is."

"He's in his cabin in the stern, deck two."

"Right." Nathan grinned knowingly, then clapped his

hands, still unwilling to turn his back on these men. "I don't even know what a stern is. Go ahead. After you."

"Either you go," one man with red hair said, "or we drag you there. Mr. Niles doesn't like to wait."

"I care more about myself than Mr. Niles." Nathan rested his hands on his hips. "Now, I'll gladly go talk to Mr. Niles, but it won't be with you clowns behind me. I may be new on board, but I have the distinct feeling there are some who wouldn't mind if Mr. Niles is informed of my violent death on my way to talk to him. This cabin is pretty tight. If the four of us get to wrestling, someone's liable to get hurt. After what happened downstairs, I'd put my money on you bozos coming right now with more knives. And what do I have? I'm a cripple with a leg brace."

The instant their eyes dropped to his brace, Nathan shot between them—faster than a man with a leg brace should've been able to move. He reached the stairs and descended in three leaps down to the control room. As he opened the door to the quiet engine room, he heard the men stomping down the stairs after him. Nathan hustled through the engine room and down the corridor to the stern cabin—usually reserved for oilers and engine mechanics. Niles probably picked it for its solitude, Nathan guessed.

After Nathan knocked on the metal door, it was opened by the broad-shouldered man who had run the identity check on him.

"Mr. Niles sent for me."

The man moved aside to allow Nathan to enter. Nathan looked back and smiled at the three men as they caught up to him.

The cabin door closed, leaving the three in the hallway, and Nathan was directed to sit on a bunk facing Niles, who sat at a desk. Two goons were behind Nathan, but he was fairly certain he wasn't there to get jumped. According to the black man, Guntari, there was a struggle for power on board. Nathan could care less about the power struggle. What bothered him was that he hadn't seen Chen Li on board.

"Thanks for coming, Patrick." Niles folded his hands. "How's your cabin?"

"It's nice, thank you." Nathan looked briefly over his shoulder. "The men seem to be really taking to me."

Niles and his men exchanged glances, a corner of Niles' mouth turning up.

"I'm an entrepreneur, Patrick. After what I know you did on the coast this morning—and your skills as a military man— I want you close as we proceed with this enterprise." He leaned forward. "You trusted me with your money, to store it for you in the armory. Can I trust you with my plans?"

Nathan considered the proposal. The conflict on board was forcing the two sides to make rash decisions, like trusting him. By the grace of God, because of the power struggle, Nathan hoped he could be enlightened to Chen Li's whereabouts sooner rather than later.

"You know my situation, Mr. Niles." Nathan shrugged. "I need to lay low for a while. I'm good for whatever you need from me."

"Good. I knew you and I could work together. I have, after all, harbored you—a wanted criminal, a violent offender." Niles stood and walked back and forth in the space between the desk and his bunk. Sun shined through the tinted port window, and next to the window was a sonar map of the ocean floor—meaningless to Nathan without explanation. "Imagine if there were a place in this world where people could hide and be guaranteed their safety. How much would you pay for that safety, Patrick?"

"Well, I guess quite a bit!" Nathan laughed. "I mean, look at me. I have half a million bucks, but I'm hiding out in the belly of some boat!"

"And you can't enjoy the luxuries the world offers because you can't feel safe spending that money. Am I right?"

"Yeah, you're right. It's too dangerous."

"Patrick, look at me. I come from an island in the Mediterranean where all people on the island enjoy the same benefits. Freedom is enjoyed equally, communally. Morality isn't a problem because everyone has what he wants and needs already. Take you, for instance."

"Me?"

"If you were taken care of, if you had the same as those around you, do you think you would've stolen that money from the bank?"

"Well, I guess not. Things haven't gone too well for me since I came back from Afghanistan."

"Exactly my point. If you were treated fairly, equally, there would've been no need to rob that bank. Personally, I blame the system for what you did. Capitalism is to blame, not you."

"You do have a point. I just wanted to take care of a few things and retire. It's not like I took millions."

"Now convert that example to the ideal environment. Men and women shouldn't be condemned for doing what they want. I'm not against people working hard for what they want, however they want to get it, like you've done. But then those same people should be able to retire and live peaceably, equally and safely in a place where the world no longer pressures them to buy and sell and upgrade."

"Sounds like heaven."

"And that's what we're creating here, on the bottom of the sea floor, where few have ventured, let alone explored. There're just some stubborn people who are standing in our way."

"You're creating heaven?" Nathan smiled. "Seriously? The kind of place you're describing, underwater?"

"A utopia, of sorts. The only one in the world, at least of this size."

Nathan acted as if he were gullible, considering the offer. This had to be a test. He needed to maintain a balance between being too anxious for information and not caring for anyone but himself.

"I would say . . . fate brought me here." Nathan nodded. "I do have a lot to offer to a project like this. I'm used to being just the muscle for people, but maybe I can do more?"

"Why don't you focus on being my muscle for now, since I have all the plans worked out already?"

"Okay." Nathan shrugged again. "What do you want me to do?"

"You need to prove your loyalty."

"I've already offered what I can—myself." Nathan held out his open palms, feeling this was the moment he'd been waiting for. "What more could I do?"

"There's a dangerous man on board. He's already killed two of my people."

"What?" Nathan felt his pulse quicken. This was it. He was getting intel no one outside the ship seemed to have. But now his biggest concern was which two people had been killed?

"As you understand, I can't go to the authorities. Our whole operation would be exposed. We have an investment here, a purpose for the future."

"Who is this man?"

"His name is Guntari, an African. I'd rather not waste any more of my men trying to dispose of him when you may be able to do so yourself—with ease, if you handle yourself as well as you did this morning."

Nathan bit his lip. He was being recruited to kill a man? Joining Niles wasn't something Nathan could turn down if it would get him closer to Chen Li—though it was beginning to sound like he was merely on board to find out what had happened to her since she obviously wasn't on the ship. Clearly, murder was the key to Niles' side, but it was just as clear to Nathan that murder wasn't the answer to anything, especially to gain information. The ship seemed too small to do any snooping for that information, so he'd have to play ball. It wasn't the first time he'd trusted God to move forward without knowing how He would work out the details.

"It's been a few years." Nathan clenched his teeth. Luigi had trained him for this—the moment when he'd become even colder than he himself knew he could be. "I'll need a weapon or two."

"Exactly what will you need?" Niles gestured to the broad-shouldered man. "Marlon here is in charge of our armory. Marlon, give him what he needs."

"Yes, Mr. Niles."

Niles smiled and offered his hand to Nathan.

"Glad to have you as part of the team, Patrick. You'll be rewarded. Trust me."

Shaking his hand, Nathan tried not to cringe as he felt the icy grip of Niles—which matched the man's cold eyes. Sharks seemed to swim around him, and Nathan hoped he could swim amongst them before they discovered he was no shark at all—and they turned their teeth on him.

✝

CHAPTER THREE

Nathan Isaacson lay on his bunk on deck three in the bow cabin that he shared with two other men. Though he hadn't moved for two hours, he occasionally snorted to give the impression of snoring. But he couldn't risk sleeping just yet. He had to tune his senses to the noises of the explorer ship, *Materia*. And he had to pray. Prayer had been one of the first disciplines Corban Dowler had instructed the COIL field operatives to practice regularly.

No matter what danger Nathan was in, communing with God helped him grasp the spiritual perspective over the worldly. Through dozens of missions for COIL, Nathan had often faced death with his team of Special Forces Christians. But he'd never been entirely alone on a single mission—until now. This solo mission forced him to depend on God even more, to abide in Christ, and rely on the Comforter inside him to counsel and help him in subtle but profound ways.

The dangers on board were immense. To make a statement to gain the fear and respect of some, he'd made enemies of others. The unknowns would've made an average man implode with stress, but Nathan wasn't an average man. He'd been an operative inside most closed-border countries in the world. God wouldn't abandon him, and God knew well the events surrounding Chen Li's whereabouts, or her death.

29

Nathan had only to trust and stand as Christ's agent.

His watch beeped twice and he sat up. Diagonally from his bunk, one of the crew lay on his bunk reading a car magazine. But Nathan wasn't fooled. Until he proved himself to Niles, Nathan would be watched closely by the men. And to prove himself, he'd been tasked to kill the man called Guntari.

Stretching his braced leg, Nathan stood. The man reading the magazine held the periodical a little higher, avoiding eye contact.

Out in the hallway, the sounds of the vessel's giant crane under strain vibrated down the corridor. It was after ten at night. What exactly was Niles up to that he had to wait until darkness to operate? Nathan hardly believed the underwater secure habitat story—with the socialist twist.

On deck, Nathan avoided the stern from where the crane was being used, and where he could hear men and women's voices as they worked. He was anxious to spy out their secret work, but too much snooping would alert men already suspicious of his true intentions. Instead, Nathan went to the bow for his first task ordered by Niles.

Leaning against the slender communications pole at the bow, Nathan watched the various approaches to the bow. He'd been told to rendezvous there with Marlon at ten-thirty. Was it a trap? The lights in the bridge and captain's suite above would illuminate a shooter, and if an aggressor approached on either side of the deck, he'd be noticed when passing a number of lit cabin windows.

A woman shrieked with laughter. Nathan was forced to consider the complexities of the crew. Corban Dowler had known so little about the *Materia* people, but had suspected them to be such a dangerous threat to Christians that he'd sent in Chen Li. Something was amiss, and though his mission was to find out about Chen Li, Nathan understood Corban would also want him to disrupt whatever anti-Christian motives the *Materia* crew might have.

"I didn't believe you would show." Marlon's broad frame blocked out a dim deck light as he approached. He wore a coat, though the January summer breeze was warm, and he spoke with a British accent. "I've been looking forward to speaking with you alone."

Nathan moved from the comm pole and put his back to the deck railing. If need be, he could jump overboard and swim west toward the reef islands—about five miles away. Most of the islands were uninhabited, but it would be a step toward staying alive. Three months earlier, he'd spent a week training in the pool, learning to swim with his brace, compensating with his arms. Without the brace, walking any distance over a few hundred feet was painful and he risked further injury.

"Do you have the weapons I asked for?"

Marlon thrust his hands into his coat pockets and made no move to offer what he had.

"You understand that guns on board are strictly policed—by me. I'm the only one with the access code and the keycard. The armory requires both."

"Why all the security? Mr. Niles controls the ship."

"The equipment we use would be ruined if men fired weapons indiscriminately at the few enemies we have on board. Only three of us have firearms—Mr. Niles, myself, and Captain Sardan."

"And the man I am to . . . dispose of?"

"He has one or two knives, unless he's in possession of the captain's semi-automatic. I'm sure it's nothing for you to worry about." Marlon turned and checked the deck. Was he expecting someone or merely being paranoid? Nathan was glad he wasn't the only one on edge. "With Guntari out of the way, we can move forward with the underwater operation without any threat. Captain Sardan will concede to working with us once Guntari is removed. Mr. Niles wants to control the whole operation, but there are other things for the rest of us. The engineers on board want to reverse-engineer the habitat and make more of them. Me? I can't lie. I'm like you; I'm in it for the money. Imagine the money involved in this thing."

"Of course." Nathan had been trusting God to illuminate a direction in which to proceed. He wasn't about to make things easier on Niles—whatever he was up to. Rather, the best way to destroy two enemies was to turn them against one another. Clearly, Niles and the captain were each fighting for control. But first, Nathan needed some security of his own. "I'll do my part."

"Can you do it without a gun? Mr. Niles doesn't want any equipment damaged. We can't lose any more crew, and returning to the coast for people and equipment is out of the question."

"I'd prefer a gun as backup, naturally." Nathan swallowed nervously. Firearms always escalated a situation, but if he could gain a few arms and throw them overboard, that would be fewer arms for others to use.

Marlon stepped closer to Nathan. His shoulders seemed to

swell, as if he were a bull gathering his bulk before a charge. Nathan rested his right hand on the steel port railing, prepared to move aside rather than receive Marlon's attack directly.

"Let's get one thing straight, Patrick Gibson. I don't know why you're on board or how you knew to be here, but I know your presence is no accident. It's too coincidental—on the eve of our success."

"You don't believe in coincidence?" Nathan scoffed. "Maybe you should be sharing this with a shrink, Marlon. I'm just here to do a job."

"All I'm saying is, I'm onto you. You're not as dumb as you make yourself out to be."

"That seems like a good reason to get along with me, Marlon." Nathan held out his left hand. "Just give me what I need to do my job."

"Mr. Niles said to return the gun when you're done, for all of our sakes." Marlon offered a handgun and a knife, one in each hand. "But you can keep the blade."

"You're the only one with the key and code to the armory?" Nathan hesitated to take the weapons. "I want to make sure Guntari doesn't have more than I do."

"The code is digital, and I alone know it, and the keycard never leaves my body." Marlon held out the weapons farther. "Here, take them."

"Just so we're clear, I hate violence." Nathan sighed, feeling that his statement didn't justify what he was about to do. As a Christian, he did abhor violence, but sometimes roughing up men who were as disobedient as children was like taking the rod to rebellious sons.

Nathan reached out, but instead of accepting the weapons, he took hold of both of Marlon's wrists. With his good leg, Nathan kicked Marlon in the solar plexus while drawing the man by the arms into the kick. The gun and knife—a diving blade in a nylon sheath—clattered on the deck.

Marlon collapsed and gasped for air. Nathan considered using a tranquilizer on the thug—one of four darts built into his leg brace—but Marlon was already incapacitated. With little resistance, Nathan frisked Marlon and checked his pockets until he found a metallic keycard on a chain around the man's thick neck. Before Marlon recovered, Nathan collected Marlon's sidearm and knife, as well as the knife and gun he'd offered Nathan.

"Well, you're right, Marlon. I'm not as dumb as I act. Take your time." Nathan checked the deck. No one seemed to have heard the confrontation. "Take deep breaths. You might be bruised for a couple days, but your diaphragm will recover in a minute."

Sticking the weapons into his waistband, Nathan stepped back to lean against the railing again. Marlon finally caught his breath, but the trauma continued. The crewman held his gut as he rose to his knees, then his feet, though his legs were visibly shaking.

"You'll pay for that!"

"Keep your voice down, Marlon." Nathan felt a deep sense of calm wash over him that kept his own voice from trembling. He was the Lord's ambassador, and as such, doing right by God would be followed by a spiritual confirmation, even when the right thing was a hard and dangerous thing. "I'm not your puppet. I'm not Mr. Niles' puppet. Now I have weapons and I have the keycard to the armory. Are you familiar with the word 'leverage'?"

"Patrick, you're . . . a dead man!"

"Just remember when you come for me, I'm well-armed." Nathan stepped briskly forward, making Marlon flinch away and fall over backward. "You tell Mr. Niles I'm siding with Guntari and Captain Sardan until I get a cut of whatever's going on under the water."

"But we've got the money you stole." Marlon struggled to his feet again. "What about that?"

"And where might my money be locked away?" Nathan smiled and tapped a finger on the armory keycard. He saw the look on Marlon's face. "Exactly. It's in the armory. It looks like you don't have leverage over me anymore, do you?"

"Mr. Niles won't stand for this. He'll think of something, then you're dead. I'll be glad to offer my services to end you!"

"Does Mr. Niles even have to know?" Nathan felt the rush at using the espionage tactics Luigi Putelli had taught him. Now, to turn an enemy into an asset, though it wasn't without its share of risks. "You've got good instincts, Marlon. You're right. I'm not here by accident."

Marlon took a moment with that information, and his head lifted a little. Knowledge was power, and Nathan had just given Marlon a piece of guarded truth.

"I knew it." Marlon swore and ran a hand across his unshaven jaw. "Who out there knows?"

"All the right people. Or, all the wrong people, depending on how close you are to Mr. Niles and the recent deaths." Nathan let that sink in before he continued. "Niles is going down, Marlon. You ever heard of the inter-governmental detainment centers in the Ukraine? No windows. Deep underground. No outside contact. They make Interpol look like toy agents."

Suddenly, Marlon's eyes became downcast, and he stared at the deck.

"Why didn't they come in with choppers and gunships?" He sounded broken. "Why you?"

"They want to be sure when they do swoop in that they know who the real players are. Trials need not be dragged out. Besides, there are lives in the balance, right?"

"Yeah." Marlon glanced up. "They're after Gilgal, aren't they?"

"Marlon, I'm just a grunt like you." Nathan had to proceed carefully. The framework of his bluff was fragile, but he was slowly getting what he wanted. His trained mind recorded specific intel that might lead to Chen Li and the spoiling of Niles' ambitions. "But Gilgal has been a topic of some discussion."

"I did prison time in Morocco years ago. I'm not too excited about facing some secret prison in the Ukraine."

"The best way to move forward is quietly, Marlon. No more killing. You're going to help me." Nathan watched in the dim lighting as the mercenary's eyes lifted and he stood up a little straighter. A clear conscience and hope, Nathan reflected, didn't impact only the heart; it changed a man from the inside out. "I've seen everyone on board at least from a distance. There are a few faces I expected to see who aren't here."

"Defectors. Three of them. About two months ago. They're gone now."

"Who killed them?"

"Guntari and Mr. Niles killed three, but I think one or two others made it into Gilgal."

Nathan's curiosity was screaming to find out what Gilgal was, but carefully. If that was where Chen Li was, then Nathan's objective was nearly met.

"Mr. Niles and Guntari used to work together?"

"Yeah, before we uncovered a plot by Captain Sardan to take over Gilgal for himself once we gained control of it. That's when the lines were drawn. The whole crew but Guntari has joined Mr. Niles."

"And what's kept Captain Sardan alive?" Nathan watched Marlon's face and posture. Body language, under a trained eye, could betray a lie, but Marlon seemed to be telling the truth.

"Are you kidding? You've seen how digitalized this ship is. Captain Sardan controls the power—electric and propane, solar and wind." Marlon's eyes focused on Nathan's new keycard necklace. "You apparently know all about leverage."

"What's the current status of Gilgal?"

"We cut off their surface buoy two months ago, so their communications are down with anyone they may know in the world, but they have a rebreather oxidation system that could last for years. Their food and water are presumably unlimited with hydroponics and the salt water desalinator plant. Those Gillies might be religious crazies, but they know their engineering." He looked over his shoulder. They were still alone. "We're drilling the last few habitation sub-chambers right now, working around the clock. Mr. Niles wants to be done in three days."

"You need to stall." Nathan finally understood why he was there. Religious crazies? He'd been called that before as well when standing up for Christ. "No one else can die, Marlon."

"It won't be easy. We can see the Gillies through the top of the central dome. They're in a panic, and Mr. Niles means to take advantage of that. We've been forcing them into the central chamber a little at a time, but they're still barring us from access to their submersible port. Mr. Niles wants to take control of Gilgal without damaging the central dome, but those Christians are stubborn—or suicidal."

"How many Gillies are we talking about here, Marlon?"

"Capacity is eighty, from what I've seen. Our guess is they have about half that, maybe a few more with our defectors joining them."

"Is Chen Li one of the dead or one of the defectors?"

"So, you really do know what you're talking about." Marlon frowned so deeply, Nathan could see his angled brow in the deck lights. "She was wounded. But I don't know if she made it into Gilgal. I liked that girl. She was one of yours?"

"Who wounded her?" Nathan quickly checked his anger. He'd never met Chen Li, but she was a COIL operative. "Never mind. Knowing that won't help. What are the chances she made it into Gilgal?"

"Hard to say. Anything could've happened down there that night. We've wrecked three submersibles and lost four men and two women. It's black as night and the atmospheres are beyond human tolerance at three thousand feet. One air lock fails and—" Marlon snapped his fingers, "you're squashed."

"Three thousand feet." Nathan whistled. He'd received his combat diver certificate at Key West in his training days, but no one could dive at that depth. "I want a diagram of Gilgal by dawn. I want to know what we're working with."

"That shouldn't be a problem."

"Why aren't the Gillies rising to the surface?"

"Impossible. They're a city resting on the sea floor, and we've destroyed all their submersibles. As far as we know, they have no more of the submersible rovers." Marlon shifted his weight. "More pressing is this Guntari thing. You're supposed to kill him for Mr. Niles, and I'm supposed to make sure you follow through."

"I'm not killing anyone, Marlon." Nathan paused, but Marlon didn't object. "How much does Mr. Niles trust you?"

"He doesn't trust anyone much, but me more than most, I guess, since he gave me charge of the armory."

"Tell him you told me to defect to Captain Sardan's side. Instead of killing Guntari, Mr. Niles can think I've joined them to secretly work from the inside for Mr. Niles."

"This is getting too complicated." Marlon shook his head.

"Let me handle the complications." Inside, Nathan prayed that God gave him the wits to endure. Such a mess of unknowns could only be sorted out by God Almighty.

"And how is this supposed to end?"

"You work inside with Mr. Niles, and I'll work with Captain Sardan, except we both pretend things are normal. When it's time, you and I will make our move. We'll take over the *Materia* and rescue the Gillies. I'll work it out."

"That's it?" Marlon chuckled. "I mean, what's to gain?"

"We walk away, knowing we saved lives and put away some bad people. And you probably won't do much prison time if you follow through."

"I'm either desperate or stupid to be doing this with you." He scuffed his shoe on the deck. "Mr. Niles promised us the Gilgal, not to mention whatever wealth came from what they have down there—technology the rest of the world may not know about."

"Think of it this way: you're about to do the first honorable thing in a long time. Am I right?" Nathan offered his hand, and Marlon accepted it. Marlon had a grip like the weathered mercenary he was. "Knock on my cabin wall twice when we need to meet. Our primary meeting place will be here. Our secondary will be on the helipad."

"The helipad's in plain sight of the stern operators."

"Secrets are best kept in plain sight."

Nathan started toward the port walkway and Marlon began to walk toward the starboard, when Marlon snapped his fingers to get Nathan's attention.

"Hey, why did your people send you all alone?" he whispered. "Why not a team?"

"You've tasted what Patrick Gibson has to offer." Nathan smiled. "I think you know the answer to that."

"One Patrick Gibson is enough?" Marlon nodded. "Right."

"Stay sharp, Marlon."

✝

CHAPTER FOUR

Marlon had never felt like this before—or if he had, he certainly couldn't remember. He was happy. He was actually joyful! But he had to keep it suppressed. Patrick Gibson had changed his life! As Trevor Niles' chief security officer, Marlon had to remain the way he'd always been—scowling, angry, depressed. Though he wasn't the tallest man on board, he was the broadest in shoulder. And his hand of discipline had been firm on those who lacked their own discipline on the explorer vessel.

Donning a fleece jacket, Marlon stepped onto the stern dive platform for his early morning shift underwater in one of the two submersibles. It was a warm January night on board, but the bubble-like rover temperatures often dropped below fifty degrees at three thousand feet.

Niles was keeping pressure on the Gilgal habitat, unsure of what those in the submerged and capsulated civilization might try to do. Taking no risks, he kept their two submersibles on an irregular dive schedule to ensure no one from Gilgal escaped or sent another buoy or message to the surface in a call for help—though the jammers were sure to block any outgoing signals.

"Only five chambers left, Marlon," a shorthaired woman said as Marlon climbed into the deep-sea submersible. Sam was a Scandinavian who competed with him to see who would force the Gillies to surrender first. "Save some for me tonight, huh?"

"You only drilled two overnight?" He scoffed, keeping up with their familiar banter, though his mind was on other priorities now. "Why do you even take a shift if you're going to waste it like that?"

As Marlon eased himself into the pilot control seat, she punched him hard on the shoulder. Before he could respond, Sam blew him a kiss and slammed the access door—sealing it with a twist of the wheel lock.

"She flirts with you," Stajner accused with jealousy in his voice. The skinny Czech had attempted to verbally spar with Sam like Marlon always did, but she'd humiliated him by calling him a toothpick, which had become his new nickname on board. He hated it. "It's not genuine, Marlon. She says you're lazy."

Ignoring the man, Marlon strapped himself into the seat in the two-man pod. If it were possible to operate the cutting torch and submersible controls with only two hands, Marlon would've gone alone.

"We're ready for dive." Marlon gave the operators on the *Materia* a thumbs-up. The twenty-ton capacity crane lifted the submersible upward with a jerk, then swung it over the water.

The water encased the bubble, then the crane released them with a muffled metallic clang. Stajner flipped switches as the rover tractors started up, driving them at a steep angle into the murky blackness below. He turned on lights and digital oxygen gauges. Regardless of his sour mood, Stajner was the best submersible operator on board the *Materia*.

In seconds, they were lost in the darkness, surrounded only by the thick glass bubble. Marlon felt the familiar exhilaration of being cut off from the world in the most dangerous environment known to man—second only to outer space.

"Watch our horizon," Stajner said.

Correcting their angle of descent, Marlon was aware that an underwater current often caused drifting, distorting their equilibrium. If a pilot didn't focus, he could be lost forever in the ocean depths.

Before taking his dive shift, Marlon had given Patrick the schematics of Gilgal, though the two men hadn't spoken openly again as they had on the bow the evening before. Marlon knew that having such a secret from Niles was reckless. The man had a sense for defectors. But Marlon hoped honor was on his side now. He'd been a ruthless soldier of fortune for as long as he could remember. Only when Patrick had given him another option did Marlon realize how much he truly craved the path less traveled. Patrick had opened the door for him to be a hero.

"To starboard." Stajner pointed to the right, and Marlon decreased the rover's descent by stabilizing the horizon, the rest accomplished by automated atmospheric ballasts fore and aft.

They were at depth, and the green glow of Gilgal's internal lights directed them to the multi-chambered habitat.

Wiping condensation off a digital screen, Stajner used the touchpad to program their next target for drilling.

"Two more nights, and they're finished." Stajner rubbed

his hands together, the sensitive controls not permitting him to wear gloves. "What are we going to do with them when they surrender?"

Marlon piloted the rover over Gilgal's main living chamber, a thick plastic dome two hundred yards in diameter. He leaned over to look straight down at people among a jungle of equipment and vegetation, the two sometimes merging inside the close quarters. For months, Marlon had dreamed of what it would be like to be a secret citizen of Gilgal. Now, he anticipated redemption—a door Patrick had opened.

"Look at those fools!" Stajner cursed, working the joysticks on his armrests that controlled the robotic arms extending off the front of the rover. "Wait until they realize their God won't let them breathe water!"

This time Marlon didn't laugh with him, not even a chuckle, as he may have in the past. He was finished justifying the evils of Niles. Marlon had hated the Gillies for a long time, envying them for reasons separate from Niles. The Gillies were Christians, isolating themselves from the world, waiting for Christ's return. Having seen their website, Marlon wondered if all Christians had such tendencies nowadays—to hide from the world. Under so much persecution, maybe hiding was what all serious Christians did anymore.

In contrast, Niles had recruited his underwater mercenaries, like Marlon, to operate Gilgal once they took it over. Now, for the first time, Marlon was disturbed that he hadn't cared if the Gillies lived or died in the attempted takeover. Children and women were down there, according to the website, though the site hadn't explained where Gilgal might be. That was something Niles had discovered himself, using the *Materia's* communication system.

Stajner switched on the external cameras, two angles, to record their drilling and cutting operation. Once they reached the far edge of Gilgal's central dome, the spider-like arms of its twelve sub-chambered autonomous living quarters came into sight wherever the submersible's spotlights shined through the hazy water.

Descending to one of the five sub-chambers not yet drilled, Marlon looked in on the lit dwelling quarters through its twenty-foot-high dome roof, as if spying like God through the rooftop of a residential condominium. Several Gillies pointed up at the roof, the submersible made visible to them no doubt by its many bright lights.

While Marlon watched, the residents fled the sub-chamber, a couple adults pausing on their way into a tunnel passage to power down the sub-chamber—which they seemed to know from experience was about to be flooded with sea water as the other seven already had been.

"Run, little fairies!" Stajner cackled. "Hold your breaths!"

As Stajner turned away and looked down, Marlon lifted his arm and elbowed the Czech hard on the side of the head. He slumped unconsciously against his seatbelt straps. An instant later, Marlon jerked the navigational controls back, then shut off the camera recorders. Marlon had tried to think of a way he could stall the operation for Patrick; he'd have to say Stajner was knocked unconscious when they were bumped from behind, and the cameras malfunctioned. And now Stajner's head bore the welt to prove the attack.

Steering the rover down to the sea floor, Marlon found a

jagged piece of reef encrusted with sea vegetation, mostly seapens and crinoids. He turned the submersible around and backed up to the reef until he heard a scraping and creaking sound, just enough to cause minimal external evidence of a possible collision with another vehicle—but not so much that Marlon couldn't still reach the surface.

Next, he piloted over the central dome and dropped down to the partition of plastic where he could look straight ahead into the chamber of the commons area. A congregation of residents already had gathered there. Marlon watched them flee from the room at the sight of his lights, perhaps afraid he was about to drill the main chamber, but a few residents remained. Perfect! He didn't have long until Stajner awoke.

The submersible idled automatically as Marlon switched off external pod lights so they could see him better. From inside his jacket, he drew a month-old folded newspaper. Unfolding the paper, he held it up to his glass, showing the few residents of Gilgal who were still in the commons area a message written in red marker: "You have friends. We won't let you die."

It was the only message Marlon could imagine that would mean anything—a message of hope. If the *Materia* wasn't already jamming frequencies by a buoyed jammer on a cable, he could've spoken on a channel directly to the Gillies, but Niles didn't want any communication in or out of Gilgal.

Marlon folded up his message and tucked it into his jacket. One of the people inside the dome seemed familiar. A short woman with straight black hair, but bold in posture—it was Chen Li! She was close enough to the plastic to rest a hand on the dome shell. Her other hand was preoccupied with a crutch. So, Chen Li was still alive, her crutch presumably the aftereffects of an injury incurred when escaping the *Materia*. Patrick would be pleased to hear it since he'd asked specifically about her. But what about the other defectors?

For a few seconds, Chen Li did something with her hands, then she pressed a response against the dome plastic for Marlon to read. He had to switch on one headlight and squint to read the black lettering: "How can we trust you, Marlon?"

Initially, Marlon was offended, but then he considered the situation. Chen Li had known him on board the *Materia* as Nile's ruthless security officer in charge of weaponry. Two months earlier, he'd tried to kill her, along with other defectors, and in the last couple weeks, he'd been actively involved in drilling the sub-chambers of Gilgal in an effort to force their surrender—or death.

Since he didn't have a way to write another message for them, Marlon grabbed Stajner by his collar and shoved his unconscious face against the bubble. Chen Li would know him as well, Marlon guessed, since the skinny European who had a sneering remark for everything was always getting on people's nerves.

As he watched, Chen Li conversed with two Gillie men. Marlon wasn't as concerned about being trusted as much as he wanted his message of hope to be realized. Now, Patrick's plan was real—the Gillies were expecting rescue or relief. But would they open up their underwater submersible port on the belly of the city? That couldn't be tested yet. Stajner could wake at any moment. It was time to go.

Chen Li held up a second communication: "How many are there?"

Hesitating, Marlon didn't want to tell her it was just him and one man with a leg brace who claimed to be some sort of secret agent. So, Marlon held up seven fingers. Seven defectors. It was better than two, though it seemed that Patrick was worth six men!

Out of time, Marlon pulled back on the controls and switched on the tractors. As the rover crawled upward, Marlon turned on the cameras for more run-time. Twenty minutes later, the surface above came into sight. The shadow to the west was the *Materia*, and Marlon navigated toward it. Surprisingly, Stajner was still unconscious, but Marlon had checked his steady pulse several times to ensure the man was still okay.

When the submersible surfaced off the stern of the *Materia*, the divers weren't prepared for hauling her aboard since he was two hours earlier than expected. Drilling one or two sub-chambers of Gilgal took time, and sometimes debris had to be cleared from the flood holes and new holes drilled.

Divers jumped into the water to assist the attachment onto the crane. Niles stood on the back of the helipad, hands on his hips, his face hard. Marlon fixed a frown on his own face, reminding himself that liars were often discovered by overreacting or exaggerating. And he wasn't used to lying to Niles.

The rover settled on the stern, the top was unhinged, then Marlon climbed out hastily, slapping away any helping hands—including Sam's.

"Just help Stajner!" he ordered. "And check the electronics. We were attacked!"

Instead of using the interior stairs off the vehicle hangar,

Marlon climbed up the equipment grating and swung onto the safety bars to reach the helipad.

"The Gillies attacked us." Marlon stood next to Niles and watched the divers and crew lift Stajner out of the pod. "They hit us from behind. Stajner hit his head and I lost power. As soon as I gained control, I came back up. We hadn't even started drilling!"

"How could the Gillies still have a submersible?" Niles took a deep breath. "You saw it yourself?"

"No, but I noticed their lights right afterward. They approached without lights, then fled. It was a stealth attack, Mr. Niles. Either they built a new vehicle or had one hidden in their docking chamber."

"This changes things." He cupped his mouth. "Sam! How bad is the damage?"

The woman climbed onto the back of the rover.

"Some scratches. A few dents." She shook her head. "It looks like they hit him hard enough to do damage to their own hull. I'll get the techs to check out the equipment, but none of the cables are broken."

"You're a lucky man, Marlon." Niles glanced at him. "But we've got another problem. Patrick Gibson still hasn't disposed of Guntari. You gave him a weapon?"

"Last night. A handgun and a knife." Marlon felt his pulse quicken. "He may be waiting for the right opportunity, though we discussed that it might be better to get close to Guntari and Captain Sardan, even act like he's on their side."

"Well, I don't like it. I wanted Guntari dead. Patrick's up there in the captain's suite and in the cockpit with Captain Sardan. If I wanted to give Sardan the crew, I'd jump overboard myself! You messed this up, Marlon. There was already ample opportunity for Patrick to kill the African. We don't have time to cuddle up with our enemies when there's so much at stake."

"You want me to take care of Patrick?" Marlon asked—a gamble given his current play. "We were doing fine without him."

"But this guy is good, Marlon. Even with that leg brace, he moves like a veteran of more than he admits. I don't want to lose any more people—even people who don't follow orders." He growled loudly over the wind. "When it's time to move into Gilgal, we'll need to disperse weapons to the others. Captain Sardan isn't dumb enough to take us all on. But if Patrick isn't still with us, then our job just became a lot harder."

"I'll keep an eye out." Marlon felt a tremble deep in his stomach. Patrick had the keycard to the armory. Working with the government man could easily blow up in his face. "What'll we do about the drilling now?"

"We'll need four operators down there, one submersible drilling while a second one watches for an attack." Niles cursed. "That means putting more people at risk down there, and fewer loyal people up here to hold the ship. I feel like something is working against me."

"When Gilgal falls, I want to be down there." Marlon grit his teeth. "They tried to kill me this morning! When my instruments went dark, I was in total blackness. They'll pay for that!"

"You'll get your chance. Just do your part to gain access to their docking chamber. Nothing else matters right now."

"So, you haven't said what happens after that, Mr. Niles. I've assumed, of course."

"Well, we're not going to ferry them to safety, if that's what you're suggesting. You'll be in charge of disposal. I don't want any bodies washing up on Australian beaches."

"Okay, I'll take care of it." Marlon scoffed, as if he wasn't ready to vomit at the order to massacre and dispose of the Gillies. "Plenty of sharks around."

"Any of the defectors still alive in Gilgal, bring them to me first. I want to look them in the face when they realize they've lost and I've won. I will rule Gilgal. No one will stop me. No one can."

†

CHAPTER FIVE

Nathan Isaacson chewed his tuna sandwich slowly as he sat on the *Materia's* settee. The dining table was ten feet away, where Niles' men ate. No one spoke. Everyone seemed to sense the tension from the presence of Captain Sardan, who sat between Nathan and Guntari.

The news of the Gilgal attack against Stajner and Marlon had reached Nathan hours after Marlon surfaced. At least, Nathan had heard the report, but he hadn't yet spoken to Marlon in private to discover how much of it was true—since Stajner had reportedly been unconscious. There was always a risk that an asset might reverse his loyalties and turn on his handler, so Nathan remained cautious as to Marlon's potential betrayal of him. Joining Captain Sardan and Guntari didn't necessarily make Nathan safe, nor did the keycard under his shirt, though those matters certainly helped.

Trust. That word kept repeating itself in Nathan's mind, and he knew it was of God. There were no accidents with God, and there was certainly no waste. Nathan had come aboard the *Materia* to find Chen Li, but God would use him to move in the lives of all whom God desired—for God's good pleasure and glory.

Rising from the dining table, Marlon walked to the galley where he washed his plate in the sink. Nathan took his opportunity, even in sight of the others, to speak with Marlon. Opening the fridge, his back to the dining table, Nathan spoke quietly out of the side of his mouth.

"We need to talk."

"I can't get away. There've been developments." Marlon turned the water pressure higher. "I may've made things worse for all of us, even the Gillies."

"They attacked you?"

Marlon shook his head and sighed loudly for the others at the table.

"I got them a message that we're about to rescue them." He glanced at Nathan. "I saw Chen Li. She's alive."

Nathan's body tensed. That meant his mission was ready to move to the next level, however cautiously. Only a couple days ago, he'd thought the idea of an underwater habitat was a joke, or a test for him. But this was real. Chen Li was three thousand feet below the surface of the water, living in a plastic, dome-shaped city with other Christians.

"Captain Sardan wants Guntari and me to take out at least five of you to even the odds." Nathan studied a carton of powdered milk. "We're running out of time. Something big needs to happen, and fast."

"You've got to give me back my gun!" Marlon shook his head in frustration. "How am I supposed to defend myself?"

"Trust. Just keep the Gillies alive," Nathan whispered, and noticed the woman named Sam craning her neck and approaching the galley. Marlon, however, had turned away from her, and opened his mouth to speak again to Nathan. Speaking anything within earshot of another crewmember could expose their alliance, so Nathan interrupted him by tossing a food container at Marlon. "What'd you say to me?"

Shock flashed over Marlon's face, but then he noticed Sam. Appearances had to be maintained. He rushed Nathan from three paces away.

Though Nathan had instigated the mock fight, he wasn't braced for Marlon's mass when he tackled him. Sam screamed and the others started shouting as Nathan grappled with the man built like a bull. They exchanged blows to the body, bruising but not damaging, until three divers jumped between them and pulled them apart.

"I'll kill you!" Marlon growled and pulled against the two men who held him back. "You're dead, Patrick!"

"That's enough!" It was Niles, absent until then. He stepped past Captain Sardan and Guntari, moving through his own men and women to reach the galley. Nathan looked down at the shorter man, who held his semiautomatic handgun across his chest. "Patrick, is this how you react to your hosts? We don't need this! Not now! The enemy is down there! The enemy is Gilgal! We need to work against them, not against each other!"

"Get your hands off me!" Nathan shook off the diver who held him, and forced his way through the crowd to reach Captain Sardan and Guntari. The three of them left together.

In the captain's suite, Captain Sardan applauded lightly, a rare smile on his lined face.

"We have them so scared, they're ready to explode!"

"Yankee." Guntari smiled, showing discolored teeth. "Warn me next time you are to cause a distraction. I'll be ready to take one or two of their number."

"It's a plan." Nathan slapped Guntari on the shoulder. "I

just reacted to what he said. It was something about burning us off the boat tonight."

"They wouldn't!" Captain Sardan looked at Guntari. "They can't touch me while I still have the access codes to the power systems. I decide when the lights come on. I decide when they dive. They have to keep me informed on the progress with Gilgal or I shut them down. They don't shut me down!"

"Everything from the hot water to the oxygen tank compressor, we control it, Yankee. They can't burn us out." Guntari sat on the edge of the captain's bed. All three men, including Nathan, had moved into the captain's suite for better protection. "They can't do anything without power."

"Unless they've figured out a reroute." Nathan nodded at the captain. It was time to put more pressure on the crew. Pressure meant mistakes, and with all the lust for blood on board, Nathan needed every edge he could get. "Are we sure they haven't found a reroute? Are we now expendable?"

The question stung Captain Sardan's pride, and Guntari was silent as well. The captain paced the cabin, then paused to stare out the window at the afternoon horizon.

"If we want to control Gilgal, we must get inside first." Captain Sardan stood like Napoleon at the window, his hands braced behind his back. "If Mr. Niles has changed tactics, we need a new plan."

"I don't see how we can get into Gilgal first." Nathan frowned, though inside he was rejoicing. The layers of tension he'd added since coming aboard had disrupted both parties' plans, and Marlon's misinformation about the Gillies' attack had changed everything. "Gilgal has turned offensive, and we have no access to the submersibles."

"Patrick and I can hold them off, but not forever." Guntari said. Nathan had come to realize the man was valued more for his physical skills than for his mind. "I agree—it's time to either take the ship completely or abandon ship and find a way into Gilgal ourselves."

"Mr. Niles will never let us gain access to the submersibles." The captain resumed his pacing. "We'll have to take them by force, both submersibles. Patrick and I in one. Guntari, you in the other."

"How will we get into Gilgal?" Guntari shook his head. "Mr. Niles and his men have already tried everything. The Gillies will die before they open their docking port."

"We could raise the jammers to communicate a threat by radio," the captain suggested as Nathan bided his time. "We'll tell them we'll blow the central chamber dome with explosives if they don't open the docking port."

"But once we're inside Gilgal," Guntari said, "Mr. Niles will control us from the outside, like he does with the Gillies now."

"No, we can't pull up the jammers." Nathan tightened a strap on his leg brace. "A distress call could reach the coast and the Coast Guard would be on us inside an hour. We need something that helps us take over the *Materia* and Gilgal both at once."

The men were silent in thought for a few moments. Nathan prayed he'd remain receptive to ideas from God, guidance one way or another that would give him peace while his companions were in complete turmoil. In his life, Nathan didn't stand on a reality based on the ups and downs of experience. Rather, he based his reality on what God's Word revealed to him as truth. And only that which came from truth was worthy of swaying him to act or respond.

From what Nathan remembered about Gilgal in the Bible, it was a transition camp for the Israelites after they crossed the Jordan River into the Promised Land. As Nathan understood it, the Gillies were Christians, but with a view of the world that wasn't God's will for Christians. How could God's people, who knew the truth of Jesus Christ, shine like lights in the darkness when they were hiding from the world?

However misplaced their zeal to be separate, the Gillies needed to be saved from Niles and the captain—before one or the other of them got the upper hand and killed them all. Nathan had to do something and quick. If he continued to fuel the fires between the two sides, they'd only explode and do more damage. A sufficient amount of instability and heightened level of division had been attained, he decided. Now, it was time to conquer, to use his achieved position to gain his objective.

"I have an idea." Nathan stood, a confident smile on his lips, which he hoped would persuade his companions if his words didn't. "For a moment, we make peace with Mr. Niles and his people."

"What?" Guntari swore in his native tongue. "No! Never!"

"Wait." Captain Sardan held up his hand. "You have a plan, Patrick?"

"For the good of us all, we make peace until we get control of Gilgal—until we're inside."

"Mr. Niles will never let us inside to take control." The captain squinted in thought, making his wrinkles multiply. "How can we take Gilgal?"

"Everyone knows Marlon and I are enemies."

"That's clear."

"If he and I agree to work together to be the first ones inside Gilgal's docking port, then I'll turn on Marlon and take Gilgal for the three of us."

"But what about Mr. Niles destroying Gilgal after we get it first?" the captain asked.

"Once we control Gilgal, Mr. Niles will disable the jammers and open a channel of communication. He knows we won't call the authorities, not after we've shed the blood of the Gillies, unless we want to keep them alive. We can make any demands we want once we run Gilgal—and admit only who we want through the docking chamber."

"It's ruthless." Guntari looked to Captain Sardan. "I like this Yankee."

"This could work." The captain set a digital notepad on his lap. "The terms for peace will have to appear authentic, or we risk an ambush ourselves. To amend your idea, Patrick, I suggest you and Marlon enter Gilgal first, yes, but then Mr. Niles and I will be in the second submersible. By the time we dock, you'll have subdued Marlon, and you can take Mr. Niles captive when he enters Gilgal with me. The rest of his people will concede to my leadership if he's dead."

"Are you certain you can kill Marlon?" Guntari asked Nathan. "He's a powerful man. You felt his strength earlier."

"I'll crush him." Nathan clenched his fist, hoping his face displayed a hatred he didn't have. It was harder to pretend to dislike people than show the compassion he truly had. If an opportunity opened to share the gospel with just one of the crew, he wouldn't hesitate. Nothing more would show the hand of God on the mission than a miracle of repentance in a man's heart.

Nathan was ready.

...✝...

From one end of the dining table where Nathan was seated, he counted those present. The whole crew on board was there, even Marlon, who sat across from Nathan with a cold stare on his face aimed at Nathan. Most of the crew stood aside and a few were seated at the table, but all seemed to hold their breath while Mr. Niles studied the document.

Proverbs 21:5 was on Nathan's mind. He'd been patient and diligent, trusting the Lord. Prayer had been his constant pastime, and examining his personal motives had kept his heart seeking after God's will. Other men with his same abilities could've strayed into the realm of seeking glory for themselves or compromising standards, but Nathan sought God's glory. True, he didn't have a Bible on board, but he'd been instructed by Corban Dowler to read and memorize Scripture daily for just such a mission. The Word was in him. It saturated him. He lived by it. And now he faithfully waited to see what God worked before him, then he'd prayerfully step forward again. Chen Li and the Gillies had to be protected.

After Trevor Niles read the agreement, he pushed it away from him.

"I agree to this peace accord," Niles finally said, spoken through an exhale as if involuntary. But his crew wasn't so comforted by the idea, it seemed. They exchanged whispers until Niles held up his hand. "Look at me. The agreement is sound. Marlon and our new friend, Patrick, will enter Gilgal first, after we convince the Gillies to open their port to us by threatening with an explosive detonation. Then, Captain Sardan and I'll enter Gilgal second, at which time the four of us will use our firearms to take command of Gilgal. Once we control Gilgal, Captain Sardan will return to the surface. Is this agreed, Captain?"

"It is." Captain Sardan played his treachery so well, Nathan noticed. He wasn't the only actor by far. Marlon glared at Nathan with what anyone would guess was genuine contempt. "I am a ship's captain. Gilgal can't operate without a surface tender. With me controlling the surface and Mr. Niles controlling Gilgal, we can manage a profitable partnership to provide for future projects and clients."

"We'll all need access to the armory," Captain Sardan said. "Used with discretion, of course."

"Of course." Niles nodded, and looked to Marlon. "Marlon, portion out the appropriate weaponry from the armory for the first boarders, though I'm aware the four of us are already sufficiently armed."

Nathan didn't respond. He'd actually thrown all the bullets for the two guns he had over the side of the ship, but if the plan went well, there would be no need for them, especially in Gilgal.

"Very well." Niles rose from his chair. "At midnight, we detonate an explosive to get the Gillies' attention. They'll open the chamber port or there'll be a second detonation, and we'll be rid of this place. They have to know we're not bluffing. My dreams—your dreams—will be realized tonight. I will rule Gilgal!"

†

CHAPTER SIX

All of Gilgal shook, but Chen Li knew it wasn't an earthquake since the rumble of an explosion still thundered in her ears. Rolling out of bed, she tugged on the deck shoes she'd worn since fleeing the *Materia*. She joined the other gathering residents of the underwater habitat. They all looked up at the plastic dome and around at the equipment, whispering in fear, expecting a breach.

"It was an explosion—somewhere close," Nicholas Astroff said, holding his wife's hand. He and Lana were like father and mother to everyone in Gilgal, even to Li, who was their most recent arrival. "Check the sub-chambers. Look for flooding and contain it. Quickly!"

Most of the seventeen men scattered, but Nicholas, a sixty-year-old native of Michigan, remained next to the entrance of the food processing section of Gilgal—one of six sections, not counting the five sub-chambers that hadn't been flooded.

"Li?" Nicholas drew her to the side to speak in private. "What do you think they're up to now?"

"Well, it's midnight . . ." She shook her head. "Detonating ordnance at this depth makes no sense unless they're trying to send us a message."

She looked over her shoulder at the group of nineteen

women and fourteen children who Lana was leading in prayer. There were far more souls in Gilgal than Li had first supposed—and more than Trevor Niles and Captain Sardan were aware of. Supposing she could make a difference inside Gilgal, Li had left her undercover COIL assignment on the *Materia* two months ago. But she'd made no difference. Now, she was just a prisoner like the rest of them. Li was reminded how far God had brought her from living on the streets of Hong Kong, and the British Christians who'd given her a new home. Then she'd met Corban Dowler. Her training had been extensive, but only her faith in God and His loving arms gave her any stability now.

"Since we won't let them in, will they really destroy us?"

He'd asked her the question many times. The City of Gilgal had options, but not safe ones until the jammers were removed and buoys could be sent up to the surface to restore satellite communication.

"I wish I could say no." Li bit her lower lip. "It's not below Mr. Niles to blow the dome, especially if he's receiving pressure on the surface to move on."

"What about the other defectors up there?" Nicholas' stress was at its peak. Li wasn't sure he'd even slept for two days. "If you have friends up there, why aren't they stopping this?"

"Nick, I don't know." Li looked up at the dome. For two months, she hadn't made contact. Where was COIL? Had Corban Dowler abandoned her to die? What had happened to COIL's rapid response teams? "There may be men up there right now risking their lives for us."

"Well, we're risking our lives by waiting, knowing others want to kill us. I've been patient, Li." He accepted a cup of tea from his wife, the leaves picked from their own garden. "At first, I refused to leave the sub-chambers behind. Those cost millions of dollars. And then you joined us and assured me others would come to help us. But help hasn't come. I'm sorry. Even if we can't establish geosynchronic communication with the surface, we'll take the risk and navigate through the water. We leave in twenty-four hours, Li. Staying here any longer is death."

The man stood beside her a moment—perhaps expecting her to respond—but Li had no answers for him. He certainly didn't need to apologize to her; he carried the city's expectations for safety on his shoulders. The Gillies had come to Gilgal to escape the evils of the world, but instead, evil had hunted them down.

Li was left to stand alone to reflect on the time that had finally run out. Now they'd risk everything. Nicholas was desperate.

Unknown to Trevor Niles, Gilgal had a simple ballast and jet turbine system that enabled it to rise from the sea floor, then move at a slow speed through the ocean to another settlement site. Li hadn't been aware of the system until the fifth week she'd been in the habitat. The Gillies had hoped to reestablish the satellite link to safely relocate, because moving blindly through the blackness of the sea was madness. However, Gilgal had been pushed to that point—to loose the ballast and fire up the turbine drives. The cost would be the twelve sub-chambers attached to the central dome, but seven of them had already been drilled and flooded by Niles' teams.

The citizens of Gilgal listened to Nicholas as he explained his plans. Moving Gilgal up the Great Barrier Reef was dangerous business, but Nicholas and the rest of them understood from Li just how deadly those above were becoming. Only the day before, Li had abandoned her crutches, the bullet wound on her calf still tender from her escape from the *Materia*. The other defectors had been killed in a submersible collision, or from Niles' over-anxious shooters. The Gillies could expect no better treatment from those aboard the *Materia*.

Gradually, the Gillies returned to their sleeping pallets, or one of the five sub-chambers still livable. Whatever Niles was planning wasn't coming yet. The explosion had rocked the nerves of the Gillies to the point that they were willing to risk everything as soon as the generators were fully powered.

Walking around the central control console of Gilgal—a massive elevated cockpit—Li sat down on a bench in the hydroponics quarter. The plants and garden had been a place of peace for her to pray and meditate over the slow weeks. But tonight she found no peace or answers, and she fought the feeling of abandonment and loss. The cause for which Corban Dowler had sent her no longer depended on her. Had she failed? She'd kept the *Materia's* mischief in check until she couldn't hide her inner feelings to preserve life. Instead of saving anyone once the danger was apparent, she'd become another life that Niles was about to take in order to gain control of the world's only underwater city.

Where were the COIL heroes she'd heard of?

Nathan stood with his back to the wall in the *Materia's* dive locker. Next to him, Marlon inserted the keycard into the armory's locking mechanism.

"It's still not working, Mr. Niles." Marlon was visibly sweating. He inspected the card as if he didn't know Nathan had damaged the card with a welding torch before giving it back to Marlon. Arming the crew on the *Materia* before they entered Gilgal wasn't an option for Nathan. "It's no use."

Ripping the card from Marlon's fingers, Niles glared at him, then shoved his weapons officer aside. Repeatedly, he inserted the card into the slot and turned the handle of the oversized safe. Behind him, half of the crew waited with bloodlust to be armed for the takeover. The delay played on their nerves.

"The Gillies have made us look like fools for the last time!" Niles jerked on the handle harder than necessary. "We just detonated an explosive to shatter their courage! We must take Gilgal now!"

Pausing for a breath, Niles studied the card more closely.

"Has this card left your person?" Niles moved closer to Marlon, and two of the larger divers grabbed Marlon by the arms. "What did you do to this card?"

Marlon opened his mouth to respond, and Nathan prayed he'd say nothing of their pact. Nathan looked around him for his own escape if the mercenary confessed to his tactics with Nathan, but there was nowhere to run.

"It's been tampered with!" Niles held up the card. "What have you to say for yourself? I always wondered if we had more defectors on board. But you, Marlon?"

Niles was losing control. So determined was he to conquer and rule Gilgal, he wasn't able to consider anything but evil in those around him. Worse yet, Niles was armed with a handgun, as was Captain Sardan. Though Nathan and Marlon had guns visible in their waistbands, Nathan had thrown the bullets overboard.

"I didn't do anything to the card, Mr. Niles! We can still board Gilgal!" Marlon tried to shake off the men who held his arms, but they held him tightly. "We can bluff our way inside with the arms we do have!"

Before Nathan could think of something to diffuse the situation, Niles drew his gun on Marlon. Marlon looked down at the gun aimed at his chest.

"This armory keycard was your only responsibility!" Niles shook with rage. "I trusted you, Marlon! Now this key is useless! How could you do this to me?"

"Mr. Niles, I'm as frustrated as you!" Marlon's voice was steadier than Nathan expected it to be. "We still have some plastique left. I can blow the door hinges."

"No, you can't! The armory door is tamper proof! Only a fool would try to blow a door on an armory where bullets and guns are stored!" His finger tightened on the trigger. "You betrayed me, Marlon."

Marlon glanced at Nathan. Nathan didn't move, still unsure whether to save Marlon for the sake of the facade, or save all the Gillies. By some miracle, Marlon wasn't crumbling before even a drawn gun. Nathan had to do something!

"Fine." Marlon sighed. "You may as well know, if you're going to kill me. I couldn't let you kill all those Gillies."

From the doorway, Guntari sneered. He and Captain Sardan seemed glad to see Niles' trusted man fall. That would leave mostly outlaw oceanographers, divers, and a few techs at Niles' side. But Nathan had come aboard to disrupt their operation, not to see lives lost.

"Not here, Mr. Niles." Nathan stepped around Niles and snatched Marlon's gun from his waistband—before anyone else could find it unloaded. Since Nathan felt he couldn't expose his hidden motives quite yet, Marlon would simply have to keep playing along. "Let me take him out in the tender."

Niles clenched his teeth. He kept the gun against Marlon's chest, but Nathan didn't wait for his answer. Taking a length of nylon rope out of a locker, Nathan cut it and bound Marlon's wrists behind his back while the divers held him by the shoulders.

"Please, you can't kill him, Mr. Niles!" Sam fumed. She tried to get through the crowd, but Stajner held her back. "Marlon hasn't done anything!"

"He was against the truce the whole time." Nathan shoved Marlon toward the closed tender door and smacked him on the head. "Why'd you turn, huh? A weak stomach?"

"Don't do this, Mr. Niles." Marlon looked at Nathan, maybe for a signal, but Nathan gave him nothing. Spitting at their feet, Marlon tried to kick those nearest him. "Killing me will solve nothing!"

"You may have single-handedly destroyed this entire operation." Niles himself opened the access door in the starboard hull. The divers wrestled Marlon to the floor and bound his ankles. Nathan took the opportunity to take an emergency five-ounce dive tank off the wall, and hide it in his shirt. "Fine time for you to grow a conscience, Marlon—on the eve of taking over Gilgal!"

Nathan moved to the access door, the morning sunshine pouring through.

"I'll do it, Mr. Niles." Nathan yanked Marlon to his feet and held him by one arm. "Someone lower the tender!"

"Patrick, this is personal." Niles held up his gun. "It's just between Marlon and me."

Leaning closer so only he could hear, Nathan spoke quietly to Niles.

"This is an opportunity to show the crew what happens to traitors." Nathan winked at Niles as the man's blood thirst seemed to bring a sparkle to his eye. "Get everyone on deck. It'll help bring the group together, especially since we recently drew a truce. Make sure they all see me take care of this for you."

"My authority will be confirmed . . ." Niles' head lifted in pride, then he turned to the others. "Lower the tender. Patrick will be feeding the sharks this morning!"

"Don't do this!" Marlon screamed as Niles' henchmen wrestled him to the edge of the door. "Mr. Niles, you'll never get away with this!"

"I already have." Niles chuckled. "Come on. I want the whole crew to see this from the helipad."

The tender—the same red and white inflatable that had picked Nathan up—plopped onto the water outside the access door, and the davit cables were released. Nathan and two others forced Marlon out the access door. He dropped two feet to the bow of the outboard.

"Just me." Nathan set his hand on one of the diver's shoulders and jumped down to the tender. He pushed away from the *Materia*. Only he and Marlon were on board the little motorboat. "This will be quick."

Starting the motor, Nathan piloted away from the *Materia*.

He looked back once and saw the crew lining the starboard deck of the helipad. Fifty yards out, he cut the motor and allowed the boat to bob in the gentle waves.

"What are you stopping for?" While still bound, Marlon twisted around to look at Nathan. "We're busted! Keep going! We'll be halfway to—"

"To nowhere before they catch us, or we run out of gas." Nathan looked over his shoulder. "The chopper would catch us in five minutes. Besides, I'm not about to leave the Gillies in Niles' hands. No, we have to follow through with this."

"So I risked my life because you want to stay undercover?" Marlon fought his binds as Nathan moved from the stern to the bow. "I should've never trusted you! What was I thinking siding with a government spook?"

"That's right. Make this look real." Nathan struggled with Marlon, even in his bound state, to lift him over the edge of the inflatable side. I'll throw a life preserver off the bow within an hour. Just give me some time. Can you tread water that long?"

"Huh?" Marlon frowned and stopped fighting. "Not tied up, I can't!"

"Just stay under water for a few minutes until everyone goes inside."

Greater fear and misunderstanding swept over Marlon's face as Nathan rolled him overboard then reached into the water to hold him by his shirt collar. On the far side of the inflatable, those on the *Materia* would hardly be able to see him.

"Can you swim five miles west to make land?" Nathan drew a diving knife from a sheath on his belt. He raised it high overhead for effect, and leaned far overboard to hold up Marlon's dead weight. "Lizard Island is west by northwest."

"Patrick! Don't!"

The knife plunged, sliced through the water, ran along Marlon's spine, and split the nylon that bound his wrists behind him. Three more splashes into the water cut through his ankle binds as well.

"Keep your head under and swim for your life!"

Nathan pulled the dive canister from his shirt and thrust it in Marlon's face. Marlon grasped it as Nathan shoved the man's head under water. Bubbles seeped from Marlon's mouth. The last image Nathan saw was Marlon fitting the mouthpiece of the little canister into his mouth, then diving into oblivion.

Standing in the boat, Nathan raised his knife to the *Materia*, as if he were the victor of a great battle. The show was over, and with nothing left to see, those on the helipad began to disperse. Only Niles remained.

After piloting the outboard to the access door, Nathan rode the inflatable to its place where it hung from a davit arm.

"The sharks will tear the body apart." Niles' dark hair blew in the sea breeze. "You continue to impress me, Patrick Gibson."

"I just want my place in Gilgal." Nathan looked at Niles. "You and I are alike in that respect."

"Is that so? How?"

"We'll do anything to get it."

Niles held Nathan's gaze for a moment, and then looked out to sea again.

"I believe you."

CHAPTER SEVEN

Marlon sucked on the mouthpiece of the miniature dive canister and rolled over on his back under water. He was fifteen feet beneath the surface, treading water in the shadow of the *Materia*. If anyone on board switched on the fish finder, he imagined the crew's curiosity at the large stationary fish under the hull.

Ten minutes earlier, the man Marlon knew as Patrick Gibson had saved his life by orchestrating a mock execution. Ever since the tall man with the leg brace had come aboard, he'd been tangling the whole operation into knots. Even Marlon had been the victim of his mastery. But now more than ever, Marlon was intrigued. The man certainly had guts to face Niles.

Even though Marlon had been slow to discover how Patrick was reacting to the chess game on board, Marlon saw how the government man had worked his way tightly into Niles' good graces. However, Marlon had been removed from the equation to the point that Marlon could now do as he pleased. At the present, he swam at a crosscurrent between escaping to the reef islands to the west, and inserting himself back into the fray of fighting over Gilgal. If he did enter the fray, he might expose Patrick as a fraud, and Marlon knew they'd both be killed then. The facade had to be maintained.

Clearly, Patrick had intended for Marlon to swim for his life, never to return. But Marlon wasn't so hasty. Patrick was quite a strategist, but Marlon had known Niles off and on for years, even before he'd left his native Greek Island of Zalzuna to build himself an empire. That was fourteen years earlier. Niles didn't understand the word defeat, even to the point of killing one of his men—Marlon himself—who'd known him longer than anyone! Well, at least Niles thought he'd killed him.

No, Marlon decided. He'd stick around to personally see Niles fall. If not his downfall, then at least he'd see his defeat over Gilgal. Somehow, Marlon was certain Patrick would win—maybe just to send Niles defeated back to Zalzuna—but Niles would put up a fight. And when Patrick needed someone, Marlon would be there to repay the favor he'd been shown. Patrick had saved his life in more ways than one.

A donut life preserver plopped on the water above him. Marlon let go of the now empty dive canister and rose to the surface, his head emerging in the middle of the preserver. He swam backward, clutching the donut, and hid from sight under the awning of the pointed bow of the *Materia*.

It had been almost twenty years since Marlon had been home to the British coast of Plymouth. For years, he hadn't the nerve to return home, knowing in his heart he was an international criminal. His father would've sensed trouble in an instant. But now he was on the side of right, and the hope of returning home was something that intensified in Marlon's heart like it had never soared before!

...✝...

Something deep inside Nathan was instantly revealed to him—a sense of confidence that guarded him, preserved him in the will of God, no matter what he might face.

He'd had this feeling many times when he'd led COIL's primary extraction team. When triumph was in sight, when God's hand was evident, when the fruit of love was lived out by faith—a man pushed concern for himself aside and a spiritual determination became the driving force.

Stabbing a piece of sushi, Nathan held the very knife blade with which he'd supposedly retired Marlon. Using his teeth, he plucked the raw meat off the tip and chomped on it. He was aware of the stares, whispers, and questions the others shared about him as he stood at the kitchen counter. They sat at the dining table or on the settee, eating their own meals.

The engineer on board had unsuccessfully tried to remove the door on the armory, so Niles was in a fit again. No one wanted to cross him now, yet everyone was anxious to take from the spoils of Gilgal. Even Captain Sardan was keeping to himself, though Guntari had inquired of Nathan earlier to ensure their plan against Niles was still intact.

"I'm working myself into the right position," Nathan had promised him. "Gilgal will be ours by midnight."

All on board seemed to give Nathan a little wider girth now. They'd witnessed him murder a man in cold blood. Chances were, if Niles wished it so, he would do so again. No one dared speak ill of Niles or his plan—or the one they knew as Patrick Gibson.

Nathan walked to the windows that faced west. It had been three hours since he'd sent Marlon swimming toward the Reef. As long as he was reading the sun right, the man was probably near one of the islands by that time. Guessing that Marlon was a wanted man, Nathan figured he wouldn't see him again.

And somewhere out there, Corban Dowler was orchestrating other operations, seeking God's will in the lives of the afflicted, sometimes asking men and women to pay the ultimate price to help the persecuted.

"Everyone listen up!"

It was Niles. Nathan had never seen the man's face so dark, as if the drive to kill the Gillies and rule Gilgal was making him ill. If the man had any conscience at all, Nathan considered, he'd be bothered by the blood he'd shed and terror he'd caused.

Captain Sardan and Guntari joined the crew. Nathan crossed his arms as he found a place among the men and women drunk on Niles' dream.

"We refuse to be detoured!" Niles browsed the faces, as if daring them to defy him. "There are only two underwater charges left. We'll use one more to unsettle the Gillies, and the last one we'll slap against the central dome plastic so they can see it from the inside out. Then we'll arm ourselves with everything we've got and take Gilgal!"

A man raised his hand.

"Who's entering Gilgal first now that Marlon is gone?"

"Here's what I've decided—" Niles nodded at Nathan. "Patrick and I will enter Gilgal's docking port first. Any objections?"

"As long as Guntari and I are in the second submersible," Captain Sardan stated. "Keep the port open until a few of us can get inside and take the whole city."

"The submersible pilot can shuttle only one passenger at a time, so the four of us will take Gilgal ourselves, since we're armed. Then we'll shuttle down one at a time those of you who already have assignments in Gilgal. Patrick, can four of us take the dome? There are about forty people living inside."

"I'll draw up an attack plan." Nathan nodded curtly. "Shouldn't be difficult. They're just Christians."

"Excellent." Niles' face seemed to grow darker, as if he'd passed into a deep shadow. "Prepare the submersibles. Make ready the oxygen tanks for prolonged submersion. We'll detonate the next explosive and move directly to taking the dome without surfacing. Rattling them with another blast should open that submersible port, or I swear I'll blow the whole city!"

…✝…

Nathan shivered against the chill inside the submersible as Niles used the armrest joysticks in the pilot seat to guide them down into the murky blackness of the sea. The tractor drive system under the bubble in which they sat created a whine that sounded like a high-pitched scream—a tribute, Nathan imagined, to the wickedness for which the submersibles were now employed.

Behind their submersible was the second one, Guntari steering it for Captain Sardan, their pod lights giving Nathan's pod the feel of daylight.

"You seem very calm." Niles dove the submersible so steeply that Nathan placed one foot on the glass in front of him. "Once we're inside, it'll be you and Guntari performing most of the dirty work. I'll back you up as much as I can."

"That's what I'm here for."

Indeed, Nathan was calm. Though he was an operative with countless missions under his belt, it was his trust in God's hand over the situation that gave him such resolve. He was simply the vessel through which God was working—Christ in him tending to the weary and comforting the broken. In that case, the Gillies were the ones he imagined were weary and near breaking from their underwater siege.

On such missions, Nathan tried not to imagine the gratitude of those he was about to rescue, but he couldn't help himself where Chen Li was involved. Though Nathan had never met the pretty Chinese agent, she was a Christian and a COIL operative. That made her family. She'd come to infiltrate the *Materia's* secrets, and no doubt her defection from Niles, along with others, had stalled his takeover of Gilgal since he had fewer hands.

While in Afghanistan, Nathan had learned to fly a chopper, and the hand controls Niles was now using seemed quite similar. Though Nathan had only a general plan on how to rescue the Gillies, and take Niles and Captain Sardan's crew into custody, he had to remain alert for the first opportunity to take action—not waiting too long or starting too early. As a Christian, he didn't wish to compromise God's desire for kindness, even toward enemies. Thus, Nathan considered non-lethal avenues by which he could take everyone into custody. He had the four tranquilizers in his leg brace, but how and when to use them was in God's hands.

Gilgal seemed to rise from the darkness, and Nathan was startled at the size of the glowing plastic orb that stared up at them like a giant eyeball. He felt a little foolish now for not believing such a place existed. It was a whole city!

"That's the same expression I had when I first saw it." Niles chuckled. "And just think: it'll be mine inside of an hour! With Marlon gone, you'll be my right-hand man."

Nathan reached down to his leg brace as if to scratch his knee, but instead, he loosened a tranquilizer dart from his leg brace. He would've liked to have Marlon at his side as originally planned for this next stage, but he had to work with what God had given him. Once inside Gilgal, he could count on Chen Li, no doubt trained in martial arts and various defense techniques to assist him in subduing Niles, as well as Captain Sardan and Guntari when they entered second.

The two submersibles cruised over the top of the dome. Nathan looked down at the upturned faces of Gilgal below. Chen Li was there somewhere. It was nearly midnight, but the Gillies were awake and active, perhaps not aware that on the surface, the sky was dark and their part of the world was asleep.

"We got their attention," Nathan said, a little glee in his voice that he hoped Niles interpreted as dark intention rather than righteous zeal. "How are they powered? So much light!"

"Their light-emitting diodes are powered by current turbines. See the blades that look like windmills?" Niles pointed down one side of the central dome. "We considered disabling their power to force them to surrender, but we're not sure how much damage it would do to the other systems. You've seen Gilgal's specs. There are some unknowns about the habitat. I intend to find out those secrets."

As they reached the far edge of Gilgal, Guntari sped past Nathan's submersible and piloted across the sloping sea floor. It was sandy except for reef formations covered with colorful vegetation. In Guntari's submersible robotic arm he held the detonation package meant to shake Gilgal into submission. The robotic arm in front of Nathan held a similar explosive, the second and final package—enough bundled power to crumble a bridge, which Nathan knew from experience.

Niles set their submersible on the ocean floor as Guntari continued a short distance farther so as not to damage the dome. Nathan leaned forward and dimmed the lights in their own rover to see Guntari's operation more clearly.

"Don't worry." Niles flipped a switch, exhausting carbon dioxide and filling the pod with fresh oxygen. "Guntari has been a devil on my back for months, but when it comes to this stuff, he's an expert. Be glad we're working together now."

"He's set the package on the ocean floor," Nathan said. "I sure wish we could detonate it remotely."

"We can't take the risk of turning off the frequency jammers. The Gillies could send a communication buoy topside and alert the Australian Navy. Besides, those pincers are so precise, they could tie your shoelaces."

Snorting at Niles' description, Nathan wasn't so sure of the accuracy as he watched Guntari struggle with the package and the left-most robotic arm.

"Something's wrong." Nathan felt icy sweat on his back.

"Nothing's wrong. He'll just pull the fuse. The fuse is sixty seconds long once he's pulled it. It's more than enough time to get away."

"I get that. I think he already pulled the fuse!" Nathan looked at Niles. "He pulled it, but he's not letting go of the thing!"

As if to confirm Nathan's words, Guntari's submersible jerked left and right, as Guntari obviously tried to dislodge the explosive, but the robotic pincers were clasped tightly.

Nathan reached for the controls, but Niles blocked his hand.

"We can save them!" Nathan stated. "We have forty seconds left. Just pull the package from their—"

"No." Instead, Niles turned their submersible and started back toward Gilgal. "The job is done. The explosive will still work as intended. You and I can take Gilgal alone."

Unstrapping his seat harness, Nathan turned to see Guntari's submersible continue to shake the package loose, even scraping it roughly on the sea floor. Dust from the bottom clouded his last attempts from Nathan's sight.

The concussion hit Nathan and Niles like a collision. The more sensitive gauges and indicator lights blinked off then back on. Nathan fell to the floor, then climbed back into his seat and strapped in. Stunned, he looked at Niles.

"You sabotaged them."

"Very good, Patrick." Niles steered them up to Gilgal's central dome. "A sovereign cannot share his sovereignty. They weren't allies. You're not the only one who can be cold-blooded."

Feeling his anger rise, Nathan closed his eyes and prayed briefly for God's wisdom. Though he wanted to control all the variables, he couldn't. Niles was responsible for their blood. Soon, Nathan had to witness the ruthless man's defeat. There could be no other way.

✝

CHAPTER EIGHT

"Seal the sub-chamber doors!" Nicholas Astroff ordered. "We're leaving now! Lana, get me another head count. I don't want to leave anyone behind who's still in one of the sub-chambers."

Chen Li gazed out the plastic at the ocean as Lana began to count aloud the number of citizens of Gilgal. It wasn't easy since several of the men were racing about, checking pressures and the dome's integrity sensors.

"Someone's coming, Nicholas!" Li called.

He stalked over to her side and they watched together as the bright lights of a submersible rover approached the dome. A metallic bundle in its starboard robotic arm was conspicuously marked BOMB.

"God help us," Nicholas whispered. "We're too late. He's going to blow the dome."

"Nick, we can't leave yet!" A man ran up to him. "The battery bank hasn't recharged the drive yet. Without enough power to go to the next potential site, we'll have to set down on an unstable sea floor. It could be our death."

"I've failed everyone." Nicholas moaned and shook his head. "These people are forcing us to choose between death and death."

Li peered beyond the bomb at the two men in the

submersible. She recognized Niles' deceitfully gentle features, but she didn't recognize the broad shouldered man with thick eyebrows, angled toward the bridge of his nose. Niles had taken on more men? It wasn't like him to share the spoils with more than he had to.

"You're the expert, Li." Nicholas didn't take his eyes off the rover. "Can we stall until we're fully powered again, or do we have to open the submersible port? It seems they're waiting for an answer."

"The one on the left is Trevor Niles. There's nothing good in him, and half the people on board the *Materia* are no better. If we let in two, the rest will come."

"And we saw the other submersible before this latest blast. It's out there somewhere, too."

"A dozen more people on the *Materia* just waiting to get in here . . ."

"When I built Gilgal, I never imagined I'd be forced to hand it over to a ship full of maniacs." Nicholas sighed loudly. Behind them, the Gillies were quiet, watching their leader and the rover that could only mean havoc. "If they blow the dome, we all die. At least, if we let them in, we'll have a chance to talk to them. Maybe they'll listen to reason."

"Right." But Li didn't agree. If Nicholas let Niles in, they were all dead, sooner or later. The Gillies' passive stand against violence would lead to their demise. Li—a Hong Kong street scrapper from childhood—was trained by COIL to love the enemy, but they'd also schooled her in the art of hand-to-hand combat to use when necessary, always to preserve life, never to kill.

With an edge, she guessed she could take Niles. He was a

pampered villain who usually stood by as others followed his orders. Usually. But the tall stranger in the copilot seat had a hard, weathered look about him. Definitely a mercenary, like Marlon, Niles' right hand back on the *Materia*. Perhaps Marlon was on the other submersible. Niles was rarely separate from his number one goon.

"If I make a move against the boarders, your men have to back me up." Li flexed her small fists. She'd fought grown men before. "Will they?"

"To what end?" Nicholas shook his head. "Violence only begets violence. Until we can relocate Gilgal, the *Materia* will just send more people if we capture one or two of theirs."

"They have only two submersibles, Nick. We can use that against them. Or, if we could get our hands on one of the submersibles, I could get to the surface and outside the range of the jammers, then radio for help. We can do this!"

"Not by violence, no. Pray for God's mercy, Li. I won't sink to their level, or yours, if that's your way. I have to open the port." Nicholas waved his arm at the submersible, signaling he would open the port. As a broken man, he walked toward the center console. The siege was over.

Li remained at the dome wall and watched a broad smile spread across Niles' face. Niles shook his finger at her. He didn't know the extent of what her assignment had been on the *Materia*, but he'd never let her go unpunished for her defection, especially since it had caused the defection of others on board, though they were now dead. Worse yet, Niles hated Christians, and Li had sided with them against him. There would be no mercy.

Suddenly, the tall man in the copilot seat adjusted

something in his hand, and swung it at Niles! Niles' smile disappeared as he gaped at his copilot, whose fist slammed into his chest. The copilot removed his fist from Niles' chest, and Li now saw the man held a small device the size of a pen, which he placed into some sort of sheath on his leg.

Niles wavered, his equilibrium seemingly lost, then he fell forward onto the joystick. The submersible lurched forward two feet. The bundle marked BOMB slammed into the dome. Li's eyes met the copilot's, as if they both understood their next conscious reality would be the afterlife.

But the explosive didn't detonate. Unstrapping Niles, the copilot changed seats with the sleeping man.

With her mouth gaping, Li focused on closing it to hide her confusion and shock.

The stranger, now in control of the rover, waved weakly, as if a little embarrassed he'd nearly blown them all to pieces. Li held up her hands and mouthed the words: *WHAT ARE YOU DOING?*

Smiling, he held up a cupped hand in the shape of a *C* and mouthed back one word that nearly made Li's knees buckle: *COIL.*

Placing her hand to her heart, tears came to her eyes. *THANK YOU* was all she could manage to mouth back; it seemed so little compared to the danger this stranger had surely faced to join Niles' campaign against Gilgal.

They were saved. COIL had come for her after all. But she suddenly didn't feel presentable to greet her handsome rescuer.

...✝...

As Nathan piloted the submersible underneath Gilgal to

the port, he felt like a fool for nearly blowing the whole operation—literally—and in front of Chen Li, too!

He could barely contain his elation over how God was working out the details to preserve His people. The bitterness he felt for Captain Sardan and Guntari's demise was pushed to the back of his mind as he reached the port chamber opening. Nathan drove the rover into the lit interior of the pressurized dive chamber.

A red light flashed as the port door closed beneath him, then the water was pumped out around the submersible. The tractors settled on the floor. The light switched to green and Nathan powered down the submersible. An airlock door slid open across the garage-sized chamber, and a number of men and Li entered. The men's faces appeared weary and grim, but Li was smiling, her brown eyes meeting Nathan's as they shared a secret no one else knew.

Two men helped Nathan unseal his door, though when he saw it done, he realized he could've done it himself from the inside. Nathan left Niles in his tranquilized state and climbed out of the top of the submersible. The men stepped back, but Li rushed to him.

Nathan returned her embrace, though she was much shorter than he was.

"You're a godsend! You don't know how much I've been praying for you to come!" Li took his hand in hers and pointed at one man with a broad face and small eyes. "This is Nicholas Astroff, the leader of Gilgal. Nick this is . . ."

"Uh, Patrick Gibson."

"How many COIL agents are on the surface?" Li asked.

"Oh, right." Nathan surveyed the men who gazed

expectantly at him. "Is there somewhere Li and I could speak in private?"

"Come on inside." Nicholas waved his hand. "We both have a lot of questions, no doubt. You saved our necks, young man."

Li released his hand and Nathan reached down to take the explosive device out of the robotic pincers. Tucking it under his arm, he followed the others from the dive chamber. Inside, more than a dozen men, women, and wide-eyed children regarded him as if he were an alien. A few of the men stepped forward and shook his hand.

"Thank you for coming," one said.

"God has sent you to us," another said. "Praise Him!"

Though Nathan had a few choice words in mind for them, he remained quiet for now. How could they think following a recluse to the bottom of an ocean wouldn't end badly? This wasn't what God desired of His children!

Once again, Li took his hand and drew him into what Nathan could tell was the hydroponics section. He gazed upward at the plastic and dark water above. It seemed like they were in a colony on a distant planet. Behind him, the citizens of Gilgal waited for their turn at him, as they watched the two COIL agents from a distance.

"I hardly know where to begin!" Li laughed and blushed, his hand in both of hers now, as if he would leave if she released him. "How many COIL agents are on the surface?"

"Actually, I'm a team of one, but Corban Dowler has us under satellite surveillance. We're not alone." Nathan glanced over his shoulder and smiled at the Gillies. They hadn't moved. "How are you holding up in this place?"

"Well, I was falling apart like the rest of Gilgal—especially thinking I was here for life—but now you're here."

"We're not out of trouble yet. The frequency jammers are still engaged all around Gilgal and on the surface. The *Materia* has quite a few people who need to be dealt with, and a couple who might think it's their turn to take over leadership. Ideally, they should all be arrested."

"They won't go easily."

"With Niles out of the way, the Australian Coast Guard can deal with them as soon as we can make a call. That means we need to go topside again."

"We?"

"Unless you want to stay here." Nathan bent his head toward her. "The *Materia* isn't under my control yet."

"If we take the submersible, we could go to the coast."

"It's miles away. We wouldn't make it but halfway. No, we have to take the *Materia* before they do anything else foolish."

"How?" She drew back a little, as if she were disappointed in him. "How long have you been a COIL agent?"

"A little while." He did his best to withhold a smile. "Long enough, I think."

"This isn't the job for one man who's been with the COIL agency for only a little while. No offense, but we need a lot more than we have."

"Okay." Nathan frowned and took his hand away from her to place both of his hands on his hips. Li's cuteness was beginning to fade. "What exactly do you foresee as a problem as I move forward?"

"So, you've subdued Mr. Niles, but he's hardly the only problem. There's Captain Sardan, and his bodyguard,

Guntari, and the worst guy named Marlon, though as of late, I can't tell whose side he's on."

"I see." Nathan counted each one on his fingers. "Dead, dead, and as good as dead."

"*What?*" She cringed and gawked at him. "You . . . killed them?"

"Of course not! Well, maybe the last one, kind of." Nathan frowned at himself, sorry for the confusion he was creating. He took her by the shoulders. "I can take over the *Materia* with your help. They think I'm a killer and a fugitive. That sort of thing brings respect from people like them. They think I'm capable of terrible things. All we have to do is shut down the jammer and make a call. You know the people on board better than me. We can do this together."

"How long were you on board?"

"About two days."

"You won them over and gained Mr. Niles' confidence in two days?" Her original smile returned. "So, you're a little better than you give yourself credit for."

"It's not me. I'm just—"

"Hey!" One of Nicholas' men called to them. "Wasn't that guy in the submersible dead?"

"Who? Niles?" Nathan felt the blood drain from his face. He walked quickly out of the hydroponics section. "No, he's just been tranquilized for—"

His gaze fell upon the red light blinking on the dive chamber wall.

"He's awake! What did you use on him?" Li dashed to the wall and hit the control button to open the door. "Oh, he's taking the submersible! We'll be trapped again!"

The door didn't respond, so Nathan tried to fit his fingers into the inner chamber door crack to pry it open. Almost as quickly, Nicholas shoved him back.

"Let him go or you'll kill us all! If you open that door, we'll be flooded. We'll all drown!"

Nathan put his ear to the door and listened to the pressurized chamber fill with water. Had it been twenty minutes already? He'd overestimated the effects of the tranquilizer. Behind him, the citizens were silent, and Nathan turned around slowly. They stared at him as if he'd single-handedly sentenced them to die. Though it would mean little to them, he was glad he'd at least taken the explosive from the submersible robotic arm. But that was the only right thing he felt he'd done.

"What will he do now?" Nicholas asked Nathan.

"He'll return to the *Materia* and think of another way to take Gilgal." Nathan had difficulty meeting anyone's gaze directly. "I'm sorry. I should have—"

"Our generators will need a couple more hours, Nick," a mustached man said.

"Patrick, do we have until dawn before Niles tries another attack?"

"I think so, but what can you do that you haven't already tried?"

Nicholas turned to his people and began giving orders. He said they had a two and a half hour deadline to secure anything that could move. Nathan felt like a failure who wasn't worthy of an explanation as to what they intended to do.

Li seemed downcast, but at least she approached him

when the others just turned their backs and walked away.

"Gilgal has a drive system. We're moving up the Reef, even outside the perimeter of Mr. Niles' jammers."

"A drive system?" Nathan smiled. "Seriously?"

"Seriously. But it's extremely dangerous. A city this size moving through darkness, navigating by sonar only—it's not something anyone has been looking forward to. That's the reason why we hadn't tried it when we had some hope of resolution. To be honest with you, one of the things I've been telling them is that COIL would come for me."

"But we can surface now, right?"

"Only as a last resort," Nicholas answered as he was walking by and stopped. "We've learned a hard lesson here. We won't make any more contact with the surface unless it's an emergency, and that includes sending a buoy topside. Our communications via satellite were probably how Niles tracked us down in the first place. We'll rise from the ocean floor in a couple hours, just enough to move northwest along the Reef."

"I don't understand." Nathan chuckled uneasily. "You have no other submersibles, and you don't want to surface? No offense, but you guys may have signed on to a life in a bubble, but what about Li and me? We can't swim out of here; we'd be crushed under the weight of so many atmospheres of water."

Nicholas glanced at a few of the older men, elders of the community, who shook their heads.

"No, we won't be surfacing. But we will be going to new coordinates where we won't be found again if we remain at depth. You two can submit to God's plan for you inside Gilgal if you let Him open your eyes to the blessings of living a sanctified life here. Ask Li. She's lived here for two months. It must feel like home now, doesn't it, Li?"

Nathan looked at Li whose eyes were wide with shock, as if she wanted to scream. That was Nathan's sentiment as well. This time, he was the one who took her hand in his. God's will couldn't be for them to hide from the world at the bottom of the ocean. He leaned down to whisper in her ear.

"Don't worry. I'll get you out of Gilgal. God's already given me an idea. We'll do it together. I'm not leaving your side."

†

CHAPTER NINE

Marlon had shed his clothes overnight, with the exception of his shorts. He clung to the donut life preserver, too exhausted to tread water any longer in the portside moon-shadow of the *Materia*. He'd witnessed the deployment of the two submersibles around midnight, and though it was nearly dawn, the two pods had still not returned. That meant either the divers were dead from the last explosion, or they'd entered Gilgal. Whatever the case, Marlon decided if he didn't sneak aboard the *Materia* for food and water soon, he was shark bait—for real this time.

The only place for a diver to crawl onto the *Materia* was at the stern where the tall crane cast an arching shadow over the dark sea. Marlon drifted down the hull, kicking only occasionally for cautious propulsion. He wondered if he'd made a mistake by remaining with the *Materia* to help Patrick Gibson. By now, Marlon could've been in an island cafe drinking some chilled coconut beverage.

The deck at the stern was four feet above the water surface, so Marlon had to climb up a panel, then lunge for the crane neck to reach the deck. He rolled against the waiting racks where the submersibles would be set once removed from the water. A woman laughed from the helipad overhead as two men spoke in low tones.

He had no friends on board, except maybe Sam. The close relationship he'd had with Niles as his right hand had made him the disciplinarian more than a few times. As a disciplinarian on a ship full of ex-cons, fugitives, and rebels, he hadn't been too popular, least of all with Stajner.

Rising to his feet, Marlon padded quietly into the vehicle hangar, then paused against the wall, which was cluttered with cables and dive machinery. His weariness was replaced by excitement. Who was left on board while the others were under water? The thought made him shiver with anticipation. If just the crew and Stajner were aboard, what stopped him from taking over the *Materia*? When Niles and Guntari returned, he could demand their capture or refuse to board them altogether. Or submit to Patrick's decision. If Patrick had successfully entered Gilgal as planned, and subdued Niles in the process, all that was left to do was to call in the authorities. Patrick would need a compliant crew for that.

As he moved against the wall, he peered through the doorway of the mission control room. For now, it was empty. If the crew were exploring the hidden recesses of the Reef, the control room would've been up and operating, its several screens bearing images of colorful fish and plants transmitted from the submersibles. But the frequency jammers ruined any capability to receive such pictures from the rovers below.

Finding overalls hanging in a closet, Marlon put them on, along with a pair of deck boots two sizes too large. From a counter drawer, he sorted through a number of knives he'd used in the past to fillet fish he'd caught off the dive platform. He tucked one knife into his shoe under his pant leg, and the other up his sleeve for quick access, the tip close to his elbow.

Someone on the helipad was drunkenly singing a filthy sailor's song. Alcohol was supposedly prohibited on board, according to Niles, which further confirmed no one of authority was aboard. The helipad was a frequent place for fraternizing on warm summer nights. Whoever else may have been on board was probably still asleep, waiting for the others to wake them when the submersibles returned.

There were few actual assignments handed down for the crew when the submersibles weren't on board. Most of the crew had been hand-selected, some by Marlon personally, for their specific expertise once inside Gilgal. With Patrick on the scene, Marlon didn't think any of the crew would see the inside of Gilgal, now.

Avoiding the helipad, Marlon moved deeper through the vehicle hangar and past the waste incinerator room. The galley was three steps farther down the corridor, but he stopped against the wall. Someone was in the galley. It had to be Rob, the cook, or his assistant with the red hair. Too famished to wait any longer, Marlon stepped around the corner and into the doorway. It was Rob, an Aussie with few actual culinary skills. The man looked up from a mixing bowl of powdered eggs, and froze.

"Marlon?" Rob's initial shock passed quickly. Though he was in his sixties now, Rob was a circumnavigator from his early years spent on various monohull racing crews. He was a tough man, recently having gained a belly, but otherwise sturdy. "Thought you were dead. I guess Sam can stop crying her eyes out now."

As Marlon moved farther along the counter, Rob set his egg bowl aside and glanced at a butcher knife nearby.

"Don't do it, Rob. I'm not here to deal with you." Marlon shook his head. "Bigger things than you know are happening right now. Mr. Niles is about to meet his end."

"Does he know you're alive?" There was a little gleam in Rob's eye. "That was some show you and the new fellow put on."

"You can join me or fall in with Mr. Niles."

"And you'll lead us?" Rob grinned.

"No. There's no one leading anymore. It's over."

"Says you." Rob's smile vanished. "I'll take my chances with Mr. Niles. He's been good to me so far."

Marlon didn't get a chance to respond. Rob grasped for the knife, but missed the handle, scattering the blade up the counter. Before he could actually get a grip on the knife, Marlon flung open the freezer door and knocked Rob unconscious. The noise had been significant, and perhaps others would've come to investigate, but a shout was made from the helipad.

"They're back! It's Mr. Niles! He's alone! He did it!"

A bell clanged and the ship-wide intercom announced the same message. The crew dashed for the stern dive platform from every direction, many of them running past the galley without noticing Marlon gulping down the powdered eggs and milk.

If Niles was back already, that foiled Marlon's plans to retake the *Materia*. He'd be better off leaving the ship again, but he wasn't too keen about going back into the salty water. His skin felt clammy and burned at the same time—one from the moisture and the other from the sun during the day before.

A week earlier, in the same situation, Marlon might have killed Rob to keep him silent. But already, Marlon recognized the difference inside him. After years of brutality, his conscience was crying out for relief. Even though it would've been to his benefit to finish Rob off, Marlon left the galley with a jug of water and a sealed bag of cashews.

While the crew was at the stern to hear the latest from Niles, Marlon crept down the stairs to the second deck and into the dive locker. The on-board mixing and storing of dive gas provided Marlon with his pick of a dozen oxygen tanks, full scuba gear, and rebreather systems. Using a netted tool bag, he bagged six tanks and two rebreather packs. He also donned a wetsuit to protect his skin, and a set of flippers, with a backup set in the bag.

Quietly, so as not to attract a look from the stern, Marlon opened the access door. Any moment, Rob would gain consciousness, and the ship would be searched for him. He dragged his bundle of breathing equipment to the door, then returned to the dive lockers. Anything he wasn't taking for himself, he didn't want anyone else to use to come after him. No doubt, they'd try to capture him, unless he made it impossible to do so.

The tanks and rebreathers he wasn't planning to take, he carried to the access door and dropped them as gently as possible into the ocean. Without buoyancy gear attached, the tanks sank instantly.

Finally, he was ready to leave, yet he hesitated. Sam. Could he just . . . leave her? They were hardly an item on board, but their relationship was building into something. So much depended on what Patrick had planned. Sure, Marlon knew he should wait for whatever Patrick was doing, and he could do so under water, but with another person? He had to try to help Sam. In many ways, he felt she was like him. Since no one had really opened the door for him to do the right thing, he'd only done bad. What if he gave Sam the same opportunity Patrick had given him?

In a hurry now, Marlon tied a rope to his dive gear bag and lowered it off the side of the ship into the water. He tied the other end of the rope to a hinge on the access door so when he closed it with some force, the rope was invisible from inside.

Marlon fit a dive mask over his face and pulled up the dive suit hood around his head. Though he was intent on disguising himself as much as possible for as long as possible, he planned to be prepared for a hasty abandonment of the *Materia*.

With an extra dive mask in his hand, he walked casually from the locker room and ascended the portside stairs to the third deck. He emerged from the shadows of the vehicle hangar as the crane operator worked with six men to bring the submersible aboard. Others were gathered around the A-frame crane, waiting for the latest news on Gilgal.

He spotted Sam in the pre-dawn light with the help of the stern deck lights. She worked as a free dive technician at times like these, and her work was now done. The crane's tether had been attached to the submersible, and she was drying her hair with a towel on the starboard side. Stajner approached and offered her a second towel. Marlon smiled to himself as she rejected his offer and moved away to the head of the vehicle hangar.

Seeing his moment, Marlon cupped his hand to his mouth.

"Sam, you got a minute?" he called casually, appreciating the nasal distortion the dive mask created on his voice. Still drying her hair, she walked into the hangar. Marlon backed up the stairs a few steps to get out of sight of the others.

"Hello?" She rounded the corner. Her eyes squinted, then her hands went to her mouth. After glancing toward the stern, she bounded into his arms. "You *aanklager!* I saw you die!"

He tolerated her kisses for a moment, hoping to remember later to ask what she'd called him in her native Dutch, then held her at arm's length.

"I don't have long. Listen to me. Are you listening?" He guided her farther up the narrow stairs. "This is life and death."

"What's going on?"

"Government agents are on their way. Interpol, others—I don't know everything. Anyone at Mr. Niles' side will be arrested for what we're doing here to the Gillies. They know all about the operation."

"Is that why you sabotaged the armory keycard?"

"What? No. Long story. I'm leaving the ship. You have to come with me. Please, Sam . . ."

"Where is there to go?" She smiled and looked down the stairs, suddenly seeming distrustful of him. "You have a boat we haven't noticed on the horizon?"

"No, we'll go under water. We'll stay in the second atmosphere. We can wait there for a few hours until this business blows over."

"That's . . . insane, Marlon. How do you know this stuff?

Where are the agents?" Sam shook her head. "Marlon, I'm not sure you're making any sense. If Interpol knew about us, we'd be arrested."

"I can't explain everything right now. You have to trust me. Are you coming or not?"

"But . . . Mr. Niles just came back from Gilgal. He's obviously been there! Inside Gilgal! Think of it!"

Marlon blinked in frustration.

"Sam, there won't be any Gilgal for us. Listen! Patrick Gibson is a federal officer of some sort. That's how I'm still alive. Mr. Niles won't be allowed to rule from Gilgal."

"What? No!" She pushed him away and stepped down the stairs. "Marlon, you're not making any sense. I don't believe you. We've been working so hard on this. Mr. Niles said you'd lost your mind. Just look at you!"

"Aren't you listening?" He held out his hands. "Mr. Niles is about to be busted! The whole crew will be imprisoned with him!"

"Sam? Are you up there?" Stajner was at the foot of the stairs. "Mr. Niles says Captain Sardan and Guntari are dead. Patrick joined the Gillies, but Mr. Niles jammed open their submersible port. We're in, Sam! Sam?"

Continuing to back up the stairs, Marlon heard Stajner climbing up.

"People are dying, Sam!" Marlon said quietly. "Come with me. Mr. Niles will do anything to get what he wants."

"Who are you talking to, Sam?" asked Stajner. "Everyone's out here."

Suddenly, Sam grasped Marlon's wrist, and Marlon was too shocked at first to shake her loose.

"It's Marlon!" she cried. "Marlon's alive! Help me! He's trying to sabotage the operation again!"

A few steps above her, Marlon planted his foot on her shoulder and shoved. She lost her grip and fell into Stajner. When Marlon turned to escape, he instead dodged a sweeping knife from above by Rob the cook. Since there was no way to fight Rob, who was armed and had the higher ground, Marlon lunged after Sam and Stajner as they tumbled down the steep steps to the deck below. He leaped beyond them as they tried to cling to him, their screams for help drawing others.

Since the water was Marlon's only escape, he dashed across the vehicle hangar, only to meet Niles' chief diver known as Salt. He was lean and bitter, and when his eyes fell on Marlon, Marlon knew he had his hands full—not to mention that Rob was still pursuing him and others were gathering.

Salt's fist bounced off Marlon's dive mask, which sent Marlon staggering into the arms of two technicians. Rob sliced at him again, cutting instead one of the men from collarbone to ribs. Marlon dodged then fell to his knees and crawled toward the edge of the deck. Others clawed at him, but he kept moving, his dive suit too tight for their fingers to find purchase.

"Stop!" Niles yelled.

At the edge, Marlon was ready to slide into the sea, but he heard the hammer pull back on Niles' gun—the only gun now on board, he guessed. Stopping, Marlon looked up at Niles as the man approached. The others crowded in as well, scowls on their faces rather than joy at seeing him alive.

"So, you and Patrick have a few tricks!" Niles shook his head, smiling down at Marlon as if Marlon were a prized fish recently landed. "What are you thinking, Marlon? The years we served together!"

"That didn't stop you from trying to have me killed!"

"He knocked me out upstairs!" Rob held his head with one hand, the knife in his other. The man he'd sliced was being tended by others who scowled at Marlon as if he'd injured the man himself.

"And he demanded I go with him!" Sam folded her arms. "He said Interpol was all over us."

"Interpol?" Niles laughed, and the others joined. "Where's Interpol, Marlon? And where were you going? Swimming to Gilgal? Go ahead. You'll save me a bullet. Better yet, I'll send you on your way. Someone get me chains and some weight!"

Two men went into the vehicle hangar, and Marlon heard chains rattling. He had to get off the ship now!

"Is it true?" one of the scientists asked. "Could Interpol be onto us?"

"It's not likely." Niles holstered his gun. "Marlon's just trying to take Gilgal from us. He and Patrick have been working together. I think that's obvious, now."

"Where is Patrick?" Marlon asked. Without a gun on him, his leap overboard was all that waited. They still didn't know he had a bag full of dive equipment waiting for him.

"In Gilgal. They're stuck inside, at our disposal. We've won. I just returned to pick up Stajner. Now, the two of us can take Gilgal easily."

"Patrick won't allow it." Marlon scoffed. "You don't know who you've crossed this time, Mr. Niles. You think I would've defected if Patrick weren't for real? Look what the man's done in just a few days! You're all going to prison."

"Hold him down!" Niles ordered as the men approached with a piece of iron and thirty feet of chain. "If he wants to go to Gilgal, we'll send him to Gilgal!"

Stajner moved forward first, then Rob with his knife. Marlon gulped a breath of air as he dove for the water. A few seconds later, he was under the *Materia* and untying his gear from the access door. Once again, Marlon was faced with the choice to either swim to safety, or stay near the *Materia* to help Patrick—unless the mysterious agent man was already lost . . .

†

CHAPTER TEN

Everything in Gilgal that could be tied down and secured was done so by Nicholas Astroff's able men and women. With battery reserves nearly fully powered, Gilgal was ready to relocate.

"This is all my fault," Nathan mumbled. "If I would've bound Niles' hands or something, none of this would be necessary."

Chen Li, seated beside him on a sofa in the living quarters of Gilgal, took his hand in hers. Though they'd just met, it seemed a natural gesture—especially if Nicholas really was intent on keeping them in Gilgal for however long they were in water too deep in which to swim. And the disabled submersible port door made an escape impossible.

"I've been in hopeless places before," Li said. "I was a little girl in Hong Kong. No family or anyone to look out for me. Looking back, I see how God brought me up, provided people, and eventually I met Corban Dowler."

"I'm not disagreeing with you about God," Nathan said, "but we're three thousand feet under water. The only people who know Gilgal exists are outside trying to kill us. And once we relocate, even our killers won't know how to find us, let alone our friends."

"Patrick, I've been here for two months waiting for rescue.

The Gillies always knew they could relocate, so it wasn't like a prison to them. They accepted what situations arose, and that included me. I was given a place, mostly taking care of the kids, but I'll tell you this: it was a lot harder being here as the only outsider."

"Two makes it better?" Nathan sighed and smiled at her. "You're right. I'm overlooking the good, I guess. I mean, who wouldn't dream of being trapped in an underwater city with a coworker and a bubble full of isolationists?"

"Coworker?" She tilted her head and elbowed him. "You sure that's the word you want to use to describe the beginning of our relationship?"

"Relationship?" Nathan sat up straighter, his eyes wide.

"We're stuck in Gilgal, Patrick. Together. You figure it out."

She stood and strode away, leaving Nathan feeling like an insensitive lug. It wasn't the first time he'd misunderstood a woman's signals, but any other time, people could get away from one another. In Gilgal, there was no getting away. Were they a designated couple now in Gilgal? Would Nicholas preside over a marriage ceremony and expect them to live happily ever under water? Sure, Li was a catch, but this wasn't how Nathan had imagined he'd settle down.

"We're lifting!" someone announced.

Not knowing what to expect, Nathan moved off the sofa to sit on the floor. Gilgal shuddered and vibrated, and he stared up at the dome, half-expecting it to implode. At least then, he thought, Li would be spared from marrying him. He was an international operative, not husband material! Bad guys and bullets were his forte, not betrothals and babies.

"Vertical drive is operable!" someone voiced. "Commencing horizontal propulsion . . ."

Something fell off a shelf and broke. Gilgal vibrated more, and a child whimpered.

"Shut her down! Shut her down! We've got debris in the drive!"

Whatever motors were engaged were shut off abruptly, and Gilgal slammed down onto the ocean floor. Women muffled their screams and more children cried. Nathan gasped for air, realizing he'd been holding his breath while praying.

As Gilgal settled again, Nathan climbed to his feet and walked to the central console.

"It's the horizontal drive," an engineer explained to Nicholas. "It's either been damaged intentionally, or there's natural debris in her."

"How can we fix it?" Nathan asked. "Can we access it from inside?"

"Patrick! Not now!" Nicholas held up his hand. Nathan took a step back. More Gillies gathered to hear the news. "How bad is it? We came back down pretty hard."

"We're on different ground." The engineer rubbed his jaw. "Those few seconds of lift shifted us in the current only a few feet, but it was enough to put us on an uneven plain. We had the luxury of originally founding Gilgal on an even plain when we could shift her with the help of the submersibles.

"Tell me our options."

"Well, we've got vertical drive, due to buoyancy, but nothing horizontal."

"Then go vertical," Nathan suggested, "and let the current carry us away. We can relocate that way."

"That'd be pure death!" The engineer gasped. "What if we're carried farther off the continental shelf into deeper waters? When our power runs out, we'd try to set her down and realize her dome isn't built for greater atmospheric pressure."

"The dome would collapse," Nicholas said in simpler terms for Nathan. "Would you please let us discuss this?"

Again, Nathan had been rebuked, but he felt indebted to help them find a solution since he'd blown the rescue. He was about to say more when Li moved to his side and shook her head. Did no one trust him at all?

"If we remain here," Nicholas said, "we're certain to be captured or worse. We'll have to take our chances in the current."

"Okay, Nick." The engineer checked a gauge. "We'll have about ten hours of vertical drive power to find an even plain within our atmospheric limitations. Beyond that, we'll have to set her down wherever we end up and recharge."

"Even a couple miles away should be enough." Nicholas set his hand on the engineer's shoulder. "I know we'll be flying blind except for sonar until we can send up a buoy that isn't jammed, but even that isn't an option, anymore. We don't want to be tracked. Just do your best with what you have."

"I will, Nick."

"All of you, listen up!" Nicholas clapped his hands three times. "We're going to find a new location for Gilgal, but it'll take some drifting in the current to get there. We can only control our vertical depth. It may get bumpy. I suggest we break up into prayer groups while Mr. Monroe prepares for another lift, this one more prolonged."

Fearfully, the Gillies separated into groups to pray. Nathan felt more of an outsider as he and Li were left aside, but then Li started to leave to join Lana Astroff and three children who were kneeling nearby.

"Wait." Nathan took her by the wrist and drew her aside. "I have an idea that doesn't risk the lives of everyone in Gilgal. Well, not as much, anyway . . ."

"Patrick, seriously." She smiled, her hand on his arm. "Mr. Monroe is one of the best engineers probably in the world. If there's a safer way, he would've thought of it."

She left him to kneel with the others. Wandering over to Monroe, Nathan browsed the console and studied the screens.

"All automated, huh?" He fingered a red switch labeled *ENGAGE*.

"Don't touch that, please. Haven't you done enough damage, sir?"

"Sorry." Nathan moved around the circular console, feeling that edgy sensation deep in his gut when a plan began to formulate. He came to a keyboard and screen clearly identified as the vertical drive control. The computer was set to maintain a height of thirty meters off the ocean floor, meant to interface with Monroe's sonar program, which he was calibrating.

Touching a couple keys, Nathan found a calculation entry still possible. By a depth gauge, he saw Gilgal was 2,987 feet below the surface. For the automated vertical drive, he set it to ascend and stop at only forty-five feet under the surface.

"Very nice system, Mr. Monroe," Nathan said over the console. He could see only the technician's head. "You must have security available as well, right? You wouldn't want one of the kids to implement the vertical drive in the middle of the night, right?"

"Yes, there's security, Patrick, but we have no enemies here. Let us work."

"Security . . ." Nathan scanned a menu of options. "Let's see here. Locking. Ah, yes."

The secure function could be locked according to a number of variables. Nathan set it for uninterrupted operation, until otherwise commanded. When the locking prompt appeared, he typed in his own name for the password—followed by three random numbers. He closed the window and continued around the console. Peering over Monroe's shoulder, he noticed the sonar program was ready.

"Engaging vertical lift!" Monroe punched the red switch. "Hang on! God help us . . ."

Nathan stepped away, that reckless feeling expanding to his chest, but it felt better than the hopeless and helpless feeling he'd felt earlier.

Gilgal trembled, and the Gillies prayed louder. Nathan set a hand on a support beam that led to the water treatment section. Deep down, he felt as if he'd taken advantage of the Gillies, but being unreasonable was no way to function. His idea hadn't even been explored—until now.

"We've reached adequate drifting height!" Monroe announced. "We're in the flow of the current. Wait . . . We're still ascending! This isn't right. How can this be?"

"What is it?" Nicholas joined Monroe. "Is the sonar malfunctioning?"

"No, the vertical drive accelerated beyond the maximum setting I set for our height off the ocean floor. We're one hundred feet up! One-twenty . . . and increasing! We could go all the way to the surface!"

"Stop it!" Nicholas ordered. "We can't surface! They'll be able to attack us at will! Our submersible chamber is still jammed open. We won't be able to keep them out!"

"I'm trying!" Monroe went to the vertical drive control. "The settings have been changed. Looks like we're set for . . ."

Monroe's eyes met Nathan's.

"What's wrong?" Nicholas demanded.

"Patrick has changed these numbers. We'll rise to within forty-five feet of the surface. That is, Gilgal's foundation will be forty-five feet under water. The top of the dome will be only five feet under the surface."

"How could you do such a thing?" Nicholas shook a finger at Nathan. "Switch it back, now!"

"Not a chance." Nathan crossed his arms. "Go ahead, Mr. Monroe. Tell him why I may have just saved everyone's life."

Monroe's face went from fury to enlightenment.

"That's it! In shallow water, we can repair the horizontal drive ourselves!"

"Yeah." Nicholas scowled. "A by-product, no doubt, of Patrick leaving. He's only thinking of himself. Patrick, if we're attacked or damaged up there, it's on your head!"

"That was a dumb move." Li nudged Nathan's arm. "You're not familiar with Gilgal's controls."

"It was worth a try." Nathan watched Monroe monitor their ascent. "Trust me, you don't want to be partnered with me for an indeterminate number of years."

"First, we were coworkers. Now, we're partners?" She shook her head. "Maybe a couple more missions together and you'll actually figure out who we are to each other."

She left him again, but Nicholas was quickly before him.

"I won't lie to you, Patrick. I'll be glad to get rid of anyone who doesn't want to be in Gilgal, but only if we can do it safely. Do you have a plan? This Niles character is no fool."

"We need to wedge open the inner submersible door just enough to get me into the chamber. I know, we'll get flooded a bit, but it'll be for only a few seconds. Once in the chamber, I can close the outer port and empty it of water."

"There's no dive gear in the dome. It's all in the dive chamber. You'll have to hold your breath for as long as two minutes in there!" He sighed, seeing Nathan wasn't declining. "Okay, then what?"

"Then I come back in here and you can decide who will fix the horizontal drive. You'll have your dive gear by then, right?"

"Mr. Monroe will do that part. Fine. What about you and Li?"

"Well, we're only about five miles from the Reef Islands. If we aren't too close to the *Materia*, we can surface without attention and swim for land."

"Your contacts can have Niles and his crew arrested?"

"That's my plan."

"Patrick, I'm not looking for a headline." Nicholas moved closer. "I don't want anyone knowing where we are."

"Where you go after I'm gone is your business."

"How long until we reach the intended shallows, Mr. Monroe?"

"Less than five minutes."

"I want to do this as quickly as possible. Get the tools,

men! We have to open the submersible door as soon as we're in place. Everyone, we're about to make a mess in here; expect some flooding."

"Are you sure about this?" Li asked as Nathan joined the procession to the submersible chamber door. "You can hold your breath for two minutes—while active? Your stunt may just drown you."

"Don't worry, Li. I won't leave without you." He smiled down at her. "We have this companion thing to work out."

That made her laugh—a sound that Nathan made a mental note to hear again very soon. But for now, he oversaw the selection of potential tools that Nicholas had available for opening the chamber door by force. Two of the sturdier men selected thick metal rods, and another man held an actual seal-spreader that looked like a pair of giant scissors with flat ends.

"We're there!" Monroe called from the console, though the mid-morning sunshine was obvious through the dome ceiling and the five feet of water overhead. "Gilgal is holding depth. Go!"

Teams with towels backed the men with tools. Nathan took off his shirt and shoes to leave them with Chen Li. Li stared at his chest, then reached out to touch one of his scars on his torso.

"So many . . ." Her face saddened, but then reversed, and a smile crept across her lips. "You're no beginner, Patrick Gibson. You're one of the men Corban Dowler told me about a couple years ago."

"If you've learned anything from my antics," Nathan said for her ears only, "then you'll know I'm nobody special, but it's a good thing God is a big God to fix my blunders."

The children were on the other side of Gilgal, far away from the certain intake of water. Nathan rubbed his hands together and nodded at the men. Li moved aside with several other women. With no more time to prepare himself, he stood over the man with the seal-spreader.

"I'm ready." He flexed his fingers, ready to grab the edge of the door to draw himself through as it opened. "Let's do this!"

They inserted the spreader into the seam, assisted by a couple swift kicks. A trickle of water seeped through. The men with rods were ready to insert their braces.

The spreader opened the door one inch. The direct burst of water hit the man so hard, his head snapped back and he lost his grip on his tool as he flew into the flood control crew. The door slammed shut. The man covered his eyes with his hands and Nathan understood instantly what had happened. The water was so pressurized, it had shot under the man's eyelids. Nathan moved to speak privately to Nicholas.

"We're inside three atmospheres of oceanic pressure. It's going to take some ingenuity to beat physics here—and maybe some brute force."

"Two men on the spreader!" Nicholas ordered. "Stand aside from the spray when it opens again. Patrick, brace yourself!"

Again, they spread the door an inch. Water shot into Gilgal. The men with the rods inserted their tools and forced the door wider, wider . . . Other men joined in the effort, holding the workers' legs, supporting them. Nathan knelt under one rod holder, trying to avoid the gush of gallons pouring in.

"A few more inches!" Nathan yelled over the noise. "A little more! Come on! Nick, push me through!"

Nicholas poised himself like a linebacker and nodded. Next to him and behind him, the flood controllers were overwhelmed with water, many of them forced aside like toys in a child's tub.

Nathan saw his window open just wide enough. Closing his eyes, he tucked his head and ducked into the flood. He dragged himself through the door—the water warmer than he expected—and fought to move past waist level into the chamber. Suddenly, hands were on his legs giving him enough thrust to get one foot far enough on the outside of the door.

An instant later, he was all the way through, and the door behind him slid shut. The roaring in his ears and tearing pressure of rushing water was gone. And Nathan suddenly realized he hadn't taken a deep enough breath for what was to follow.

The door to the ocean stood open before him, so he went to that first, since it had to be closed before the pumps could empty the chamber of water. It was then that he discovered what had jammed the door open—a giant conch— intentionally placed during Niles' departure in the submersible. But removing the crustacean shell was no easy task, especially as Nathan's mind was focused on his burning lungs. Turning from the conch, Nathan swam to the top of the dive chamber in search for a pocket of air, even a single breath—anything!

Bubbles escaped his lips. Frantically now, he searched the ceiling. There was no air! He was about to drown. Pushing away from the ceiling, he consigned himself to death. His mind no longer seemed to function without the right amount of oxygen, and he was near unconsciousness.

He would be in the presence of his Lord and Savior in a few minutes. It wasn't a troubling thought. Nathan had believed in the complete redemptive work at the cross for some years now. This was an end he was ready to face.

†

<u>*CHAPTER ELEVEN*</u>

Marlon was so utterly shocked to bump into an object under water that his first instinct was to draw a diving blade and turn on the whale shark that intended to swallow him. But before he blunted his blade on the thick plastic bubble, it dawned on him that he was looking into the confines of Gilgal, rising from the deep.

The closer Marlon peered into the hovering city, the more he realized something had gone drastically wrong inside. Though Marlon's own life had hung in the balance as he'd circled the *Materia* explorer ship while waiting for Patrick Gibson, whatever tragedy had caused a degree of flooding within Gilgal now seemed to require Marlon's urgent attention.

Immediately, Marlon oriented himself with his past experience and charts he knew of Gilgal, and kicked with his flippered feet straight down the dome toward the city's foundation, under which he knew lay the submersible chamber. Turning under its belly, he had only to swim thirty yards with his gear still in tow before he came upon the port that was jammed open by a large conch shell—Niles' doing, by his own confession. Whatever else was happening inside, Marlon attributed it to other damage Niles had caused to Gilgal as well.

But then Marlon spied Patrick near the ceiling of the chamber. Marlon let go of his dive bag to settle on the chamber floor, and surged up to the man who was without scuba gear whatsoever. As Marlon grabbed hold of Patrick's arm, it seemed to frighten the agent, but Marlon thrust his safe second air regulator into Patrick's mouth. Patrick's eyes bulged, and he seemed to cough for the first few breaths, but the man had extreme mental discipline, Marlon noticed, for not lapsing into panic. Another few seconds, and Patrick would've been a drifting corpse!

When Patrick seemed to have recovered adequately, Marlon gestured toward topside. The two shared air as they left the chamber. Marlon took up his bag of dive gear once again as they rose to the surface.

…✝…

Nathan exhaled carefully as he ascended, his head breaking through the surface above Gilgal before Marlon's. His immediate concern was for the *Materia's* location—whether it was close or far away from Gilgal—and discovered the explorer vessel was about one hundred and fifty yards northwest.

Marlon's masked face joined him, and together they stood on top of the dome of Gilgal in five feet of water, varying a few inches now and then according to the fluctuations of the vertical drive turbines.

"I've never been happier to see someone I've killed!" Nathan laughed, his nerves still unsettled over his unlikely rescue—only by God's providence. "Can you spare a rebreather there? I'd say you had enough for a platoon."

"Didn't know how long I'd be waiting for you, so I took

what I could off the *Materia* and sunk the rest." Marlon handed him a dive mask, flippers, and a rebreather with four hours of dive time remaining. "What does the rising of Gilgal mean?"

"They're relocating the city." Nathan strapped the rebreather onto his back and tugged on the flippers. "They have two problems: their horizontal drive turbine is malfunctioning, and the submersible chamber is jammed open. That's what I was supposed to be fixing when I decided to try to breathe water."

"Yeah, I saw the conch. So, we're two men with two problems." Marlon looked over his shoulder. "Our heads might be two dots in the water to them, but I wouldn't stay up here for long. You attack the conch. Where's this horizontal drive?"

"Under the power section. From what Mr. Niles has said, I don't think he's damaged it—or even knows it exists—so I'm guessing there's just some ocean debris clogging it."

"Okay, I'll check it out. Then what?"

"I'm kind of winging it." Nathan smiled, still trembling from his near death experience. "With three of us, we could probably retake the *Materia* come nightfall, if we use our heads. I figure Mr. Niles will take advantage of the jammed-open chamber, so when he leaves in the submersible, we board the *Materia*."

"All right, but three of us?"

"Chen Li is with us. Gilgal is moving on. We need to shut down the jammers and get on a sat-phone."

"Patrick, to be honest with you, I'm just a no-good—"

"No." Nathan spit on his mask to keep it from fogging,

then inhaled through his nose to seal it tightly to his face. "You and I don't know one another too well, but trust me when I say I'm not the one you need to confess your sins to. That's between you and God. He's the One who gave His life for you. For now, we're a team. In one hour, we meet back here, the three of us, to make a plan to retake the *Materia*. Can you handle that drive?"

"I'll do my best."

They submerged together, then separated over the dome to attend to their individual tasks, Marlon trailing his dive gear. As Nathan swam below the dome, he considered how his recent experience was a sign from God. The Lord obviously intended him to continue His work on earth since He'd provided a rescue.

He returned to the chamber and worked for several minutes on the conch before it came out in pieces. The door closed with such force that Nathan was glad he wasn't in front of it as it sealed. The red light flashed on the wall as the water pumped out, and Nathan knelt to shed his dive gear. When the inner chamber door opened, Li was the first to rush in, already in a wet suit.

"If I didn't know any better," she said slyly, "I'd say that was Marlon I saw through the dome. You said he was dead!"

"Dead to Niles, but alive and thankfully an asset to us."

"Praise God, you've done it, Patrick!" Nicholas grasped Nathan's elbow and pumped his hand heartily. "You've saved us all!"

"Give me a few more hours, and I'll have a new submersible for you as well. No point in moving on without the safety of a rover."

"Oh, you will, will you?" Li guffawed. "Mr. Niles is just going to roll out the red carpet for you and give you his rover?"

"You need another submersible for safety reasons, Nick." Nathan said, ignoring for the moment but appreciating Li's sarcasm. "My guy will have your horizontal drive cleared in a few minutes. Come midnight, Lord willing, I can deliver that submersible. There are lives to consider."

"Now, don't you tell me—"

"Nick." Monroe interrupted Nicholas. "With the horizontal drive functional, we can navigate where we need to, set Gilgal down for a recharge, and come back to the coordinates at midnight. We do need at least one submersible. This could set us up for years to come."

"Assuming you let me disable the jammers so you can determine GPS coordinates." Nathan nodded with the men, knowing he was asking them to communicate with satellites and risk exposure again. "I'll do my best. If you must seclude yourselves from the world and God's plan of spreading His Word—"

"Don't preach to me, Patrick!" Nicholas raised his chin. "I know God's sanctifying call. No one will detour us."

"So be it. Midnight, then." Sometimes, Nathan reflected, he met pockets of Christians who refused help, refused rescue, or even freedom from bondage. All he could do was assist them and let them go.

Nathan was given his shirt and a wet suit, but he left his shoes behind. As the chamber filled with water, he and Li stood in their dive gear, facing one another. It was moments like this, with confidence in God, that Nathan thanked His

Lord he was His servant. And sharing such a moment with a stunning agent . . .

"That's a pretty tall order, Patrick." Li donned her mask. "Shutting down the jammers and delivering a rover? A very tall order."

"We serve a tall God." Nathan smiled. "He specializes in tall orders."

...✝...

Trevor Niles pushed the joystick straight forward and forced the submersible to dive at such a steep angle it made Stajner strain against his chest harness in the copilot seat. But Stajner didn't complain. Now that he thought about it, Niles realized no one had spoken to him directly even as the *Materia* crew had readied the submersible for the most important dive yet. Their lack of communication meant they now shared his destiny, his desire, his determination. And they feared him. He wouldn't stop until he ruled the empire he wanted; the underwater bubble city of Gilgal would be his own! It wasn't too much to ask for. Fantasizing, he pictured the clientele and the millions he would preside over. All his!

The afternoon sun on the surface was quickly left behind, and Stajner flipped on the rover's bow lights. Niles was ready for a fight, but he hoped the Gillies took their defeat as the Christian cowards he knew they were. Those who resisted, would die. Those who wanted to share his reign, would die—like Captain Sardan and Guntari.

"We're at depth, sir," Stajner said twenty minutes later.

So busy was he contemplating his triumphal entry that Niles had nearly plowed straight into the sea floor! He eased back on the joystick and leveled the submersible. His own genius surprised him sometimes—this time particularly in regard to the conch he'd found and jammed into the door of Gilgal's dive chamber. Now the Gillies were trapped inside their habitat until he deemed it time to make the chamber operable again. There were rulers, he thought, and there were the ruled. He was definitely a ruler.

"Maybe we've drifted off course in an ocean flow." Stajner twisted in his seat to look around. "Usually the lights of Gilgal are visible within one hundred meters."

Niles wasn't too concerned. The Gillies might've powered down their lights to hide in the darkness of the ocean, but it was only a temporary state of hiding. Their fall was inevitable. After more than a two month siege, the castle was about to be claimed once and for all by its rightful king!

In widening circles, Niles piloted the rover in search of Gilgal. Since he hadn't come upon the dome yet, he surely must have been thrown off course during the dive. Seriously, he chuckled to himself, how far could a sunken city run?"

"I don't believe it!" Stajner cursed and wiped condensation from the glass. "Are those the sub-chambers? Where's the city?"

Now, Niles felt like puking. Sure enough, a large circle on the ocean floor, like a shadowy eclipse, marked where Gilgal had once rested. The twelve sub-chambers that had been attached to the central dome now lay dark and alone on the ocean floor. Gilgal had vanished!

"It isn't possible . . ." Niles looked directly up, suspecting Gilgal might drop from the surface and crush them. But that was absurd; Gilgal had no piloting capabilities, no drive, or thrust! They had to be there somewhere!

Refusing to be defeated, Niles continued down the Reef to the southeast. If Gilgal had somehow moved, perhaps it had followed the current and was still nearby. Or it had slid off the continental shelf even farther, and had imploded under crushing pressures. The surface would be strewn with debris if that were the case, and he'd seen no debris.

The longer Niles searched, the more he felt his hatred rise. Fools had done this. Religious fools! *Christians*, no less. Men and women who believed in a great Being in the sky had outsmarted him time and again. These Christians were nothing like the Christian converts on the island of his birth, Zalzuna, whose communist rule easily shut the mouth of any confessor. Once Niles had ventured into the world from the island, he'd expected to find a similar breed. He'd even targeted Christians because he knew they were weak. Christians weren't smarter than he was, nor more crafty, by any means. Yet, they boasted that a Spirit watched over them, and if Niles hadn't shown that such ideas were complete fiction, he might've begun to believe it.

"They think they've won," Niles mumbled, not caring if Stajner heard him. "They think I won't go after them—or others like them. I'll make them pay. I'll find them, or trap them, wherever they are. Maybe not the Gillies, but there are other Christians. I'll get them . . ."

Boiling with anger and defeat, Niles turned back, and began the ascent to the *Materia*. He wished he didn't have to face the crew under such a defeated state—again. At least he could use their own frustration with the Christians to reignite their fervor for another enterprise elsewhere. No one would deter his destiny to rule!

$$\dagger$$

CHAPTER TWELVE

Silently, Nathan and Marlon climbed aboard the *Materia* by way of the stern dive platform. They didn't have long to take over the ship, not with Niles due back soon when he didn't find Gilgal where he thought he would. There were men and women on the helipad near the tail of the two-man chopper, but the late evening crowd was nowhere else on deck.

"Captain Sardan was using his electrical codes as leverage to keep himself alive," Marlon said quietly as they walked into the vehicle hangar. Nathan, Marlon, and Chen Li had spent the last hour of darkness treading water a short distance away from the *Materia,* waiting and planning these very moves. "Once he left the power activated to dive to Gilgal, he became expendable to Niles. That's my guess as to why Niles blew him up."

"I think you're on to something there." Nathan pointed at the upper deck. He wasn't used to talking much during an operation. "Just get those jammers turned off and make that call to my people. Li can't hold off Niles forever."

Marlon nodded and, still in his wetsuit, bounded up the stairs to the bridge above deck three. Nathan, however, descended the stairs cautiously and prayerfully, knowing that which lay ahead would require much more than his own careless tongue to end the conflict on board. God Himself was the only One who could bring true peace to the rebellious hearts on the *Materia*.

On deck two, Nathan moved uncontested through the engine room to the four-man cabin in the bow. Two men were lounging in their bunks when he stepped into the doorway. One of them was the goon from Nathan's first day on board who he'd bested in the dive locker.

Both men set down their magazines and looked at one another, then swung their feet off their bunks. They paused before standing when Nathan raised his hand.

"Now, you know it'll take a lot more than you two to take me down. Hear me out." Nathan glanced down the corridor, wary of more men who could become potential problems, especially when he was as tired as he was. "Niles has been thwarted. Gilgal has a drive engine and they've flown the coop. They got tired of the assaults and took off, probably never to be found again."

"You're lying, Patrick," one man said. "Gilgal is a city. I've seen her. Cities don't have drives."

"If you don't like the drive scenario, then the city vanished from the sea floor. Those are your only two options. Believe what you want." Nathan shrugged. "The point is, Niles' plan blew up in his face, and now the authorities are on the way."

"Yeah, right. The authorities don't even know we're anything but explorers."

"Really?" Nathan chuckled. "You're one of those aboard who still thinks I crashed my plane by accident? Near one of the only vessels within fifty miles? Come on. Neither of you believes that, anymore."

Both exchanged looks.

"Where's Mr. Niles?"

"He's about to be arrested." Nathan placed his hands on his hips. "There was an underlying conflict here. Are you guys aware of it?" They looked on with uncertainty. "No matter how misplaced the Gillies' determination was to be separate from the world, they're still Christians—God's people. Evil certainly wins a lot of battles in this world, but how can you expect to take on the Creator of the world and win? Christians were targeted here, and that means God was targeted."

"I don't believe that garbage."

"Sure, you do. Deep down, you've known you were no accident, that there was some purpose for your life. You each have a conscience, which science can't explain. You both stand accused or excused as individuals. Maybe you've grown a little calloused, but some part of you has questioned the afterlife. Here you've risked your lives to take something below the water. You've stared death in the face, so you've both thought about death. When you stand alone before God, do you think you'll throw some good deeds at a perfect God's feet and demand heaven based on those deeds?"

"Patrick, you're out of your mind. You're as crazy as those Gillies."

"Be quiet and listen." Nathan gave them a fierce stare, a daring look. Though he hadn't rehearsed this conversation, it was one he'd had with countless captive audiences around the world during some of the worst missions to rescue God's people. "Both of you have some ugliness inside of you that can't be solved by penance or the claim of anything good in you or your past. It's time to take account and call out to God for forgiveness. He made a way through Jesus on the cross. All that sin you're carrying—it's time to hand it over to a wrathful but also a merciful God." He checked his watch. "I'd say you have ten minutes before the authorities get here from the coast."

Nathan moved aside for them to run for the inflatable, if they chose to. Marlon would ensure no one used the bridge to take the *Materia* herself away. Her electronics had stores of evidence that the actual Interpol agents would use to prosecute Niles.

One of the men took the opportunity to leave, looking back once to shake his head at Nathan, then ascended the stairs. The other rose from his bunk more slowly. He was the young man Nathan had pummeled on his first day aboard.

"You know, my grandmother says she still prays for me."

"Maybe I'm an answer to her prayers."

"I'd say I have some things to confess."

"Not to me—or to any man." Nathan pointed to the man's chest. "That's between you and God. That kind of new birth can come only from Him. I'd say I was just planting the seed, but it sounds like your grandmother was being faithful at planting the seed long before this."

"Should I run for it?" The man looked suddenly weary. "I doubt using the motorboat to go for the islands will avoid arrest."

"Sometimes there's more mercy found when you take responsibility." Nathan smiled. "I know from experience you'll have a clear conscience if you don't run from this."

"Then I'm staying. What should I do?"

Nathan set his hand on the young man's shoulder. He recalled the story of Corban Dowler's forgiveness towards Luigi Putelli for trying to kill him—and the friendship they now had.

"Help me clear the boat. Anyone left aboard or associated with Mr. Niles will be arrested."

…✝…

Chen Li had been thrilled that Patrick had entrusted her with the responsibility of intercepting Niles' submersible on its way to the surface. It was certainly better than boarding the *Materia* where most of the men and women would look at her as a traitor. Sure, Patrick seemed confident enough in his plan, but those on the *Materia* were nearly twenty persons!

Li watched her depth gauge. She was holding steady at thirty feet, near the threshold to the next atmosphere of pressure where the prolonged breathing of diving gases would require a lengthy stay in a decompression chamber at the back of the *Materia's* vehicle hangar.

At the first flicker of light below her, however, Li dove to meet the rising submersible. *Forty feet.* She kept kicking. *Fifty.* Her ears popped as she released pressure. *Sixty.* It was hard to believe she'd been so helpless on the streets of Hong Kong twenty years ago. *Seventy feet.* Now, she was diving into darkness, trusting God as she faced men who bore lethal hatred for her and anyone else who stood in their way. *Eighty.*

The submersible swerved to avoid her, but Li wore flippers. As a swimmer, she easily outmaneuvered the rover as it sought a way past her to reach the surface. She collided against the front of the submersible glass and saw Niles and Stajner inside. Niles drew a firearm and aimed it at her through the glass, but Stajner slapped it away, visibly screaming at Niles. If the rover's glass broke, they'd both die.

Content for the moment, at least, Li drew a dive knife that Marlon had given her. As the submersible continued its sluggish ascent, now with three bodies, its tractor propulsion churned wildly. But then Li carefully shoved the blade into the left tractor track. It jammed, making a grinding sound that made Li flinch away, worried the track would violently tear apart or explode.

The rover churned in a gradual circle, only one of its tracks now operable. Still attached to the front of the bubble, Li noticed they were at a depth of seventy feet. It was such a formidable depth from the surface that a submersible cockpit implosion would mean certain death. Far above, there was an orange haze. To the men trapped in the bubble with oxygen depleting and no scuba gear, it would surely seem to be miles to the *Materia*. And before either of the men could initiate the emergency buoyancy surfacing routine, Li reached to the back of the rover and unscrewed two hoses, their compressed air suddenly hissing bubbles wildly.

Sliding over to the side of the submersible's glass, Li could see the central monitor dials. Niles had been under water for two hours looking for Gilgal. He was down to forty-percent oxygen, and they didn't have any supplemental tanks on the back. She'd dived enough times in the rovers to know to take emergency tanks, but such was Niles' haste to take over Gilgal.

The right track stopped spinning, and the automated depth-ballast adjustment system held them at the seventy-foot depth.

Triumphantly stalling a fuming Niles, Li smiled around her air regulator and pushed off the rover glass to head for the surface. Though reluctant to board the *Materia*, she did want to be with Patrick again. Was it because he'd rescued her that she was attracted to him? There was definitely more to her attraction to him, even if the idea of living as a couple in Gilgal was long past. They were cut from the same mold— COIL agents, Christians adventurists, and more than a little lonely.

But as Li left the submersible, her right fin caught in something. She looked down and saw the left robotic pincer had grabbed her fin. And the right arm was closing quickly! Li struggled frantically to get her heel out of the fin, but she wasn't fast enough. The right pincer closed around her calf, making her scream. Her regulator fell from her mouth and bubbles escaped her lips.

Li twisted her leg around. The pincer bit down harder. She fit the regulator back into her mouth and took a quick breath as the other pincer reached for a hold farther up her leg. Like a nightmare, she imagined the pincers walking up her body and tearing her mask and oxygen from her.

Instead, Li reached past the second pincer to the arm that controlled it, and took hold of the cable that gave it power. With a desperate tear, she yanked the cable from the socket, disabling the pincer but not the arm. Though she'd won a little victory, she was still trapped in the first pincer, the cable unreachable. Her leg throbbed with pain, more so since the pincer was over her two-month-old bullet wound, but she managed to think past it to the more pressing danger of suffocating. She had less air than the rover had.

Niles tapped his watch, a signal to her indicating he was aware of her dilemma. He then pointed at the tractor that was disabled by the knife. But even though she wouldn't have pulled out the blade, she couldn't even see it now, which meant it wasn't within reach.

She gazed yearningly upward. Patrick had come for her once. Would he come for her again, or was he too busy with the crew on the *Materia*? The three of them had agreed that giving the crew a chance to escape would be safer than trying to detain them all. They were primarily after Niles, anyway, though as COIL agents, she and Patrick had a concern priority for lost souls and preserving life.

Twisting the robotic arm, Niles flung Li like a rag to one side, the strain on her leg testing the breaking point of her bones. Her mask fogged as her temperature heated and tears trickled against the seal. This wasn't the death she'd imagined facing. Recently, she'd merely looked forward to dying as a senior citizen of Gilgal—beside Patrick. She couldn't die like this—in darkness, in pain, in the company of hateful men. What was God doing?

Closing her eyes, she prayed as the arm tossed her again. The pain was unbearable. Under stress, her oxygen would deplete more quickly. At seventy feet, she was already using three times more volume than she would be on the surface. Where was Patrick?

...✝...

"Do you think they'll reach land?" Marlon asked Nathan as they gazed off the bow of the *Materia*. Twelve men and women had taken two inflatable tenders with outboards to run for land—at night.

"Doesn't matter. We've made the call. Every Coast Guard vessel from Brisbane to Cairns will be watching the beaches. My people will be here in a few minutes."

"Are you sure me and the others will be okay?" Marlon's brow seemed more lined in the dim deck lighting. Four men and two women had declined to run as well.

"Lives were lost while you guys stood by and continued to participate. But with Mr. Niles in custody, your cooperation and testifying against him will help."

"So, you and Li will testify for us? Those of us who are surrendering voluntarily?"

"In person, we can't. We don't exist. You understand." Nathan frowned at Marlon, wishing he could do more. "My report should suffice, though."

"Report?" He looked hopeful.

"Yeah, I can write a convincing report. Without your help to take the *Materia*, I would've died, and the Gillies would've probably perished on some reef at three thousand feet. Regardless of what happens, I want you to think about what we discussed. God has a purpose for you, Marlon. The cross of Christ is before you."

"I appreciate it, Patrick." He looked afar off. "If I don't sit in prison too long, I have family I've avoided for more years than I care to admit."

"You know, I haven't heard Li come aboard." Nathan walked along the deck and reached the stern where the A-frame crane hung out over the dark water. "Li, you here?"

Marlon pulled at the deck ladder they'd hung overboard for her.

"No wet footprints here. She's still under."

"It's been over an hour." Nathan clung to the crane and leaned out over the water. "Kill the lights, Marlon. I think I see something."

Turning off the stern lights, Marlon left only some interior and bridge lights on. Nathan squinted at the surface. Every couple of waves, he could see a shimmer of light far under water.

"I think the submersible is down there. She stopped it." Nathan zipped up his wetsuit, donned a mask, and pulled on a pair of free diving flippers. "Get the tanks. Something's wrong."

Nathan took a deep breath and dove straight in, trusting Marlon to follow with oxygen.

He swam toward the light below—which looked closer from the surface, but now he realized was much, much deeper. As he descended, his chest compressed and his ears popped. A splash far above told him Marlon was indeed coming as backup for whatever lay below.

The submersible gradually took shape, and the wriggling form in the lights made Nathan surge deeper than he would've felt safe doing under any other circumstances. Li was trapped, but at least she looked alive.

Then, other silhouettes passed between Nathan and the submersible lights—silhouettes with fins and long, sweeping tails. When Nathan looked around him, his heart pounded in his ears. More gray bodies dimly reflected the rover lights. Sharks circled all around, dozens of them—tiger sharks.

Only when he was closer to Li did he see the red film drifting in the water in front of the lights, and more blood coursing from her leg trapped in the robotic claw. Nathan forced his fear aside and clenched his teeth. He reminded himself God was here, even here, where all seemed to spell tragedy and loss.

✝

CHAPTER THIRTEEN

Nathan arrived at Li's side, but barely. She seemed to anticipate his need for oxygen and, even in her state, gave him her safe second regulator. He took slow, controlled breaths and glared in at Niles and Stajner. Both men sat quite contently, much to Nathan's fury, as they tortured Li with the robotic pincer. Niles pointed at the track. The rover's propulsion on the port side was disabled and too damaged for Nathan to fix in such a situation. Li had done her job to capture Niles at depth, but no one had foreseen this predicament. The evil man seemed determined to hold Li hostage until the track was operable. Unfortunately, Nathan couldn't convey to Niles the extent of the damage of the track.

A shark flashed across Nathan's back. He elbowed it hard in the side. Other sharks crowded the edge of the light—and wherever there was light, that haunting shimmer of crimson drew them ever closer. The blood tempted them, and Li's wounded appearance of twisting and turning to free herself seemed to only excite the predators further.

Another shark moved gently up to Nathan from above, but he held back a punch with his fist when he saw it was Marlon with a dive tank of his own and another single. Nathan strapped it hastily onto his back and buckled it in the front.

Marlon moved into a defensive position beside Li, his back to the submersible lights and his face to the sharks.

Moving up and laying against the rover's glass, Nathan gestured to the robotic pincer. Niles shook his head.

If they wanted to die stubbornly, so be it. But Nathan had to save Li's life. And if Niles wouldn't release Li, Nathan would get inside the rover and do so himself.

Removing his regulator so Niles could see his mouth, with as much emotion as Nathan could broadcast in his face, he screamed through the water, "Do it!"

Niles visibly chuckled and seemed to make a joke to Stajner as he pointed to the disabled track.

That was their last warning, Nathan decided. He positioned himself on top of the submersible where the hatch was sealed closed. Niles and Stajner scrambled out of their seatbelts to stand and try to brace the door from opening. Since Nathan was outside, his legs gave him stability so his arms could force the door open on its hinges. Niles and Stajner didn't have a chance against Nathan's strength as they fought for a handhold. But it hadn't been designed to lock in the anticipation of a shark-infested battle of wills to the death.

There would be no death, Nathan hoped, if Niles and Stajner each took a deep breath and exhaled during their ascents.

He broke the seal and heaved it open so quickly, the submersible pod filled with water in one second. A giant bubble of air wobbled toward the surface, expanding as it ascended. Niles and Stajner looked as if they'd been punched. Disoriented, they swirled in their new watery atmosphere like dolls in a washing machine.

Niles seemed to gain his senses first, and Nathan saw him draw his firearm. The man reached out of the open door and fired at Nathan. The explosion was muffled, but the projectile was certainly deadly within a few feet of the muzzle. Nathan gripped Niles by the wrist and twisted his arm, but Niles' other arm shot up to grab Nathan's air regulator. Not willing to lose his air, Nathan shoved away from the door to let Niles escape to the surface unimpeded.

But Marlon wouldn't allow Niles to escape, surely knowing how dangerous such a man could be if free. Marlon kicked forward and caught at Niles' clothes, turning him in the water, restricting him from rising to the surface. Niles planted his gun against Marlon's shoulder and fired.

In that instant, the situation exploded. Nathan watched wide-eyed as Marlon floated backwards, his face full of shock and pain, his shoulder gushing red. Niles darted upward, reaching for the surface, but not before a shark opened its mouth at Niles' head. The side of Niles' face seemed to peel away under the shark's teeth, but the shark wasn't getting a bite of Niles without Niles fighting back. He fired at the shark until the gun was empty. Then, with his face bleeding horribly, Niles kicked toward the surface.

As soon as Niles was out of the way, Stajner kicked off the copilot seat of the rover. No sooner had he left the submersible hatch than a shark swiped past him, spinning him sideways. With no air, and in his haste for the surface, Stajner passed through the cloud of red where sharks were biting indiscriminately anything in their grasp—even each other. Nathan had to look away from what followed—the flurry of flesh and blood that poured into the water.

Ducking into the submersible hatch while he could still see, Nathan unlocked the robotic pincer with a simple double-tap on the joystick trigger. Li swam free below the rover instead of upward into the bloody fray. Then Nathan noticed Marlon above. Though wounded, Marlon was swimming frantically for the surface. Nathan prayed for God's help.

Li slipped into the submersible beside Nathan, and he pulled the hatch closed. Indicating that her air was depleted, Nathan shared his second regulator. They waited long minutes as the frenzy outside dissipated. Shedding his tank, Nathan cut a leg off his wetsuit and wrapped Li's damaged leg tightly. He checked her depth gauge and gestured to her that she was due for the decompression chamber for a while since she'd been beyond the safe threshold—but they weren't about to ascend with such company all around.

Enjoying the thought of sharing the decompression chamber with Li, Nathan settled into the pilot seat for another twenty minutes before he signaled Li that it was time to exit. The sharks had calmed, and most had moved on. Those in sight were no longer frenzied, perhaps now only curious about the lights.

They surfaced together, side by side, just off the stern of the *Materia.* An Australian Coast Guard motorboat flashed a light on them, and men in life jackets and fatigues came to their aid.

"Get her to the decompression chamber, now!" Nathan ordered.

"Are you Patrick Gibson?" a man with bars on his collar yelled over the noise of a chopper landing on the helipad.

"Yeah, I'm Patrick."

Two men in fatigues lifted Li off her feet and carried her into the vehicle hangar.

"Yes, sir," the lieutenant said into his radio. "He's here."

"Hey!" Nathan pointed at the helipad. "Where's the little chopper that was up there?"

"I arrived first." The lieutenant shook his head. "Never saw a chopper, except ours."

Walking into the vehicle hangar, Nathan wondered how Niles could've survived such an injury to his face and yet still fly out in the chopper. A familiar face stepped out of the stairwell on his left while other agents hustled all about.

"Thank God, you're safe!" Corban Dowler gave him a brief embrace. "Chen Li?"

"Decompression chamber, where I'm headed for a while. She'll be okay. You have a pen?"

"Here." Corban offered his sat-phone instead. "You get to the bottom of this mess? Nobody on board is talking yet. We can't figure out what this vessel was doing out here."

"Oh, I got to the bottom of it, but the mastermind just escaped ahead of you—in a two-man, white and blue helicopter. His name is Trevor Niles. We don't want him going free." Nathan typed in a message onto the phone keypad. "There. Those are coordinates for a position a few hundred yards from here. It's two hours from midnight right now. There's a submersible rover seventy feet straight below. That submersible needs to be functional and at those coordinates on the ocean surface by midnight. One of its tracks is currently jammed, but it's nothing a couple dive techs can't fix in a few minutes."

"Okay, I'll get on it." Corban smiled and cocked his head. "I can't wait for this debrief. Anything else I need to know right now?"

"I'll tell you in the report—even the unbelievable details." Nathan backed away toward the decompression chamber wherein Li was being helped, her leg already temporarily bandaged. "Just get that submersible up and repaired by midnight. Lives are counting on it, Boss!"

Nathan climbed into the chamber and sat down facing Li as the men outside sealed the door shut. For the first time, Nathan felt the weight of the night's events. Marlon had risked his life for him and Li, and his about-face against Niles had been something Nathan wouldn't soon forget.

"Was that Corban Dowler?" Li peeked out the two-inch oval window. "How steamed is he?"

"Why would he be steamed?" Nathan acknowledged blood clotting on his shoulder and a gash in his shirt. It would be another scar to add to all the others, but his first as a lone COIL operator—and his first shark wound.

"That depends on how badly we blew the op." Li stuck out her lower lip. "I didn't stay on the *Materia* like I was assigned."

"Our missions were different, weren't they? Mine was to make sure you were safe. Yours was to keep tabs on a group who'd voiced hostility toward Christians. You're now safe and no Gillies died."

"Mr. Niles got away, and Marlon was injured. That's a failure to me."

Looking at the floor of the chamber, Nathan prayed his anger at Niles didn't turn into hatred.

"Don't keep score," he suddenly blurted, as much for himself as for Li. "That's something Corban taught me a few years ago. Trust God to do what you can, and let God worry about the consequences of things out of your control."

"Then we won't get reprimanded?"

"For saving the lives of the Gillies?" He tried not to sound too critical. Li had obviously not been on many missions in which hardly anything ever went as planned. "No, we won't be reprimanded. We'll debrief, and our report will help Corban and others at COIL assign us to the next mission."

"*Us?*" She smiled and nudged his foot with her own. "You think they'll assign us to something together?"

"I . . ." He felt himself blush. "I may have spoken out of turn. There are so many needs and only so many operators. Pair-ups are not irregular, but they're usually male-male teams, not unmarried male-female teams."

"So, as long as we're not unmarried?" She bit her lip as she tried to hide her smile. "Oh, relax, Patrick! I'm trying to make you squirm. I just know a good teammate when I see one."

"*Teammate?*"

"It's a process." She sighed, and Nathan was relieved that her bout of teasing was over. Regardless of his romantic notions toward her, now that the mission was over, he realized he'd probably be assigned to something else alone, for which he'd been trained to do.

"What will COIL do about Niles?"

"We're not international police." He settled more comfortably into his seat, though he wished he was in a chase chopper hunting down Niles. "COIL responds to threats against Christians. If Niles persists on persecuting believers, we'll come across him again someday, no matter where he goes."

"Well, I won't feel this mission is truly over until Niles is in custody, somebody's custody. He killed others, you know, who tried to defect from the *Materia*."

"I know." He folded his arms and closed his eyes, sleepiness finally setting in. It had been a hard few days. "We have to be patient about these things. God is just. Vengeance is His. Niles will fall when it's time, but not until God says it's time."

"How long until we're assigned to another mission, with other COIL agents or individually?"

Nathan heard her question, but he didn't remember his answer as he drifted off. What seemed like seconds later, before he was fully rested, the chamber door opened, and Corban's frame appeared in its stead.

"Patrick, can I speak to you for a moment? You're needed in Belarus. Excuse us, Chen Li. I'm glad you're okay. We'll talk as soon as your levels are down."

Rubbing his eyes, Nathan squeezed Li's hand as they parted. She reached for him, but he moved out of the chamber and looked back inside.

"Goodbye, Li." He wondered if that was her real name, though he guessed it wasn't. But it didn't matter, knowing the rarity of experiencing such a connection in the field—and an even rarer event of seeing such a connection again. Nathan was a special agent for COIL, a shadow who passed in and out of the lives who needed him most—and disappeared.

"Someday," he said with a wink, "we'll work out that partner thing."

PART II

<u>*CHAPTER FOURTEEN*</u>

Two years later . . .

Nineteen-year-old Lacy Jamison held her breath and ducked under the surface of the water as the armed men prowled above her on the floating dock. The moon's reflection danced off the harbor's rippling waves. Lacy knew it was this reflection that saved her, as one gunman stared directly into the water. He surely saw only the moon instead of her wide eyes staring up at him.

She flinched as the sound of muffled gunshots reached her submerged ears. The subtropical waters of Zalzuna weren't cold, but she shivered nonetheless. Gunshots could mean only one thing: they'd found her parents, Albert and Sarah Jamison. Acting as a diversion, Lacy had drawn the enemy from her father as he'd helped his already-wounded wife away from the water's edge.

Lacy's lungs began to burn; she needed air! Reaching up, she gently touched the dock to check for vibrations. Were they gone? If her parents had been caught, Lacy didn't want to be free, either. She wouldn't know life without them, even if they'd been separated when she'd attended school in the States. They were missionaries, and while most of the world may have forgotten their efforts, Lacy couldn't.

Allowing herself to float upward, her head bobbed

through the surface. She took a deep breath, trying not to pant too loudly. Trembling, she tried to steady her nerves as she eyed the shoreline no more than fifty feet away. An ancient stone wall blocked her view of the cobbled street where men yelled and shadows danced before car headlights.

Another burst of gunfire made her jump. Silence followed, but it was broken by the wailing of a man. It was her father. Albert cried out in Burmese, which he knew fluently. Even though Lacy had visited them in the troubled country, she knew only a few words. They'd been missionaries in Myanmar for five years before coming to Zalzuna, and it was only natural that Albert would lapse into the foreign tongue to mourn his wife. Lacy understood: her mother had been killed. She tried to find satisfaction in the fact that the soldiers didn't understand her father's words of grief. That was something Albert and his daughter alone shared.

"Bye-bye, Mamma," Lacy whispered, her tears mingling with the salt water. "See you in heaven."

Too late, Lacy heard the man on the dock above her. She'd been too focused on the sounds of the soldiers dragging her father from her mother's body when suddenly she looked up at a grinning gunman. He pushed his gunstock aside and reached into the water with both hands. Grasping Lacy by her shoulders, he nearly crushed her collarbone. She was only an inch over five feet tall, and weighed less than one hundred pounds, so the man easily pulled her from the water below him.

However, once Lacy had been tossed roughly onto the dock and recovered from the shock of pain to her shoulder, she fought like a wildcat. Another soldier joined the first to escort her to shore. She kicked viciously at their hands as they tried to hold her ankles and wrists. A lucky heel caught one of the men on the chin and sent him sprawling into the water.

"Daddy!" she screamed, but there was no response from the shoreline. Other soldiers gathered to watch the single soldier struggle against Lacy's claws and kicks. Many of them jeered at their comrade until he pinned her down with a knee and punched her square in the nose.

As Lacy's head was spinning amongst stars and blood, she prayed for bravery. Whatever was to come, she'd come to Zalzuna with her parents to help the people, and she could die with a clear conscience. She'd been serving Jesus Christ.

On shore, she was bound and thrown into the back of a truck.

"Be still," a tender voice comforted as she gained her senses. It was a voice she knew. After trying to move her limbs, she found that they were tied securely. She blew her nose down her shirtfront to clear her nostrils of caked blood. "Be still, Lacy."

"Daddy?"

"I'm here."

The truck bounced over a pothole and rounded a corner. Behind the truck, a Jeep followed with armed men. The Jeep's headlights shined into the back of the truck to show Lacy that she and her father were alone.

"Momma?"

Albert's silence confirmed what she already knew, but this time she held back the tears. She shifted her head to rest against his knee.

"God is with us, Lacy," Albert said. "We're not alone."

Lacy squeezed her eyes closed. She knew God was with them, but it didn't help at that instant as her imagination ran wild. They were going to prison for sure. The only question was how much torture and abuse they'd have to endure before the steel doors slammed shut and they were left to rot in peace.

For the first time in her life, Lacy hoped she would die. She wasn't strong like her parents.

What if she gave away secrets she'd been trusted to keep? What about the other Christians on the island? Would they know to go into hiding now?

"I can't do this, Daddy." Lacy sobbed. "I can't. . . ."

"You *can*, sweetie. Hey, they didn't search me. I still have a colored pencil!"

A colored pencil? Lacy scoffed to herself. Albert was an artist. If anything would give him satisfaction at a time like this, it was a drawing utensil. Even when he arrived in a country where he couldn't speak the native dialect, Albert could still draw a wide range of biblical events to share the gospel message.

"Maybe you can draw us a way out," Lacy said.

"Hey, remember Nigeria? God watched over us then, Lacy. Besides, if we're finished on earth, we'll only see your mother that much sooner, right?"

Though Lacy didn't answer, she did remember Nigeria. She'd been nine years old when Muslim extremists with machetes had hacked through the thatched hut, killed her pet dog, and kidnapped their family of three. Most of the natives who'd converted to Christianity had been slaughtered, but the Jamisons had survived. They were held for four weeks. Lacy's earlobe was still torn from the earring that had been ripped out during the ordeal.

Sure, she remembered, but this wasn't Nigeria, which had been more accessible to the Special Forces team that had rescued them. There weren't any Special Forces teams storming the Island of Zalzuna to save a father and daughter who'd been warned time and again to avoid the communist island in the Greek Isles.

Lacy rolled her head away from her father's knee. For a moment, she despised him for his bravery, his faith, his indifference for life as he served his Lord. She felt only despair and fear of their looming death.

As the truck's brakes squealed, Albert began to pray aloud for God's protection. Lacy closed her eyes, shutting him out. There seemed to be no hope. She wished she were a child again, back in Oregon—playing in the surf with the neighbor boy, Walter, and her cousin, Brad, searching for starfish, hunting for shells, climbing the rocks up to the lighthouse . . . Anywhere, but Zalzuna!

...✝...

Nathan Isaacson flicked a bead of sweat off his brow and shifted his two hundred and twenty pound body under the camouflage netting that hid his position on the brown hillside. Squinting through his field glasses, he focused on a Range Rover with bad shocks, bouncing along the dirt road toward him. He checked his watch. They were right on time. It had to be Ron and Sandy Colson. Against the *jagina'en's* wishes, the Colsons had been in the eastern province of Cameroon distributing food and supplies to refugees fleeing from the Central African Republic.

Licking his lips, Nathan gazed beyond the aid workers from Binka, Cameroon. Two miles back were two more plumes of dust. The *jagina'en*, Central African Republic's armed bandits, were in pursuit. Unbeknownst to the Colsons, they were about to be butchered so they'd never return to help the refugees later—or share with other aid workers about the atrocities they'd witnessed.

Three days earlier, Nathan had met Ron and Sandy. They thought he was only a touring photographer, but he was there to protect the American couple and their work. In Garoua-Boulai, they'd distributed sacks of food, blankets, sleeping mats, soap, and other urgent supplies to the refugees. No one else was helping the twenty-five thousand displaced persons.

As soon as Corban Dowler had learned that missionaries in the Eastern Province were in jeopardy, he'd notified Nathan, and Nathan had been sent in to neutralize the situation. In most countries, any neutralizing was only temporary, but sometimes a short reprieve was all that was needed. Circumstantial misdirection, Nathan called it.

After three years of extractions with COIL, when Nathan had taken the bullet in the knee in Malaysia, he'd been forced out of fieldwork indefinitely as a team leader. Corban had put him into low-level spy training under the Italian master, Luigi Putelli, and for the last two years, Nathan had been a team of one. The knee brace he still wore no longer encumber him, and he'd gradually come to accept the calling that required his skills. Yes, he was lonely, but in the last two years since meeting Agent Chen Li, his loneliness had been tempered by coded contact with her—not in person, but contact, nonetheless.

Having grown his handlebar mustache back, it tickled his lip, but Nathan dared not reach a hand up to smooth it down, not with the enemy this close. He was a mound of grass on the slope, but if he moved at this point, he could be spotted. The *jagina'en* would be aware of him soon enough, and he certainly didn't want to give them an edge.

He glanced to his left where the road wound around the hill then came back into sight. The Colsons' vehicle disappeared for five minutes, then reappeared. They weren't traveling fast; there was no reason they should as they returned from a successful week of distribution to the Fulbe people. And they had no reason to suspect the bandits closing quickly on their bumper.

The bandits were Nathan's concern.

As they neared Nathan's position, he could see Ron was driving. He wanted to wave at the missionary—an ex-welder from Montana who'd heard his calling for God later in life, then had come to Cameroon when the natives needed him the most. Nathan admired the big man who'd greeted him with a friendly bear hug in Garoua-Boulai days before—not because they knew each other, but because Ron had a big heart. But today, Nathan didn't wave at them. That would cause them to stop, and then they'd be in worse danger. Not to mention Nathan's cover would be blown. Whenever possible, COIL's operatives were to remain hidden. If ever questioned, the missionaries could honestly admit they knew nothing.

The Colsons drove past, dust in their wake.

Nathan threw off the camo-net, rolled down the slope once before he found his feet, and bounded down to the road twenty feet below his former position. Skidding to a stop, he bent down to scratch at the dirt at the edge of the road. Finding the planks he'd buried the day before, he tipped them on end, one at a time, and flipped them off the roadway. Where the planks had been, Nathan revealed a deep ditch he'd covered until the Colsons passed. Sooner than expected, Nathan heard the bandits approaching, but he didn't look up. He hefted the last of the planks off the road and down the steep slope that continued down to a seasonal gulch.

Pausing, he admired his work. The ditch was four feet wide and four feet deep, stretching all the way across both tire ruts. The bandits wouldn't be able to stop in time once they came around the curve. It would buy the Colsons enough time to reach what little civilization did exist in that region of Cameroon. Even the border-hopping bandits didn't want witnesses to their crimes. When, or if, the Colsons ever went back to the refugee camp—a trip of several-days—Nathan or one of the other operatives would be contacted again, but today, he was merely supposed to make sure the Colsons arrived safely back at their village.

With his trap in place, he scrambled up the bank to where he'd left his backpack. He threw his net over his shoulders and collapsed into the hillside as the *jagina'en* vehicles came into sight.

Gasping for breath from his exertion under the hot sun, Nathan watched as the first vehicle with three soldiers saw the ditch across the road, but only an instant before the front wheels fell into the trap. Their speed was just enough to break the front axle from the chassis on impact. The second vehicle rear-ended the first, probably causing a few bumps and bruises, but the bandits poured out of the vehicles unharmed, though cursing and seemingly confused. They pointed after the Colsons' Rover now miles away.

Doing his best to suppress his laughter, Nathan settled into his position to out-wait the *jagina'en's* departure. They worked together to tip over the disabled vehicle, allowing it to tumble down the far slope where it would sit abandoned until the earth itself melted away. With a final curse yelled after the Colsons, the bandits climbed into the second vehicle and turned around. Only when they were a dust plume five miles away did Nathan throw off his net.

From a strap on his pack, he removed a trenching shovel with an adjustable head. He slid down to the road to pack the discarded soil back into the ditch that was now the coffin for the broken axle.

Once finished, Nathan returned to his spot on the slope and sat down to guzzle from his canteen. He picked up a satellite phone and called a secure number to leave a scrambled message: *Mission accomplished.* When he reached the coast, he would call in for his next assignment, hoping again to be reunited with Chen Li. Maybe the next one . . .

Shouldering his pack, Nathan climbed the hill until he reached the summit. An ATV and a trailer burdened with fuel and water waited for him. He paused to gaze at the vast terrain from his elevated position. Such beauty. But that was enough sight-seeing for Nathan. Another mission awaited his attention.

†

<u>*CHAPTER FIFTEEN*</u>

Brad Alden tested the weight of the green apple in the palm of his hand. He cracked his neck to the left, then to the right, while his eyes stayed focused on the knot on the birch tree.

"It's the ninth inning." The nineteen year old lowered his voice as would a commentator. "Bases loaded. The Pacifics are up by one. If they're going to pull this game off and win the championship, ladies and gentlemen, it's up to Mr. Alden, the high school pitcher who's been getting the attention all night. This pitch very well may decide this young man's future. He must feel the pressure. He knows the Major League scouts are here. He's seen the little men in suits checking the speed of his fastball. He can't believe they're here for him. They can't believe his fastball. The stands are packed, but you'd never know it; they're so silent. I think I heard a cricket chirp. Here's the wind-up. And . . . the pitch!"

Flinging his arm forward, Brad led with his hip, his chest, his shoulder, then, like a whip, he snapped the apple from his fingers. An instant later, the apple exploded over the knot in the birch tree. He didn't imitate the cheer from the crowd, but it was still loud in his ears.

Tomorrow was the day. The whole State of Oregon would be at the evening game. Why? They'd read the papers. They'd heard the stories. Now, they would find out for themselves. Could the teenager just out of high school really throw a fastball like the Major League pitchers? Brad hoped so. Everyone Brad knew was rooting for him; everyone in Bandon, anyway. The tourist town's natives needed a hero, and they'd found one in the tall, two-hundred-pound lefty. With a nicely trimmed goatee, few believed he was only nineteen. The goatee itself was dark with hints of red, though his hair was dirty blond with long bangs.

"Hey, does Bandon's savior have time for a home-cooked meal?"

Spinning around, he saw his mother standing in the back door. She was a strong woman, a hiker, and headstrong enough that anyone but Brad's father shied away from tangling with her.

"Mom, how long have you been standing there?" Brad started toward the house, hoping his face wasn't too red.

"Long enough to know we're going to have to feed you and your ego tonight." She laughed with him, and playfully pushed him into the house. Though she was shorter than his six-foot frame, he would bet against himself in an arm-wrestling match. "Get your dad. Sweet potatoes are on the table. Gotta get you carbed-up for your big day tomorrow."

Brad yelled for his father, Frank, as Brad washed his hands. He stared at himself in the mirror. Tomorrow was the big day. Should he lose the goatee? No, he looked older, maybe even tougher, with it. His mother wanted him to get a haircut, but the girls liked his longer hair. All eyes would be on him tomorrow. Especially, Josie's eyes.

Josie was the only girl Brad had ever cared about through

high school. He hadn't figured out how to say goodbye to her, though. She was going to a Bible school in Illinois. Brad was going to the highest bidder. Different priorities pulled them apart.

He left the bathroom of their middle-class home and opened the door to his father's study. His dad worked from home as an editor for a book printer in Portland. The studious man didn't look up as Brad poked his head into the dimly lit office. Many who didn't know the family often mistook father and son as brothers, since Frank was a young-looking forty-three with brown hair. And he was fit enough to play the part, too. But when it came to wisdom, Brad relied on his father.

Frank was an elder in their local church, and even preached occasionally. Brad didn't know how his father did it, but the man balanced being a friend and a conservative father at the same time. Now that Brad thought about it, he didn't know any other father who regularly fished with his son, or played racquetball at the club. Actually, every bit of Brad's pitching skill he owed to his father. If they hadn't played catch when Brad was still in grade school, bought him his first mitt, and taught him not to fear the ball, Brad would be a nobody. He was Brad the Pitcher now.

"Dinner's ready, Dad." Brad noticed his father was deep in thought over something on his desk, or maybe he was praying.

Looking up, Frank met his son's gaze. Brad swallowed over a lump in his throat when he noticed the concern on his father's face. Something was wrong. He slipped the rest of the way into the office and shut the door.

"What's going on?" Brad eased himself into the chair opposite his father. "Still no call?"

"Nope." Frank sighed and leaned back in his chair, his hands behind his head. "For twenty years, your Aunt Sarah's never missed a call-in."

Brad sighed also, his baseball fantasies fading away in light of this greater concern. Frank's sister, Sarah, had married Albert Jamison twenty years ago, and the two had become overseas missionaries, most often in Asia and Africa. They'd be strangers to Brad since they were always in the mission field, but their daughter, Lacy, had lived with the Aldens during every school year. Lacy was more like a sister to him than a cousin, and if something had happened to his aunt and uncle, Lacy was certainly in trouble, too.

Shame suddenly swept over Brad. He searched his memory for a hint as to which country the Jamisons were currently reaching for Christ, but he couldn't remember since he'd been too focused on his own success. But this was all different. His father wouldn't be this concerned unless something was seriously wrong.

"Um, how do you pronounce that country again?" Brad asked, masking his ignorance. "Where are they?"

"Zalzuna. I checked a few websites, but all I've found are the normal governmentally controlled press releases characteristic of a communist nation. Nothing about foreigners or political prisoners, which is usually how they're classified when caught."

"What're you gonna do?"

"Not much I can do, Brad, but pray. I called Washington and talked to a Christian public relations liaison for international crises. They're too swamped to pay any mind to it. Albert and Sarah picked one place this time that's so out-of-the-way that the US government isn't going to waste their time on it. Besides, they were told not to go to Zalzuna. It was too dangerous."

Fidgeting in his seat, Brad knew all too well the stories. There were dozens of countries where the Bible and Christians were simply not permitted. If caught, torture, imprisonment, or death often followed. Brad's own future seemed insignificant when considering the danger Lacy could be in at that very minute.

"If you're not doing anything else, maybe you could talk to the Kassvineys. Walt's dad knows a lot of people, Dad. He's been around the world a time or two."

"They were the first ones I thought of, too," Frank said. "When all else fails, ask for help from the genius family who goes to your church, huh?"

"It's worth a shot."

"After dinner then." Frank stood and stretched. "We'll pay them a visit, you and I. They were in church last week, so they're probably still in town."

Brad's anticipated game the following evening quickly faded as a priority. If he wanted to pitch at his full potential, Brad needed a full night's sleep. But tonight would be a late night if they were going to the Kassviney mansion. Well, sometimes sacrifices had to be made. And he felt it was the right kind of sacrifice to make, even though it regarded his own future.

Dinner—usually a rally time for the family to discuss the day—was solemn as Frank shared his concerns with Jennifer.

She was usually optimistic, but this time, she didn't have much to say except that she supported him in getting to the bottom of his sister's silence.

"Little Walter might even be of more help than you think," Jennifer said. "He knows Greek. During Sunday school, he used to always scribble in that tablet of his, making notes in Greek. That was years ago, though."

Frank and Jennifer continued to talk as they ate, but Brad was lost in thought over the Kassvineys. William "Bill" Kassviney was a retired physicist, having won a Nobel Prize a few years earlier. He was a balding, sixty-year-old widower. Many younger, well-known scientists relied upon him as a consultant.

But it wasn't necessarily the genius of the father that made the Kassviney family unique. The older man had a son, Walter, who'd been in Brad's class in school—before he was found to be a chess prodigy. At one time, the two had been playmates, but once Walter had been "discovered," the two had grown apart. Walter had graduated from college with three degrees before Brad had picked out a prom suit. However, when either of the two Kassvineys wasn't traveling the world and sharing their wealth and knowledge, they attended the small fellowship down the coast in Bandon, Oregon. No matter where they went, Bandon was always home to the Kassvineys, and that gave Brad a sense of pride—that he knew Walter.

"Don't let your dad keep you there all night." Jennifer wagged her finger at Brad. "You can't throw straight if you're sleeping on the mound!"

The Kassviney estate was up the coast from the Bandon

Lighthouse where Brad, Walter, and Lacy had played as children. The white lighthouse—now a museum—was barely more than a gazebo with a roof and a short tower, but it drew Brad's attention as they passed it, forcing him to remember a more carefree time of his life. Then his eyes were drawn to the house that hung over the cliffs far above and to the right. Even in the closing darkness, the house seemed to be teetering on the edge. As children, the three had often joked that Walter's father had accidentally built the house on the wrong cliff, for it was in fact overlooking the highway rather than the ocean's crashing waves. Whether the right bluff or not, the Kassviney mansion was the nicest house anyone in Bandon had ever seen. Brad had played there as a child, but hadn't been inside since.

There were many theories and rumors in Bandon when it came to the origin of the Kassviney fortune. Inheritance, stock market, or just plain genius money management were among the top guesses. Mrs. Kassviney had died when Walter was a baby, which further added to the mysterious nature of the secluded Kassvineys. Whatever the case, Brad knew their fortune wasn't squandered on themselves. Guests from around the world frequented the mansion, and at least once in the early years, Mr. Kassviney had taken in a homeless family after their house had burned down in the harbor city of Bend. The estate itself had no fence or gate, though as Frank drove their family blazer onto the elevated property, Brad noticed cameras mounted on a gardener's shed and the garage roof. He also noticed an additional wing he'd never seen, which nearly doubled the size of the mansion on the eastern side.

Frank parked in front of the walkway next to a dry

fountain. A butler exited the front door, leaving the door open, and walked on bowed legs toward the visitors. Behind the butler, the mansion's tall windows glowed with white light as if a banquet were underway.

"Hope we're not interrupting anything," Frank mumbled as they climbed out of the car. "I don't see any other vehicles."

"Me, neither." But Brad noted the garage seemed large enough to hold more than a dozen SUVs.

"Good evening, gentlemen," the butler said. "How may I be of assistance?"

Brad thrust his hands into his jean pockets and couldn't help but grin. They hadn't thought to wear anything but their casual, afternoon clothes. The butler was suited in his Sunday best, outclassing Brad and Frank on their best day. Frank didn't seem to mind, though. Anyone who attended the Bandon Brethren Church regularly knew better than to judge a man by his clothing.

"We were hoping to talk to Bill," Frank said. "It's not too late, is it?"

"Bill?" the butler asked, glancing at Brad.

"Mr. Kassviney," Brad said, covering for his father. "Is he home? It's pretty urgent. We'll just be a couple minutes if he's busy."

"Of course. Follow me, if you please."

Frank stepped in line behind the butler and Brad brought up the rear. As they neared the open front door, Brad glanced to the left and noticed a parking lot behind the spacious garage where two limos and a number of BMWs were parked. They were interrupting something after all.

The butler led them into a den that seemed under-furnished in comparison to the grandeur of the exterior. There was only one soft chair and two padded benches—the type a barbershop might afford its customers. Brad and Frank each sat on a bench. The rock hearth was cold, though the mantle displayed the true riches: numerous pictures, mostly black and white, of unsmiling men, women, and children.

As soon as the butler left the room and his steps could be heard moving toward a giant library from where voices were heard, Brad was on his feet to inspect the photographs on the mantle. Mr. Kassviney was in most of the photos, though he was much younger. Brad recognized several senators and even one president. He was about to say as much to his father when a shadow filled the doorway from the rotunda. It was Mr. Kassviney, looking a lot older than Brad had remembered him, even though he'd been at church the week before. Usually, Brad was too preoccupied with Josie or the guys his age to notice such things, but he noticed now.

"Bill!" Frank jumped to his feet. "Good to see you."

"Hello, Frank, Brad." The older man was dressed in a sharp suit. He shook hands with each of them. "What a surprise. To what do I owe this pleasure?"

"First of all," Frank said as the three took seats, Mr. Kassviney in the soft chair, "I hope we're not pulling you away from anything too important. We'll make this as fast as possible. We just need a little input. Figured you're the man who may have the answers, Bill."

"Take your time." Bill dismissed his other guests in the library with a wave. "They're all Walter's crowd, anyway."

"It has to do with Sarah, my sister, and her husband, Albert Jamison."

"Oh? How are they?"

"That's the thing. I'm worried. They missed their monthly check-in. Sarah's never missed it in twenty years, not since she married into the missionary life. Jenny and I've been a sort of mission board for them, unofficially, of course, arranging packages, mail, and finances from time to time. Lacy has lived most of her life with us, as you know, and she's with them right now. My point is, it's not like them to miss a check-in."

"What kind of window have you arranged?" Bill asked.

"Twenty-four hours, give or take. It's been almost thirty-six now. Even if Sarah couldn't send me a digital, Albert or Lacy would. I contacted Washington, a few different people, but I've run into only dead ends—all on account of their present location."

"Which is?"

"Zalzuna," Frank said.

"I see. That would cause some to shy away from the issue." Bill looked away to gaze up at the mantle photos, as if he sought the wisdom of his youth, or the men pictured with him. "Zalzuna's government is sponsored by old Soviet money. The Chinese have made their mark on the little island, not to mention the Libyans. It's a complicated country."

"But you know people, right?" Brad folded his hands as he leaned forward. "Maybe everything's okay over there, just downed phone lines or something. We need to make a few inquiries that don't get screened out by bureaucracy."

"Yes, I understand." Bill stood and placed a hand on the mantle. He stared at the photographs in silence for such a length of time that Frank and Brad's eyes met with uncertainty. Suddenly, Mr. Kassviney turned to face the two. "I'll be honest with you both. You've been direct with me, and it wouldn't be right unless you knew the truth, though I ask you to guard this from others until it becomes public."

"Of course, Bill," Frank said. "What is it?"

"Though it's nothing official yet, I have the beginning signs of Alzheimer's. It's more of a self-diagnosis, but I know the symptoms well enough. As such, Walter has assumed many of my responsibilities. God has blessed him with more wits than I ever had, anyway. I don't trust myself enough with phone numbers, so it would be wrong to lead you both to trust me with any information I may volunteer regarding your relatives in Zalzuna. As confident as I might be, I could still be relaying twenty-year-old data as sure as if it were yesterday's news, and I'd only steer you wrong, maybe even on a deadly course. Walter's your best move. He knows the Aegean Sea's politics better than most, and even played chess in Athens and Izmit."

"Well . . ." Frank cleared his throat and glanced at Brad. His father was a trusting man, but Brad could see the internal struggle in his eyes—Walter was only nineteen. What could a teenager do to help? "I suppose it wouldn't hurt to hear what he has to say, Bill. Might give us a lead we wouldn't otherwise have thought about."

Mr. Kassviney called the butler to fetch Walter, then Frank and Bill made small talk about the previous week's sermon as they waited. When Walter arrived, Brad barely recognized him. He was five-ten, about one hundred and fifty pounds. His short-cropped, black hair was greased and combed straight back. The thousand-dollar suit and cuff links gave the chess prodigy the look of a cheap gangster or card hustler. But it was his thin lips and robotic-like movements that gave the young man an air of awkwardness. Brad had once joked that the boy was really an android, but the days when they'd chased the surf's bubbles were long gone. Walter Kassviney was now a man.

Rather than ask the butler to fetch another chair, Walter claimed a spot on the rug between Brad and Mr. Kassviney. Taking his time, Bill methodically repeated the details of the dilemma. Walter's eyes didn't stray from his father's face until he was finished speaking. At that point, Walter tugged a bulky calculator out of his breast pocket and pecked away on it for a few seconds. Satisfied with his findings, he pocketed the device and stared at the floor in front of him.

Frank cleared his throat.

"What do you think, Walt? Is there something you know that might help us proceed?"

He looked Frank in the eyes. Everything about the young man was intense, completely focused.

"When foreigners arrive at one of the three ports on Zalzuna, all belongings are searched. Electronics like cell phones and computers are confiscated. Magazines that promote freethinking, religion, or independent thought are seized. Depending on the contraband with which a visitor arrives, charges may be filed against the accused. A place like Zalzuna—international calls are monitored if not banned altogether. Tell me—I know Lacy, but her parents . . . they're experienced enough to know better than to have Bibles in their property and whatnot, right?"

"Absolutely," Frank said. "Even if they were going to smuggle some into the country, they'd run a few dry-runs first. Like your father explained, they just finished a five-year term in Myanmar. They know the politics involved. They wouldn't risk anything that would jeopardize their ministry on the island."

"Then, we can safely conclude . . ." Walter stated slowly, "if they weren't allowed into the country, they would've returned to a Greek island whence they came to make the scheduled phone call. Since this didn't happen, we can assume they're on the island. Not only are they on the island, they've been cut off from any outside contact, on which missionaries rely heavily. The probability is high they would've tried to find a way to make this scheduled call. The attempt itself would've raised flags for the government, and it's probable their request for an outside line is why they're still held on the island. If one of them was able to leave the island, would you be the first they'd contact?"

"Yes." Frank nodded. "Absolutely. She's my sister. It's all arranged. There's no one else."

"Okay. This is the first time she's missed a scheduled call," Walter said thoughtfully. "What were you to do if this scenario arose? Is there a plan in place?"

"Well, we had a loose plan that I'd start making phone calls until I had some answers. Embassies, heads of state, foreign ambassadors, whomever I could reach, even the media. But Zalzuna is isolated. They don't communicate with the West as it is, so I ran into dead ends real quick. The missionary and human rights groups that would otherwise be able to assist in this type of situation are flagged already because they're well known as Christian or some other advocate against communist ideals."

"So, we need to implement a fact-finding protocol." Walter nodded.

Mr. Kassviney smiled, a proud twinkle in his eye as he obviously admired his son.

"Whoever claimed chess was just a board game, huh?" Bill chuckled to himself and slapped his knee. "What do you think, Walter? You have someone in mind?"

"Yeah." Walter stood, all eyes on him. With one hand in his pocket and the other touching his fair-skinned chin, he began to pace from the mantle to a stuffed steelhead fish on another wall, then back again to the mantle. "It could be worse than we imagine. I'm compelled to send in two waves. The first will be for reconnaissance. We need eyes on the island. The second will be for extraction. That'll take more time to put together, but they can't move until later, so that's okay."

"Excuse me?" Frank interrupted with an uncomfortable smile. "Waves? Recon and extraction? You're serious, Walt?" He raised his eyebrows at Bill. "You have those types of resources, Bill?"

"Don't look at me," Mr. Kassviney shook his head, then nodded at his son. "This is his expertise: strategy."

Walter continued to stare at the carpet, seemingly deaf to the conversation around him.

"We need to be closer—at least in the same time-zone as Zalzuna."

"Athens," Bill offered. "Jasper O'Shottie lives in Piraeus."

"Who's Jasper?" Frank frowned.

"I'll need to make some calls." Walter ignored Frank's uncertainty. "I know a professional who might help us. It all depends if he's busy right now or not. His skills are in high demand—the state of the world being what it is."

"What about the symposium?" Mr. Kassviney asked his son. "You're supposed to be in Berlin by Sunday."

"They'll find a replacement."

"On photoclinometry, Son? I think not."

"Well, they may not have a choice." Walter drew out his calculator again and punched buttons. He walked out of the den. "I'll get started."

The three watched Walter disappear around a corner.

"Consider me confused," Frank said. "I don't understand. Is he—? What's he doing? Is he going to help?"

"Can't you see?" Bill said with a chuckle. "The boy has a one-track mind. You two had better go pack your bags if you want to keep up!"

"*Athens?*" Frank asked as if it were a fictional place. He shook his head. "I can't. It's—"

"I'll go!" Brad tried to ignore his father's stare. "When's he leaving, Mr. Kassviney?"

"You have a game tomorrow evening, Brad." Frank stood. "The most important game of your life!"

"I can hold him off until tomorrow night," Mr. Kassviney said. "But any later than that, nothing will hold him back!"

"Bill, we don't have money for this type of expedition." Frank touched his pants pocket.

"Sounds like it's become more like a rescue mission, Frank. Ah, to be young again, to run off and save the world . . ." There was no denying the light in Bill's eyes. Then he looked

Brad square in the face. "Tomorrow night, ten o'clock, be at the airport. You know Walter. He can handle issues of the brain better than issues of the body. He'll need someone to look after him. I can't think of anyone better than you, Brad."

Frank looked from Mr. Kassviney to Brad, then sighed loudly as he ran his fingers through his hair.

"Oh, boy. I hope you're going to help me explain this to your mother."

†

CHAPTER SIXTEEN

Nathan Isaacson was treading water in the South China Sea next to fellow believer, Hu Jian. Half an hour earlier, both men had been on a passenger jet destined for Hong Kong. Jian didn't know he was to be arrested when he arrived there until Nathan informed him. Setting up an early departure from the flight, they parachuted out of the jet for a dip in the sea. Instead of an execution now, Jian would be debriefed by COIL representatives in Japan, then taken back to Malaysia where he was a pastor in the underground Christian church.

After splashing down, they waved at a Japanese fishing vessel trawling nearby. Though the small ship was rigged for fishing, the crew wasn't in the fishing industry at all. Pulling the two from the water in one pass, the vessel then continued toward the Philippines in the east. On deck, Japanese fishermen played their roles of maintaining nets in case satellite cameras passed overhead.

Immediately, Nathan and Jian were whisked below deck to join a number of Japanese and other technicians who were operating computer monitors and comm devices. A Canadian—evidenced by the flag on his breast pocket— handed Nathan a towel as Jian was given a change of clothes. The man introduced himself as Graham Lordue, a COIL operative who worked the Pacific Rim. He had a long neck and eyes that looked like they'd seen too much suffering. Graham led Nathan into one of the cabins where they could talk privately. Nathan changed clothes as Graham briefed him.

"We'll be in Manila by midnight, maybe a little after." He handed Nathan a cup of coffee. "How've you been since New Guinea?"

"Too busy to remember when I even did that job," Nathan joked. "You keeping safe out here?"

"In the Lord's will." Graham shrugged. "Had a little scuffle in Brunei a couple months ago." Graham pulled up his shirt to show a four-inch scar over his bottom rib. "The sultan's niece wanted out of the country after converting. Should've been a quick grab. Walked right into it. They jumped us after we tied off. Lost two men and a good dash of blood, but some of us got away."

"And the sultan's niece?" Nathan gulped his coffee, thankful for something warm.

"Scheduled to teach Malay to Australian missionaries. Speaking of Australia, did you check your messages? They want you in Sydney for something."

Accepting a PDA from Graham, Nathan logged into COIL's message service. He read through information on a recon job in Zalzuna. There was also a firebombed church in Germany that needed some hands-on assistance with the locals.

He took a deep breath before opening a third message. It was from Chen Li. Having rescued her during the Gilgal operation two years earlier, he constantly worried and prayed for her safety. What was her current assignment? Would his next mission be to rescue her again?

But her message was brief. She missed him and wondered if he considered her his teammate yet. It was an ongoing jab he knew was meant to be flirtatious. He didn't mind at all.

Nathan responded to the first two requests, but decided to wait to respond to the third one. It would be a negative to Germany. Since he had a past there, he was the wrong man for the job. But he planned on accepting the Zalzuna recon job. Basking in the Greek Isles for a week or two? No problem! He tossed the PDA back to Graham.

"Looks like I'm on the plane tonight, already."

"Something I can help you with?" Graham raised his eyebrows, perhaps hoping for a little more action.

"Nah. Shouldn't be much. Might even call it a vacation."

"Well, good. Sounds like you deserve it, Nate. I'll let you catch some sleep. See you tonight."

As soon as Graham was gone, Nathan relaxed on the bunk and reflected upon the message from headquarters. This was the first moment of peace he'd had in days. Though he'd told Graham the next assignment would be something like a vacation, running a recon for an infiltration team was never a walk in the park. Granted, Nathan was the best man for the job. Having led dozens of his own missions into foreign countries, he knew what to watch for. The message hadn't said much—*Recon Zalzuna. Jamison Christians arrested. Details in Sydney.*

This time of the year, Zalzuna would have the best weather, but running recon in a communist country was something like taking point in a jungle full of ambushes. At the least, he'd need a fake identity and an escape route. In the past, as part of the special ops teams, he was rewarded with the gratitude of freed captives. But not now. Doing recon, he would note traps and safe-houses, friends and foes, then walk safely away. No one would know he'd been the forerunner.

The Zalzuna mission had been accepted for other reasons as well—reasons that pointed to his past. Trevor Niles was from Zalzuna. Had he returned home? Was he still bent on destroying others to achieve his own goals? If Nathan could get word to Interpol, an arrest of Niles for murder was long overdue. For two years, the killer had been on the run. Christians worldwide would be safer with Trevor Niles behind bars.

"Please watch over me, Lord . . ." Nathan covered his face with his hands. He meant to pray longer, but instead, he lapsed into a dead-man's sleep.

...✝...

Albert Jamison woke with a start. He shivered from the cold in the wide cell, his back against a damp, cement wall. As he turned his head to look at Lacy, his neck hurt, but he didn't care. His pain was nothing compared to what the interrogators had done to her.

Lacy lay in the fetal position next to her father, his hand on her shoulder. She'd said nothing since he'd crawled into the cell. They'd both been beaten. Her clothes were torn and she was missing a shoe.

The authorities wanted to know why they'd come to Zalzuna and who their religious contacts on the island were. Albert hadn't betrayed Trevor Niles, the man who'd invited them to the island, but Albert wasn't sure if they'd made Lacy talk. Touching his face with his unbroken hand, Albert felt that his jaw was broken, too.

"*The Lord is our Shepherd*," Albert whispered, but he choked on the words. His throat was bruised from when they'd strangled him into unconsciousness. He squeezed his eyes shut, a tear trickling from his battered face. "We praise You, Lord, even in this suffering . . ."

As afflicted as he was, Albert wasn't disoriented. Now, away from his torturers, he could sort through what he knew. They'd been in Zalzuna only a few days. Trevor Niles had been their only contact, but other Christians might've also been involved. Someone had rented them a house in New Manchester, the little English town on the northern shore of the island. Again, Trevor Niles had been the liaison. Albert frowned at the thought. Perhaps Trevor Niles was the betrayer? It made little sense, but he'd been the only one who knew they were visiting the capital city of Zalzuna on the eastern coast. He was the only one who'd known of the other Christians they were supposed to have met at the docks.

Suddenly, Albert's eyes opened wide.

"There was no one at the docks." He groaned in realization. His lips cracked as he continued to talk, but he couldn't stop now. Perhaps his words would comfort Lacy. "It was a trap the whole time—the island, the house, the docks, Trevor Niles . . ."

His daughter didn't move as he continued to consider the conspiracy behind his wife's murder and their arrest. A single light bulb in the center of the ceiling lit their cell, and Albert stared at it for symbolic enlightenment as he spoke aloud. But still, Lacy didn't move. She'd witnessed atrocities before. The body found ways to heal, and she'd know that. But he was worried about her mind. If she could maintain her wits, he'd worry less. This body was temporary, but the mind had a way of increasing the torture exponentially.

Obviously, Trevor Niles wasn't whom he portrayed himself to be. Albert tried to remember what he knew about the man. He'd been secretive, which was only natural for an underground believer. But his secrecy had been for a much different reason, Albert now understood. They'd made contact through the Internet. Niles had been an invisible man named Zal, but they'd eventually shared their real names. Then Niles had met them at the airstrip on the southeastern corner of Zalzuna. Albert remembered that polite, dark-haired man with the flattering words and a scar down the right side of his face. He'd seemed confident, too sure of himself. Usually, underground Christians were reserved, more cautious, and ever humble. Sure, Trevor Niles had been secretive when it came to information, but his personality had been too outgoing!

"I'm such a fool," Albert said.

He should've known, seen the signs, felt the awkwardness! Albert may not have been able to flee the island once they were in Niles' hands, but if Albert had known the man was an imposter, Albert could've alerted the outside world to be more wary than he'd been. Who else might Niles entice to the island?

"Now what?" Albert asked the light bulb. "I saw other cells down the hallway. This is some sort of old hospital. We can't be the only ones held here. Maybe that's why God allowed this, huh? There are people we need to reach here!"

Straightening his right leg, Albert drew the colored pencil from his pocket. Though it was broken in two places, the ends could be sharpened and used. He moved his good hand away from his daughter and touched the rock wall. It was whitewashed rock, perfect for a masterpiece. What would he draw? Something about Calvary, where all hope lay. Perhaps Jesus carrying the cross to Golgotha. Albert held the pencil up to the light. It was a green-blue color, dark enough for the wall, but a difficult color to shade. Should he start now? No, he decided. He'd wait until Lacy could help him brainstorm the details. Such a project would help her focus on Jesus.

Albert touched Lacy's shoulder again, but she flinched away.

"We're going to be okay, sweetie." He forced a chuckle through a sob. "God's on our side. These people don't know what they're up against."

...✝...

Brad Alden was pitching a perfect game. They were in the ninth inning. One out. The score was two runs to nothing. He cracked his neck left, then right. The wind-up. Then, the pitch!

The ball was hit high into left field. Pushing the bill of his hat up, Brad watched the ball fly into the night sky. His outfielders were converging perfectly . . .

Then . . . they missed the ball! Brad covered second base as the runner slid headfirst. Safe.

Tossing the ball into his glove, Brad walked back to the mound. He had trouble focusing on what was surely the biggest game of his life. Yesterday, he would've been focused, but that was before he'd become involved in the Zalzuna inquiry to find his aunt, uncle, and cousin. Instead of thinking about the scouts measuring the speed of his fastball, his mind was on catching the plane after the game. While reporters waited to talk to him behind the dugout, Brad wondered what he was going to tell Josie. They'd had plans to go out afterwards with their old high school friends. Would she understand?

He nodded at the catcher's sign. A change-up pitch. Brad cracked his neck again. The wind-up. Strike!

For the next two pitches, Brad mixed it up. He sent a fastball skipping off home base, then an insider. The batter swung at each. People in the stands were on their feet now. His mother and father were clapping.

Brad had the best life. Did he really have to fly to Greece? He could skip the search for his relatives and stay in Bandon where he could secure his future as a well-paid athlete.

The next batter had been trouble for Brad in years past. The guy was wiry with a good eye. Shaking off the first sign, Brad nodded at the second. Outside fastball. He checked over his shoulder at the runner leading off second base. A home run at this point wouldn't only tie the game, it would send them into overtime, and Brad would miss his flight.

Again, he cracked his neck. The wind-up. The pitch. Strike!

Backing away, the batter cast Brad a dirty scowl. But Brad never took the scowls personally. After the game, they would all greet each other as fellow ball soldiers.

The second pitch was right down the middle. The batter swung and nicked the ball. The umpire heard the contact and counted it as a foul as the catcher scrambled through the dirt to grasp the ball. He came up in time to see the runner slide into third base.

Catching the ball, Brad stood on his mound. All eyes were on him. Everyone was cheering for him. He smiled. They thought his mind was on his final pitch. Instead, he looked up at the night sky. It was daytime in the Greek Isles at that minute. Was Lacy dead or alive? What kind of trouble could she and her family get into on such a little island? Since it wasn't on his father's office globe, he'd had to pull out the almanac to find the island. Though it looked like any other island in the Aegean Sea, it was unlike other Greek islands. Zalzuna was a sovereign nation, an independent dictatorship that had returned to communism after being a French colony for nearly a century.

The catcher's sign was for an inside fastball. It was a dangerous call since the batter was crowding home base.

Brad cracked his neck. The wind-up. Even as he released the ball, he saw the batter's smirk. He'd forced the inside pitch, hoping the catcher would call for a base-crowding pitch to scare the batter away. As the batter swung, Brad grit his teeth. The batter cut his follow-through short as he braced for the connection of the ball on the bat. The third base runner was tensing for the run home.

The crowd was quiet as the ball shot forward. Brad saw a blur of white flashing toward his head. Instinctively, he threw up his open mitt, then closed it an instant later when the ball slapped leather.

People in the stands were on their feet. Surprising even himself, Brad opened his mitt to look inside. He'd caught the ball! The batter threw the bat away. The game was over. The team ran onto the field to carry Brad toward the dugout. They scooped him up as the crowd from the stands flooded the diamond. Riding on his teammates' shoulders, Brad searched for his parents. He waved at his tall father. Frank smiled and waved back, as did his mother, though he could see only her hand in the air.

"You did it, Brad!" a particular female voice cheered.

Knowing the two were a couple, Brad's teammates deposited him on the ground in front of Josie, a bright-eyed brunette with a wide smile. He hugged her, though he wasn't nearly as enthusiastic as others about the win.

"Alden!"

Looking beyond Josie, Brad saw the short, white-haired man.

"Yeah, Coach?"

"They're waiting." He pointed at the dugout. "The scouts, son. Get to it. Make us proud."

"Good luck!" Josie smiled and wrapped her arms around his neck, pulling herself up to kiss him on the cheek. "I'll wait with your parents, okay?"

Entering the dugout, Brad found three men from the Major League Commission.

"Fine game, Mr. Alden," Mr. Daniels greeted as they shook hands. The other two men hung back, watching. "Have a seat. I know we're not the only folks who want to talk to you tonight, so I'll try to make this quick before you go off and celebrate. We want you. Five million a year for three years. If your young shoulder is still firing ninety-mile-an-hour balls after that, we can discuss another extension with the franchise."

Brad felt light-headed. *Fifteen million dollars?* With that kind of money, he could do anything, go anywhere, have anything! He'd never have to work a day in his life, and never have need of anything, never have to worry about anything—ever! His father could even retire.

"When do you need an answer?" Brad asked.

"A week," Mr. Daniels stated. "You might have a fist of lightening, but you still need some refining. That means training, Mr. Alden. You up to it?"

"I'm not afraid of hard work." Rising to his feet, Brad offered his hand. "But I need to think and pray about it."

"Pray?" Mr. Daniels shook Brad's hand, a cynic's smile forming on his lips. "Serious? You're religious?"

"Mr. Daniels, I'm a Christian, if that's what you're asking. It was nice meeting you. If I'm interested, I'll call you within a week." Brad turned to leave the dugout.

"Wait," Mr. Daniels called, confusion on his face. "What about the other scouts? You're only meeting with us?"

Brad checked his watch. He didn't have long.

"I have to catch a plane." He shrugged. "If they want me, I guess they can wait until I get back."

"That's not very responsible, Mr. Alden," Mr. Daniels said. "A lot of these people are reporters. They came from miles around. Like I said, it's not very responsible."

"Well, no offense, Mr. Daniels, but that all depends on what sort of emergency I'm running off for, doesn't it?"

Climbing the steps out of the dugout, Brad jogged across the expanse in front of the backstop rather than tempt the lingering crowd near the bleachers. He found Josie and his parents in the parking lot.

"Wow, that was quick!" Josie hopped off the hood of the blazer. "You talked to them all?"

Checking his watch yet again, Brad walked around Josie and stepped up to his father who sat in the driver's seat with the door open.

"Dad, I've got to get going. I'll see Josie off."

"Call when you can," Frank said.

"Now you mind your manners." Jennifer wagged her finger. "And watch what you eat. Your system isn't familiar with that spicy food."

"Keep your focus, Son." Frank shook his son's hand heartily. "Thank you for doing this, Brad. We'll be praying."

"Thanks, I'll need it."

"Spend wisely," his mother said, though she'd been told the Kassvineys were footing the bill. "You run out of money over there, you'll be up a creek!"

"I know, Mom." Brad chuckled and hugged his mother. Though she was a tough woman, she still shed a tear over her departing son. "Don't worry. I'll probably only be a couple days."

His parents left, and Brad faced Josie. He took a deep breath and exhaled, knowing she had a million questions.

"You mind telling me what's going on? We're supposed to be going to the party at Jeremy's."

Noticing the time, Brad took her hand and led her toward her car parked nearby.

"Come on. You drive. We'll talk on the way."

It was a short drive out to Bandon's airport. Along the way, Brad explained the possible dilemma facing his relatives. Josie knew Lacy well, the two having attended school together most of their lives, so she shared his concern. But she wasn't happy about being left behind.

"Well, you know I'll be in Illinois when you get back, depending on how long you'll be," she said as they parked at the airport.

"Yeah, I know." Brad took her hand in his and looked into her eyes. "I was hoping I'd be seeing you off, not you seeing me off."

"Maybe when you get back, we can get together at some point, discuss things?"

Brad nodded. He knew they'd never go back to the way things had been. They'd never discussed the future. Was she the girl for him? Was marriage in the picture?

"We'll find time, one way or another."

"Why do I feel like this is goodbye forever, then?" Her voice quivered.

"I don't know. I guess I'm just being rude, Jos. All I can think about is getting to Zalzuna."

"Be safe over there, huh?" She tried to smile, then pulled him close for a hug.

"I will."

"Don't forget about me, okay?"

"I won't, Jos. I won't."

He waved as she drove away. As soon as she was out of sight, he turned toward the airport's only terminal since he'd checked his baggage earlier. Licking his lips, he walked through the sliding doors. Josie, friends, and his baseball future faded from his mind as he focused on what lay ahead.

✝

CHAPTER SEVENTEEN

Walter Kassviney turned in his swivel chair to see Brad Alden enter the PT7 Turbo Jet. It was one of three trans-Atlantic aircraft the Kassviney family owned. The PT7 was for Walter's use, while his father used the other two to shuttle guests to and from his home when he wasn't up to traveling himself.

Waving Brad into the cabin, Walter couldn't greet him since he was on hold on the phone with someone in the Ukraine. The pilot poked his head into the cabin from the cockpit and Walter gave him a thumbs-up to let him know they could take off. Brad slumped into one of four seats in the small jet. Walter didn't think it odd at all that Brad was suited in a baseball uniform. He knew Brad had always been something of a jock in school. Occasionally, he saw his old classmate in the sports section of Bandon's rag.

As the jet engine started up, Brad fiddled with the strap of his duffle bag. Walter held up one finger at Brad to let him know he'd be only a minute more, though he'd already been on hold for ten minutes. Before they reached the end of the runway, the line clicked through.

"Hello?" a woman answered in English, which surprised Walter. He'd hoped to have a chance to use his Ukrainian or Russian. "Is someone there?"

"Ms. Kooper?"

"Yeah? Who's this?"

"My name is Walter Kassviney. Jasper O'Shottie said that you were the one to call about a problem we have in the Aegean."

"Jasper! What is this, some kinda joke? How old are you, kid?"

"Excuse me?" Walter cleared his throat, hating the fact that yet another person thought his young voice was that of a ten-year-old. "I assure you, Miss, this is no joke. We're flying from Oregon right now, to meet Jasper O'Shottie in Athens in twenty hours. What'll it take to get you and your team there?"

"Well, I'll have to make some calls. It's summer, so everyone's scattered, ya know? What kinda job?"

"Possible missionary extraction. Family of three. Zalzuna."

"Zalzuna? I'll see who I can scare up. That all?"

"Yes. Thank you."

Click.

Walter wiped his brow. He hated talking to women—let alone talking to them over the phone. They always thought he was a child, no matter how sophisticated he spoke, and he was so rarely taken seriously. Dealing with people in person was usually another matter altogether. With an IQ that doubled most, it was simply a matter of seeing him in action.

"This still isn't sinking in," Brad said with a grin. "A jet to Athens? Unbelievable."

Forcing a smile, Walter was nervous about how he and Brad would work together. Most youths didn't understand Walter, and he certainly didn't understand them. He hoped this wouldn't be the case with his childhood friend.

"Maybe you should change." Walter pointed toward the tail of the plane. "There's a decent bathroom, then you can stow your bag in the overhead compartment."

As soon as Brad was in the bathroom, Walter pulled his calculator from his suit breast pocket. He always wore a suit. It was the most fitting attire for his type of business, which usually involved management. Though he didn't know what it was like to mow the lawn or dig a trench, laborers didn't know what it was like to analyze a graduate student's physics thesis, either. A suit fit his social status.

On his calculator, he measured the distance between Bandon and Atlanta, their first layover. He inserted the earth's rotation and wind speed into his calculations. The PT7 wasn't the fastest jet, taking five and a half hours to travel from New York to Miami, but it did the job. After calculating the flight time to Athens, Walter linked via satellite onto the net and studied a map of downtown Athens on his small screen. It was much more than a calculator, of course, but at a glance, it appeared to be merely a student's trigonometry tool.

Over the years, Walter had gutted the handheld device and inserted his own hardware to compete with, if not surpass, the most advanced commercial communication devices. He could type with one hand as fast as most could with two on a full-sized keyboard. For security, since a child, he'd been logging personal notes in Greek. This trip to Greece was an exciting opportunity to put his Cretan knowledge to work.

"So, what's up?" Brad stowed his belongings. "You've obviously been busy."

Quickly, Walter studied Brad. The over-sized teen had

changed into jeans and a t-shirt. He had blond hair, bleached from time spent in the sun, but the shadow of a goatee on his chin had a hint of red. Walter's eyes stopped thoughtfully on Brad's left hand—his pitching hand. It looked strong, though his nails were dirty. His hands were probably calloused, too. Thinking back, Walter had played with Brad enough as a child to know Frank Alden had raised Brad to work and play hard. And now that they were practically adults, they were each prepared for what was to come.

As an analyst, and from everything he knew about Brad, Walter decided he'd stick close to Brad if circumstances abroad became hazardous—and Walter was nearly certain things would become hazardous. Walter couldn't foresee any way to stay out of the storm that brewed around the Jamison family—and those in Zalzuna who'd abducted them didn't even know the storm was coming.

"We have an old friend named Jasper O'Shottie. He's ex-Coast Guard." Walter folded his hands. "He retired in Piraeus, a port city east of Athens. He has a boat that'll get a team to Zalzuna. Jasper also knows the type of people we want for the job."

"Team? What kind of people? How do we fit in?"

"This kind of operation requires people who function on the edge of society—any society. Jasper knows them. Sometimes they work in the shadows. Jasper himself has worked for Father several times, for jobs that are under the radar, so to speak. You understand?"

"Yeah, I think so. They don't have names, right?"

"Yes, but they're not criminals, either," Walter said. "At times, legit businessmen need special tasks done overseas.

There's a database of people like that. Most would kill you as soon as look at you, but we can select people more qualified for this type of operation."

"Christian operatives?"

"They're out there. Like I said, we've used Jasper before. We don't have to kill the enemy to help your family."

"Dad would approve of that type of offensive."

"So would the Jamisons. If we proceed wrongly, we ruin everything they've worked for, which is to share Christ."

"I hadn't really thought of that—their testimony for Christ. All I can think about is getting Lacy out alive and unharmed. When Dad and I left your place last night, he told me we need to keep our anger in check. I think he was talking to me more than to you."

"Us geeks—we have tempers, too, you know."

A couple seconds passed before they both burst out laughing, the tension from their years apart, forgotten. They were still the boys who'd posted a stick flag on the sandy beach, promising to be comrades for life.

"Remember that time Lacy beat us both in the foot race?" Brad reminisced. "I thought you were going to box her!"

"But I didn't, did I?" Walter laughed. "You know why?"

"Because she would've boxed you back?"

"Exactly! Why do you think I became a bookworm? I have no temperament for physical exertion—or the physique for it!"

Recovering from their laughter, they both sighed.

"Man, I sure hope this trip is worthwhile, Walt. I know you're putting a lot into this."

"It's nothing, for Lacy." Walter shrugged. "Trust me—if I

didn't believe this was a reasonable risk, I would've never left my doctorate party."

"What did you say?" Brad blinked several times. "Your *doctorate*? That's what that party was last night? It was for . . . *Dr.* Walter Kassviney?"

"Lacy needs us, right?" Walter turned to face a laptop. "It was just a party. Right now, we have other things to go through."

"So, what kind of doctorate did you get?" Brad asked. "I haven't even received my official high school diploma, yet!"

"Forget about it. Look." Walter pointed at the screen. "You need to familiarize yourself with the Island of Zalzuna."

"I thought we were only going to Athens and Piraeus, leaving the rest to some team you're bringing in."

"Do you want to know what's going on or not?"

Brad stood, then knelt next to Walter's seat to view the screen.

"Tell me what I'm looking at."

"This is Zalzuna, the island. Population, five thousand. The whole island is only two hundred square miles. Mykonos, a tourist hotspot, is to the southwest about twenty miles away. Zalzuna itself is over eighty miles from Piraeus, which makes for a two-hour boat ride. They speak English, Greek, and French—and some Arabic. Most of the citizens are European, but down here on the southern tip of the island, Libyan refugees have populated one of the three small cities on the volcanic rock. That town is called Sankaddan.

"The other two cities are New Manchester, here in the north, and the capital, Zalzuna, here in this eastern natural harbor."

"What's this hill here in the middle of the island?" Brad pointed at the map.

"It's a volcano, and yes, it's active—one of the few active volcanoes in the Aegean, but it usually only smokes. There are just two fresh water sources, north, and south. New Manchester and Zalzuna share the northern source, which has resulted in a number of violent skirmishes in the past. But right now, the troops in Zalzuna run the island. Most of them are Cretans. The Europeans have populated New Manchester so there's obviously a degree of ethnic controversy that hasn't been remedied by their lack of diversification."

"Talk to me about my aunt and uncle. What kind of line do you think they crossed on this island?"

"Religion is banned on the island. The Libyans are making a surge with Islam, but the Cretans are brutal and repressive, backed by Chinese, Cuban, and North Korean fascists. Without a doubt, if Sarah, Lacy, and Albert were discovered to be Christian missionaries, they've been arrested. Most people have sense enough to avoid countries like this, but there've only been rumors as to how Zalzuna treats their religious prisoners. Human rights groups graded this country with an F, same as Saudi Arabia and North Korea."

"Which is why we're expecting the worst." Brad returned to his seat. "Maybe I wouldn't mind going to that island after all. Maybe they'd like to try pushing me around."

"You're not a soldier, Brad, and they're not high school punks."

Walter held Brad's gaze until Brad looked down at the floor. He shook his head and rubbed his face with both hands.

"It's getting late. Does this seat recline?"

As Brad dropped the seat back to its horizontal position, Walter studied his laptop screen once again. He pulled up additional satellite images of the island to study the terrain and alternate approaches to the island. Zalzuna wasn't known for its tourism, so a rescue party couldn't arrive and expect to blend in. Tourists did happen upon the island, but they regretted it later.

Ten minutes later, Walter heard snoring from Brad. Closing out his research windows, he opened an email he'd already read twenty times. For someone with a photographic memory, twenty times was the most he'd ever read anything in his life:

Wally,

Gonna be in Zalzuna for about a month. Write back if you're not too busy. Sure like to catch up with you when I'm back in the States after summer.

XO

Lacy

Checking the date again, Walter confirmed she'd sent the note only one day before Brad's dad had reported a problem. Wally. She'd always called him that. But the email was Walter's secret, for now. Brad wouldn't understand, he figured. And he certainly wouldn't understand that Walter loved her. He'd always loved Lacy Jamison.

✝

CHAPTER EIGHTEEN

"Just tell us the names of the other Christians you were meeting with, Mr. Jamison," a giant bald man with a British accent said soothingly to Albert, "and we can end this pain. We won't even bother with your daughter anymore. Why would you want to hurt your daughter?"

Albert hung from a chain attached to his wrists. He was naked except for bruises and welts. His head hung forward, his chin on his chest, and his lips moved in a silent prayer. It was just pain. It would pass. He'd been saved in Christ, so the sting of death was no sting at all, but a very real taste of salvation.

A second man swung a thin broomstick at the back of Albert's legs. Before it connected, he could hear it whooshing through the air. An hour earlier, when the interrogation had begun, he'd been able to brace himself for the strikes. But he was exhausted now. The broomstick connected. His whole body rocked on the chains. Albert was certain he'd gained another welt, but that part of his legs was already numb from previous blows.

"This will last for days, Mr. Jamison." The bald man stepped close to Albert and took a fistful of his hair. The man was as tall as Albert, even though Albert was suspended a foot off the floor. "What is it that makes you so resilient? The others understood the gravity of their situation. Help yourself. Help your daughter."

The bald man stepped away for the other man to strike him. This time, Albert's abdomen was the target. It was unmarred flesh and the pain made Albert's entire body quiver. Blinking away tears, he kicked and swung around on his binds to glimpse the second man before the bald one steadied the chain. The second soldier wore a uniform. He was young, possibly no older than Albert's own nephew, Brad. The young man gripped and regripped his stick as he looked with uncertainty from Albert to the bald man.

"It doesn't seem to bother him much, sir," the younger man said. "Maybe we should take him down. Maybe . . . try something else."

The giant stepped up to the other, towering over him. The younger one cringed against the stone wall.

"No stomach for a little discipline, Soldier? A hundred others would kill to have this position! Look at him! You want these cultists to take over the island with their lies? Sure, what we do is a little distasteful, but you learn to enjoy it for the good of the country. All weaklings! They can't stand alone so they cling to an imaginary Leader who is not this country's leader. If that's what you are, Soldier—a coward, a weakling—then get out of here! Get out if you can't fulfill your duties!"

The young man gathered himself and slowly raised his head to meet the dark eyes of the bald man.

"I'm no weakling, sir. Don't— Don't question my loyalties again, sir, or I'll—"

The bald man slapped the broomstick from the youth's

hands. It clattered onto the floor as the interrogation room door opened. Albert could only see trousers until he lifted his head.

"Niles . . ." Albert whispered, but the tall, dark-haired man with a scarred face still heard him.

Trevor Niles chuckled and walked around Albert, examining his body. The bald man stepped forward after shoving the young soldier aside.

"If he knew anything, Mr. Niles, he would've talked by now. No one's lasted this long."

Stopping in front of Albert, Niles tapped his classy shoes to some unheard beat. He was dressed in a suit now, though when Albert had first met the imposter, he'd been clothed in rags.

"I'll pray for you, Niles." Albert gasped, unable to bring himself to say his first name, as if the evil man had lost the privilege. "God still loves you."

"He might be one we can't rehabilitate, Fredrick." Niles' accent was also British. "What about the girl?"

"She's not recovered from the first questioning."

"Unresponsive?" Niles smiled. "Isn't that the way we like our religious fanatics?" He shook his head at Albert. "This one's different, huh? Doesn't matter. Work on him until he breaks. When that happens, we'll see him in court. Until then, label him as uncooperative."

"Yes, sir." Bald Fredrick saluted.

Taking one last disappointing look at Albert, Niles then left the room.

"That's it," Fredrick said to the young soldier holding the stick. "Take the prisoner down and move him into the holding pen. I have paperwork and other important things to do."

Fredrick began to leave.

"What about the girl?" the soldier asked.

"We don't want her to become a burden. Put her in with the others. Let them take care of her."

When Fredrick was gone, the soldier used a pulley to lower Albert to the floor. He reached overhead and unhooked the missionary's hands from the chain. With his legs crumbling beneath him, Albert fell to the floor.

"Come on." The soldier knelt next to him. "You have to walk back. Get your clothes on, old man."

Albert wheezed a little laugh at the thought of him being an old man, since he was only forty-six. His life's work had made him old, though. No doubt, he looked sixty with his graying hair and thinning mustache. He crawled into the corner where his clothes lay. After feeling the cuff of one pant leg, he thrust his foot inside. Yes, his colored pencil pieces were still there, hooked in the inseam.

"You don't need to be afraid," Albert said to the waiting soldier.

"I'm not afraid of anything!" The soldier stomped his foot, then after a moment, he cleared his throat. "What are you talking about?"

"Your commander, Fredrick—you don't need to be afraid of him. It's not always easy to do what you know is right. But easy or not, if you're afraid of doing the right thing, you'll be afraid your whole life instead of accomplishing what your Creator has planned for you."

"Shut up! There's no Creator!" The soldier glanced at the

door, but he didn't strike Albert. Instead, he moved closer. "What do you know? You're just a prisoner. They'll kill you, you know."

"Only if my God permits it." Albert took his time dressing. This was why he'd been captured, he was sure—to share the gospel even with his torturer. "I would gladly die for my Lord, because He died for me, the sins of the world on His shoulders. You believe it would be a small thing to turn my back on my God? No. That would be turning my back on life itself. That's why you can beat me to death, my young friend, and you'll only bring me that much closer to what awaits me after this brief life."

"How can you be so certain?" The soldier's voice showed concern. "No one ever comes back, so you can't know what exists afterward."

"Look around you." Albert stopped dressing to meet the soldier's eyes. "Just believe what you see. This world, creation, is no accident. We're intelligent beings, created uniquely. We're more than tissue and impulses. We can feel and imagine intangible things like love and hope. And we have a conscience. But why? When Jesus Christ came to earth during the Roman era, His friends, family, and many witnesses who'd never met Him, wrote about Him, His arrival, and all He would do for mankind—and did do. He was the Son of God, God Incarnate, my friend.

"He experienced this life so He could righteously judge us after death because He is loving, but He's also just. But He didn't only come to be a Man to know what it was like to live on earth; He came to die for mankind Himself. He was perfect, sinless, and He shed His blood so you wouldn't die the eternal death. It's every man and woman's choice, to accept by faith that gift of eternal life, or reject Him in indecision, which is to choose eternal death."

"You speak boldly, more than the others I've read about in reports."

"There've been many others?" Now that Albert had shared his most important information, he would make his own inquiries. "Christians? You know of others?"

"Some. Some have been caught with crosses, but Fredrick has forced many to recant. Others remain silent and defiant—traitors to Zalzuna and General Yousef. Fredrick is an expert at rehabilitation, but those of you who can't be shown the right way are executed."

"Lacy, my daughter, is your age. You can see she's innocent. Don't put yourself in danger for our sakes, but will you consider helping her?"

"How?" The soldier withdrew several feet from Albert. He nervously glanced at the door again. If someone heard him talking with the prisoner, he could be disciplined. "She can't be helped. Get dressed."

Albert pulled on his shirt. He used the wall to stand shakily. For a few minutes, as he'd shared Christ with the soldier, he'd forgotten his pain. But now it was back, and he winced and began to fall. The soldier caught him, and Albert leaned heavily on him as they left the room.

From the interrogation room, they entered a long corridor with a high ceiling. Instead of returning to his previous holding cell, the soldier helped him down the corridor toward a heavy steel door. The closer they came to the steel door, Albert could hear several voices distinctly. Another soldier emerged from a different door, shaking a ring of keys until he found the right one. He drew his pistol and leveled it as he opened the steel door.

"Get in there!" Albert's soldier barked as he shoved Albert inside.

Taking two shaky steps into the spacious room, Albert's muscles and tendons were too abused to support his weight. He fell forward, breaking his fall with his hands as the door behind him slammed shut. Sighing, he rose to his elbows. The torture was over for now. Maybe he could rest for a while and pray for strength and—

"Sir?" a gentle voice called. A shadow moved over Albert. He was a small, black man with a missing eye. "We take you. Come."

Before Albert could object, three men and a woman—all of them thin from bare rations—lifted and carried Albert to recline against their perfectly whitewashed, stone wall. Being touched made him hurt worse, but Albert was grateful for their kindness and compassion. It brought tears to his eyes. Taking in his surroundings, he hoped to see Lacy in the room as well.

The room was half the size of a basketball court. There was a toilet and one faucet without a sink in the far corner. The lingering odor told Albert the toilet was broken. The faucet dripped continuously, but a number of bowls had been placed to catch every precious drop. Along Albert's wall were the four who'd carried him to the wall—the black man, a white woman with ratted hair, and two men who looked to be Greek. On the wall opposite them, three other men sat. By their features, they were Libyans, Albert guessed, which meant they were probably from Sankaddan. To Albert's right, two men and two women huddled together on that wall. One of the women lay sick or unconscious, presumably from a beating. They appeared to be Cretan-Greeks.

All eyes were on Albert.

"My name is Albert," he greeted with a genuine smile, a friendly wave, and a nod to each group. "May God give us all the strength to endure even this, yes?"

The Libyans across from Albert looked away. The Cretans and those on Albert's wall next to him continued to stare at him.

"I knew you were Christian!" The black man's pearly whites gleamed, though two were missing. His missing eye had been gouged out recently, the flesh around the socket still red. "Twice, I heard them scream at you to betray Jesus. I am Paul."

Surely no older than thirty years, he offered his hand.

"Albert." The missionary shook the man's hand. "It's a pleasure to meet you, Paul."

"When I was on that wall," the man said, pointing at the opposite side of the room, "I used to be Mohammed. But now, I am Paul. You know of Paul in the Christian book?"

"Oh, yes. I know Paul very well. Who are your friends here?"

"We are Christians on this wall." Paul introduced him to the woman and two men by name, though they were now more reserved. "They are Orthodox over there." He pointed at the wall to the right where the four Cretans sat. "And they are the Muslims." He gestured to the opposite wall. "It is not simple to follow any god today in Zalzuna."

"That's true," Albert said. "But the Christian book, the Bible, told us this would happen. All who live godly in this present world will suffer persecution."

"What?" Paul frowned. "You have read this?"

This wasn't the first time Albert had found a man who'd never seen a Bible. There'd been villages in Myanmar where one Bible had been shared between ten villages. The ten rotated pages every month.

"Yes, I've read this." Albert nodded. "God has sent me here to share with you all of what the Bible says, no matter which wall you sit against right now. I've read the Bible since my youth and I know it well."

"You are a prophet?" Paul's eye grew very wide.

"No, just a believer, one of the many faithful of Jesus Christ. How did you come to know about Jesus, Paul?"

"A man here, gone now. I was arrested when I was caught with a Koran in Sankaddan. But Allah never fulfilled me. Jesus is love. I believe He died for me. This is enough for salvation, yes? It is what the other man said—it is a free gift."

"That's true, Paul. Confess with your mouth and believe. You've done this, my friend. Look." Albert reached into his pant leg and withdrew a piece of his broken colored pencil. "I'll draw the Bible for you, for everyone here! It's why I'm here—to share the Bible with anyone I can, even with the soldiers and guards!"

Turning around, Albert rose to his knees as he faced the wall, a perfectly white slate. He licked his cracked and bloody lips as he drew a line from left to right. Using short strokes, he consumed himself with his work. Speaking as he drew, he explained every object: a star in the sky, a virgin giving birth,

Baby Jesus in a manger, an evil king seeking the Baby's demise. The Muslims and Orthodox prisoners were drawn into the presentation. They left their walls and moved toward the Christian wall. After twenty minutes, Albert had filled his section of the wall, then he shifted to the right and began to draw the first of the seven miracles of Jesus, the wedding feast in Cana from John's gospel.

Suddenly, a key turned in the lock of the steel door. Fearfully, the captives scampered back to their walls. Albert hid the colored pencil piece in his hand and spun around to sit casually against the wall. He prayed the guards didn't look into the room. This was supposed to be the holding pen for anti-religion rehabilitation, not the Bible picture room!

Two soldiers entered the room, one carrying the arms of Lacy, and the other carrying her legs. They dropped her roughly onto the floor two paces inside the room, then retreated and closed the door. Albert lunged toward his daughter's still form.

"Lacy!"

"Come!" Paul ordered the other three Christians, then rattled off Arabic to his old companions on the other wall. They moved forward to help, as did the Cretans.

Albert cradled Lacy's head. Her eyes opened as his tears fell on her dry cheeks.

"Baby, I'm here." He tried to comfort her. "You're okay. We're with friends, see?"

She peered at the many people who crowded around her. It was her first real response he'd seen her make since she'd returned from her first interrogation. When she saw the two women, the Cretan and the one with ratted hair, her focus rested on them. Albert followed her gaze and understood. Lacy needed a woman's reassurance at this point, someone who knew what Lacy had been through, the treatment she'd endured.

"Bring her." One of the Cretan women waved them toward the back wall next to the other sick woman.

As one, the captives thrust their hands underneath Lacy and picked her up off the floor. Albert forced himself to his feet and supported her head as they carried her to the far wall. They laid her gently down next to the ill woman, who may have already died.

"Give us your shirts!" the same woman ordered. "She must be cleansed."

Albert was the first to shed his top. Paul and the other two Christians and two of the Muslims did as well. Dismissing the men, the women crowded around Lacy for privacy, one of them holding the shirts to make a makeshift curtain.

Returning to his place on the Christian wall, Albert couldn't draw anymore that day. He bowed his head and prayed as he listened to the women fuss over Lacy. Lacy wept unintelligibly, which Albert believed was a good sign. Paul knelt next to Albert and folded his hands, nodding at the missionary.

"We pray together, yes? We defy the soldiers to stay faithful to Jesus?"

"Yes, we pray." Albert placed a hand on Paul's young, bony shoulder, and bowed his head until their brows touched. "Lord God, we're grateful for Your mercies in bringing us here to these friends. Paul and I pray we remain examples of Your love and boldness throughout this experience. Teach us

Your ways, Lord, even here. I pray for Your healing touch upon Lacy. Bless her, we pray, and these men and women around us. May we not seek strength outside of Your strength alone . . ."

...✝...

Stepping out of the plane, Nathan Isaacson rose to his full height as he surveyed the only airport on the Island of Zalzuna. He'd been the lone passenger aboard the single-prop plane from Ellinikon International Airport outside Athens. From his vantage point, he could see the volcano in the middle of the island, its plume of smoke rising slowly into the cloudless sky.

On the eastern slope of the volcano, green vegetation covered the ground, but there was nothing as tall as a tree. On the western side, the ground was barren rock, evidence of the toxicity of the volcano's fumes. It was a fine place for a communist country—one of poisonous air, Nathan thought. And a fine place to find Trevor Niles, if he had the opportunity.

Nathan flexed his knee with the brace. Though he had a reputable identity to uphold, if the authorities figured out he was a Christian spy, he might have to move quickly. He had to keep his faulty knee loose so it would adequately support him. COIL's Berlin office had prepared flawless papers for him. On this mission, he was Dirk Salverskein, a socialist party advocate in Berlin, which had already apparently been confirmed by Zalzuna authorities. He wouldn't have been welcomed in Zalzuna, otherwise.

Scowling, Nathan put on his game face as a Jeep zoomed up the tarmac from a small hub of buildings. He stepped away from the plane as the pilot set his luggage on the tarmac beside him. The Jeep, driven by a soldier in uniform, screeched to a halt, and a bald passenger climbed out. The man was several inches taller than Nathan, and seemed to be about ten years older. With dark eyes and a stern look on his face, he marched toward Nathan.

"Stupid drivers! I'm sorry I'm late." The man didn't offer his hand. "You would think they'd learn to drive. I'm Fredrick. General Jalway Yousef sent me. It is Salverskein, correct?"

"Call me Dirk," Nathan stated with a rich German accent. "This doesn't look like the paradise I imagined."

"Maybe not, but it's ours." Fredrick turned to his driver. "Get his bags, you fool!" He cursed at the man as he scuttled for Nathan's belongings. "The general is anxious to hear your proposal, Dirk. We have accommodations for you at the fortress in Zalzuna. I think we can convince you we have a bit of paradise, after all."

"I hope so." Nathan climbed into the Jeep. "I'd like to view more of the island as well. If my constituents are to support your endeavors, we want to make certain it's worthy of our interests."

"Of course. I'll make the arrangements." Fredrick signaled the driver that they were ready to depart. "Will tomorrow be adequate?"

The Jeep left the runway, turned onto a dusty, gravel road, and headed north.

"That will be fine." Nathan scowled a little, reminding himself to stay in character. "But, I'll know if it's a staged tour, so don't bother. I'm the money, don't forget. I'll inspect what I wish on my own."

From his peripheral vision, Nathan saw Fredrick study this cocky German who flaunted his position. The general had probably told Fredrick to accommodate the German. They needed Nathan's socialist wallet.

"You know, Dirk, you're not in Germany anymore."

"Yes, I know." Nathan looked the giant in the eyes. "I'm in the toilet of the Mediterranean."

Figuring he'd successfully laid his presence out before his hosts, Nathan relaxed in the Jeep's bouncy seat and surveyed the countryside. Cretan farmers worked the land with oxen as if from another century. They all wore *vrakas*—the baggy, seat-dragging, black pants. He wouldn't mind wearing a pair of those rather than the Berlin-styled suit he'd been assigned a day earlier by his operation coordinators. Passing a small village, he saw a father and son working on the engine of an old Chevy, and half-naked, thin children playing soccer with a ball of trash.

The road curved to the east and followed the cliff overlooking the ocean just before they dropped down into the capital. Nathan sat forward for a good view of the town he'd already memorized from aerial photographs. Fredrick watched Nathan's face as he admired the small city.

"What do you think now?" The bald man swept his arm across the view.

"Impressive." Nathan was careful not to show too much satisfaction. He wanted them to earn his approval.

In fact, from a distance, Zalzuna was impressive. As desolate as the volcanic cone was, the greenery of the town was startling. Vines and bushes grew from the flat rooftops, pouring over the sides of houses and onto the streets. The whole town was built on the edge of the harbor where a number of sizable yachts were anchored amongst dozens of ancient fishing boats. The water was a beautiful marble-green.

A moment later, they were within the town itself and Nathan got a closer look at the modern culture. Electricity seemed scarce. Hand pumps provided water access from a large underground pipe that rose above the ground in places.

The Jeep swerved left and climbed the volcano foothills to a fortress where the Turks had made a final stand during a historic battle. But the current dictator, General Jalway Yousef, had renovated and improved the fortress, incorporating electricity and the purest water from the pipe before it was pumped into the town. The Zalzuna flag waved in the sun: a red star on an ocean of blue. They drove through a tunnel and pulled into the large keep of the fortress. The driver climbed out of the Jeep and grabbed Nathan's bags. Fredrick moved into the driver's seat. He pointed at the driver.

"He'll show you to your quarters. We'll have dinner together tonight, but I have business in the city right now."

Nathan nodded.

"This way, sir," the driver directed.

Using an iron handrail, they climbed a long flight of rock steps. On the landing, Nathan paused at the balcony to admire the view. He stood on an old battlement and felt the rush of ancient conflict upon the land. Nathan had known much conflict in his adult life. It seemed he'd been born for it—as well as to save others from it.

From the battlement, he could see over the fortress walls.

The town was quiet. Other places in the region took their siesta time very seriously, though he wasn't sure if Zalzuna recognized such a practice. It was the typical communist atmosphere, Nathan reflected, and he'd seen many of them. Supposedly, everyone lived equally, communally, yet somehow the rulers lived in luxury while the peasants barely managed. They couldn't buy a boat ride off the island if they wanted to.

He spotted Fredrick's Jeep winding into the town. Nathan would keep his eye on the bald giant—probably the general's goon. Fredrick was nothing to Nathan, though; just someone to work around. What he really needed to do was prowl through the streets of the small city to hear the local banter. If he needed to, he'd use Fredrick to gain access.

Turning, Nathan entered the fortress. He would meet the general that evening. And if Nathan was still alive at sundown, he'd get to work. Though locating the Jamisons was his operational priority, he ached to bring Trevor Niles to face the world court.

†

CHAPTER NINETEEN

With steely eyes, Heather Kooper gazed out of the commercial jet window as it descended upon the Balkan Peninsula to land in Athens. She'd been in Athens dozens of times—none of them for pleasure, always for work. Or maybe it was for pleasure since she loved her work so much.

She exited the plane on the tarmac and waited in line as the baggage handlers unloaded their belongings. From the corner of her eye, Heather acknowledged Bruce Lavers' bear-like frame. The third member of the team, Clifford Lavers, was to her right. The two brothers were nothing alike, and neither of them fit into the crowd as she did, but she'd worked with them often enough to know they were dependable.

Heather secured the strap on her backpack. One never knew what to expect when called out for an operation, so she'd brought everything she might need. Rarely was she called unless a mission demanded her expertise. As a professional Canadian spelunker, she'd brought climbing rope and scuba gear. But if a job didn't fit her exact qualifications, she was always ready to prove herself amongst the mostly-male operatives with whom she worked.

"Hey, honey," a Frenchman greeted as he approached

Heather. She figured all he saw was a wiry, brunette with broad shoulders, nearing forty years old. "You all alone in Greece, babe? I'll show you around, if you want."

The Frenchman stopped in his tracks when he was met with the coldest eyes he'd probably ever seen.

"Touch me and you'll regret it." Heather clenched her fists, not bluffing a bit.

"My apologies." He raised his hands defensively as he backed away and lost himself in the waiting crowd.

Glancing at Bruce, Heather nodded at him. Since they were in operative mode, he would've moved in like lightning if anyone bothered her. Clifford, on the other hand—the younger of the brothers—was the type to let her fend for herself, which she appreciated.

Bruce nodded back and crossed his arms as they waited for their luggage. The three-person team had arrived together to meet on Jasper O'Shottie's yacht. Jasper had been one of Heather's principals for over twelve years. Heather, in turn, was the handler for the unofficial team of which Bruce and Clifford were members. There were five others, but at the present, they were actively contracted elsewhere. As requested, she'd come with whom she could round up—which was just the two men. The last time the three had worked together was in Hong Kong two years earlier on a COIL intelligence grab.

The brothers made up their own army. Bruce was forty with a square jaw and bald head. At six-four, he weighed in at a muscled two hundred and fifty. He was bright, quiet, and thoughtful, unlike Clifford, who was four inches shorter, and shot his mouth off as quickly as the thought occurred. Clifford was a skinny one-hundred-eighty pounds, with a limp left over from a terrorist attack in London where he'd been a city policeman. He was too handsome for his own good, even with a bump on his nose, but Heather could barely stand him. She preferred quiet Bruce, regardless of his troubled past.

Those who learned about Bruce's past usually feared him, but only until they took the time to get to know him personally. He'd been convicted of murder, and spent twelve years in a prison outside Liverpool. It was during his incarceration that he found Christ, and upon his release, he and his brother went into business together for themselves, since Clifford was wounded but had a healthy amount of money from the settlement. They contracted out their expertise—everything from picking locks to covert operations. With these skills, the brothers served Christ inside countries where Christians were regularly targeted and in need of specialized relief. In fact, Heather knew of no other two men who'd successfully assisted more troubled Christians than the Lavers brothers. As opposite as they were, they made a perfect team. COIL offices around the world called on them several times a year.

Heather's attention was suddenly drawn to someone she thought looked familiar—a young man a couple inches short of six feet with short-cropped hair, and wearing a suit. She guessed he was as young as fifteen, but what concerned her was that she'd seen him before. As she watched, the young man drew a device from his suit pocket and tapped away.

A moment later, he returned the gadget to his pocket, then leaned close to speak to another young man, a little older and much taller than he was. Heather browsed the other passengers. These two young men were traveling alone. Though the shorter, younger one seemed familiar to her, the taller one in a t-shirt and jeans wasn't. Who where they? She caught Clifford's eye and gestured toward the young men twenty yards away amongst the passengers. He spotted the two who didn't fit in with the rest of the tourists, and nodded. Clifford would know she wanted him to keep an eye on the two strangers, having trusted her instincts on other operations.

Frowning suddenly, Heather realized the two young men hadn't been on the plane with them; they already had their luggage with them at their feet! Heather's heart thumped with anticipation. She turned, her eyes sweeping the tarmac where jets came and went noisily every thirty seconds. Yep, two hundred yards away was a small, private jet parked outside a silver hangar. The boys had arrived separately from them, so why were they among the other plane's passengers now? Was it a trap? Were they neo-generation assassins? All sorts of people had been targeting Christian operatives lately. Heather had a lengthy list of enemies all of her own.

As fast as she thought it, the taller youth stepped up to the baggage clerk and handed him a claim slip. The clerk found a package and hefted something wrapped in brown paper. The freight was the size of a pillow. After that, the rest of the luggage came for the other passengers. The crowd surged toward the clerk and the mountain of baggage, but Heather stood to watch the two strangers depart with their parcel.

"Friends or foes?" Clifford reached her side, following her gaze across the tarmac.

"Don't know." She checked on Bruce and saw he was

fetching their gear. "Look at that kid's suit. He's no tourist. And I know I've seen him somewhere before."

"I'm on it." Clifford didn't hesitate to start away. "See you at Jasper's."

Striding across the tarmac, Clifford followed the two youths. Heather knew him to be an adequate tail, unless his patience was in demand. The man was sometimes too hasty. But tailing the two unsuspecting young men would be easy.

Seeming to pay her no mind, Bruce passed her by. He carried four suitcases in his arms, and Heather's scuba gear was strapped to his back. She watched the other passengers for a moment longer to ensure she hadn't missed anything, then she walked across the tarmac toward the terminal entrance. Once inside the air-conditioned terminal, she stopped to dig her cell phone from her backpack and slipped it into her pocket for easier access . Only then did she chastise herself for not snapping a quick picture of the two youths. Heather was more curious than concerned about them, but in her business, there was no room for error.

Outside the front entrance of the airport, Bruce was busy loading their bags into a taxi with the help of the driver. Hailing a second taxi, Heather climbed in.

"Piraeus," she instructed the driver. "Toukolimano."

No more needed to be said. Toukolimano was one of the two most famous yacht basins in the port. The taverns that specialized in seafood were favorites of tourists and wealthy locals alike. The cafe tables were mere feet from the water where yachts bobbed. It was the perfect cover for the party to gather with Jasper O'Shottie to prep for the mission.

Before she reached southern Athens, her phone rang.

"Yeah?"

"It's me." Clifford's voice was strained. "Um. They're some of ours. Those two, uh . . ."

"What? Those two kids are with us?" she asked. "How do you know? You're sure?"

"Well, the big one has me by the throat right now, and the shorter one is searching my pockets. I walked right into them."

Heather smiled. She appreciated such boldness. Clearly, she'd underestimated the two young men. Clifford was an ex-policeman who'd worked covert ops for several years. He wasn't the type to be outsmarted by a couple of youths. But they'd nabbed him, which meant they were more than they seemed.

And as she considered it further, she realized from where she knew the odd-looking boy.

He'd been on the front of some Euro-magazine, something to do with science. Was he the "child" who'd summoned her to the Aegean in the first place?

"Put him on the phone, the young one."

"Good evening, Ms. Kooper," the familiar young voice greeted. "I hope to witness more sophisticated work than this once we begin to deal with Zalzuna. This is your man we have?"

"Yes, he's one of the members of the team you asked me to put together. What do they call you? Are you Walter Kassviney?"

"I am. We'll discuss more at Jasper's."

Hanging up, Heather clenched her jaw. Though she appreciated boldness, she didn't like taking orders. For years, she'd asked God to help her with her pride, but she trusted no one besides herself, and that forced her to rely only on herself. A youngster who'd never shaved was already outsmarting her team? That bothered her. But she'd been bothered before. What usually helped her get past her attitude was to engulf her team in a mission. Once she found out what this mission was, she could take charge and be herself.

Until then, she would be bothered.

The sun had set over Athens by the time the team gathered for prayer in Jasper O'Shottie's houseboat in the Tourkolimano Basin. As the six settled into their seats, measuring one another with uncertainty, they could hear the folksongs from the shore a stone's throw away. *Bouzouki* peasant musicians and singers were among the tourists, teaching them the old lyrics of gods and battles and seafaring people.

Brad was the only one of the six not sitting. He'd also been the one to take the initiative to lead in prayer. Since they all claimed to be Christians, he saw no reason why they didn't dedicate their safety and decisions to their sovereign God. Nevertheless, he stood protectively close to Walter, with his thumbs hooked in his jeans pockets where he could react in an instant.

He and Walter had spotted the tail before leaving the airport. Outside the terminal, Brad had lain in wait around a corner, while Walter had continued on. Brad was twenty pounds heavier than the operative Clifford, though much lighter than Bruce, whose hand he'd shaken only moments ago. Bruce sat comfortably next to Heather Kooper, who sat next to sulking Clifford. Heather was pretty, Brad judged, but those eyes were too cold for him to consider her attractive.

Jasper O'Shottie burped but didn't excuse himself. The retired Coast Guard agent in his sixties wore a rusty-red beard, and a potbelly tempted the seams of his red and white tank top. But as lazy and unaware as the old sailor seemed, Brad saw thoughtful, wary eyes—eyes as green as the sea— under his red brows. He'd briefly shown them around his double-masted yacht, saying he would rename her if they could think of a better name than *Sealion*. The name fit, though, since Jasper rarely sailed anywhere nowadays, and his boat played the part of a beached sea lion.

Walter seemed to take Jasper's burp as his cue. From behind his chair, Walter dragged out the pillow-sized package he'd collected at the airport, and set it on a cooler in their midst. Heather sat forward with curiosity on her face.

"I'd like to thank Jasper for hosting us." Walter folded his hands before himself, maybe a little too formally. "We're staging from here until I receive intel regarding Zalzuna. Then you guys can move in."

"Zalzuna!" Clifford said. He glanced at his team, then clamped his mouth shut.

"So, what's in Zalzuna?" Heather asked. Brad noticed the team looked to her for leadership, except him and Walter. "Nobody goes to Zalzuna. Everyone with a brain knows that country's been off-limits since 1945. It's too unstable. It's a death zone—a D-Z."

"Well, what's off-limits to the world is a door waiting to be opened for Christ." Walter dropped three photographs on top of the package. "This is the Jamison family. They're missionaries. Albert and Sarah. Lacy is their nineteen-year-old daughter. They missed their scheduled call a few days ago. Only death or imprisonment would stop them from calling in once a month. That's why you're here."

Heather and the Lavers brothers studied the pictures, then handed them to Jasper.

"For those of you unfamiliar," Walter continued, "Zalzuna was founded in 1945 after the communists retreated from the British during the guerrilla war that raged for two years. Eventually, the communists were defeated by US forces, but Zalzuna remained their one and only stronghold. It's been largely overlooked by the world, but other communist nations such as Cuba, China, and North Korea have sponsored various enterprises on the island, mostly money laundering. The terrain is rocky with patches of dense, unkempt vegetation where crops don't grow. The one-thousand-foot-tall volcano has become more active in the last few months, but from the seismic reports I've read, I don't believe it's a threat."

From a number of glossy pictures, Walter provided the team various angles of the island.

"Seismic reports?" Clifford scoffed. "You read seismic reports? Who are you again?"

"Can it, Cliff," Heather hushed. "That's the sort of thing I'd like to know, as a matter of fact. There are enough earthquakes in this region to mess us up. We won't run into problems, right?"

"Correct." Walter nodded. "Notice, there are only a few approaches to the Zalzunian coastline—thanks to the high, vertical cliffs. In three of the four places where there are no cliffs, three small cities have sprung up, which I've labeled for you. If the Jamison family is being held as prisoners, or for trial, they're probably in the capital city of Zalzuna."

"What's this on the western part of the island?" Clifford tapped a finger on the map. "Looks like a . . . desert?"

"The volcano spills poisonous sulfuric vapor. It rolls down the west side of the slope, killing everything in its path, though it's not a problem for humans to breathe, short term. The shelf that looks like a desert is honeycombed with tunnels and tombs. It's an optional approach to the island since it's not guarded. The few olive trees that are tough enough to survive the vapors are only harvested every two years, so we won't have to worry about stumbling upon peasant farmers."

"You said you're waiting for intel from the island?" Heather looked from Brad to Walter. "You have someone there already? That's impressive."

"Yes, I sent him in several days ago." Walter collected his notes. "He'll make a quick assessment, hopefully locate the Jamison family, then notify me. There's no point going in blind, right?"

"Depends who the guy is." Clifford shook his head. "If he's a flunky, we could be just as blind as without him."

"I assure you, he's a professional." Walter didn't seem ruffled by their doubt, but Brad was feeling the tension. "Now, let's—"

"No," Clifford interrupted. "I want to know who this guy is. We're trusting our lives on some sort of . . . What are you, a high schooler?"

"Did you arrive from the States in a plane, Clifford?" Brad

asked suddenly. He'd gone to public school, so he knew a bully when he saw one. Even if the man was a Christian, he obviously had a few personality flaws.

"Yeah. So?"

"And you trusted that plane to get you to Athens?"

"Of course I trusted the plane." Clifford scoffed again. "What does—?"

"Two years ago, Walter here designed and patented a safer combustion engine that burns less fuel." Brad smiled. "It hasn't been implemented in the US, but it's widespread throughout Europe. You look at him and you see a youth, a geek. I look at him and I see a genius who's so intricate in his planning that millions trust his design every day without even knowing it. You have already trusted your life in his hands. Why are you questioning his intel now?"

Clifford sank into his chair, defeated again. Jasper smiled, looking from person to person. Walter had told Brad that Jasper knew the Kassviney family well. Brad also knew Walter could take care of himself when it came to his wits, but sometimes Walter needed to be stood up for in other ways.

"Jasper charted a route from here to Zalzuna eighty miles away." Walter clicked keys on his calculator. "For the next day or two, until we get Zalzuna intel, we need to prepare for anything. Study the aerial photographs and analyze the public information I've already gathered. For instance, we can't parachute into the island without alerting the authorities. The Chinese installed a sophisticated land-to-air radar system. We need to prepare for a number of different approaches, and when we know more, we can focus on the most adequate to touch down closest to the area where the Jamison family is being held. That's subject to change, though. There are many variables."

"And what if they're already dead?" Clifford traced a finger across his throat.

"What do you mean if they're dead?" Brad fired back. He'd teach Clifford to shut his mouth one way or another. "So, what do you think? If they're dead, we go home. Did you want to hang around?"

"Look here, kid!" Clifford rose to his feet, fury on his face. His fists were clenched as he started forward.

But Brad was ready. He plucked a plum from a window basket and side-armed it into Clifford's forehead. If anyone else had thrown the plum, the impact would've only angered the operative. But since it was Brad the Major League pitcher, the plum exploded on impact and sent Clifford staggering backward to sprawl over his chair. Before Clifford could gather his senses, Brad plucked two more plums and braced himself for an assault from any other direction.

"That wasn't necessary." Heather looked critically at Brad, then at Clifford, who was now even more furious. "Sit in your seat, Cliff, and shut up. Unless we start acting like a team, I'm going home. Brad, Walter, you guys are young, so give us a break as we adjust, and we'll give you a break for your unprofessionalism. We're all Christians here, so act like it. Let's get the Jamisons out of Zalzuna. That's all that matters for the next week or two. Jasper? Can I have my usual forward cabin?"

"Absolutely," the old man said. "Just push the fishing gear under the bunk."

"There's one more thing." Setting the pillow-sized package on the table, Walter tore the wrap to expose a leather case. It opened like an accordion with tri-level foam trays that encased ordinary-looking devices. "This is a shipment from COIL, the missionary assistance organization. These are non-lethal weapons. Some of them, like these pens, are designed to be taken through customs as mere writing utensils. I know they're not the tranquilizer guns you're probably used to working with, but select one or two of these items for yourselves. I'll supply you with the specs for each item in the morning, if needed."

Clifford quickly reached into the case and snatched up one of the pens. It appeared to be a layman's calligraphy utensil. Removing the cap, he scribbled on a knee of his pants. Ink flowed normally. He inspected the ends, as the others looked on, fascinated. Plucking off the writing tip, he exposed a hollow tube the size of a .22 barrel. Carefully, he inspected it, but resigned with a shrug as he rested it on his leg.

"How's it—?"

Before he could finish, he looked up, startled, pale, and frightened.

"It . . . shot me!"

"See you in about twenty minutes." Walter checked his watch as Clifford fell over. He picked up the pen and smiled triumphantly at Brad. "Thanks to Clifford's live demonstration, let me explain to you all as to what happened to him. He accidentally pressed this tiny pinhole switch underneath the pen's clip. A water-soluble dart loaded with sleeping toxin shot out of the barrel, propelled by CO2, and it passed through his pant leg into his leg muscle. I'm sure it was intended to be used on non-team members, though."

Bruce, who'd been quiet until then, broke the silence with a breathless laugh. Soon, they were all clutching their stomachs in laughter, as Clifford slept unaware.

†

<u>*CHAPTER TWENTY*</u>

Nathan Isaacson sat at one end of a large banquet table. He was the guest of honor, but not the only guest of General Jalway Yousef. Fredrick's giant frame leaned over the table, his elbows on either side of an empty plate, and one of his gnarled fists drummed the tabletop every few seconds as they waited for the general to arrive. Across from Fredrick sat a man and his wife who spoke excitedly in Greek about the invitation they'd accepted to be at the general's table. Beside and across from them were a number of Libyan, Cretan, and Turkish guests, men and women who seemed less enthusiastic—or perhaps were just hungry—about having to wait for the general, whose chair at the other end of the table remained unoccupied.

Soldiers stood along the walls, doubling as servers this night. Nathan had already surveyed their attire, but he couldn't keep his eyes off of them. The general seemed to favor the Cretans in his small armed forces, though the officers were mostly European—specifically British. The Cretans were recognized as a dark and fearless sort. They served the general with purpose and loyalty since the dictator had spared them from a life in the fields. Throughout history, they were known to be lively, warm-hearted people, but under such circumstances as these, their ruthless lust to feud was revealed—as much as their desire to prove their worth.

The servers were armed with both holstered pistols and short, ornamental swords, which they were certain to be skilled in wielding. Nathan had no wish to tangle with them.

An hour passed, which was obviously driving Fredrick wild. He kept knocking his knuckles on the tabletop and checking his watch. One other guest snored lightly. Nathan sat calmly, though inside, he was concerned about his mission. Intelligence gathering was never what one hoped. It usually didn't happen fast enough, nor was the information as thorough as desired. There was also the presence of danger, of course.

Though the world of special operatives believed Nathan was dead, he expected someday to run into someone from his past. How would he react? Would he be able to react?

Regardless of his own safety, his constant underlying directive was to spread the gospel of Christ. For this reason, he was unarmed when he infiltrated most countries. COIL supplied him with various tranquilizers and non-lethal weapons, but if they were discovered, his cover would be blown. Rather, he most often relied on the wits God had given him to get in and out of situations. Sometimes he used false identifications, but he always depended on the Holy Spirit to settle his temperament. If Nathan relied on his own temperament, he'd simply kill the enemy and save the good guys.

It was toward this lack of respect for his enemies that God had changed his heart. Nathan didn't hate Fredrick, General Yousef, or those who might be holding the Jamison family. He had to believe Christ had died for them as well, loving them beyond any sin they could commit, wishing they'd come to Him rather than perish eternally.

A fat man with heavy boots and a crisply ironed uniform marched into the room from the kitchen, and stomped his right foot sharply.

"Enter! General Yousef!" The man saluted, then sidestepped.

Behind the herald, a man entered clothed in battle dress, his military uniform sparkling with medals and bars and ribbons. The guests at the table rose to their feet and clapped, as did Nathan. General Jalway Yousef smiled and nodded, acknowledging his guests one by one. He appeared to be in his late fifties, a little shorter than Nathan, and had a beaked nose that would shame the boldest falcon. Sinister, though amused, eyes peered from either side of the monumental nose. When those eyes fell on Nathan, the man nodded extralong, probably to show his gratitude to the alleged German for accepting a place at his table. But Nathan wouldn't miss such an opportunity to pry information from the general or the guests. Beneath the general's uniform, Nathan noticed a thin but rigid frame. COIL's own intel said the general was a Turk, though Nathan was certain the man had more European blood than anything.

As the general seated himself with his guests, the kitchen doors opened with a parade of platters.

"Mr. Dirk Salverskein!" the general called in accented English over the activity. Nathan decided the man had French heritage. The guests became silent. They surely wanted to know who the brown-haired stranger with the mustache was. "Your accommodations are satisfactory?"

"They are splendid. Thank you!" But Nathan had stayed in better suites in war-torn Serbia during the war. However, to an impoverished Zalzunian, the accommodations were splendid.

"I knew we had friends in Germany," the general said, referring to the socialist underground in Berlin. "It is pleasing to know I am not alone here."

"We are few, General, but we are mighty." Nathan raised his wine glass to salute the general. General Yousef returned the gesture. The servers placed a number of foods before Nathan. "Tell me, General, what is this we eat tonight?"

The general seemed pleased at the question, his eyes narrowing slightly, probably at Nathan's informal tact. Most often, Nathan guessed, those below the general accepted what they were given without question. But here was a foreigner who wouldn't know the customs. Nevertheless, Nathan sensed General Yousef had already taken a liking to him.

"You have two cheeses before you." The general pointed with a knife, his mouth already full. "The robust *feta* and *manouri*. The *marida* is the best here—better than in all the Greek Isles. It is fried fish mixed and basted in *retsina*, a wine native to the mainland. For dessert, we have *baklava*, the sweetest you have ever tasted. The honey is from our own bees, I must admit."

"It looks delicious, more than I could find on Friedrichstrasse." Nathan saluted the general again with a swig of wine. He didn't drink wine often, but he could hold his own. This wine was cheaply diluted to the point of tasting like watered-down grape juice, so he didn't worry that his senses would be blurred.

"Tell me," the general said, "it has been so long since I was in the Mitte. How is the city of twenty-three boroughs?"

Nathan smiled as he finished chewing a bite of cheese. General Yousef's question was a test, for which he'd been prepared. Though not a Berliner, Nathan had spent enough time in his cover-city to use it for that purpose: a cover. He knew the coffee shops, the main banks, the publishing houses, and largest stores.

"There are only twelve boroughs now, General." Nathan hoped his amusement was apparent. The general seemed to enjoy the sport. "Really, you should visit soon. It's been too long for you."

"You would be my host?" The general leaned forward.

"Me? No. I am merely a squire, General. My employers would gladly host you, with whatever entertainment you desire."

"Dirk, you are too modest. But tell me: your employers— when will I know the mysterious men in the shadows? Or are there women involved? I do not discriminate, but I do wish to know names."

"In due time." Again, Nathan saluted the man with his cup.

"Fredrick tells me you wish to tour my fine country."

"I do." Nathan took a bite of fish. "The idea of Zalzuna as a socialist state is much more significant than the reality I've seen. That's not meant to be an insult, General, but what I've witnessed thus far is not a country of wealth, but of poverty, with the exception of your residence."

With surprise on his face, Fredrick stopped chewing and stared at Nathan. No one dared speak such words to General Yousef, Nathan guessed. And he was certain Fredrick had killed men and women for less. However, Fredrick seemed not to know how to react—to attack or defend. The general studied Nathan's face. For the words Nathan had spoken, the general could've imprisoned him, but Nathan hoped they remembered their German guest had come with the impression of great riches. Money sometimes could buy a wealth of restraint.

"What do you propose, Dirk?" The general stabbed his fork into his food and left it there. "Your sponsors feel the same as you? That this is an impoverished country, and the idea is grander than the reality?"

"They do," Nathan stated, "but we hope to assist you with the development, though subtly, so as not to take credit ourselves, of course. It's your country and it has great potential. We don't wish to detract from this potential."

The general nodded briefly, relaxing some. Fredrick, however, had obviously taken the insult to heart. He glared with hatred at the foreigner, his bald head red with fury.

"How will you do it?" General Yousef resumed eating.

"You have a wealth of natural resources." Nathan felt in control again, but he had to be careful. "Properly managed, if you exported them to Berlin, we would pay exorbitant prices. The wealth would be shared with the citizens. There is also a need to improve living standards—sewage, electrical, and communication."

"Communication with the world of evil permits the errors of imperialism." Fredrick growled. "We will never allow it."

"No one will force you to compromise." Nathan ignored Fredrick and gazed at the general. "But you'll find with greater giving comes greater gratitude."

"Are you saying our citizens are not grateful?" Fredrick began to rise from his chair. "Ask anyone! They owe their lives to this administration! How dare—"

"Fredrick." The general held up one hand, calming the bald man enough so he relaxed in his seat a little. "Dirk, naturally, we welcome ideas. We welcome your financial assistance even more. However, I do not welcome your presumptions or your forced ideals upon my rule here. My people are comfortable. Yes, they are simple, but they live in a past you cannot understand. They love the past. I will not force them to change, nor will I allow them to change. Only I know what is best for them."

Everyone at the table had stopped eating, diplomats and guests alike. Now, they looked to Nathan for a response. He had hoped to make subtle suggestions, obvious imperfections within Zalzuna that needed improvement, but the resistance to change seemed immovable. Such was the communist mind set against the international community and its advancements socially, technologically, and medically.

"Of course, General." Nathan didn't mind giving a little ground. "We would never want you to force change. You have a fine island. Regardless of what you change, or do not change, because of the fact that your ideals parallel my employers', we will contribute to your efforts."

Frowning, Fredrick was apparently unable to follow the swing of conversation. But it was obvious General Yousef knew a politician's tongue when he heard one, so he nodded with satisfaction. Nathan enjoyed reading them as a cardsharp reads amateur card hustlers.

"It is for this wisdom we welcome you." The general

initiated another solute with his glass of wine. The guests continued to eat, maybe a little disappointed the excitement hadn't continued. "Tomorrow, I will arrange a complete tour of the island. Fredrick? Can you spare the time?"

"Permit me to request one of your sergeants instead," Nathan said before Fredrick could respond. "I'm sure Fredrick has more important things to do than to escort me."

"I'll arrange a sergeant . . . gladly." Fredrick clenched his teeth, obviously unwilling to act as a tour guide for the arrogant foreigner. Nathan guessed Fredrick would restrict him from certain places on the island, whereas a sergeant assigned to the task would be less inclined to argue with Nathan's interests.

"Very well." The general slapped the table. "We will talk again tomorrow."

Though General Yousef had hardly eaten, he rose from his chair and walked around the table, shaking hands with each of his guests.

Nathan returned to his quarters, yawning often so the others would think he was suffering from jetlag and extreme exhaustion. In reality, he was waiting for his opportunity. Once inside his meager suite, he turned off the lights and dressed in baggy *vrakas*, which he'd found in a complimentary closet. While they may've been meant for pajamas, he intended to blend in with the locals. He donned a straw-woven hat, also from the closet, and stepped onto a small balcony outside his bedroom. It faced to the west, the volcano appearing as a shadow against the night sky. He looked over the balcony railing, then vaulted over.

Landing softly twelve feet below, he rolled once, and

found his feet without pause. Two strides later, he was across an uncut lawn and stood next to a shrub as two soldiers walked past. As soon as their voices could no longer be heard, Nathan squeezed through the shrubs, climbed over the wall, and ran, limping down a cobbled pathway to the keep of the ancient fortress. Even in the darkness, he could see the low point in the eastern wall. He watched the keep for several minutes from the moon-shadows against the base of the battlements. There didn't seem to be guard dogs. The soldiers only wore sidearms since the threat of invaders was very low, but they were sure to have rifles in an armory somewhere. Since they were a police state, they expected no resistance to their overwhelming authority.

The two guards walked along the base of the wall on the opposite side of the keep. Nathan saw no one else keeping watch of the general's compound—except for the entrance, where a heavy, iron gate was locked and more heavily guarded.

Sprinting across the expanse, Nathan reached the eastern wall's stone stairs, which he ascended three at a time. Reaching the top, he crouched low, hoping to make no silhouette against the night sky. Squinting in the fading light, he studied the lit windows of the fortress behind which General Yousef and maybe even Fredrick resided. Seeing no immediate danger, he stood and hurried to the battlement to look down at the hill that sloped toward the town's outskirts below.

It was much farther to the ground here than it was from Nathan's balcony. He climbed over the battlement edge, then hung from his fingertips and dropped. Turning as he fell, he landed with his back to the fortress wall, rolled twice before he stopped himself, then looked back. Getting out was the easy part.

$$\dagger$$

CHAPTER TWENTY-ONE

Brad Alden suddenly sat upright. Orange light poured in through two different starboard scuttles in the aft stateroom he shared with Walter Kassviney. Rubbing the sleep out of his eyes, he listened for Walter's steady breathing. Moving so as not to disturb his friend, Brad peered out of the round window to where a super-sized motorboat idled. The engine was muffled, but it had still woken him from a dead sleep. After pulling on his jeans, he checked his watch—two in the morning. What was Jasper O'Shottie up to?

It was a warm night, so Brad didn't bother with a shirt as he climbed the cabin steps to the deck. Who was up and about in the middle of the night? He thought everyone had gone to bed when he had just before midnight.

Toward the stern, he saw the bear-like frame of Bruce Lavers lean over the rail of the yacht. The operative spoke in a low voice to someone below on the speedboat. Bruce saw Brad approaching and straightened to his full height of six-four—two inches taller than Brad and fifty pounds heavier.

"Thought I heard someone out here." Brad looked over the rail. "What's going on?"

He was shocked to see the length of the speedboat below. It was over seventy feet long! Three diesel engines revved under the control of Jasper on the roofless bridge.

"Just testing," Bruce stated. "Didn't mean to wake you."

Jasper killed the engines and ran to the bow. Throwing a line up to Bruce, Jasper's throw was off and Brad caught the line easily in one hand. He gave the bowline to Bruce and together they pulled the two boats together to tie off. Using a rope ladder, Jasper climbed onto the yacht with surprising agility for an aging, overweight man.

"What're you doing up, kid?" Jasper slapped Brad on the back as he passed him to check Bruce's knot on the deck cleat. Bruce didn't seem bothered as Jasper belayed the rope again.

"Heard the engines." Brad leaned against the rail as the three of them admired the speedboat. "Is it yours?"

"Her?" Jasper chuckled. "If she was mine, we'd be living on her instead of on this tub. No, she's just our transportation to Zalzuna on Kassviney's dime. Sleeps six in three staterooms. She's a few years old, but Sunseeker made their best Predator models back then. We'll outfit her to be our floating base of operations off the coast of Zalzuna, or maybe anchor off Mykonos. Just need a few provisions and fuel. We can find most of that in Mykonos, which is the closest island to Zalzuna in the Cyclades Islands."

Without saying good night, Bruce simply walked away and off the deck toward the stateroom he shared with his brother.

"Doesn't say much, does he?" Brad looked after the bulky man.

"Nah, but he's dependable, and he's a believer. Just be thankful he's on our side, kid." Jasper clucked his tongue and shook his head. "Usually, you'd have to get through Bruce to hassle Cliff like you did earlier tonight. I suspect I know why he didn't defend his little brother, though. Be glad he didn't."

"Why? Because I'm young?"

"No. Age doesn't mean much to Bruce, I suspect." Jasper buffed the deck rail with his sleeve. "A man like Bruce, he probably sized you up in the first few minutes after he met you—tested the strength of your handshake, saw how you move on the balls of your feet. And anyone who defends someone he cares about like you did Walter, well, that means something to Bruce. He's defended his little brother for years. Some say that's why he went to prison—defending Cliff."

"Bruce was in prison?" Brad frowned.

"Sure. Did a dozen years somewhere up in the British Isles. The irony is that Cliff went on to become a policeman in London. Got injured during a terrorist bombing."

"So, that's why he limps?"

"That's why, kid."

"Maybe I should feel fortunate I'm still alive, humiliating Cliff like I did—twice!"

"We're all Christians here, kid, but this isn't the world you know. Seems you got the right stuff. You think like they do, like an operative. I suspect Cliff was testing you, anyway—maybe to see how far he could push you and Walter. Even I thought you might get pushed around a little, but you held your ground. You got gumption. Bruce said so, too. Heather's saying they'll use you since their team is a little short."

"What? Use me?" Brad gulped. "You mean, when they go into Zalzuna?"

"You don't expect me to go, do you?" Jasper chuckled. "No, my days of belly-crawling up beaches are long past. And Walter wouldn't be of much use, either. I'll keep him in the

Predator with me. He and I can monitor your movements once you guys hit land."

"I didn't really come prepared for anything like that."

"Better get prepared. Heather's going to put you through some training tomorrow. We'll be leaving in two days."

"Two days?" Brad blinked with a puzzled look. "Wait. What about Walter's inside man? Did we hear from the island? Am I the only one who slept tonight?"

"There's something about intel you have to understand, kid." Jasper faced him directly. "It never stacks up to what you expect it to be. Walter says he sent in a pro to study the island, find those missionaries. That's fine. We have other intel, and our intel says we can go in two days."

"Oh, man." Brad moaned. "Walt doesn't know about this, does he? You guys have done this behind his back?"

"Look, kid, I know he's a genius, but this is a world he doesn't know. You can't prepare for a mission by reading a spy book. I've known the Kassviney family for years. Believe me when I say I admire their tactics, but experience rules out here."

"What kind of intel do you have?" Brad felt like his catcher was second-guessing his next pitch. "It's solid enough to really go in two days?"

"Sure. Someone on the island gained Internet access and left a message, something about Zalzuna needing Bibles in English and Greek. The website was a few months old, but we found a drop box and left a message. They responded a few minutes later."

"This all happened tonight?" Brad shook his head. "That doesn't make you nervous?"

"Nervous? We text-messaged with the fella for a few minutes and found out he knows right where those missionaries are being held. This guy is connected with the Christian underground on the island."

"He knows the Jamisons?"

"Yeah. It's done. We found the warehouse in New Manchester where the Jamisons are being held—used some of your fancy satellite photos."

"New Manchester?" Brad felt a sinking feeling in his stomach. Who was he to correct professionals? But he couldn't let it go. "They wouldn't be in New Manchester. They'd be in the capital, Zalzuna. They're political prisoners."

"Intel is intel, kid. We have a shot here. The sooner we go in, the better. Trust us. We've done this a few times."

Brad turned away from the old sailor and walked up the deck in thought as Jasper waited for a response. Frustrated, Brad sorted through what Walter had explained to him about the island's politics. Could it be that easy—an Internet connection? Walter had said Internet access was strictly policed on the island. Only the communist administration had access to the net—and very few of them! He returned to Jasper.

"You're telling me that someone with Internet access now knows we're attempting a rescue of the Jamisons?"

"Gotta trust somebody, kid. This fellow is even going to light a fire on the beach east of New Manchester where the team can go ashore. You'll be with 'em. We know what needs to be done. Now we're just working out the details."

"So, what's the name of your contact on the island?" Brad asked.

"Niles. Yeah. Trevor Niles. Hey, he's legitimate, kid! Even while we were typing back and forth, he was concerned about someone listening. Bad guys don't care who's listening on a commie island. It's legit."

"It could've been an act!" Brad felt his temperature rising. "You guys should've trusted Walt! He thinks of everything, every angle. And he wouldn't have missed the Zalzuna contact on the Internet. I'm no brain, but I'd say you just warned the enemy we're on our way. You might've just killed the Jamisons!"

Jasper was speechless as he stroked his red beard.

"What's going on?" sleepy-eyed Heather asked as she crossed the deck to them, wearing sweats and a hooded sweatshirt. "You get the boat, Jasper?"

"Yeah. Seems the kid here has a few concerns, though."

"Well, what is it?" Heather rested her hands on her hips as she stood next to Jasper.

Brad searched for words. He was out of his league, but he trusted Walter's strategy to the utmost.

"If Walt sent someone to the island to scope everything out before we arrive—risking his life to find the Jamisons—then it's only because there was no other way." Brad pointed at Heather. "You guys had no right to go behind his back to contact whoever this Trevor Niles character is. Citizens don't have computer net access in Zalzuna. You've all betrayed the Jamisons before we even gave them a chance—or gave ourselves a chance to get them out."

"I'm sure it's not a trap, Brad." Heather's voice was cold, like her eyes. "I read the text messages carefully. So did Cliff. Niles is for real. He's a Christian on Zalzuna. Though he didn't know much about the Jamisons, he told us where they're being held since they'd in fact been arrested, which was more than Walt gave us. You know what that guy kept asking for? Bibles. He said if we were coming to help the Jamisons, we might as well bring some Bibles with us to give to the citizens. The enemy doesn't ask for Bibles."

"The kid thinks we're beginners." Jasper scoffed. "You sure you want him along?"

"You know what?" Brad raised his hand like a traffic cop. "It doesn't matter. I'm done talking about this tonight. In the morning, we'll see what Walter has to say. He can think straighter than any of us put together on our best day."

"Have it your way, kid." Jasper shrugged.

Squeezing between Heather and Jasper, Brad reached the companionway and looked back at the two as they whispered between themselves, planning things beyond their ability. They'd been spies too long, Brad decided, as he descended the stairs.

Reaching his stateroom, Brad woke Walter. In hushed voices, Brad shared everything he'd learned. When finished, Brad waited in the shadows of the orange lights while Walter computed all the facts. He was silent for so long, Brad reached for him to see if he'd fallen asleep, but Walter cleared his throat.

"When I want a chess adversary to fall into a trap, I feed him every piece necessary to distract him from my strategy."

"Okay." Brad nodded. "Keep going. What are you saying?"

"Trevor Niles. It's too perfect. Zalzuna's administration has access to the Internet. They'd have shut down such a site right away. It's a decoy—maybe even the entrapping decoy your uncle pursued when he arrived in the country. Misinformation is the most useful tactic within the intelligence world."

"How sure are you?" Brad asked. "I mean, would you gamble with three lives? Are you that sure?"

"I'm a horrible gambler, Brad." Walter nibbled on a fingernail. "But I rarely lose a worthwhile bet. If Heather is putting everything on someone she met on the Internet who claimed to be a Christian from Zalzuna, she forgets how many Internet predators pretend to be someone else. It's a trap. I'm certain of it."

"So, how long until your guy in Zalzuna calls in?" Brad paced in the narrow cabin. "Will he call before we leave in two days?"

"I don't know. It all depends on his phone access. Could be a week, or an hour." To emphasize his point, Walter checked the phone clipped to the waistband of his shorts. "If Heather's plan is a trap—and I'm certain it is—we'll have a half-dozen people to rescue from Zalzuna instead of three. That is, if we go along with Heather's plan."

"This is insane!" Brad sighed and ran his fingers through his hair. "Jasper's totally backing Heather, too. It's you and me against a bunch of adults who think they can out-think you."

"Well, I've been known to be wrong before . . ." Walter paused, as if recollecting a few instances. "But I'm right about this. Only a fool would go to New Manchester to rescue prisoners. Countries as small as Zalzuna hear legal matters at the government seat, and that's the capital."

"They're going to ruin any chance we have, Walt!" Brad punched his palm. "How can we convince them? Heather's plan won't work, I know it! We have to wait for better intel!"

"You've already said what could be said to them, I believe." Walter stood and patted Brad on the shoulder. "I wouldn't have much more to add. In the morning, we could talk about everything again with that Clifford guy, but what use is that? We'd get nowhere." Walter turned, dug through his suitcase, then pulled out a pair of overalls. As he tugged them on, he looked up at Brad's face. "What? You know I don't own a pair of jeans. I bought these before we left Oregon. Overalls are all-purpose."

"Yeah, it's . . . cool." Brad smiled. "I've just never seen you wear anything but a suit since we were kids."

"Do you still remember how to pilot a boat?" Walter zipped up his suitcase. "Remember that time we went deep sea fishing? You were seasick until the captain let you pilot."

"Oh, I remember. That was your dad's idea. But I've driven a hundred water ski crafts since then, Walt. Yeah, I can pilot."

"Fine. That's what I needed to know." Walter sat on his bunk and opened his laptop. "We have clear weather. It's eighty miles to Zalzuna. The Sunseeker Predator you described to me, with three diesel engines, can do over sixty miles per hour. If we leave now, we can refuel in Mykonos around dawn. We'll harbor there until we get the call, then decide how the rescue should proceed."

"What are you talking about?" Brad whispered. "You and me? We can't do anything alone, Walt! We need—"

"Listen!" Walter hushed him with surprising force. "Who do you think is financing this? I am. The speedboat out there? It may be a rental, but I'm paying for it. This whole team is here because I wired money to Jasper. It's ridiculous it's come to this, but when employees can't follow orders, they get fired. If we do it their way, Lacy rots in a prison for sure. If you and I go on our own, we at least give her a chance, and we won't be expected by whoever this Trevor Niles is."

"Heather'll just find another boat and come after us," Brad said. "This isn't the way we should resolve this."

"I'm very familiar with people underestimating me, Brad, but you need to realize we're not among individuals who care how fast you can throw a spherical object. They are similarly indifferent to my God-given intelligence. Besides, if we take their boat now, we'll buy time for the whole team. We're saving their lives, Brad. By the time they catch up to us in Mykonos in a day or two, hopefully we'll have heard from Zalzuna."

"All right." Brad took a deep breath. "But I sure wish my dad were here. You and I might think we have everything figured out, but Dad would have some wisdom of his own to throw in."

"Your dad would tell us to pray right now. That's what he'd say."

In the semi-darkness, Brad and Walter looked at each other and nodded. They'd all been leaving God out of their plans. Yes, they wanted the same thing as Heather and the guys, but God was sovereign, and denying Him His place in their plans—they were acting no different from the world around them.

"Okay. I'll pray." Brad bowed his head next to Walter's. "Dear God, we ask for Your blessing on this plan of ours. We don't have much ironed out by any means, so we ask You to give us wisdom and insight along the way. Please watch out for Uncle Albert, Aunt Sarah, and Lacy. Please keep us safe as we go forward with the extreme, Lord. After we're gone, maybe Jasper, Heather, and the others will see some of the wisdom we've tried to share with them about Zalzuna. Thank You for everything You continue to do for us daily. In Jesus' name, amen."

"Amen." Walter moved to the door. "Take everything, my stuff, too. I'm going to get some of their gear to take with us. See you on deck."

Brad needed no more than a minute to gather his own belongings. He shouldered his duffel bag, and Walter's laptop case and suitcase. Outside the stateroom, he moved quietly through the galley to the companionway. Ascending the stairs, he found the deck empty. A drunkard whooped onshore, then broke glass, but it was nothing that concerned Brad.

He moved to the rail where the speedboat bobbed in the water. Brad dropped his duffel down the few feet onto the Predator's bow, then climbed down carefully with Walter's belongings. Carrying everything to the bridge, he set it on the floor as his face lit up at the sight of the technologically advanced controls. While the vessel itself may have been a decade old, the controls had been updated.

"Don't start the engine." Walter set two cases of gear on the floor next to the rest of their baggage. "Loose the ropes and let us drift away."

Reaching onto the deck of the yacht, Brad untied the knots Jasper had tied only ninety minutes earlier. He went to the tip of the bow, shoved off the yacht's hull, then returned to the bridge. Behind the Predator, the basin's mouth was narrow, but there was no traffic. Eventually, they'd have to start the engines to maneuver out of the basin, though.

"What do you think?" Walter seemed to be trembling. "I can build a gyroscope, but I'm not—"

"Don't sweat it." Brad caressed the throttle and browsed the dials and controls. It was the largest vessel he'd ever piloted. Checking the distance they'd drifted from the yacht—about twenty feet—he then looked at Walter. "Ready?"

Walter nodded, a rare grin on his young face.

"Punch it!"

$$\dagger$$

CHAPTER TWENTY-TWO

Nathan Isaacson paused to gain his bearings. Mentally, he retraced his steps since leaving the fortress. He'd traveled straight to the shoreline first. Well, as straight as the streets of Zalzuna allowed him to travel. Many of the cities in the Greek Isles had intentionally designed their streets to wind and curve like a maze to thwart pirate invasions. From the shoreline, Nathan had snooped around a number of warehouses, then gradually worked his way inland, keeping his eye out for large buildings with foundations that could double as a jail or prison. He ran into no civilians on the streets, only a few straggling soldiers stumbling home or leaving for an early watch. A few dogs yelped at Nathan for a pat on the head, but they left him alone when they sniffed his baggy clothes and found nothing edible.

It was time to return to the fortress. There was no telling how long it would take to find a way back into his suite.

Kneeling next to a whitewashed stone building, he checked his watch. He peered around the corner of the building at the entrance. It wasn't guarded, but it was some sort of official building. A Zalzunian flag hung on a flagpole and there was Greek print on a plaque next to the door.

Quickly, Nathan stepped back as a man in uniform exited the door and lit a cigarette. Licking his lips, Nathan tensed for action as he heard the crunch of gravel under the man's boots. The soldier rounded the dark corner. Nathan attacked before the man could see Nathan's European features. He jabbed him hard on the chin and spun him around by the shoulder to slam the man into the wall, though out of sight from the front door. The soldier went limp from the blow to the chin.

By one arm, Nathan held the man as he inspected his surroundings. No one seemed to have noticed the subtle commotion. Crushing the man's cigarette into the ground, he inspected the soldier's face. He was just a boy, and his uniform was pressed as if new.

With little effort, Nathan threw the young soldier over his shoulder in a fireman's carry. He walked swiftly across one of the streets barely wide enough for an ox cart. Quick-stepping down an alley, he sniffed the air for the sea breeze, then ran down a winding street, pausing in a doorstep as an early-rising farmer set out for his tobacco field north of the volcano. Nathan continued until he reached the water's edge. The sea lapped gently at the sandy beach, but everything else was quiet and still.

Drawing the young soldier's sidearm from his holster, Nathan hurled it into the water. Then he heaved the soldier into the shallows of the sea. The youth splashed with great commotion and became alert as the water choked him into gasping breaths. Wading up to his ankles, Nathan drew the youth into the moon-shadows of a boat winch. He was careful to keep the boy's face to the ground so he couldn't identify Nathan later.

"Let me go!" the soldier demanded in Greek-accented English.

"Quiet!" Nathan hushed him with his own Greek accent. He slapped the soldier on the head, his other hand firmly holding him by the back of the neck. "I have a couple very simple questions for you, then I'll let you go. Understand?"

"I— Okay. I understand."

"What's the building you came out of? Answer me!"

"It's just— It's just a hospital. That's all!"

"Don't lie to me!" Nathan called his bluff. "I saw no medical signs on the building!"

"Okay, okay! It's just a hospital, an old hospital. But they made it into a rehabilitation center."

"Rehabilitation? You mean torture?" Nathan had seen it before, even experienced it personally. "Are any prisoners housed there? Who are you guarding in there? Tell me!"

"Just . . . political prisoners. Nobody important. What do you want?"

"Are there any foreigners being held?"

"Yes."

"Who? Talk!"

"Um, I don't know! Foreigners? A girl. Young, about my age. Um. Curly blond hair, short. And her father, an old man."

"What about the old man's wife? Where is she?"

"She . . . They shot her. I heard they executed her when she resisted arrest last week. That's all I know."

"Don't lie!" Nathan did his best to disguise his voice. "The father and daughter, they're well? You'd better not be harming them!"

"No, no! I'm not doing anything! I just stand guard! Honest!"

"If you're lying to me, I'll be back for you, boy! And if you tell anyone you talked to me, they'll know you're spineless enough to answer all my questions because I'm letting you live. You know what will happen to you then?"

"What?"

"They'll rehabilitate you!" Nathan jerked the youth upright, then forced him to run toward the water's edge. At the last instant, Nathan hurled the soldier out into deeper water, then turned and ran before the soldier could catch his breath and clear his eyes to see him.

Nathan knew he'd taken too long with the soldier. The horizon was already beginning to glow. He ran through the winding streets to the west. His knee brace squeaked slightly from the salt water in the hinge joint, but he was otherwise a ghost flying through the streets.

After taking two wrong alleys and backtracking, he finally emerged at the bottom of the slope below the fortress. Slipping through the sparse vegetation, he circled around the outside wall to the uphill side. It was morning now. The sun was up. Down in the town, men, women, and children had begun their day of labor for the country, for the general.

Directly at the back of the fortress, the wall was only ten feet high. It took Nathan three tries to hook one hand over the edge, then the other hand. Drawing himself upward, he checked the lawn and rear side of the fortress for activity. His own suite balcony seemed so far away, so far up. To his right, one of the guests from the night before appeared on the balcony of that guest room with a cup of tea. Nathan lowered himself to avoid being seen. He could never climb the wall and reach his balcony with an observer loitering only yards away.

Suddenly, the wall against Nathan's cheek began to vibrate. A woman inside the fortress screamed. The wall shook harder. A man yelled. A dog barked. Nathan pulled himself up the wall again and saw the man on the balcony flee back into his suite.

Wasting no time, Nathan scurried up the wall. For an instant, he crouched on the top. He couldn't help but look back over his shoulder at the mountain. The wall trembled under him as the volcano burped smoke and even a degree of fire. Having seen enough, Nathan leaped off the wall to the other side and rolled to his feet on the grass below. At the most, he had a few seconds before others appeared at their windows to peer up at the violent mountain threatening them all.

At a full run, Nathan planted a foot on the windowsill of the first-floor window and jumped straight up. With one hand, he clutched a vertical bar of his balcony's railing. He swung his body and pulled himself up until he could throw a knee upward to help his struggle. After collapsing onto his balcony, he crawled into his suite as he gasped for breath. Though he'd torn the skin on his palm a little, he was safe and his cover was hopefully still intact.

There was a knock on his door. Nathan took off his straw hat and whipped it toward the closet. He peeled off his shirt and threw it on the bed, then kicked off his boots and shoved them under the bed.

"Come in," he called sleepily, yawning for emphasis.

Fredrick and two soldiers entered the room, sidearms drawn. They stopped short at the sight of Nathan in what appeared to be his sleeping apparel.

"What's the meaning of this?" Nathan barked.

"Have you been anywhere overnight?" Fredrick's face snarled as his eyes studied the room and Nathan.

"What?" Nathan made an effort to scowl. "First an earthquake and then I'm interrogated? This is my wake-up call? Have you forgotten I am the general's guest here?"

Gesturing to his men to lower their weapons, Fredrick and his soldiers backed out of the room. However, Fredrick stopped.

"My apologies, Dirk. One of my men was attacked in the city. We wanted to . . . ensure your safety."

Barely withholding a burst of laughter, Nathan raised his chin proudly.

"Well, I thank you for your concern. The earthquake is over now and I wish to dress for my tour today."

"As you wish."

Lingering a second longer, Fredrick scoped the room thoroughly, then turned around and walked out, closing the door behind him.

Nathan looked left and right. His bed was still perfectly made and one of his muddy boots was sticking out from under the bed. Fredrick was no fool. The soldier boy in town had talked, as Nathan had assumed he would.

It was time to get off the island. His job here was finished. He'd found what he'd come for: the Jamisons. Even without locating Trevor Niles, he had to leave before he became a permanent guest of the rehabilitation center.

Heather Kooper was awake and on her feet two seconds after the Predator's diesel engines began to rumble. Someone was stealing the speedboat! She bounded up the companionway two steps at a time. The boating community in Piraeus was close-knit and they watched out for one another; such closeness usually kept criminals at bay.

When she reached the starboard rail, Heather realized she wasn't the only one who'd been alerted from sleep by the commotion. Jasper was already there, with Clifford and Bruce arriving on Heather's heels.

"Slow down." Jasper gazed after the stern lights of their disappearing boat, now leaving the Tourkoimano Basin. "It's the boys."

"*What?*" Heather gasped. "What do they think they're doing?"

"And they took half the gear, too." Jasper shrugged. "Guess they were more upset than I thought about the change of plans."

For once, Clifford was speechless. Heather watched him run to the yacht's stern as if he were about to jump into the water and swim after the Predator. He leaned over the rail and peered into the horizon's darkness.

"Those guys are ruining everything!" Heather examined the other boats moored nearby. Was there anything they could borrow to chase the boys down?

"I don't get it." Clifford returned from the stern, shaking his head in bewilderment. "That takes some nerve. What do they think they can accomplish on their own?"

"They're mad because we didn't go along with their plan." Heather gave up looking for a chase boat. The Predator was the fastest around. "Their feelings are hurt because our intel preceded theirs."

"Ridiculous!" Clifford spat.

"You might want to back up a little." Bruce leaned against the mast. Since the bear of a man so rarely spoke, the others gave him their attention.

"What're you talking about?" Clifford moved closer to his brother. "A couple of teenagers just sped off with our two-million-dollar boat!"

"I'm just saying, back up a little." Bruce crossed his arms, apparently not irritated by his brother's fury. "Seems we've been underestimating those two ever since they arrived. It'd be mighty stupid for us to continue on that same trail."

Heather took a deep breath. There was wisdom in Bruce's few words. She looked to Jasper for advice, but he seemed concerned about the turn of events as well, and faced the water in thought. Clifford merely looked from one to the other.

"Okay." Heather held up her hand. "Let's assume they actually have a plan."

"Oh, they have a plan—guaranteed." Jasper chuckled. "A Kassviney never does anything without a plan."

"So . . . Brad told Walter about our plan to leave in two days. Walt didn't like it, so they went on ahead."

"The boys knew we wouldn't listen to their ideas," Jasper added.

"Maybe they knew something we didn't," Bruce said.

"I think we blew it." Jasper gave a long sigh, still not facing them. "If Walter did something this drastic, we really need to question our own tactics. Like Bruce said, we might've been getting ahead of ourselves. Walter doesn't do things on an emotional level. Maybe we need to re-think our Zalzuna intel source. That's what Brad was saying. Our own hastiness may have just cost us involvement in this rescue altogether."

"Unless Brad forced Walt to steal the boat?" Clifford looked from Heather to Bruce.

"You know better than that," Bruce criticized his brother.

"Yeah." Jasper took a nylon rope and began to coil it. "The kid might be a bit of a loose cannon, but he relies on Walter's brains quite a bit. They did this together."

"So, what do you think they're going to do?" Clifford held his hands wide.

"They'll wait for their own intel before they do anything rash." Jasper dropped the coiled rope on a deck hook. "After that, they might try to rescue the Jamisons on their own."

"No one has an idea who Walter sent in to gather intel?" Heather asked the others. "Let's say we went after the boys. We can't go ahead with our plan now. They have half our gear and our floating headquarters."

"I'm pretty sure now that Walter knows a lot more than he's told us," Jasper said. "An apology is probably in order."

"Well, I'm not apologizing to anyone." Clifford kicked at the mast, narrowly missing his brother's foot. "They've ruined everything!"

"We're the ones who ruined everything." Bruce shoved his brother away from him. "If the brainiac is for real, we should've stayed with his plan."

"So, what do we do?" Clifford asked.

"Well, this tub still floats." Jasper gestured at his yacht. "If we take her, we'll be a couple days behind them since we'll be trusting the breeze, but there're only so many ports near Zalzuna where they can refuel. We'll find them."

"And we need to find them before they go in." Heather nodded at Jasper. "If the Jamisons are going to have any chance, we can't let those two do it alone. They have no clue what they're really up against."

"Okay." Jasper gazed upward, his eyes on the wind speed indicator. "I'll check the sheets. We set sail in an hour. They'll be halfway to Zalzuna by then, but we don't have any other option."

...✝...

"Just tell us who is searching for you, Mr. Jamison," Trevor Niles demanded. "You don't want us to bring in your daughter, do you?"

"She doesn't know any more than I do." Albert gasped in pain.

Again, Albert Jamison hung from the ceiling chains in the interrogation room. Besides the imposter Trevor Niles, Fredrick, the bald giant, was also there. The young soldier Albert had witnessed to the day before stood in the corner next to Albert's clothes. The young man had a wicked bruise on his chin. Albert wondered if their conversation had been overheard, causing the soldier to be disciplined.

They hadn't beaten Albert with the broomstick that day. Instead, they'd tried a much more gruesome method. The younger soldier wore tight, leather gloves to protect his knuckles as he'd pounded on the ribs of Albert's torso. Albert struggled to breathe with several of his ribs now surely broken. But the soldier hadn't done all the damage to the missionary. An hour earlier, Fredrick had become frustrated with Albert's lack of answers, and had struck him with his own ungloved fists.

Fredrick drew Niles off to one side.

"If someone is looking for the prisoners, maybe we should move them."

In delirium, Albert hung his head, but it was an act. True, he was hurting, but the fact that someone was already inquiring about them gave him great hope. He couldn't wait to tell Lacy!

"That might be a little premature." Niles scowled at the young soldier in the corner who'd been attacked the night before. "Besides, where would we put them? Double the guard—with real guards this time. Tell me about this German visitor you have at the fortress."

"He moves like a soldier." Fredrick scratched his bald head. "But by the way he acts and speaks, he seems pretty naive to our ways. Besides, he has a bum leg and a knee brace. I don't think he's worth our attention."

"It could be an act," Niles said. "Anyway, I want to meet him. I even know some German. Can you set up a meeting?"

"Probably. He's touring the island today."

"I'll be in New Manchester preparing the ambush for the incoming team of Christians. You'll find me on the beach."

"All right, I'll pass it on." Fredrick nodded. "You want help with the ambush?"

"No, I'd rather keep you here just in case they try something else." Niles glanced at the soldier. "If this fool is telling the truth about last night, then there's someone already on the island. Who knows what they're doing?"

"It's hard to believe that website continues to bring in our adversaries." Fredrick chuckled.

"Only for those who insist on invading our land. It's an

easy way to learn their true intentions before they arrive. You know why I do this. I told you about Gilgal."

"Thanks for coming, Mr. Niles."

Niles and Fredrick shook hands, then Niles exited the room. Fredrick snarled at Albert for a few seconds, then slugged the missionary in the gut. Albert moaned as he swung on the chains.

"Take him back to the room," Fredrick ordered the soldier. "We'll work on him more tonight."

As soon as Fredrick was out of the interrogation room, the soldier began to unchain Albert's wrists. Albert was in more pain today than the day before. They'd intentionally targeted his bones and internal organs rather than the skin. When his wrists were free, he collapsed onto the rock floor before he could be caught by the young man. Laying there, Albert gasped for breath at the edge of consciousness. The soldier fetched his clothes and dropped them on Albert's naked body.

"Put on your clothes. I have chores."

"Who . . . did that to your chin?" Albert wheezed.

"You should know. He was one of your friends."

"My friends? I have no friends on this island that I know of, but I'm sorry for your injury. Tell me. What's your name?"

"Horatio." The soldier checked the door. "Get dressed."

Albert moved to pull on his trousers. His ribs were too painful to pull on his own shirt.

"There are really people searching for me?" Albert couldn't help his desire to know more!

"Yes, but they will fail. An ambush is being laid for them tomorrow night."

"Don't you care that others may die?" Albert raised his eyebrows. "You could warn them, or help them escape the ambush."

"Why? I don't care. I can't even chew food with my jaw right now!"

"Whoever chose to attack you could've killed you, but they didn't, did they? You were left alive for a reason. Consider that." Albert smiled, thanking God in his heart for this opportunity. "Nothing is an accident before God. Horatio, you must decide the right thing to do."

"I serve my country. That is what's right. You came here and broke the law. Others who come here will meet the same fate. Don't talk to me anymore about your God."

Horatio forced Albert's shirt over his head and thrust his arms through the sleeves. Breathless and wincing in pain, Albert was drawn to his feet and pushed out the door.

Down the corridor, Albert was shoved into the rehab holding room. He rolled onto the floor and lay still. It hurt too much to move. Paul was instantly at his side, searching with his one eye for visible injuries on the older man's body.

Against the Cretan wall, Albert noticed Lacy beside the sick woman. She looked worriedly at her father. Out of habit, she touched her earlobe that had been damaged since childhood.

"Daddy? Paul, is he all right?"

Lifting Albert's shirt up, Paul examined the bruises. The young black man would surely know from experience that some of Albert's ribs were broken. Albert's labored breathing was evidence as well. The two men's eyes met, and Albert hoped Paul understood his pleading look.

"He is well," Paul said. "Your father will catch his breath and be like new in no time." He pointed at the wall where Albert's drawings were incomplete. "Come. God will not take you from us until you finish."

Paul helped Albert to the wall on the right beneath his first drawing. He pushed a worn-down piece of Albert's colored pencil into the man's hands. Albert thanked him with a nod of the head, then Paul sat against the wall next to him.

From the Cretan wall, Lacy rose shakily to her feet, attended by one of the dark-skinned women, and walked over to Albert where they sat down on the floor in front of him. Albert forced a smile and reached out to touch his daughter's face.

"You're so beautiful . . ."

Tears came to Lacy's eyes, then she looked at Paul.

"I thought you said he was okay. Paul, I have some nursing background. I can see he's not well."

"It is nothing we can care for." Paul slumped and looked at the floor. "It is his bones."

"Mista Albert?" The Cretan woman set a blue stone on the floor in front of Albert's knee. The stone was the size of a fingernail, almost as clear as a sapphire. Albert knew many of the superstitious women in the Greek Isles carried such trinkets. "This is for you. I want you to have it. It will keep you safe, Mista Albert, and protect you from evil spirits so you can continue to tell us the stories."

Albert rolled the blue stone between his fingertips, not wanting to be insensitive.

"Jesus Christ has given us victory over evil spirits, my friends, so we need not depend upon beautiful stones such as this one. This is why enemies of Jesus can only hurt our bodies, but they can't hurt our souls." He smiled at the woman. "Thank you for your gift. It will remind me of this special time Lacy and I spent with you all, when we shared the good news of Jesus."

"Where did I leave off, hmmm? Let me see here." Albert closed his eyes, drinking in the presence of God, then opened them again.

"You were about to tell us this morning about the Man who walked on the water, Teacher," one of the Muslim men said. "The others would like to know as well."

"Of course." He looked to Lacy for help. She knew the Bible well and was able to share anything that he could. Like the others, she watched his face, surely hoping to be distracted by stories as they waited for their next interrogation, or for death itself.

Lacy still fingered her earlobe. In the past, she'd said it was a reminder of what God had brought her through. If she had survived Nigeria, she could survive this as well. Sometimes, Albert considered, God left scars like Lacy's ear to remind us how He has brought us through the fires of life.

"Go ahead, Lacy." Albert gestured to her, and her face lit up. "You tell them the story of Peter. I'll rest up for the next one."

"Me?" Suddenly, Lacy seemed self-conscious of her weakened, battered state. But each one of them was battered and abused. Albert prayed in his heart for her in those few seconds, and she opened her mouth as she positioned herself to face them all. "The day began when Jesus of Nazareth was teaching on the shores of the Sea of Galilee in Israel . . ."

The pain wasn't so bad now, not when he could hear the Word of God shared. They didn't need a Bible when God's Word was in their hearts and in their mouths.

Albert closed his eyes and rested.

†

CHAPTER TWENTY-THREE

In the dining room, Nathan Isaacson sat next to his Zalzunian driver and tour guide—a soldier under Fredrick. All morning, they'd toured the southern city of Sankaddan. They'd returned to the fortress for a noon meal before going back out again.

Poking a finger at something that looked like pita bread, Nathan watched his escort gobble up everything on his plate. From what Nathan had witnessed, the only men who ate well on the island were those who worked for General Yousef and his cabinet. Though Nathan knew why he was on the island, he was desperately brainstorming for ideas as to how he could make a difference while there. If he would've arrived with better resources—including an escape boat once things got too dangerous—he could've taken the time to find a replacement for the general and caused enough of a rebellion that the peasants would no longer support a communist regime. But that was an operation for another time.

The same server from the night before waited on them again, but Nathan knew the man was doing more than serving. He was watching Nathan. Even the driver assigned to him for the tour of Zalzuna had certainly been instructed by Fredrick to watch him closely.

Nibbling on his light lunch, Nathan glanced to his left

where the dining room hallway led to the bedroom suites. Another hall was there as well, running perpendicular to the main corridor. On several occasions, Nathan had seen a number of clerks come and go from that hallway. The satellite on the rooftop of the fortress told him he needed to venture down that corridor if he were to contact the outside world. But, he wouldn't access such technology easily. He needed to find another landline or communication device with satellite capabilities. Somehow, he had to alert his contact of the Jamison family's location. Every minute counted until he was to leave the next day. Even warning his contact a day ahead of schedule could make a world of difference, but how was he to do that?

"Are you ready, sir?" his escort asked. A Libyan-born loyalist to the general, he was nearly as tall as Nathan was, though thinner, and seemed to walk light on his feet. His left hand was never far from either his ornamental sword or his pistol. But Nathan wasn't interested in brawling with the man. He needed only to endure the man's company through the useless tour.

The tour was useless because Nathan had already found the prisoners he'd been sent to find. Instead of contributing to their rescue, he had to listen to how the olives were harvested, the tobacco was bundled, and the fish were fished. When Nathan had seen poverty, his escort bragged of triumph. When Nathan witnessed disease, his escort boasted of that year's crops. When Nathan noticed ruin, the communist's eye saw only order and achievement. As Nathan relied upon his God through life's obstacles, communists relied upon their communal efforts.

"Where are we going next?" Nathan felt his heart beating faster.

"New Manchester. It's the smallest of the three cities, but a worthy visit."

"When will you show me the rest of Zalzuna?" Nathan wanted to see the rehabilitation building in the daylight, if he could, especially before he reported to his contact. It all depended on the escort's next answer.

"We won't have time. You leave tomorrow." The driver rested his hand on his ornamental sword. "Besides, you've seen enough of Zalzuna driving through the streets, yes?"

Nodding, Nathan understood he wasn't being given a chance to see the capital city. So be it. He'd make the phone call now.

"I need to use the restroom." Nathan rose from his chair holding his abdomen. "Your food is affecting me adversely, I believe."

"All right. I'll wait here, but we must be leaving soon."

"Thank you." Nathan bowed slightly, then dashed out of the dining room and into the hallway toward his suite. He didn't know what to do, or even if he'd be able to do anything, but he had to try.

Inside his suite, he hurried straight to the balcony and looked out on the rear garden, which he now knew intimately. But he wasn't going down this time. Climbing onto his rail, he reached overhead to the balcony above. Pulling his body up, he dragged himself over the support. The drapes on this third story suite weren't drawn, so he found himself peering directly into the room. If someone were in the room, Nathan would easily be seen.

Testing the handle, he found it to be unlocked, and the door swung outward. An instant later, he was inside the suite, searching for a telephone line, laptop, or anything else useful. He guessed the occupants of this room were a married couple from Sankaddan. Their field had yielded the most crops in the south; their reward was a week's stay in the fortress.

Nathan's search ended abruptly when he heard a door slam outside the room. Tensing, he prepared to bolt to the balcony. But no one entered the room. Cautiously, he crept to the door that led out to the hallway. Cracking the door open, he looked both directions. It was empty at the moment, so he stepped out.

Spying an ornate door, he slinked over to it, opened it a few inches, and peeked into the room to see the splendor of a large furnished room. This was the general's sprawling master suite, occupying equal floor space of the kitchen and dining areas below.

Tapestries and rugs in bright Indian and African colors hung on the walls, and pillows covered giant sofas. While the civilians of Zalzuna starved on government rations, General Yousef relaxed on Persian silk.

The room seemed to be vacant, so Nathan eased inside and closed the door. His eyes studied everything hastily. There! Running to a cabinet, he opened the hinged door. A rotary phone stared back at him. He glanced back at the door. If someone came in now, he was busted, destined to be imprisoned and executed, though surely not before a taste of Zalzunian rehabilitation.

Praying through his doubt, he picked up the receiver and listened for a dial tone. He was about to hang up when he heard it, though very faintly. A dial tone so far away—Nathan figured the general was somehow splicing into nearby island telephone cables.

Though Nathan had memorized dozens of numbers, he dialed the States' number to his call-forwarding account. It was set up to connect to whomever he was to report to if it wasn't directly to Corban Dowler's Manhattan COIL office. After the line bounced off routers around the world, there were three rings. Every second was a greater risk to Nathan's life. He checked his watch. Already, seven minutes had passed since he'd left the kitchen.

"Hello?" a youthful voice answered.

Thankfully, it was the same voice that had contacted him a week earlier through COIL, so Nathan wasn't fazed. COIL wouldn't have forwarded the job to Nathan unless they'd thoroughly checked the contact for legitimacy.

"It's me."

"King David's grandmother?" the youth tested for security.

"Ruth. I'm in a hurry."

"Speak. I'm recording."

"Found father and daughter. Mother deceased, body unknown. Father and daughter one click west of shoreline in Zalzuna capital. Look for a large, whitewashed building shaped like an *L*. Do you copy?"

"I copy. Anything else?"

Nathan jumped. He could hear the footsteps. Someone was approaching the room from down the hallway!

"They're all armed with sidearms and sabers. Gotta go!"

There was no exiting the room through the door—not now. Nathan lunged across the room in search of the suite's balcony, but found none. Instead, he found a large window. He threw up the glass slider and climbed onto the small ledge. Balancing on two inches of crumbling cement, he moved to the side of the window, clinging with his fingertips to the grooved wall of the fortress. Using his right foot, he slid the window closed as he heard the door inside open.

Steadying his breathing, Nathan didn't look down for a few seconds. The phone—had he put it back? Had he closed the cabinet? Yes, he'd slammed it shut as he'd searched for an exit from the room. He'd left no other trace in the room; no one knew he'd made the call.

Only after gathering his senses did he study his surroundings. Since the sun was on his back, he was on the southern face of the most prominent section of the fortress. The ledge under his right foot crumbled under his weight. Moving more to his left and away from the window, he looked to his left. The ledge disappeared around the corner twelve feet away, but the ledge was also cracked between him and the corner. He was trapped—unable to go back to the window or go farther to his left.

Finally, he looked down. Below him, the exhaust vent blew fumes from the southern wall of the kitchen. Beyond the blower, it was another ten feet to the cobblestone ground and a small avenue that led to the keep. Carefully, Nathan turned his head to look behind him. Only ten feet below him, and across the avenue expanse, was the roof of another building that Nathan had earlier identified as a barracks for the soldiers who worked at the fortress. He looked up. The roof's edge was too high to reach. His only option was to leap for the barracks roof.

He was out of time. If his driver hadn't already checked on him in his suite, he would any minute. The only satisfaction was that Nathan had already completed his mission. If he were caught now, he'd still be victorious in having located the Jamisons.

Taking a deep breath, he planted his fingertips on the wall on either side of his shoulders, and bent his knees. Slowly, he began to lean away from the wall. As he fell backward, he gathered his strength and shoved off the wall, leaping as far as he could. Attempting to land on his hands and feet, he turned through the air, but in an instant, he realized he'd over-rotated.

Slamming onto the roof on his right shoulder, he slid down the shingled slope toward the edge. Desperately, Nathan clawed at the clay shingles, but to no avail.

Again, Nathan fell through the air. Extending his legs, he dropped feet-first from the roof. It was farther than he'd jumped to the cobbled ground before. The impact bruised his heels. Tumbling sideways, he brutally bashed an elbow on the weathered rock. Finally, he came to rest on his back. He staring up almost thirty feet at the ledge outside the general's window. Dazed, he sat up; he had no time for laying around! Nearby, he heard men talking. Though he saw no one yet, someone was coming.

Jumping to his feet, he ran down the avenue away from the keep until he reached a gate that led to the garden below the many suite balconies. Like a track star, he leaped over the gate and counted the balconies from right to left before he spotted his own. Like earlier that morning, he used the windowsill at a dead run to vault upward. He caught the bottom of his balcony and strained with both arms to pull himself up, but he was exhausted from the night's activities and his recent ledge adventure. Though he tried to swing his leg onto the balcony, he lacked the strength. Stubbornly, he couldn't bring himself to let go and fall back to the grass, nor could he climb any farther upward.

"Did you find the toilet?"

Looking up, Nathan saw his soldier escort on the balcony. The man extended a hand to Nathan. Accepting his help, Nathan was dragged over the balcony railing where he fell onto his back, gasping for air.

"What were you doing?" The escort peered over the balcony at the grass below.

Touching his brow, Nathan's fingers came away bloody, as was his elbow and a knee.

"I fell!" Shaking his fist at the balcony railing, he growled. "What do you think? You should make this railing safer!"

The soldier tested the balcony's solid railing. Nathan hoped the man would just think of him as a fool—how only a fool could accidentally fall over the railing. Then the man knelt down to inspect Nathan's brow.

"It is for certain nothing serious. Wash yourself and then we must be going. There is someone you must meet in New Manchester."

Nathan climbed to his feet and trudged into the suite toward the bathroom. He began to wash his wounds as his escort watched with crossed arms.

"You have gravel in your wounds." The soldier pointed at Nathan's elbow. "There is no gravel in the grass below your balcony."

Admiring his swollen brow in the mirror, Nathan was undaunted by his escort's skepticism.

"If you fall hard enough, you hit gravel." He winced as he touched his wounds. "Trust me. There's gravel under that grass."

The soldier didn't seem to be convinced, but Nathan could say nothing else. He'd been caught in the act. If they had any real suspicion of what he'd done, they could check the phone logs and find evidence of the phone call he'd made. That would prove very little, but the suspicious activities linked to him were beginning to pile up.

"Okay." Nathan tugged on a fresh shirt. "I'm ready to go to New Manchester."

...✝...

Sitting on the portside railing of the bridge, Brad rocked with the bounce of the vessel on the waves. For the last two hours, he'd been learning how to plot a course and operate the Predator's automated cruise control. As Walter had guessed, it was dawn and they were nearly to the island known as Mykonos, which was nearest Zalzuna. He'd not seen Walter for over an hour, though, since he'd gone below deck to catch a little sleep.

Anticipating adventure, Brad was too excited to sleep. If the team wasn't going in, that meant he'd be going ashore to rescue his cousin, aunt, and uncle. He'd be the hero—if he made it out alive.

"Brad!" Walter stumbled onto the deck, his laptop in his hands. His eyes were wide. "He called!"

"What?" Brad jumped to his feet. "Your guy in Zalzuna?"

"Yeah! Check it out." Walter set the laptop on the pilot's

seat and flipped up the screen to show an animated satellite image of Zalzuna. He pointed at an L-shaped, white building in the center of the capital city. "They're being held here, he said. It's some sort of administration building, single level."

"Okay, I see it. He's certain they're there?"

"He wouldn't have called, otherwise. But . . ." Walter stepped to his tall friend and placed a hand on his arm. "Your Aunt Sarah, she's been killed. Only Lacy and Albert are alive."

"Aunt Sarah?" Brad winced. "She wouldn't hurt a fly."

"I'm sorry, Brad. But we know now we have to get to Lacy and Albert as soon as possible."

Retreating to the railing outside the bridge, Brad sat down. More than his own emotions, he was thinking of his father. Frank Alden found a reason to talk about his missionary sister at least once a day in conversation. They'd been close, even though thousands of miles apart.

"So, he saw Lacy? She's okay?"

"Maybe, but he didn't say." Walter shrugged. "There wasn't enough time to ask him questions. He was in a hurry. She and your uncle are alive, though. That's what matters." Walter studied his laptop screen again, then opened a number of additional windows to show Brad various angles and preconceived plans of extraction from the island. "We'll refuel, then head to the island. If the authorities are beginning to execute the prisoners, Albert and Lacy could be next. We need to go in tonight."

"You're coming with me?"

"Well, no." Walter shook his head. "I'll be here, in the boat, monitoring communications and maneuvering the boat for a pickup. You know me, Brad. I'd love to go, but I'd simply be in your way. You'd be saving three lives instead of two, if I tagged along. I have a plan. Due to the constraints of darkness, you'll have only eight hours to get in and out. Can you do it?"

Sighing heavily, Brad tried to shake off his despair.

"Show me."

"We drop you off here, on the west side of the island. It's as desolate as the Badlands, except for a few olive trees and tombs. Then, you hike inland around the volcano. The south side appears to be populated, but it's shorter with easier terrain. Reach the town of Zalzuna, then extract from the bay, here, in the east."

"Yeah." Brad nodded with uncertainty. "Okay, but what about getting them out of this building where they're held?"

"It depends on what type of security they have. Whatever the case, you have to go inside, I think."

"Okay, I understand that, but what's the plan?"

The two stared at each other.

"That's it." Walter's face wrinkled as if in pain. "That's all I can come up with without calculating probable statistics regarding the number of men and weapons you could be facing."

"Use your imagination. Let's imagine the worst. Ten men are in that building, all of them armed and guarding Uncle Albert and Lacy. I have one chance. How do I get in and out?"

Walter looked down at the floor of the bridge for a few seconds, then back at Brad's face.

"I can't really do hypotheticals, Brad. You know that. I deal with hard facts. Maybe when you get there, you can report to me what you're looking at, and I can come up with a strategy on how to get in and out with the safest probability. I'm . . . sorry."

"It's okay, Walt. I'll just have to come up with something. At least I'll be going loaded with all those stun grenades."

"And you always have your pitching arm. They won't be expecting that!"

†

<u>*CHAPTER TWENTY-FOUR*</u>

"Give it to me!" a uniformed guard shouted at Albert Jamison. Behind the guard, two soldiers aimed their sidearms at the other captives in the holding room. "I know it's you! Give me the pencil, now!"

Albert moved from the wall where he'd been drawing Bible stories. The others were still gathered around him, as was Lacy, anxious to hear all he had to say about the brutality of the Jews and Romans during the crucifixion of Christ. They'd been so involved in sharing and listening, no one had heard the guards enter the room with the midday rations until it was too late.

Discouraged, Albert offered the guard the sliver of colored pencil he'd been using.

"Closer!" The guard waved at Albert. "Bring it!"

Taking two more steps, Albert held the pencil out with two fingers. Horatio wasn't among the guards, so Albert didn't trust these three. The guard snatched the pencil away with one hand, but with the other, he punched Albert solidly on the jaw, knocking him hard against the wall.

"Nobody move!" The guard drew his pistol as he and his comrades backed toward the door, taking the afternoon meal with them. "I'm reporting this to the commander! You'll all pay for this. You'd be wise to scrub the walls clean before he gets here! No food for you until tomorrow. Learn your lesson!"

The door slammed shut. Lacy and Paul ran to Albert, who groaned as he slowly sat up. Rubbing his jaw, he did his best to smile. He could feel several teeth were loose, but he said nothing of his misery.

"Now, where were we?" Albert reached into his pant leg to snatch the other half of the colored pencil from the stitching. "Oh. There were two thieves with Jesus, and they were crucified on either side of the Son of God . . ."

As if they hadn't been interrupted at all, Albert continued to share the gospel story all the way through the resurrection and ascension.

...✝...

Nathan wanted to get off the Island of Zalzuna. The next day couldn't come soon enough. His mission was complete, and he was ready for the next. But he couldn't consider the next operation until he was safely away from this one. Never before had he been such a willing captive after the completion of a job. The fact was, however, there was only one way off the island: in the general's plane to Athens. This meant Nathan had to continue to be the cool, indifferent communist sympathizer from Berlin.

"And here are the island's greatest olive trees." Nathan's escort pointed at the northern slope of the volcano as they approached New Manchester, but Nathan's mind was elsewhere. Farmland stretched inland along the cliff-side road from Zalzuna to New Manchester. Between fields of various crops were the ramshackle, whitewashed peasant dwellings— one-room houses that supported one or two families who worked the land. There were no modern machinery or tractors visible. All planting and harvesting was done by hand, cart, and oxen.

The land was rich with crops, due to the island's northernmost well and irrigation system, but without modernized equipment, the people were slaves to their own government's refusal to industrialize—the few feeding the many. The people would starve if they left their fields, but it was spiritual food Nathan wished he could give them.

The escort slammed on his brakes as two farmers crossed the road, one supporting the other who was injured. The driver honked his horn impatiently, but the farmers were too weary to move any faster. Nathan saw blood on the farmer's ankle.

"That man needs medical attention." Nathan started to get out of the Jeep. "An injured worker is no use to anyone."

"They can tend to themselves." As soon as possible, the driver swerved the Jeep around them and sped away. "Besides, only General Yousef and his army have access to the medical staff on the island."

"An injury like that—the man could die!" Nathan clenched his teeth.

"Another will replace him." The driver shrugged. "The country can't stop functioning because one man is disabled."

Now that he thought about it, Nathan hadn't witnessed any disabled or many elderly people. He wondered if the general truly did away with the weaker elements of their island society.

"This tour is more important than one man's life, anyway." The driver ground the gears as he shifted. "The assistant governor of New Manchester has requested a meeting with you. That's an honor. Mr. Niles is a demanding and important man."

"His name is Niles?" Nathan's mouth went dry.

"Yes, Mr. Trevor Niles. He'll be governor someday, and perhaps our president. Mr. Niles is a respectable leader."

Trevor Niles. He hadn't even changed his name? And he was now the assistant governor of New Manchester? Niles was finally ruling like he'd always wanted to. But what was Nathan to do with Niles now? Niles was an official; Nathan was an operative without resources. His pulse quickened as he touched his mustache. A lot could change in two years. Nathan hadn't had his handlebar mustache last time they'd met. Maybe Niles wouldn't recognize him.

Just before entering New Manchester, the driver slowed the Jeep and pulled off the road where a troop of soldiers was digging trenches on the beach. The trenches lined the edge of the shore where the sand was loose and soft.

"Expecting an invasion?" Nathan joked with his escort, but the man remained serious.

"Come. He's waiting."

Climbing out of the Jeep, Nathan followed his driver down to the beach. Only then did Nathan notice a plain-clothed man among the soldiers with shovels. Trevor Niles. Nathan's stomach felt like ice. He'd seen this man murder a man in cold blood—and try to kill many others.

Niles hadn't noticed the two new arrivals as he directed the two dozen soldiers. Most of them were stripped to the waist, their sidearms and uniform tops on a gnarled log nearby. Trailing his driver, Nathan casually looked over his shoulder, a prayer on his lips. The volcano smoked and rumbled more than usual. But Nathan would still flee toward it if he had to. He clenched his teeth when he noticed the driver had taken the Jeep keys and clipped them to his belt.

"Mr. Niles!" The driver waved. Niles looked up. "I've brought Dirk Salverskein from Zalzuna!"

As he saw recognition sweep over Niles' face, Nathan thought about running in the other direction. The man stepped away from his soldiers and approached the two newcomers. Ignoring the driver, he offered his hand to Nathan.

"Dirk. I've heard great things about you!" The man shook Nathan's hand. "Have we met before?"

"Perhaps in Amsterdam?" Nathan had never been there. He'd say anything to keep the man's mind off the Coral Sea operation, Nathan's first mission as a lone COIL agent. "Are you a book collector?"

"No, that's not it."

"I'm sorry, I don't recall." Nathan turned away a little. Why had this meeting been arranged? He gestured at the soldiers. "I know fortification trenches when I see them—the formation and depth. You're defending the island from someone?"

"In fact, it's an invasion I want to talk to you about, Dirk." Taking Nathan by the arm, Niles led him almost forcefully down the beach, leaving the driver and other soldiers behind. "I must know—how do you know the Jamisons?"

Stopping suddenly, Nathan remembered to use his German accent even in his hidden shock. Niles couldn't know his intentions on the island. How could he? Was the man merely fishing for information?

"Jamisons? Should I know this name?" He frowned. "Someone in Berlin you want me to greet for you? Family perhaps?"

Nathan watched as Niles studied his face. Niles' own face had changed considerably. The substantial scar from the shark on his right cheek was pale in contrast to the man's olive-colored skin. A dozen of Niles' mercenaries had been arrested for murder, but regrettably, Niles had escaped.

By the startled look on Niles' face, he was recalling the same Gilgal occasion. When Niles had run for his life, hidden COIL operatives had searched for him to prosecute, but no contact had ever been made. Until now.

"Patrick Gibson." Niles whispered Nathan's cover name, fury in his eyes as he backed away. "It's . . . *you!*"

Nathan uppercut the man on the chin hard and fast before Niles could call for help. The man staggered until his knees buckled and he fell over. Glancing to his right, Nathan noted the soldiers hadn't noticed anything, yet. They were still digging. Niles' eyes were open, but he was too dazed to get up.

Desperately, Nathan looked out to sea. He was on an island. How far could he run before they caught him?

"The Gillies disappeared after I gave them your submersible," Nathan stated. "They're still in Gilgal. Just so you know that."

Then, Nathan turned south and ran for his life. There was nothing but fields for a distance, yet the soldiers would be on foot as well. The only vehicle around was the one Jeep in which Nathan had arrived. Leaping over an irrigation ditch, he fell face-first in fertilizer, but an instant later, he was back on his feet. Gunshots rang out behind him. It was only small arms fire, with very limited range, but a stray bullet could still hit him.

He sprinted straight toward the volcano, and already, the ground sloped uphill. Ten years ago, he'd been faster on his feet, but even with the brace, his stride was such that the men now in pursuit wouldn't catch him easily. They'd have to hunt him down.

Crossing the main road that led into New Manchester, he jumped another ditch, landed perfectly, then ran one hundred more yards through a field of dry dirt. Panting, he stopped to catch his breath, but he paused for more than only his wind. First, he studied the terrain in front of him. He'd reach thick vegetation in another quarter mile. Once there, he could hide amongst the plants and foliage, with short trees and brush the color of celery. There were ravines running up the volcanic slope as well, and he'd find himself trapped if he journeyed up the wrong one.

Far behind, Niles shouted at his soldiers to form a line to pursue the enemy. Nathan flexed the fist with which he'd punched Niles. He shouldn't have hit the man. Violence was only the result of bad planning, Nathan recalled someone saying. And it was certainly not Christ-like—similar to Simon Peter who'd hastily and needlessly cut off the ear of the high priest's servant.

The Jeep Niles had could've run down Nathan, but there were two irrigation ditches between them now. Nathan had forced a long, drawn-out pursuit on foot. He counted twenty-five men, including Niles.

Facing New Manchester, Nathan guessed Niles would summon more soldiers from the small city. The military might even have access to ATVs, which could traverse the terrain faster.

The foot soldiers were gaining on him, but Nathan stood, still indecisive. He faced the volcano again. The numerous ravines were covered with crawling vines and wild vegetation, but he spotted two gullies that snaked straight up the mountain. Getting caught in the wrong one would mean capture. The walls would be too steep to climb out of. He could just barely identify two more ravines to the east that weaved through the greenery above the fortress. But Nathan wasn't interested in hiding himself among people. And he certainly didn't know whom to trust. So he focused on a single, westerly ravine caused by an ancient lava flow. The gulch snaked toward the west side of the volcano's cone, the uninhabited side of the volcano.

The soldiers were within two hundred yards when Nathan started running again at a steady, pace-consuming rate. Several shots were fired behind him again, but he simply prayed, ducked his head, and continued. They were too far behind to be accurate. He was more concerned that the peasant farmers working the nearby fields would meet a stray bullet. As best he could, he avoided the innocents.

Coming abruptly upon the end of the fields, Nathan plunged into the vegetation and short trees. None of the dense foliage was taller than ten feet, but it stretched all the way to the brim of the volcano.

Even though Nathan was out of sight of his pursuers now, he didn't stop. Rather, he turned sharply to the right in search of the westerly ravine. He figured those chasing him would expect him to flee straight ahead, or east. If they thought to find him in either of the two other ravines, they'd in fact find themselves at the volcano's crater and exposed to its fumes.

Slowing to a walk, Nathan wished he had a machete to chop a path through the vines. But chopping a trail would leave a path for his pursuers. Instead, he found himself slipping under patches of hanging plants and thorn bushes to lose everyone but the most expert of trackers.

Pausing, he checked the sun. It was midday. Though he searched for the volcano's highest point, Nathan couldn't see over the plants. Again, he moved steadily forward, watching the steep angle of the ground to stay in the vegetation while heading west.

Finally, he found what he hoped was the western-most ravine. The ground that led up the ravine was much more hazardous with aged leaves covering lava rocks and foot-swallowing holes. With care, he picked his way up the steeper ground and shuddered at the jagged walls of the ravine; he couldn't climb the walls if he'd wanted to. If this ravine became too difficult, he'd have to return to the mouth, which could mean he'd be caught.

Nathan hesitated to consider another possibility. Niles was a predator. Would he think to circle around the backside of the volcano to ambush him? Though he could imagine being captured, Nathan wanted to at least give them a chase first.

While Nathan should have felt helpless and hopeless, he'd already found hope in the fact that a team was inbound to rescue the Jamisons from the rehabilitation center in Zalzuna. But how soon? That would be the fastest way off the island— to catch a ride with the extraction team.

The worst-case scenario, however, would be to hide out

on the volcano for a few days until the search waned. Then he could sneak down to the coast, steal a fishing vessel, and sail to Mykonos, a Greek island only a half-day's sail away with the right breeze. That plan depended on the pressure he received from the search party. He didn't have any food or water, which would need to be remedied before he could hole up somewhere to wait out his enemies. However, Niles wasn't the sort to accept defeat easily. Memories of his zeal to capture Gilgal spoke volumes.

Suddenly, just as Nathan started forward again, the ground shook and an explosion erupted to his left. He was forced to his hands and knees on the steep hillside as the volcano spouted wrath from the depths of the earth. A number of tropical birds flapped overhead, away from the belching cone. Vapor spewed into the air, but the wind began to dissipate it. A few seconds later, it was over. Nathan continued up the ravine, sometimes scrambling with his hands on rocks and vines, clawing upward a few feet at a time.

There was an abrupt break in the foliage around him. The view was breathtaking—the green sea spanning to the horizon. But immediately below him, and surprisingly close, was the western quarter of New Manchester. It was the first clarification he had that he was in the western ravine, headed in the right direction.

He noticed two fishing vessels not far offshore. The boats were single-masted, which would be easy to sail by one or two people. All Nathan had to do was get to one of them, preferably under the cover of darkness. Nathan praised God. When all seemed lost, the Lord brought him hope with resources that were readily available. But he prayed he wouldn't be forced to steal a boat from the locals. His first choice was to catch up with the extraction team for a ride off the island.

Would it be an extraction team he knew from his past? The thought intrigued him; he was believed to be dead by most COIL personnel. Chen Li was the exception, though she didn't even know his real name—for her own safety. After this mission, he decided it was time to become better acquainted with her, at least to meet her in person again!

The walls of the ravine became more shallow, evidence he was nearing the top of the volcano. The smell of sulfur was stronger as well. Fifty yards later, the ravine ended, and he emerged from the vegetation on the western side of the cone. He could've thrown a rock over the lip of the cone, he was so close, but he didn't want to be spotted on the desolate ground. Moving on, he started down the western side, carefully placing his feet as he picked his way through the wasteland before him.

Leaving the foliage and civilization of the northern side behind, the western slope had the appearance of rocky terrain left bare after a forest fire. But there were still places to hide. Rocky outcroppings littered the countryside all the way to the shoreline, which was a mixture of beach and cliffs below. A number of tunnels used during Greece's civil wars had been turned into catacombs. If Nathan searched carefully enough, he hoped to find a hidden pool of rainwater.

Half an hour later, Nathan reached level ground and picked up his pace to a slow jog. He needed to find cover. If Niles or his men reached the top of the volcano soon, they'd be able to browse the whole island. With a good pair of field glasses, they'd spot Nathan easily as he weaved his way through the black rock.

Nathan hopped down into a cistern-shaped pit. Smiling, he praised God at the sight of a small pool of water, though only a couple of pints. But upon tasting it, he found it was sulfur-poisoned. Licking his lips, he checked his watch. Thirsty or not, this was as good a place as any to wait for nightfall. Settling onto the rock bottom, he rested. After sundown, he'd venture into Zalzuna again.

...✝...

Brad stood on the bow of the Predator speedboat and gazed to the northeast. Far away on the horizon, there was a grayish haze. Was that Zalzuna? Did the island have smog?

"There are fish on the coals if you're hungry, mister," a Mykonesian said as he refueled their boat.

Since Walter had been dying to test his Greek on the locals, Brad didn't bother to address the man.

"We'll trade you food for fish." Walter said, though the islander's hospitality was being offered free of charge, except for the fuel. "We have canned beef, milk, and sweets."

A number of local children climbed aboard the Predator and admired the oversized motors, though their curiosity was interrupted by a game of chase. Brad quickly joined in as Walter continued to converse with the islanders.

A short while later, the two Americans stood on the bridge and waved goodbye to their newfound friends. They wished they'd had more time to share the gospel of Jesus Christ with them. The island had many churches, but the churches were a remnant of superstitious vows made by sailors on rough seas, and the Bible's truth was no better known there than it was on the communist Island of Zalzuna.

Brad pointed the bow to the northeast where the smog lingered over the water miles away.

"You ready for tonight?" Walter asked a few minutes later.

Taking a deep breath, Brad glanced down at his companion, then back at the horizon as he programmed the autopilot.

"I'm scared to death, Walt."

"Good. That means you won't do anything stupid." Walter gestured ahead toward the island, which still wasn't quite in sight. "Only a few more miles, then we'll drop anchor and wait for darkness."

†

CHAPTER TWENTY-FIVE

Heather climbed the companionway to the deck of the yacht and approached Jasper at the helm. She stood beside him, feeling the wind in her hair. There hadn't been too many missions where she'd sailed through tropical waters. Though she was trying to enjoy the trip to Mykonos, her recent mistakes lingered in her mind. If Jasper and the Lavers brothers wanted to act hastily, that was their right, but she was the team leader with the most experience. There was no excuse for underestimating the two boys' determination, nor their level of intelligence.

Instead, Heather's mistakes had put more people in danger, and kept her team out of the action for which she was trained. Everything had climaxed as the Predator was swept from under their noses. That was the drastic event that had finally caused her, with Bruce's help, to see they needed to reexamine their intentions and plans.

"We're making good time." Jasper nodded at the full sails. "Good wind. We'll be in Mykonos by morning."

"Let's hope it isn't too late." Heather whispered a prayer for the boys.

She walked to the bow of the yacht to feel the spray of the ocean on her face. Too often, as a professional spelunker, she couldn't experience the open ocean like this. In a perfect world, she would put her troubled childhood of abuse out of her mind, and live a life of luxury on the coast of South Carolina. But the world wasn't perfect. Maybe that was why she'd become a caver in the first place—to hide from the world above. At thirty-six, she was still hiding. Yes, she'd found some peace in Jesus Christ, but she was still holding back.

The missions distracted her from the reality of her pain when she knew she just needed to cry her eyes out and move on. Stoically, she'd not cried since a child when she'd fled from her foster parents. She'd survived the streets of New York City until she'd come across the right people at the right church. Then, as a new believer in Christ, she'd married too young, and their honeymoon had become a reflection of her entire life. Her husband was killed during a climbing accident one week after the wedding.

Fleeing to Europe as a kind of therapy, Heather had found ways to help others in their own troubled situations. But she always returned to her caves—the darkness and scurrying rats and bats—where she could hide from her memories of tragedy and pain. Someday, she needed to leave those caves.

"We need to discuss something."

Heather turned to see that Bruce had joined her. For a man as big as a bear, he moved with remarkable silence.

"Discuss what?"

"Walter Kassviney may have been right." Bruce stood close so no one else on deck would hear him. "I don't think we should trust our Internet contact, this Trevor Niles, who told us to land east of New Manchester. It may truly be a trap."

"What do you propose?" Heather agreed with him, but she

was comforted by his insight. Now that she'd had time to reflect upon some of the boys' objections, she saw the holes in her plan. "Landing spots are limited around New Manchester. There are cliffs both to the west and east."

"That's why we go back to Walter's plan, and hit Zalzuna directly. Brad said last night the Jamisons were certain to be in the capital."

"Then why would Niles say the Jamisons were being held in New Manchester?"

"It must be an ambush."

Nodding, Heather seriously considered it all. Now, it did seem too easy—to find someone on the Internet who claimed to know exactly where the captured missionaries were!

"So, we'll target Zalzuna." She moved closer to Bruce, their arms touching. "At least we can contact the boys once we're within radio range. Without their intel, we're flying blind."

"Exactly. We also need to talk about the possibility of the boys going in before us."

"They can't. They're waiting for their own intel."

"What if they already have it?" Bruce didn't draw away from her and she felt her loneliness drift away. "They could already be on the island and going in tonight."

Her eyes drifted from the big man's face to the horizon. What if they were? It was certainly a possibility.

"We're the support team, then. Brad's the primary. Walt won't go. He'll send Brad in alone. If they have the intel already, Brad will know right where to go. We'll be outside support, their contingency for extraction if anything goes wrong. If we're not too late, that is. It's our own fault we're not involved directly, I guess. Jasper says we won't be to

Mykonos until morning. Zalzuna is twenty miles farther."

"There's that airstrip on the southeastern corner of Zalzuna Island," Bruce said. "The satellite shows two small prop planes parked there. Since we want to do this right, we should send our only pilot there."

"You want me to go to the airstrip? There are cliffs all around that approach."

"I guess you'll have to climb them, Heather. If we continue around to the capital, we can assist the boys from the east side, unless we're in contact with them before that, or receive other intel. We need the flexibility of the airstrip as a backup, though. Relying only on the sea isn't wise."

Though Heather didn't like it, she knew it was the right thing to do. The Lavers brothers couldn't fly a plane. And if Brad or the Jamisons had to flee south rather than out to sea where the yacht would be waiting, she'd have a plane ready for departure. They'd have radio contact by then. But what about the cliffs? They could take hours to scale, depending on the sheerness of their vertical face.

"Okay," Heather agreed. "Fine time for you to learn to speak up, Bruce, but you're right. We'll go over it tonight with Cliff and Jasper. From now on, we're a support team for the boys."

Bruce nodded, reached up and touched her cheek, then walked back to the stern where Heather knew he liked to watch their wake.

Taking a deep breath, she felt his lingering touch. The following day, then, would be a hard day. Everything she'd learned her whole life would be put to the test.

"Heal me of my arrogance, Lord," Heather prayed into the

breeze. "I'm listening now. Watch over us, please, and keep the Jamisons safe. And whatever the boys are up to, be with them, too, Lord. Amen." She chuckled aloud and shook her head at their boldness. They had some nerve to attempt this on their own!

She went to her cabin to rest and to think about Bruce. He'd never touched her like that before.

...✝...

Trevor Niles stood like a general over his army as his soldiers continued to dig trenches along the beach east of New Manchester. Hearing a Jeep coming from Zalzuna on the road behind him, he didn't immediately turn from his men and the sea. He wondered what the Jeep meant, if it was good news or bad. The only news he wanted was that the man he knew as Patrick Gibson had been captured. General Yousef had mobilized over one hundred troops to comb the island, particularly the vegetation on the northern side of the volcano where they'd last seen the man.

The Jeep halted behind Niles. He turned to see the bald giant, Fredrick, General Yousef's right hand. Niles would soon be the island's dictator. The whole island knew it, so Fredrick was busy trying to please Niles as well. Even the general knew Niles had loyalists that outnumbered his own. It was just a matter of time before the fortress changed hands. The only obstacle was the general himself. When the time was right, the self-indulgent man would be removed—and not by natural causes. Gilgal seemed like peanuts, now. Niles would rule his own island, his own country!

"It's not good, Mr. Niles." Fredrick stood next to the assistant governor. "Just bad news, this time."

"You mean worse news." Niles rolled his eyes. "The news is already bad, Fredrick. What makes it worse?"

"This Patrick man was certainly here to free the two American Christians, the Jamisons. We should relocate the political prisoners."

"No." Niles faced the taller man. "Look at me. Use them for bait to flush Patrick out. If it doesn't work by morning, execute the prisoners. Patrick knows his time is limited on the island. I believe he'll try something tonight."

"So, you're not worried about a team of invaders?"

"Patrick hasn't had access to a phone, so no one's been warned away. Let me worry about the ambush here, Fredrick. You take care of the Jamisons."

"Tell me about Patrick. Is he really as good as you say?"

"Two years ago, when I left Zalzuna, I had great plans. A gem was within reach. But a miserable bunch of Christians remained in my way. That's when Patrick came and turned my own people against me! He even sided with the Christians. See this scar on my face? Don't underestimate Patrick Gibson!"

"We have him outnumbered two hundred to one, Mr. Niles. No one is that good."

"You haven't found him yet, have you?" Niles growled. "Get out of here. Report his capture. Anything else, I don't want to hear it, understand? I'm tired of the ineptitude of your men. I have better things to do than stand here like a cursed officer! But your men would be on siesta if I weren't here. This will be the greatest capture in all of Zalzuna history. An American special operations team invading my country? I'll be known as the defender of Zalzuna!"

"The general's days are numbered, sir."

Fredrick drove away, leaving Niles a captive of his own fury.

"I'll beat you this time, Patrick." The sun was beginning to set. "You have no way off my island. And whoever you're spying for will never leave, either. This is *my* country now. And I refuse to be beaten!"

Using a pair of field glasses, he scanned the northern horizon. The gullible Christians would be coming ashore right there, right where he'd used the Internet to coax them to come. If needed, he'd draw all the soldiers he could from the search party to lay in wait. His soldiers had nothing to fear. The Christians wouldn't have weapons since they didn't believe in killing their enemies. What good was religion if not for conquering? That was what the religious had used the church for since the beginning of the world. What made these Christians so different?

But deep inside, Niles felt uncertainty. The fact that the Christians were braving the island at all without lethal weapons meant they were bold—very bold—bolder than he and his men were who outnumbered them many times over. And courage scared Niles. He didn't understand it. When he could, he stomped courage out from the island, because courage bred stubbornness. He'd seen it in the Gillies, as they'd zealously stolen a dream from him. True Christians— those who prayed to their God even during their executions— had the type of courage he couldn't kill. It lived beyond the grave, and it seemed to linger upon his small island.

Maybe this time he could stomp it out for good, and never have to deal with the Christ-followers again.

"Dig faster, you!" he shouted at a resting soldier. "Daylight is nearly gone. All of you, dig! These trenches are your salvation when the enemy comes ashore! Dig, I say!"

…✝…

Keeping his head low, Brad paddled toward the western beach of Zalzuna. The sky was dark and he could see the shadow of the volcano against the few stars. Now that his eyes had adjusted to the darkness, there was a strange glow from the top of the cone.

He'd paddled for ten minutes when he paused to give his arms a rest. Farther out at sea, the Predator speedboat drifted. Just barely, he could still see the boat's white hull, but only because he knew to look for it. No one onshore would see it, he felt certain. And Walter had promised not to start the motor until Brad was safely ashore, just in case the sound drew someone's attention out to sea from the island.

"You there yet?" Walter asked over their comm system. "I can't see you anymore."

Brad touched both sides of his neckband, which was wired to his right ear.

"Not yet." Brad talked in a hushed voice. "About a hundred yards to go. You see any movement onshore?"

"No. Wait! Yes! Two flashlights at the top of the beach."

Ducking his head lower, Brad didn't have much more room to lay flat in the two-man raft. He held his backpack next to his ribs. It weighed nearly thirty pounds, most of that in gear from Heather's cases since Brad had grabbed as many of their flash and bang grenades and tranquilizer pens as he could. The weapons were unfamiliar to him, but Walter had instructed him on what Brad couldn't imagine from movies.

To his surprise, Brad didn't have to paddle anymore toward the shore. The waves swept him closer and closer. He was about to be washed onto the sand when the radio clicked in his ear.

"It's clear," Walter whispered. "They're moving north. Looks like a patrol. Better watch for others. I don't think they're expecting us, but it seems they're ready, regardless."

One final wave carried Brad's raft onto the sand. Like a seal, he rolled out of the raft and dragged it farther up the beach. After climbing over a field of volcanic rocks, he sat down in a small bowl where seawater had pooled. Using a double-edged blade from a thigh sheath, he slashed the raft three times to deflate it, then stashed it between two boulders. Next, he pulled two stun grenades from his pack and clipped them onto the back of his belt where he could grab them easily. Walter had wanted Brad to dress in a full black suit, top and bottom, but Brad had chosen his jeans instead, though he wore a long-sleeve, black polyester shirt with various pockets. His Oregon hiking boots were as sturdy as any combat boots, and had excellent traction.

Shrugging into his pack, Brad mentally inventoried its contents: a canteen, a number of energy bars, his own pair of night vision goggles, and the weaponry. He touched his neckpiece.

"I'm ready. You there?"

"Yeah, I'm here. I'll see you on the other side."

Faintly, and only after Brad poked his head out of his hole, he discerned the Predator's motor over the gentle crash of the waves on the beach.

The boys had agreed to maintain radio silence except for

hourly checks or emergencies. Otherwise, each was on his own.

Studying the terrain to the southwest, Brad knew the basic features of the island well, maybe as well as the islanders. But in the darkness, he could fall into a crevice, or one of the many tomb openings, if he wasn't careful. The moon wasn't out, so he donned the night vision goggles for a red and gray contrasted view of the ground ahead. Nothing moved on the beach. He was alone, and that gave him a shiver.

"Be with me, Lord."

He and Walter had prayed together on the boat before they'd separated. Neither of them knew exactly what lay ahead, but God knew. Brad suddenly thought of Josie back in Oregon. Or had she already left Oregon for Illinois? Now that he'd come halfway around the world to take part in such an adventure, Brad couldn't imagine returning to his mundane life—even the life of a Major League pitcher. What kind of Christian would he be if he sought all-star recognition rather than God's glory on the mission field? Surely, some Christians were called to do that, but after all this, he couldn't. He was ashamed of his past selfish desires. Now, it all seemed like a lifetime ago.

Rising from the hole in the ground, he felt the weight of the pack on his back. He'd carried heavier packs while fly-fishing for steelhead with his dad below Klamath Falls. It seemed everything in his life had prepared him for this very night.

At a slow pace, Brad headed southeast. He kept the goggles on his face to watch where he placed his feet, and occasionally stopped to check his back trail and the terrain around him.

Two hundred yards later, he saw another pair of men with flashlights walking clockwise around the island. Quickly, he crouched down. The volcanic rock all around him was flat with nothing to hide behind, but the men weren't approaching him. Rather, they circled the perimeter of the volcanic rock. Shivering with fear, Brad watched them until they reached the beach and continued north. Before he moved again, he studied the terrain. Already, he was approaching the peasant farms north of Sankadden. The satellite photos had shown a slope speckled with peasant dwellings amidst farm fields.

After scanning his back trail, he rose, only to fall flat a breath later. Was that a gnarled olive tree behind him? The tree moved toward him, then stopped. It was no tree at all, but a man! The man with a frame as tall as Brad's but heavier dropped out of sight to hide in a shallow crevice one hundred yards back. The patrolling soldiers seemed to move in pairs, so where was this man's partner?

Brad's presence had been discovered far sooner than he'd planned. He wondered if he should sneak up on the man with a tranquilizer. It didn't seem like a valid option, not when he had to get so close to him. Walter had said the soldiers carried firearms. And Brad had no interest in testing a tranquilizer pen against a gun.

However, Brad still didn't see a second man on his tail. It was only one man, a man who obviously didn't realize Brad wore night vision and could see the prowler raise his head to check Brad's position. He guessed the man couldn't see Brad well, if at all, unless Brad was moving. The stranger seemed to be waiting for him to move again, but Brad didn't have time to out-wait the enemy. He had to reach Zalzuna, find a way into the rehabilitation center, and flee to the harbor. Already, he was pressed for time.

Yet, he couldn't bring himself to move onward, and the longer he waited, he feared the more obvious it would became to the stranger that Brad was aware of his presence. Had the man already called for backup? Did they have radios? Brad turned and scoped the fields to the south. No movement there. He looked back to the northwest. The enemy had risen from his hiding spot and crawled adjacent to Brad's heading, as if the man were trying to get around Brad.

Without moving, Brad watched the man crawl closer, though not directly at him. He didn't seem to have a sidearm or a uniform, but rather a suit of some type. His features seemed European, but that didn't mean much on the island since all of New Manchester had been settled by socialists from France and other European countries. What was the man doing out there in the middle of the night?

The prowler paused and peered in Brad's direction. Brad couldn't be seen unless he stood or moved, he was sure, so he remained very still. The enemy then moved east along the slope. For five more minutes, Brad watched before the man simply disappeared over a small bluff where the vegetation had begun to grow, free of the poisonous volcanic vapors.

It made no sense. Brad was confused. He hadn't been in the Special Forces for more than an hour and he found himself already stumped by a situation. Though he considered alerting Walter that he'd already crossed . . . someone, such an explanation defied reason, and Walter probably wouldn't know what to think of it, either.

Nothing else moved for several more minutes. Cautiously, Brad rose to his feet, half-expecting a barrage of bullets to mow him down. But all was silent. Evermore alert, he edged eastward in the direction of Zalzuna—and after the prowling stranger.

✝

CHAPTER TWENTY-SIX

Nathan crawled two more yards before he stopped and rolled to his feet. His hands and knees were raw from the volcanic rock. He wouldn't have been crawling at all if it weren't for the lone stranger who was also suspiciously hiding amongst the lava formations.

Motionlessly, he studied the rock to the west, certain they'd seen each other. Something told him it wasn't a soldier he'd come across. But who else would be snooping around on the southern side of the volcano? Crouching, Nathan dashed down a rock bowl and hid there. He was thirsty and famished. Praying for water, he felt around in the darkness, but found none. The peasants, in their cheerful, kindhearted way, would certainly spare a piece of bread if he inquired at one of the many farmhouses to the south, but he wished to put no one in harm's way. If he were found on a peasant's doorstep, the peasant would be executed as well.

Looking to the west again, Nathan noticed the one he'd crawled past was again on his feet, creeping to the east after him. The man was wearing a pack, Nathan decided, but he could only occasionally glimpse the silhouette of the man against the stars. The stranger didn't have a rifle, but he could still be armed.

They couldn't play tag all night in the dark, so Nathan

tensed for a confrontation as the other crept nearer. Nathan leaned against the rock below the approaching man. The shallow rock bowl was visible enough, but he wouldn't see Nathan until it was too late.

A couple more steps . . .

Suddenly, the man stopped short, just one yard away from where Nathan was about to grab the stranger's ankles and drag him into the rock bowl.

"If you move, you'll regret it," a young man's low, quiet voice said in unaccented English.

Blinking in shock, Nathan stared up at the figure. He was caught, but how had the man seen him? There was no point in getting shot by blindly running away across the dangerous rock.

"I'm not moving," Nathan stated.

"Give me your weapon."

"I don't have one." Nathan squinted through the darkness at the shadow above him. He couldn't see a gun. Rather, the man's left arm seemed to be cocked as if he were about to throw something.

Flinching, Nathan heard voices behind him, somewhere to the southeast. The stranger had heard them, too, and dropped to the rock, trying to hide. Nathan understood right away—neither of them wanted to be discovered by the patrolling soldiers.

"Get down here!" Nathan whispered. "They'll see you up there!"

The man belly-crawled headfirst into the rock bowl. Together, they held their breaths as they waited for the soldiers to pass. After not moving for two more minutes, the stranger next to Nathan then poked his head over the rock.

"They're gone," he said. "Now they're down by the beach."

"You . . . have night vision." Nathan wagged his finger. "I should've guessed. Apparently, you're not from the island. Zalzuna's soldiers have never even seen night vision."

"And I'd say you're not from the island, either—hiding with me the way you are."

Nathan licked his lips. Just because they had the same enemies, didn't make them friends.

"Do you have a way off the island? I'm looking for a boat I don't have to steal. The name's Dirk, by the way."

"Call me Brad. Why don't you want to stay on the island?" Brad asked. "Nice climate, beautiful scenery . . ."

"It's the company—with exception to yours, of course."

"So, you know the island?"

"Sure. Why?" Nathan's voice was strained, his throat parched.

"Show me around Zalzuna's streets and I'll give you a boat ride to Mykonos."

"What's in Zalzuna?" Nathan shook his head. "The whole island is crawling with soldiers tonight. You don't want to go there."

"Seems that's where you're headed." Brad touched his throat as Nathan heard a loud transmission from the young man's ear. "Yeah, I'm here. Ran into someone south of the volcano. Not an enemy."

"Who is it?" the transmitter asked. "Ask his name."

Nathan frowned. There were others nearby with this one? It wasn't a habit of his to be outsmarted. Who were these guys?

"Your name?" Brad asked him.

"Dirk Salverskein."

"Ask him how long Moses was in the ark," Nathan heard the transmitter in the youth's ear.

"How long was Moses in the ark?"

Suddenly, Nathan smiled. The question itself confirmed to whom he was talking. *Finally, some friendlies!*

"Moses wasn't in the ark." Nathan set a hand on the young man's shoulder. "It was Noah, and it rained forty days and forty nights. I think they were in the ark close to a year."

"Did you hear that?"

"Yeah, I heard him," the transmitter responded. "He's with us, Brad! That's my guy. What's he still doing on the island?"

"My cover was blown," Nathan said. "I ran into someone who recognized me. Now, I'm trying to get off the island."

"Are the Jamisons still in place?"

"I suspect so, but at this point, they're probably only being used as bait for me."

"Who recognized you?" Brad asked.

"A man named Trevor Niles. I had a run-in with him in the Coral Sea two years ago. Bad character."

"See, I knew it!" the transmitter voice said. "This guy can help you, Brad. I'll get into place. Talk to you in an hour."

"Please tell me you have water in there." Nathan gestured to Brad's back.

Brad slipped off his pack and gave Nathan the canteen and two energy bars.

"So, how bad is it?" Brad sat down in the rock bowl. "What are we walking into? Can we get who's left of the Jamison family out?"

"Don't know. Depends on how many you have in your team. If we watch the building for a couple days, we might come up with a plan. We'll need to wait until things settle down, though."

"Yeah. Well . . . a couple problems with that." Brad drew from the canteen as well. "We have until daylight. Our escape boat will be waiting in Zalzuna's port to take us off this rock. As for the team, it's just you and me. The real team fell prey to the wiles of your friend, Niles. Walt and I saw it was a trap, so we came early—as soon as we got your call earlier today."

"Walter Kassviney. That would make you . . . ?"

"Brad Alders."

The two shook hands. Nathan settled onto the rock opposite Brad.

"Well, we have a problem then. The building is well guarded. We can't approach the building as it is. Soldiers are all over the place, hunting for me."

"I noticed."

"You've got night vision, though." Nathan pointed. "We can use that to our advantage. Maybe we could try a little Trojan horse tactic to get into the rehab center, but getting out won't be easy. What kind of weaponry do you have? Maybe an NL-3 or something?"

"NL-3? I don't know what that is. I've got some stun grenades and tranq pens, but I've never used any of this stuff before."

"What? Who are you?" Nathan asked. "You're what COIL sent in? After all I've risked, they send in some inexperienced kid?"

"Hey, I'm not even supposed to be here! If the team

would've followed the plan, they could be doing this right now and you could be talking to them. But Niles duped them, so Walt and I took the boat and half their gear. If the Jamisons have any chance at all, it's you, me, and Walt."

"Give me half of everything you have," Nathan ordered.

"I'll do you better than that." Brad gave him the night vision goggles. "I'm not even sure I'm using these things right." He also handed him a number of stun grenades.

"Okay, I'll take point." Nathan donned the night vision. "You trail by twenty yards. Watch for my hand signals, if you can. A fist means stop and find cover. If you see anything, give me a low bird call, something loony."

"Got it," Brad said. "Hey, it'll be okay now, right?"

Ignoring the boy's optimism, Nathan could see through the night vision that Brad was both young and nervous. They'd be lucky to survive the night, let alone rescue anyone.

"We'll continue straight east until we reach the coast. You at least know the geography?"

"Yeah." Brad waved ahead. "Lead the way."

"When we reach the coast, we'll follow it north until it's time to cut west to the rehab center. Expect an ambush at some point. Hopefully, I'll see them first, but don't count on it. They'll be hiding on the flat roofs when we get closer to the center. They're expecting an invasion, so there's not much we can do about that."

"Did you see Lacy?" Brad asked. "I mean, I just want to know what kind of condition she's in."

"Does it matter?" Nathan regretted the words an instant later. He'd been working alone for too long. "We're taking her home either way, right? I'd prepare for the worst, though."

"Right. I was just wondering. She's my cousin. I just—"

"Wait a minute. Brad, how old are you?"

"Nineteen, same as Lacy."

"On second thought, when we get to the coast, you wait for me to come back, then we can all get to the boat together."

"No." Brad shook his head. "If it's as dangerous as you say it is, you'll need me to get them out of the center. Yeah, I'm only a teenager, but I've been through enough to know I can handle whatever is waiting for us. Just tell me what to do, Dirk."

"You keep your head down," Nathan ordered. "Hear me? Don't turn this into a failed rescue attempt."

"I won't."

Nathan nodded. Brad's face did look a little older than nineteen, but that didn't mean he could react to the coming threats without freezing.

"Do you know the terrain east of here?" Nathan asked.

"Sure. Turns into farmland. There's an airstrip on our right. The city will be on our left when we reach the coast."

"Can we expect anything from the team you left behind?"

"Not too soon," Brad said. "We took their transportation."

"Okay, let's move out. Remember: bird calls if you see something I don't. And watch my hand signals."

…✝…

As Brad watched, Dirk swept the surrounding terrain once with his goggles, then crawled out of the bowl to the east. After tightening his pack around his shoulders and chest, Brad climbed out after the operative. It took him a few seconds to spot the man ahead of him. Dirk moved quickly, nearly at a jog across the volcanic rock. Smiling, Brad was reminded of his baseball training. His coach had prepared him for this. If he had to, he could run for an hour.

Without much effort, Brad matched Dirk's pace to the east. He was grateful for a lighter pack since Dirk now carried several grenades. Every few minutes, Brad glanced over his left shoulder at the volcano's glow to ensure they were headed in the right direction. But Dirk didn't seem to need any landmark compass.

Dirk didn't slow or even look back for twenty minutes, until he raised his fist suddenly and knelt on one knee. Brad skidded to a halt and fell on his belly. What was it? Tilting his head, he strained his ears for a sound. They hadn't seen any soldiers for a while. It had to be a patrol.

Then Brad noticed a light beyond a number of olive trees. The vegetation and fields were thick now, the vaporous side of the volcano left far behind. Dirk waved him forward. Brad stood and bounded ahead to kneel next to Dirk.

"Four houses." Dirk pointed. "See them? And soldiers, too—one . . . two . . . three and four."

Brad shook his head. He could see one little light where the nearest house was, but the other houses or soldiers were beyond his vision.

"We'll have to go around to the south." Dirk swept his hand across the dark scene. "We might lose a little time, so keep moving. If we get separated, meet at the airport. Got it?"

"Yeah. The airport."

Not wasting any more time, Dirk set off to the south. Brad followed without hesitation. Every step he took brought him closer to Lacy and Uncle Albert. He prayed they weren't too late.

†

CHAPTER TWENTY-SEVEN

Straightening his uniform, Horatio Salmose made a mental note to wash off the blood before the next shift. The blood was the worst part of his job. Discouraged, he pondered why Fredrick kept him as his primary torturer. Horatio was a horrible persecutor. He acted as if interested in the politics and the defense of their communist ideals, but in Fredrick's efforts to turn Horatio into a brutal robot, exactly the opposite had happened to the young guard. Instead, Horatio was having thoughts he dared not voice to anyone.

Briskly, Horatio saluted one of the senior officers in the corridor of the rehabilitation center. Normally, he and only two other guards ran the center. On this night, however, Fredrick had called in extra hands—twenty in all—to ward off any sort of rescue attempt of the two American missionaries. And all the soldiers knew about the ambush also being staged by Trevor Niles east of New Manchester.

Horatio looked up and down the corridor from the guards' lounge. Almost everyone was outside on the roof, waiting in ambush, though there were three inside besides himself. No one was too attentive, he noticed, which would infuriate Fredrick if he made a surprise inspection. It was four in the morning. The men had been on guard all night. Some on the rooftop were probably even sleeping.

But Horatio was wide-awake. Yes, his body was weary after a double shift, but his mind was racing. He hoped someone out there was truly coming to rescue the Jamisons. And in the chaos that was sure to follow, he hoped to leave with them.

Scoffing at the idea, he knew he didn't have the courage to run away from Fredrick. What if he were caught? Horatio shivered at the thought. The torture or "rehabilitation" techniques the bald man would use on a traitor or conspirator with the Christians—was it worth the risk?

Pacing closer to the holding room where the captives slept, Horatio noticed two of the three guards in the building were in the lounge drinking watered-down coffee. Though Horatio listened to their conversation about crops and weather, his eyes were on the holding room's steel door. Policy stated that at least two guards were to be present to open the door, but Horatio had his own key. And as soon as no one was looking, he planned to break that policy. He wanted to talk to Albert Jamison again. No one had spoken to him as that old man had. No one had ever befriended Horatio before—certainly none of the captives, especially after he'd tortured them for hours under Fredrick's supervision. Albert was the first of only a couple dozen that Horatio had tortured who actually lived his faith, unwaveringly. Most Christians had recanted and vowed loyalty to General Yousef and their communal government. And Niles was always nearby, asking for whatever intel their victims confessed.

It was too dangerous to talk to Albert, Horatio decided. Albert wouldn't believe he really wanted to help him, anyway. The old man would think it was a trap or test. Even if he did get the door open and the two talked, what would the conversation be?—*I've beat you without mercy, but I want to escape the island with you if someone tries to rescue you and your daughter. Oh, and by the way, if you're not rescued, you're scheduled to be executed at dawn.*

The two guards from the lounge suddenly passed Horatio as they marched down the corridor with a thermos of coffee for the other man. The officer at the other end of the corridor looked back to see Horatio standing guard. There was no reason to suspect that Horatio was having thoughts other than absolute loyalty to the country; he was Fredrick's primary torturer! Even some veteran soldiers didn't speak to Horatio because they knew he'd be their own torturer if they were ever suspected of disloyalty.

The officer and the other two left the building by the only door, which faced south, to check on the men waiting in ambush and give them coffee. Horatio was already standing next to the prisoners' door. He cringed with uncertainty. The other guards could come back any minute. It was a stupid thing to dare. If the captives were feeling particularly anxious tonight, they might even rush the door. That had happened before, Fredrick had told him. What if it happened now? Horatio wouldn't be able to stop such a vigorous attack.

But still, Horatio didn't move away from the door. More than all the risks and threats of discipline, he remembered the love in Albert's voice. Albert had seemed wise, not stupid, for believing in his God. With such a strong belief in his God, Albert was willing to endure great agony at the hands of the enemy—and still try to share his God's love with them. Never had Horatio seen such passion, such faith.

Though Horatio knew the bald giant would never admit it, it seemed that Fredrick was afraid of this kind of faith. And it was with this faith that Horatio wanted to fill the void inside his own soul. The emptiness of the communal efforts of the Zalzunian government wasn't fulfilling Horatio. And it had taken someone like Albert to show Horatio what he was lacking in his life.

Perhaps Horatio could find salvation with Albert's God, and maybe even with Albert's rescuers.

Looking down at his hand, Horatio found he'd already pulled the large brass key from his pocket. After checking the corridor one last time, he fit the key into the lock. It clicked when he turned it. His whole body shivered. He opened the door wide enough to fit his head into the room.

The prisoners were asleep, a few against each wall. And all over the walls were drawings—more than Horatio had last seen. The guards had already taken one colored pencil away from Albert, but the sly missionary obviously had another.

"Albert!" Horatio whispered into the room. There were two overhead lamps that never went out for security purposes. No one stirred. "Jamison!"

Several looked up and rubbed sleep from their eyes. One man groaned as he woke.

"Horatio?" Albert Jamison sat up. "Is that you?"

"Come here!" Horatio waved urgently at him. Glancing over his shoulder, he wasn't sure if he would hear the front door open or not. "Hurry!"

A younger man whom Horatio had beaten only three days before helped Albert to his feet and to the door. Horatio swallowed over a lump in his throat as the two men stopped in front of him and met his gaze. Unable to hold their gaze, Horatio's face was downcast in shame.

"They mean to kill you and your daughter in the morning." Horatio didn't mind the presence of the other captive. "You have friends willing to risk their lives to save you. If they come for you tonight, may I go with you? Off the island?"

"Of course, Horatio. You may come, but what of these others?"

"I'm not sure. But I may go with you? Your friends will truly come for you? They care so much for you?"

"Yes, I have friends, Horatio, and my friends are your friends. Do you know when they'll be here? Can you help them find Lacy and me?"

"I don't know. It's very dangerous." Horatio shuddered. "If I knew more, perhaps I could help. There are many outside waiting in ambush. Perhaps no one will come at all. It's nearly dawn—two hours away. Fredrick will come then."

"Save Lacy, Horatio, please!" Albert clutched Horatio's hand. "Worry about no one else but her. Can you do this? Can you save my daughter?"

"How? No, I can't. There's no way! It would mean certain death if I were caught!" Horatio flinched at the sound of the front door opening. "I'll try. That's all."

He closed the door gently and withdrew his key in one smooth motion. Sidestepping twice, he was safe in the guards' lounge. *Safe?* Tell his trembling hands! Was it possible to save this man and the girl? What then? Even if he could get them out of the building, there was no way off the island, not without help.

After guzzling a cup of hot coffee, Horatio wiped his mouth with the back of his hand. He'd much rather die helping people who appreciated his efforts than work for men like Fredrick, who yelled at him louder the more he tried to please him.

With this mindset, Horatio left the lounge, passed the rotation of men coming down the corridor, and left through the entrance. Standing outside, he stretched in the night air. The guards in hiding were on the roof, as well as across the street on the opposite roof—a laundry. It was around the corner of the rehab building that Horatio had been jumped by one of Albert's rescuers. Albert's friends were already here! Horatio's jaw was evidence of that much. But where were they? Perhaps they were watching even now. And he suddenly knew what he had to do to help them.

"Horatio!" someone called from the roof. "Get out of sight!"

"Sorry." Horatio walked quickly across the road and behind the laundry. He watched the darkness for Albert's friends, though once out of sight from the rehab building, everything was shadows.

Pausing at the corner where he'd been jumped the night before, he saw that no one was there. Didn't they know that darkness was running out? They didn't have long to save the Jamisons.

In a jog, Horatio moved down the avenue farther away from the rehab center. None of the others cared who did what, but if Fredrick showed up, he'd want an account for every soldier's activities. Horatio stopped in front of a warehouse door and found the door unlocked, as usual. No one would steal contents from the warehouse; the island had too many informants. But Horatio had been there many times, even back when he was a mere farm boy, before he'd been drafted into his country's mandatory five-year military service.

Inside, Horatio crept around two broken-down Jeeps and a never-before-used armored personnel carrier the general had bought from the Russians. Touching a backhoe in passing, he then admired a giant bulldozer that was only taken out of the warehouse when a new road needed to be engineered. Horatio climbed up the track and into the driver's seat, ten feet off the ground. He remembered when the bulldozer had arrived on the island. It had come from Turkey on a barge when he was just a boy, and the event had produced a spontaneous parade of citizens down every street to the sea.

He pushed the start button. Having driven it once, Horatio hoped it had enough fuel for the task he had in mind. The monstrous machine roared to life, a thundering sound as the engine caught and held steady. Grabbing the controls, he raised the shovel three feet, then started moving it forward. Since he was about to do massive damage to the town anyway, he didn't bother to open the warehouse door. He simply tore through it like it was paper. In the street, he turned to the left and started toward the rehab center. Around him, lights were lit in windows as the roar of the machine woke the sleeping city.

When the laundry building came into sight, Horatio aimed the bulldozer at the middle of the building, knowing it would pass through everything until someone jumped into the seat to stop the controls. Someone would need to stop the machine, because Horatio wouldn't be there. He used a wrench to wedge the gas pedal in place, then he jumped off the crawling beast. Already, he heard shouts from the rooftop of the laundry building, but they wouldn't see him in the darkness.

Horatio ran down the avenue and circled around to the rehab center from another direction. If Albert had friends nearby, now was their opportunity. He waited in the shadows as the bulldozer emerged from the collapsed laundry building. Men ran in all directions. Several fired at the unmanned machine, but it still crawled toward the rehab center.

As the dozer reached the center, Fredrick arrived in a rush. There was fear in his eyes as he stood in the Jeep's headlights—and Horatio knew why. If Trevor Niles found out about such disorder—and he was sure to learn of it—there would be disastrous consequences for Fredrick.

Ducking behind a building, Horatio saw a man with a rifle run past. The man was known to be a brutal guard, but now he was running for his life from the bulldozer. Yes, Horatio had caused this. He couldn't help but grin. But where were Albert Jamison's friends?

$$\dagger$$

<u>*CHAPTER TWENTY-EIGHT*</u>

Brad and Dirk crouched behind the forgotten shell of a rowboat. The Zalzuna port waves lapped gently against the shore behind them as they observed the city built on the eastern slope of the volcano.

"It's quiet." Dirk looked up and down the shoreline. "Too quiet."

"It's five in the morning." Brad tapped his wrist. "Quiet is normal at this hour."

"No, not this quiet." Dirk shook his head. "We haven't seen a patrol for over an hour. I was here yesterday morning. People were awake. Something's up, for sure."

"Ambush?"

"Most likely." Dirk snatched a stun grenade off his waistband. Brad did the same, then looked to Dirk for guidance. He nodded at Brad with a mischievous smile. "I've done some foolish things in my life, but this takes the cake. We're almost certain to be going into an ambush against men with firearms."

"I know."

"You think you can toss that far and fast enough to make a difference?" Dirk gestured at Brad's grenade.

"Yeah, I think so."

"Okay. Stay behind me. Stick to the plan. Evac to the boat.

If our exit is blocked, or we get split up, evac to the airport on the southern coast, then to Sankaddan."

"Got it."

"Let's go!"

Dirk rose to his feet, then ran across the boat yard to the first row of warehouses and canning factories. Brad hung back a few seconds and picked up three fist-sized rocks.

Brad touched the comm unit on his neck.

"Walter, you there?"

"Yes, I'm here."

"We're going for it."

"Tell me when you're coming my way," Walter said, "and I'll come closer to shore. Better hurry. Darkness is fading."

"All right."

Jumping to his feet, Brad ran after Dirk. He reached the first building as Dirk moved to the second. After jogging around the island all night, his eyes were well-adjusted to the darkness. The small city had no lights, though he glimpsed a few lamps far above the city where the general lived.

Suddenly, Dirk halted his charge toward the rehab center and retreated at a run to Brad's position. He slid like a base runner behind the animal cart where Brad waited. The veteran operative caught his breath and peered up the winding avenue to the west.

"A man in uniform coming our way." Dirk massaged his braced leg. "It's dark enough. He'll probably just pass us by."

Both men lowered themselves flat beneath the cart. Sure enough, the soldier marched down the middle of the street. Passing the cart, he then stopped at a warehouse door and disappeared inside.

"I think that's the guard I questioned last night," Dirk voiced. "Wonder what he's up to all alone. Let's go before he comes back."

Dirk started forward, then jumped back at the roar of an engine from within the warehouse. They watched from under the cart as a bulldozer tore its way out of the warehouse, then turned down their street. The noise of the rambling engine was so foreign to the sleeping town that lamps were lit and residents peered out to investigate the commotion.

"What's he doing?" Brad asked over the noise, but Dirk didn't answer.

The bulldozer filled the avenue. The two didn't realize it was heading toward them until the last second. Dirk grabbed Brad by the back of his pack and together they stumbled from under the cart. They dove through a flimsy doorway as the giant machine crushed the cart and continued westward.

Brad gained his senses and found himself beside Dirk inside a single-room apartment where four pairs of eyes stared with fear at the foreigners.

"We're sorry!" Brad called to the residents as Dirk dragged him back into the street. In Greek, Brad spoke words that Walter had taught him: *"Lee-poo-me!"*

The two men left the apartment and leaped over the remnants of the crushed cart to chase after the bulldozer. The engine was too loud to communicate, but Brad understood that Dirk wanted to stay directly behind the dozer as it crawled in the direction of the center. Dirk readied his stun grenade, so Brad did likewise. There was nothing stealthy about their approach, now. Everyone could hear them coming.

The powerful machine barely slowed as it plowed through the outside wall of what Dirk had told him was the laundry building. Only then did Brad notice men on the roof scrambling to get clear as it collapsed under their feet. Bricks and mortar crumbled over the bulldozer. Dirk pulled Brad closer to the rear of the beast to avoid harm. Rarely-used electrical wires crackled and sparked to Brad's right, but he didn't stop. The dozer was now unmanned, its driver having bailed out just before colliding with the laundry building.

Several bricks fell on Brad's arms and shoulders as the bulldozer plowed through the opposite wall. Dirk tripped and fell, but Brad pulled him up. The two tucked in closer behind the machine.

Gunshots pierced the night, followed by the whine of ricocheting bullets off the roof and tracks of the dozer. Dirk pointed ahead frantically, and Brad dared a glance around the tracks to see the whitewashed wall of the rehab building. They were headed straight for it!

Two men ran across the road behind the bulldozer, but neither noticed the two infiltrators. The street was in chaos. Wounded men yelled for help from the collapsed laundry. Others shouted warnings to those on the rehab center's rooftop. More gunfire peppered the dozer, causing Brad and Dirk to duck lower. Electricity popped, the effect similar to a strobe-light show, mixed with the muzzle flashes.

Sparks caught something in the laundry rubble and flames grew. Men ran frantically left and right as the bulldozer crashed through the rehab center's eastern wall.

Brad fell. A section of wall collapsed over him and Dirk, but Brad jumped up and continued after the machine. He wiped blood from his brow. Suddenly, a passageway opened on Brad's right. They were inside the building! The lights fluttered, but stayed on. Steel cell doors lined the corridor's right wall.

He turned to guide Dirk to his find, but Dirk was no longer beside him. Looking back, Brad saw Dirk had fallen under the wall, and both his legs were caught. Dirk waved Brad to go on ahead. Nodding, Brad climbed over debris into the corridor as the bulldozer rumbled through the rest of the building and beyond.

"Uncle Albert!" Brad yelled, dashing from steel door to steel door. "Lacy!" He found all the doors open and the cells empty, until he reached the last one. Finding it locked, he beat on the outside with a fist. "Uncle Albert!"

"You!" someone behind him shouted. "Don't move!"

Pulling the pin from his stun grenade, he tossed it as he turned around, covering his ears and shutting his eyes. The grenade exploded with an ear-piercing concussion and a flash of blinding light in a cloud of white choking smoke. Brad slowly opened his eyes. Taking a breath, he gagged on the fumes, but he was in better shape than the two blind, deaf, and choking soldiers. Panicked, one of them fired a round into the wall while the other felt along the wall toward Brad.

Wasting no time, Brad ran to the nearest soldier and tore off a key ring from his belt. He had only seconds before more soldiers entered the corridor to check on their captives. The ambush had certainly been in place, but neither the island authorities nor the rescue party had foreseen the participation of the bulldozer. Brad understood that God was answering their prayers by turning events in their favor.

The first three keys didn't fit the lock, but the fourth one did. He threw the door open, only to take a step back as he looked into the face of his Uncle Albert! A small black man with one eye supported him on the left, and Lacy, with ratted, filthy hair, supported his right.

"Brad!" Lacy released her father and threw her arms around Brad's neck, sobbing against his shoulder. "I can't believe you're here!"

"We must hurry!" the one-eyed man stated as the other prisoners rushed from the room.

"Follow me!" Brad took Lacy by the hand and snatched another stun grenade in preparation. As he led the way down the corridor, he touched his neckpiece. "Walter! I have them! We're coming to you!"

"Okay. I see a lot of commotion up there. The city's coming to life."

"Walter!" Lacy gasped through the corridor's fumes. "Our Walter?"

Not answering, Brad stepped over the wall debris where Dirk had fallen, but Dirk was no longer there. He had no time to look for him now. Dirk was a professional. Brad hoped the man was already fleeing to the shore.

The sky glowed with early dawn light as Brad peered through the hole in the wall left from the bulldozer. Soldiers still ran around in a frenzy while a giant, bald man shouted orders. Suddenly, two soldiers dragged Dirk by the arms across the street and dropped him at the feet of the bald man. Dirk rose to his hands and knees, but the bald man kicked him in the ribs, forcing Dirk to roll away. The bald man pointed at the building.

"Check the prisoners, you fools!" the man roared.

Ducking out of sight before he was spotted, Brad palmed his second stun grenade.

"Get to the harbor, understand?" Brad ordered the one-eyed man. "Cover your ears until after the second explosion, then run for your lives!"

There was no time to wait for confirmation. Brad stepped into the wall opening in full view of the dozen soldiers outside. The two nearest guards stopped in their tracks as Brad cracked his neck left, then right. The bald man and Dirk looked in unison at Brad. This was his ballgame now, Brad thought with a half-smile. Dirk nodded at Brad like a catcher over home base.

Calmly, Brad pulled the pin on the grenade as the bald man's mouth opened in stupefied silence. Brad did the wind-up, cocked his arm, and fired.

The bald man could've reacted to any other man's throw, but there was no time to react to the rocket Brad pitched into the ribs of the bald giant. The collision of the grenade with the man knocked him sprawling, but then came the explosion. Dirk covered his ears, but the grenade had landed only a few feet from his head. The concussion disoriented anyone that was nearby.

For good measure, Brad tossed another grenade at the nearest soldiers, then hid behind the wall next to Lacy as the explosion rocked the street and shattered the soldiers' senses for thirty seconds. Those who were unfamiliar with stun grenades fled in all directions, certain a full battle was waging, and some screamed that an army of Turks was invading.

"Go!" Brad drew Lacy into the street. "Get to the port!"

Albert and his one-eyed companion followed Lacy across the street, passing the staggering, blinded soldiers to reach the remains of the laundry beyond.

Brad dashed into the smoky street to Dirk, who was choking and confused. But when Brad yanked the veteran to his feet, he submitted to Brad's guidance into the laundry. Once in the rubble out of the soldiers' sight, the two paused to catch their breaths.

"We have to go back!" Dirk shook his head. "The prisoners—we have to go back and get them!"

"I already got them, Dirk." Brad shrugged off his pack and hooked two more grenades to his belt. "They're in front of us, heading to the harbor."

"Well, then, we'd better catch up to them!" Dirk wiped his smoke-blackened face. "There're soldiers everywhere. Let's go!"

The bulldozer had sufficiently removed several support columns. The entire structure creaked and groaned as if about to crumble around them. Brad let Dirk go ahead as he pulled on his pack again and touched his neckpiece.

"Five coming to you, Walt. I'm bringing up the rear."

"Five?" Walter asked. "Who else?"

Brad started to answer, but he was silenced as the building collapsed around him. He scrambled and tore at the wreckage. Though he reached a hand outside the piled debris, a blow to his head was too much. Consciousness faded as a fire burning nearby flickered out.

$$\dagger$$

<u>*CHAPTER TWENTY-NINE*</u>

"Which way do we go?" Lacy asked Paul as he and her father caught up to her on a street corner.

It was daylight now. The peasants had apparently heard the sounds of battle, and while they probably would've been in their fields by then, today they hid in their small dwellings.

Paul and Albert stopped next to Lacy and looked in each direction. Albert was breathing laboriously as he clutched his ribs.

"I don't know." Paul shook his head. "I'm from Sankaddan."

Lacy peered back the way they'd come, up a winding street crowded by one-room houses with covered windows. The intersection before her made no sense. She thought the sea was straight ahead, but there was no street straight ahead, only another wall of houses. A wrong choice could mean circling back to the rehab center.

"Wait!" Albert wheezed. "Horatio. The guard. I promised him he could come with us!"

"That's out of your control, Daddy." Lacy squeezed her father's arm. "If he was coming, he would've been in place. Where's Brad?"

At that instant, they heard the sound of feet behind them. The three escapees held their breaths as a tall man with a handlebar mustache ran toward them. Lacy moved closer to her father, though he was in no shape to protect her. And Paul was barely able to support her father, let alone ward off an attack.

"This way!" The mustached man guided to the right. "Come on! They're on our heels!"

"He's with Brad!" Albert slapped Paul's back as if he were prodding a horse to move ahead. "Follow him!"

Again, Lacy glanced over her shoulder, but didn't see Brad. She said a prayer in her heart for her cousin.

The mustached man waited for the three struggling Christians at the next corner. He nudged Paul aside and took Albert by the wrist.

"My name is Dirk. I'm sorry to have to do this, but we have to move faster."

Albert nodded firmly. With a practiced tug, Dirk pulled Albert over his shoulder in a fireman's carry. Lacy saw her father manage a determined breath. Pain etched his face. An instant later, he went limp.

"Someone's coming behind us!" Lacy said.

Dirk led the way at a faster pace, Lacy followed, and Paul brought up the rear.

Lacy smelled the ocean a dozen steps before they rounded a warehouse corner and saw the blue green water of the harbor at sunrise. A long, flat speedboat bobbed in the waves ten feet off the shore. Walter was standing on the bow! She ran faster, passing Dirk and plunging into the water.

Arriving at the boat before the others, Lacy reached up and grasped Walter's slender hand. With surprising strength, he pulled her from the water.

The hiss of a rocket-propelled grenade was heard an

instant before the grenade exploded in the water next to the boat. Water erupted, then cascaded over the boat. Lacy looked up to see two men in a Jeep across the harbor reloading the rocket launcher.

"Get us out of here!" Dirk barked at Walter.

Squeezing Lacy's hand, Walter smiled at her, then scrambled toward the bridge as Dirk tossed Albert onto the deck from the waist-deep water. Lacy pulled her father away from the side and cradled his head protectively as a second RPG exploded dangerously close. Dirk grabbed Paul by the back of the pants, lifted him onto the deck, then climbed up himself. Only then did Lacy notice the man wore a leg brace. *Who was this stranger?*

The speedboat's motors roared as Walter forced the throttle forward. Lacy saw the look on Dirk's face as he surveyed the beach and the few streets they could see. She knew what it meant.

"Brad . . ."

"He knew the risks," Dirk stated, then with more sensitivity, "Brad's a smart kid. He'll know what to do. We'll come back for him. If we stay now, we're all dead. Go!"

Walter sped out of the harbor. In their wake, RPGs exploded at intervals, but none of them on target. Lacy's eyes welled with tears in fear for Brad, but pride for Walter as she watched him at the helm, piloting the boat with a fierce look on his face. Brad had freed them, but she knew it had been Walter's plan. It wouldn't have worked without him.

Albert gained consciousness and looked Lacy in the face. Though Paul lay gasping on the deck beside them, he smiled as he felt the spray of the sea.

"Did Brad . . .?" Albert asked through labored breathing.

"No, Daddy . . . No."

...✝...

It was dawn by the time Heather Kooper reached the rocky beach on the southeast quarter of the Island of Zalzuna. She unloaded her gear onto the rocks from the dinghy before checking in with Jasper and the Lavers brothers who were circling the island in the yacht.

"Come in, Jasper. I'm on dry land. Over."

"Roger that, Caver. We're picking up chatter. You hearing it? Over."

Listening for a moment, Heather still heard nothing.

"Negative. Must be the cliffs. What is it? Over."

"Good news. The boys have the Jamisons!" A few seconds passed. "Five going to the harbor. Walt, come in. This is Jasper. Over."

Waiting anxiously, Heather hated that she was missing the conversation due to cliff interference. She wondered if she'd need to climb the cliffs now at all.

"Caver, come in."

"I'm here." Heather clipped on her climbing gear. "Did I row here for nothing? Over."

"Everyone made it to the speedboat but Brad. Repeat: Brad is still on the island. Some guy with Walt named Dirk says they had a secondary evac plan to go south to the airport or to Sankaddan. Over."

Heather's heart beat a little faster. Maybe they'd see some action after all! The boys had done the hard part, but maybe her team could still be used.

"Okay, I'll get to the runway. You guys cover Sankaddan."

Heather chalked her hands. "Anything else for me? Over."

"Yeah. Walt's trying to raise Brad on his comm. Getting nothing. Over."

Sighing with a growl, Heather remembered that vengeance belonged to the Lord, but she wasn't leaving without that boy. She felt responsible, having forced the boys to go in alone.

"Jasper, we'll tear this island apart if we have to. Understand? Over."

"Copy that."

"Contact in one hour. Out."

Clapping her chalky hands, Heather tethered her bag of gear to her waist and began to climb the cliff face.

...✝...

Trevor Niles was so furious, he could barely see as he drove his Jeep from the beach of New Manchester to Zalzuna. His lack of sleep wasn't helping his anger, either. He'd been awake all night on the beach with the soldiers, waiting in ambush for the team he expected to attempt to free the Jamisons. But, his Internet ploy had fallen apart, apparently. Wasting time and men, he'd focused on the wrong part of the island.

Punching the dashboard, Niles cut his knuckle. There'd been a rescue team, indeed, but they hadn't taken the bait he'd offered by saying the Jamisons were being held in New Manchester. No one would throw his words back in his face! But Niles had been wrong about the Christians; they weren't stupid. Every time Patrick Gibson entered his life . . .

The Patrick Gibson search hadn't been handled well, either. How could Niles gather support as dictator of the country with so many failures? Fredrick and his men wouldn't follow a man who had no successes! It was Gilgal all over again!

Swerving around a corner, he noticed a column of smoke rising from the midst of Zalzuna. It was an hour past dawn, and in the daylight, the whole island would see the black smoke from the rescue team's attack. By noon, all would know the situation, of his failure. And by evening, General Yousef would be informed, and though the greedy man left the administration of the island in the hands of others, he'd feel the need to reprimand Niles. At that thought, Niles bit the inside of his cheek. He wasn't ready to do away with the general and take over the island . . . yet. That meant he'd be forced to listen to the man's chastisement.

Driving through Zalzuna, Niles stopped in the street where the way was entirely blocked by a stationary bulldozer. Behind the dozer, the rehab center was in a heap of rubble from which small fires burned. Beyond the center, another building, which had once been a laundry, had collapsed. The place was a disaster.

He climbed out of the Jeep. One soldier climbing through the debris noticed Niles and shouted to the others that the assistant governor had arrived.

Flanked by two soldiers, Fredrick marched up to Niles. Resting his hands on his hips, Niles shook his head like a disappointed father.

"Tell me we got someone, anyone." Niles felt a sinking feeling inside.

"My men . . . we're . . . still searching." Fredrick had a look of defeat on his face.

"The prisoners?"

"All are gone. Some ran away. Others escaped the island with Dirk. I mean, Patrick Gibson, and his team."

"So, there really was a team."

"Yes, sir. The men say five or six strong, but I saw only Patrick and one other." Fredrick touched his side. "The other threw a flash and bang grenade at me so hard, he broke a couple of my ribs."

"You'll live. What are you doing now, besides standing around?"

"We sent a patrol boat in pursuit, but Patrick had a speedboat waiting for him, something faster than we have in the fleet. Besides, if we start harassing vessels in the vicinity, the Greek navy will—"

"I know what the Greek navy will do, Fredrick!"

"The only good news is, I think Patrick was alone with three of our escaped criminals when he reached the harbor. An RPG squad got a pretty good look at them. Whatever team rescued the Christians, they must have gotten separated from the rest in the chaos."

"They're still here?" Niles felt a glimmer of hope. If he could catch someone legitimately classified as an enemy of the state, the reprimand from the general would be less severe. "You think they're still on the island?"

"It looks that way. Seems maybe they were in one of these buildings when they collapsed. That's why we're searching for sign."

"And what if they're not here?" Niles scowled. "You're wasting time. We could have criminal invaders on this island and you're sorting through smoldering bricks, you fool!"

"What else would they be doing on the island? If they were left behind, it's just a matter of time before someone comes across them. I've already broadcasted a reward for information."

"Obviously, they're not going to make contact with anyone!" Niles spat. "Do I have to think of everything? If the enemy is still on the island, they'll be trying to leave. Get men stationed at all ports wherever there are boats, and start policing the coasts. And broadcast this new message: the foreign enemy has already killed twenty Zalzunian children—tortured then murdered them. They want our island's resources to exploit us, to wipe us out. And double the reward for information."

"Get on it!" Fredrick ordered a sergeant on his right.

"One more thing," Niles added. "Patrick is crafty. The other Christians were probably just as sinister. An attack like this . . . they had to have help from an islander. I want a full investigation. We may have a traitor amongst us."

Fredrick glanced to his left where Horatio stood silently.

"Soldier, you see anyone acting suspiciously?"

"Sir, you were here." Horatio stood up straight. "It was too dark to see anything for certain. I chased the enemy all the way to the harbor, alone, so the others here may need to give their accounts."

"Very well." Niles nodded. "You two lead the investigation when the search is exhausted. I'll make a call and get some reserves to the coast to assist in the search." He looked up the slope where the volcano rumbled more than usual, but he had greater things to think about than a pending eruption. "I'd better go talk to the general. Of course, he won't be happy."

"I'll go to Sankaddan," Fredrick said. "My plantation is on the way. Some of the escaped prisoners fled south. We'll round up at least some of them, and keep our eyes open for foreigners."

Niles gestured at Horatio.

"Aren't you one of Fredrick's interrogators? An apprentice of sorts I saw a few days ago?"

"Yes, sir."

"Your efforts are to be commended, young man. Catch us some Christians and you'll find a sure future in my administration."

"Thank you, sir!" Horatio smiled and saluted. "I'd like that very much!"

Niles rolled his eyes at the gullible soldier. He wished he had men that were more intelligent.

…✝…

"Here they come!" Jasper O'Shottie called from the bridge of the yacht.

Bounding up the companionway, Clifford joined Bruce and Jasper on deck as they gazed to the east.

"Can you believe those boys did our job?" Clifford watched as the speedboat closed on the yacht.

"That doesn't mean we can go home quite yet." Bruce moved to the bow to catch the line from the speedboat and secure the vessel on their port side.

Peering to the north, Clifford saw where the Island of Zalzuna was only a spot on the horizon. If Heather got into trouble, they were ten miles out. He didn't like the distance. They were a team, and he preferred to be at her side to watch her back, with Bruce at Clifford's side to watch his back.

Clifford focused again on the newly arriving speedboat. His anger had settled down some, but earlier, the fury had boiled over—fury that Walter and Brad had taken such a risk without the rest of the team. Now, Clifford felt a different anger—aimed at the culprits that had possibly captured Brad, who was evidently still on the island. If he were caught, he'd surely be executed.

On the speedboat with the others was a tall, brown-haired man with a handlebar mustache. Clifford's mouth dropped. He knew this man! Rather, he knew of him. Nathan Isaacson's arm was bandaged, but the wound didn't seem to hinder the mid-thirty-year-old man. Over the years, Clifford had been on enough missions—some of them for COIL—to recognize the operative when he saw him. So, this was the professional who Walter had sent to recon for the team. Heather wouldn't believe it was Nathan Isaacson! As Clifford watched from the rail, the mysterious operative climbed aboard and shook hands with Bruce, who didn't seem to recognize the legend.

Nathan and Bruce helped lift Lacy and Albert Jamison onto the larger vessel, followed by Walter. Jasper joined the introductions, but Clifford remained mid-ship. He never knew what to say to victims, and Lacy and Albert had obviously been abused. Despite Clifford's desire to avoid the gathering, Lacy spotted him and let go of Walter's hand to walk up to Clifford.

"Hi, I'm Lacy Jamison."

"I know who you are."

"Thanks for everything you've done."

"Well, we haven't done anything, yet. That was all Walt and your cousin, so far, and . . . that guy."

"Dirk. His name is Dirk."

"Right. Dirk." Clifford bit his lip. Of course, Nathan Isaacson wouldn't mention his real name, not to civilians. "I'm glad you're okay, Miss Jamison. Sorry about your mother."

"Thank you. What about Brad? You don't know what it's like on that island, or what they'll do to him. You're going to get him out, right?"

"Yeah, we'll get him out. For sure."

"Oh, thank you." Lacy gave the British man a hug, then went back to the others.

Ten minutes later, Lacy and Albert went below deck while Jasper, Walter, and the Lavers brothers crowded around Dirk on the bridge. Dirk didn't disclose his true identity, but Clifford sensed his commanding presence. Clifford was easily intimidated by such men, as he'd been by Brad and Walter, but it was by the small lessons he'd learned in dealing with the boys that he kept his outspoken mouth shut for a change. Besides, he felt honored to be standing next to a ghost.

"Brad knows to come south, here." Dirk pointed to a map of the island as Clifford stood close by. "Sankaddan is full of unrest, so this quarter of the island is where we agreed would be a reasonable secondary evac point. Since we're not able to raise him on the radio, that means either he's been compromised, or his radio has been damaged. We need to prepare for both possibilities. You say this Heather person, a pilot, is making her way to the runway? That's good, though if Brad happens upon the airport, he'll avoid all people. My guess is he'll get to the coast, lay low until dark, then send us a message, probably by fire. He'll know we won't leave without him.

"Having said that, we also need to prepare for the other possibility: he may've been captured. If that's the case, we'll be going in hot and coming out fast. Either way, your girl, Heather, is in the right place. If Brad doesn't use her, we will."

"Heather recommended Bruce and Clifford go ashore and cover Sankaddan," Jasper said, "just in case Brad gets all the way to that city."

"That's reasonable." Nathan rubbed his chin. "The only problem with that is the port authority there. We won't be allowed to freely enter the dockyard without a thorough search under the watchful eyes of the harbormaster. And we can't take the speedboat, since they're looking for it."

"We can transfer everything of importance from the yacht to the speedboat and leave the speedboat in Walt's hands." Jasper nodded at Walter. "He seems to have the controls down to a science."

"Okay." Dirk pointed at Clifford and Bruce. "So, it's you two and me."

"If they're looking for the speedboat, they'll be looking for you as well," Walter said. "Are you sure you want to go back to the island?"

"Want to? No," Dirk said. "Need to? Yes. I know the island well, having been on all sides of it at this point. You two game? It won't be a walk in the park."

"We're with you." Bruce clapped his brother on the back. "Let's bring that boy home."

After thirty minutes, the men had transferred everything that might compromise their identity from the yacht to the speedboat, which Walter would pilot back to Mykonos with Albert and Lacy. It was agreed everyone would meet there, eventually. After Walter dropped the two missionaries off at Mykonos, he was to come back and stand by for a backup extraction, which was his own contingency idea. Dirk approved, and the yacht sailed toward Sankaddan, under the guise of a tourist vessel.

And Clifford was thrilled to be standing on deck with Nathan Isaacson.

†

CHAPTER THIRTY

Horatio Salmose was still reeling from the night's activities. Though he was shocked he'd successfully assisted in the Christians' escape, he was terribly disappointed he'd been unable to catch up to them before they'd sped away in their boat. He didn't blame Albert Jamison. The missionary was an honest man who would've taken Horatio with him had he been able.

Fredrick had gone to Sankaddan to supervise the search efforts from that city while the rest of the soldiers under his supervision spread out along the coastline. Horatio couldn't imagine staying on the island now, not after he'd already turned against his own government. He'd hoped a career in the military would save him from the fields where his own father and mother had been worked to death. But he'd learned there was no escape from the evil while on the island—only different degrees of misery and wickedness.

Too tired to walk downtown to his single-room home, Horatio sat against the only standing wall of the laundry building. He'd been given six hours off to sleep since he'd been up for nearly two days. But, if one of the sergeants saw him resting on the street, he'd be assigned a task, so it was with barely enough energy to stand that Horatio started walking. Moving through the rubble of the building, he felt a strange sort of rebellious pride that he'd caused such destruction to Fredrick and Trevor Niles' schemes against peaceful men and women.

Suddenly, Horatio froze. What weariness remained in him disappeared at the sight before him. Even the pride he'd felt disappeared. He swallowed hard and moved toward a pile of debris from which a man's hand was exposed. Horatio hadn't imagined that anyone had been in the building when his bulldozer had done its damage. Who was this?

Touching the hand, he was surprised to find it was still warm. Pushing aside several bricks to reach the man's wrist, he checked for a pulse and waited . . . There it was!

Frantically, Horatio clawed at the bricks and mortar covering the man. He knew all the citizens of the small city. Who could he be? Though Horatio had tortured and maimed men and women in the interrogation room under Fredrick's authority, he'd never wished to harm anyone himself. After each of the first dozen torture sessions, he'd vomited; he had that same feeling now.

After clearing away enough bricks, Horatio noticed the man wasn't wearing a Zalzunian military uniform. In fact, the stranger wore a torn, black, long-sleeve thermal. The thermal wasn't something that would be found in a shop on the island. Horatio stumbled backward at the sight of the stranger's face. The man was Horatio's age, maybe younger. He wore a broken communication device in his ear and a wire around his neck. As Horatio continued to unearth the young man, he found a backpack and a number of stun grenades on his belt.

"Wake up!" Horatio dragged the foreigner to clear ground, though he was careful to stay within the cover of the wall. He unfastened the backpack and used the man's own canteen to splash water on his face.

Finally, the young man sputtered once before he opened his eyes. Blinking several times, he focused on the soldier's face before him. He seemed to notice Horatio's uniform.

"I think you're one of them, aren't you?" Horatio asked. "You're fortunate I found you before the others did. They would've killed you." The man's eyes took in Horatio's sidearm in his holster. "Oh, don't worry. I'm not one of them, not any longer. Your people—do you know how to get off the island?"

The man tried to speak, but nothing came out. Horatio offered him a drink of water. He guzzled a dozen swallows, then wiped his mouth, his eyes never leaving Horatio's face.

"You're not gonna turn me in?"

"No. If I was, you'd already be in chains." Horatio scoffed. "Actually, there aren't any cells left. I ruined their ambush last night. If you were here, you'll remember the bulldozer."

"That was you?"

"It's about the only right thing I've done since I joined the military." Horatio had so many questions for this man. *Where would he live in America? Somewhere away from the ocean, he hoped. Could anyone drive a car?* "Oh! You don't know!"

"Know what?"

"The Jamisons got away! Commander Fredrick is as mad as hot grease. He's down in Sankaddan somewhere looking for you and the rest of your team."

"My team?"

"Some of the men said they saw a whole team rescue the Jamisons. Isn't that true?"

"There were just two of us. I'm not sure we could've done anything without you paving the way with that dozer." The young man looked around. "My name's Brad. You are . . . ?"

"My name is Horatio."

Brad rolled over, and with Horatio's help, rose to his feet. He was two inches taller than Horatio and many pounds heavier. Horatio reached down, picked up the backpack, and slung it over his own shoulder.

"That's not a good idea." Brad stepped forward, took his pack, and tightened the straps around his torso. Horatio didn't stop the bigger man. "No offense, but where I'm going, you're better off here. I'm not even sure I can get off this rock."

"But I can show you!" Horatio had to keep his hope alive. "I mean, depending on where you want to go. I've lived here my whole life."

Tugging the comm device off his neck, Brad examined it, then tossed it into the pile of rubble. Horatio glanced toward the street. It was midmorning and people would be about the town.

"Can you get me to the coast south of the airport by nightfall?"

"I can come?" Horatio couldn't hold back a grin.

"As long as you realize what they'll do to us if we're caught."

"Believe me, I know better than you. Come. We need to get out of Zalzuna as soon as possible."

Heather felt like a duck hunter in a blind. Two hundred yards to the south was the cliff she'd climbed—an exhilarating experience of heights and danger. Then it had taken an hour to crawl the distance from the cliff to the patch of vegetation in which she now hid. She'd built a small enclosure of scrub brush and twigs from which she could keep watch on the single runway, as well as the road from Sankaddan to Zalzuna.

A Jeep approached and passed the airport driveway. Two uniformed soldiers and a huge bald man sat in the Jeep. Heather didn't bother to duck out of sight. As long as she didn't move suddenly, her camouflage was more than adequate. Besides, this wasn't the first Zalzuna traffic she'd encountered.

Once, a patrolling Jeep had cruised slowly past her and even checked the runway expanse for activity. Another pair of soldiers on foot had trekked along the cliff. Had they peeked over the ledge, they would've found Heather's climbing gear and harness hanging from a pin six inches below the ledge. She could rappel down the two hundred foot cliff in ten seconds. It was a fast, though temporary, getaway. The Zalzuna military had at least one good patrol boat they could use to intercept her on the beach, or to catch her soon after she launched her small dinghy.

"Jasper, come in," she hailed.

"Go, Caver. Jasper here. Over."

"Status report. Over."

"We're almost to Sankaddan. Walter's taking the Jamisons to Mykonos, refueling, then he'll be on standby. Anything on your end? Over."

"A lot of patrols, which is a good sign. Over."

"Roger that. It means they haven't caught Brad, yet. Over."

"Hey, Jasper, the guy Walt sent in—who was he? Over."

"Calls himself Dirk. Big guy. Handlebar mustache, knee

brace. Pretty quick with orders, but he seems to know what he's doing. Over."

"Did you say handlebar mustache? Over."

"Roger that. Why, Caver? You know him? Over."

"Nah. It can't be him. Reminded me of someone who died long ago. Listen: if Brad is alive, he'll make his move come dark. Over."

"We'll be ready to sail. You have a bird? Over."

"Roger. I have my pick of a fleet of two. But one of them probably wouldn't make it to Mykonos. Over."

"You have everything? We need to tack before the wind once before docking. Over."

"I'm good. Be careful. Caver, out."

Heather sighed. That would be their last contact for hours. If the yacht was taken, and the four men were arrested, Heather would have to flee in her dinghy all the way to Mykonos. From there, she'd try to find another team to form a secondary rescue operation. The chance of finding another team willing to risk so much at a moment's notice was unlikely. They had this one opportunity.

Behind Heather, the volcano rumbled louder. She imagined it was mimicking the tension the whole island felt.

Brad and Horatio jogged alongside one another across a field of young olive trees. They'd agreed that crossing the field was dangerous, but they were pressed for time. Up until an hour ago, they hadn't moved but half a mile from Zalzuna due to pressing patrols scrutinizing the routes in and out of the capital city, and even more so along the coastline.

They'd crawled through brush and thorns along the

coastal cliffs to journey beyond the most dangerous zone. But Horatio promised the farther south they journeyed, the danger would grow worse. The problem wasn't necessarily the number of soldiers searching for Brad; it was the lack of cover to conceal themselves. At that moment, if someone came along in a Jeep at the end of the orchard and looked to the right, they'd spot the two fugitives sprinting south.

The young men dove into the brush on the other side of the grove and gasped for breath.

"Water." Brad handed Horatio his canteen.

Horatio sloshed the water in the bottom of the canteen. They were nearly out. He handed it back to Brad.

"I'm okay. I'll wait until we get on the boat."

"Come on. That could be hours. Finish it off. You said yourself you've been up for two days."

"You drink half, and I'll drink half."

The young men were parched, and with nowhere to refill the canteen, they both felt the urgency of getting where they were going. Brad took one swig of water, just a mouthful, and gave it to Horatio, who did the same. The canteen was now empty.

"How far from the airport are we?" Brad asked.

"Not far." Horatio pointed south. "One more plantation. The runway is on the other side. You can fly a plane?"

"No. It's just a landmark. My friend said to reach the airport, then go to the nearest coastline."

"The nearest coastline to the south is on the way to Sankadden. There are cliffs all along the coast there."

"Then, from the airport we'll head west, following the road."

"There isn't much cover," Horatio said. "Darkness would help. Your friends will wait?"

"They'll wait."

"You're certain?" Horatio looked doubtful. "They're loyal?"

"Yes, I'm certain." Brad couldn't help but smile. By now, Heather and the Lavers brothers would've found a boat and arrived at Mykonos. Walter wouldn't leave him behind, either. And whoever this Dirk was, he seemed to be the type who wouldn't leave a fallen comrade behind. Besides, Uncle Albert and Lacy wouldn't go home until his rescue had been successful. They'd bring him home, one way or another.

"I've never had friends like this."

"Well, you do now." Brad rose to his feet. "Let's go."

Leading the way, Brad set a swift pace, but they'd traveled no farther than one hundred yards before the plantation came into sight. A peasant woman in the nearest field saw him at the same time. Brad dropped to his stomach on the ground, but it was too late. Horatio belly-crawled up to Brad's side.

"Oh, man, I messed up!" Brad checked his pack straps. "I was impatient. When I saw the clearing, I didn't think there'd be anybody there."

Horatio raised his head to look over the sparse grass, which was the only cover they had nearby.

"She's running toward a cottage. I know who lives there. We can't stay here."

"Why? Who lives here?"

"My commander, Fredrick. He's very important. You saw him last night—remember the tall bald man?"

"Yeah, I remember. And I don't want to see him again. Which way do we go?"

"West, then around."

Hopping to his feet first, Horatio hadn't taken a step before gunfire thrashed through the grass and Horatio hit the ground. Brad closed his eyes and clung to the earth, praying to be spared. As soon as the thunder was silent, Brad reached out and shook Horatio's still body.

"Come on, Horatio!" he called. "Horatio!"

The Zalzunian guard was silent and still. Touching Horatio's shoulder, Brad's hand came away bloody. He'd been hit somewhere in the left side. Bullets raked the grass again. Daring a glance up, Brad saw four soldiers spread out, advancing with machine guns. There was no way around them. He could only retreat.

"Horatio!" Brad found no pulse when he touched the young man's neck. "Goodbye, Horatio. Thank you for everything."

Brad lunged to his feet, his grieving heart bringing him to tears as he turned his back to the four soldiers and ran back the way he'd come. Rounds whistled past his head. A force like a freight train hit him in the back, and he went down on his face, sliding to a stop at the edge of the olive tree orchard. A round had hit his backpack! He collected his wits quickly, jumped up, and weaved through the orchard, putting as many short trees between him and his attackers as possible.

On the other side of the orchard, he dove into the brush. In his panic, he cut his face horribly on thorns, but he felt no pain. He paused for a few breaths. North was out of the question. West would send him into the desolate part of the island where there was even less cover than he had now. South was where his attackers were. To the east was the busy road and cliffs all the way around the island to the city of Sankaddan.

Choosing east, Brad crawled through the brush. Now that he'd been spotted, he guessed reinforcements would be brought in to swarm the area. He had mere minutes to escape the vicinity. Frantically, he clawed at the ground and twigs as he crawled. The knees of his jeans were torn and he was bleeding, but he didn't stop. A burst of gunfire sounded behind him, but it was nowhere near him. It only served to push him farther and faster. The soldiers had lost track of him temporarily, it seemed, and he meant to take advantage of it!

Sooner than he realized, he arrived at the road's edge in a shallow ditch. He couldn't see far down the road, so he trusted his ears. A vehicle approached from the north. Measuring the distance, he calculated his chances. Did he have enough time? Deciding to risk it all, he rose to a crouch and sprinted across the road of packed gravel. But it was fifty more yards before he saw a patch of brush behind which to dive.

With the last of his energy, he surged forward, tripped the last few steps, then crawled the rest of the way. The patch of brush was only two feet high and not wide enough to conceal his legs. With a gasp, he tore off his pack—figuring he'd stay in place for a spell—and hugged the ground as the vehicle passed. He didn't bother looking up to see who it was. Surely, it was more soldiers arriving from Zalzuna. A moment later, another vehicle passed.

As he steadied his breathing, Brad considered his options. Horatio was probably dead, which was better than the alternative of torture, if he were still alive and caught. Nevertheless, Brad wasn't certain. He'd run away and left

Horatio behind, only because in his state, what could he do now to help Horatio?

His watch said it was seven o'clock already. Darkness was a couple hours away—if he lived that long. What then? Turning his head, he gazed to the east. There was no cover all the way to the cliff twenty-five yards away. From the charts, he knew the cliff was a two-hundred-foot fall to the ocean. No one could survive that; he'd jumped off Oregon's coastal cliffs his whole life. He had little rock-climbing experience, only the coral rocks he'd climbed around the Bandon lighthouse, so scaling the cliff in the dark was out of the question. His only option was to wait for darkness, then follow the cliffs around to Sankaddan where he could access the beach to send a signal to the team. He was certain his team was somewhere off the coast, waiting for that signal.

Brad prayed as he heard men's voices across the road. They spoke in Greek, which he didn't know but a few words. He guessed they were debating whether Brad had crossed the road or not. They'd see there was nowhere for anyone to hide across the road, and they'd conclude that he'd remained where there was more cover to the west. At least, that was Brad's prayer. And with the assumption his lone shrub would be scrutinized, he remained as still as possible, even when a leg cramp painfully plagued his right thigh.

The first hour passed. More soldiers came and went. Since Brad didn't know when one of them might eye his bush, not once did he dare to peek at the searching soldiers who combed the brush no more than a stone's throw away.

During the second hour, more vehicles arrived with fresh reinforcements, probably from New Manchester, he guessed.

Brad tried to sleep. As tired as he was, he still couldn't find peace enough to drift away. He kept his eyes closed, meditating on where true peace and security rested: at the cross of Christ. And the more he thought about Horatio, the more firmly he decided he couldn't leave the island without knowing for certain if the young man were dead or not.

When darkness finally settled across the land, three vehicles drove north. Their search had turned up nothing, but Brad knew the military wouldn't give up. Finally, for the first time in hours, Brad moved. He rolled over, eased himself into a sitting position, and massaged his leg muscle. For several minutes, he took in his surroundings and familiarized himself with the shadows. The moon was out, casting a clear reflection off the sea to the east. There were no clouds in the sky to cover the light of the moon. Even with the darkness, he'd have to move carefully along the cliffs because a watchful eye would still see him.

Far above and to the northwest, the volcano rumbled and spit fire. It quieted a moment later, as if it were biding its time for the prime occasion to erupt.

With difficulty, Brad swallowed. He needed water. Digging into his pack, he ate his last energy bar, choking it down without a drop of liquid.

Still seated, he fit his pack onto his back, though not without taking inventory first. He still had three stun grenades and two tranquilizer pens. Using a meager medical kit, he applied alcohol pads and antibiotic ointment to his scrapes and scratches. Though he was close to exhaustion, he felt a sense of exhilaration at the thought of meeting up with his friends. If Heather, Jasper, and the team were anywhere in the region, Walter would've made contact with them by now. Walter would know how best to find out about Horatio's status, perhaps by intercepting a radio transmission.

With his eyes on the terrain inland, Brad cautiously rose to his feet. Nothing moved. No cars. No soldiers. No barrels flashing gunfire his way.

He crept to the edge of the cliff and looked down at the waves frothing against the rocks far below. And farther out to sea, the Predator was one of those floating lights he could barely see, bobbing in the water. If his radio still worked, he could've briefed them on his plans, but he had to assume they'd know he'd reach out to them the best he could as soon as he could. Communication devices failed sometimes. They'd know that. Or would they automatically assume he'd been captured? His mind was ready to burst under the pressure of doubt.

Slowly, Brad followed the cliffs southward. He stayed only a few feet from the edge, which wasn't to tempt fate, but to stay as far away from the road as he could, which snaked along at his right. It wasn't long before Brad saw headlights approaching from the north, but he had time to run ahead and hide behind a small boulder until it was safe again. When Brad came upon a driveway that veered off the coastal road, he guessed he was below the airport. He was farther along than he'd estimated. Pausing south of the intersection, he wondered if he should dare to deviate from his way to search for water at the runway. If he found himself too distracted, however, he wouldn't reach Sankaddan that night at all. He was thirsty, but it was best to bypass the airport altogether. There was nothing there for him but risk.

As Brad turned away, he spotted movement in a stand of brush between him and the runway. Dropping to his stomach, he rolled twice, in case gunfire followed, but he was sure he'd been spotted. Against the backdrop of the sea and horizon, he was surely more visible than anyone else inland.

And yet, no gunfire followed, no screaming bullets sought his hide. He rose to his hands and knees and crawled westward. When he paused again, he looked toward the airport. More movement, but not just from one spot; there were many bodies moving toward him! Silently, ghostlike, at least thirty soldiers rushed him. They'd lain in wait, as if Brad were their prey.

Brad rose to his feet, with only the cliffs behind him. He wouldn't leap into the sea unless all else was lost. Calmly, he plucked a grenade off his belt and pulled the pin. They'd underestimated his will to live—and the accuracy of his arm.

The volcano exploded fire and cast an eerie, orange-red glow across the island. The illumination distracted the charging soldiers. Brad picked out the bald head of the one Horatio had called Fredrick, and pitched the first grenade at the giant man.

†

<u>*CHAPTER THIRTY-ONE*</u>

Fredrick wiped the sweat from his baldheaded brow. All evening, he'd been leading the search for the missing Christian. Finding Horatio had been a surprise, but now he wanted the man who had talked Horatio into helping him escape the island! Horatio was unconscious and terribly wounded, so Fredrick couldn't interrogate the young soldier yet, but Fredrick was fairly certain he was accurately reading the intentions of the remaining foreign invader.

Since they hadn't been able to find the missing man, Fredrick had gathered his soldiers at the airport—over fifty men. Then he'd sent all the vehicles away to make it appear they were pulling out of the vicinity. Thirty men remained, all hiding in the brush. He was certain the missing foreigner was hiding nearby, and so his ambush was laid.

His mobile phone buzzed. It was Trevor Niles.

"Everything in place?" Niles asked. "Sure want to see at least one of our ambushes work this week!"

"Yeah." Fredrick was in the center of his ambush line of men. "If we don't see anything in the first couple hours of darkness, we'll go closer to Sankaddan."

"Where did you take that traitor? What was his name?"

"Horatio, sir." Fredrick was angry that his own interrogator had betrayed them all. The young soldier would pay as soon as he was conscious. "We took him to the Sankaddan clinic. He was a weak man. I was trying to toughen him up, but I see my time spent with him only made him weaker."

"The general has been briefed. He awaits news. Call me when you have something."

Pocketing his phone, Fredrick narrowed his eyes in thought, as he looked south. Both he and Niles were responsible for the failings lately, but Niles had rushed to the general's side and was surely putting all the blame on Fredrick. If Fredrick didn't succeed this time, he knew Niles wouldn't hesitate to discipline him publicly. Worse yet, they still hadn't caught any of the other escapees, either, mostly because they were spending so much time searching for this cursed man who so evaded his men. Fredrick didn't know how the man had gotten away after stumbling upon his plantation. He'd had nowhere to run, and yet Fredrick's men hadn't found him—only a few traces of blood and fabric clinging to thorn bushes. And by the time Fredrick had arrived on the scene, his men had so trampled all sign, it was impossible to track the evasive intruder.

A moment earlier, Fredrick had finally spotted the foreigner—a tall, lanky figure across the road near the cliffs. One by one, the message was passed down the line, every soldier preparing to attack. The lone man lingered at the roadside where it intersected with the roadway to the airport. No better ambush could've been planned. His men were perfectly placed. The invader had nowhere to run!

Silently, Fredrick signaled the advance by rising to his feet and starting forward. Like a wave, the thirty soldiers moved on either side of Fredrick, sidearms and rifles in their hands. When the lone man sensed the danger, Fredrick saw him reach for his side, then cock his arm, as if to throw something. Fredrick felt as if his heart skipped a beat when he realized the man was about to throw another grenade! With his side still painful from the last grenade the operative had thrown at him, he took comfort in the fact that no one could be that accurate twice.

Along the line of men beside Fredrick, one of his soldiers moved up, then passed him. In the darkness, it was too hard to see which of his men it was. But from the silhouette, this man had longer, loose hair. He suddenly realized it wasn't one of his men at all! It was . . . *a woman!* The infiltrator was two steps ahead of Fredrick when he reached for her, but she was moving faster, even with a pack on her back. He didn't know where she'd come from! She just . . . was.

Behind him, the volcano that had been rumbling for days, belched such fire that half the men became distracted. For an instant, they took their eyes off the lone man against the cliff.

Looking ahead of the woman, Fredrick saw his foe on the cliff release the grenade with the expert snap of his wrist. Though Fredrick opened his mouth to warn his men about the woman and the grenade, it was too late. The grenade hit him squarely on the chest and stopped him in his tracks. He couldn't breathe. Falling to his knees, Fredrick looked down at the grenade in front of him. Everything in his head told him to look away, but he was staring directly at it in unbelief when it exploded.

When Heather noticed the Zalzunian troops begin to

congregate around her at the airstrip, she knew Brad had to be near. Thirty soldiers were spread out in a line from east to west to the south of her. She was hidden only twenty yards away, but in the darkness, she felt adequately protected since their focus was toward the cliffs.

Though she felt safe, Heather worried about how she would help Brad if he encountered the deadly ambush. Would she be able to get him to a plane and start it up in time? Straining to hear, she listened to a large, bald man point and gave orders to the others. She caught no signal as to their specific intentions. But Baldy was definitely in charge.

In the moonlight, Heather saw Brad at the cliff edge an instant before Baldy did. When the troops rushed toward Brad, Heather was on Baldy's heels. Silently, even with her heavy pack, she overtook the man and his soldiers.

Once in front of them, she saw Brad throw a grenade at the men behind her. She was temporarily deafened, but her eyes were unaffected. With both hands, she tossed two of her own grenades, one to each side. They exploded simultaneously, blinding Brad, as well as the rest of the soldiers, who stopped their attack in fear and confusion.

Heather had only a few seconds when she reached Brad, who was kneeling on the ground, covering his eyes with his hands.

Grabbing Brad by the back of his collar, Heather pushed him toward the cliff rim. She reached over the edge and found her rappel rope, then fastened it to her harness.

"Brad, I'm here!" she yelled. "C'mon!"

He crawled toward her and stood. Grabbing at his waist to find his belt, she hoped the leather was sturdy enough to hold his weight. Then she clipped her harness to him, kicked his heels from under him, and they tumbled over the cliff together.

For two seconds, they free-fell before Heather twisted the rope in a *Z* to manage their decent. Brad's arms were flailing, then he clung to her torso as she bounded thirty yards at a time down the cliff face.

Unable to see much besides shadows in the darkness, they hit the beach hard, then crumpled in a heap of limbs as Heather struggled to loose Brad from her harness. Once they were free from the rope, Heather jumped up and pulled the dinghy away from the cliff wall into the water. She waited for Brad's senses to return, then he followed her and climbed into the narrow bow. Heather hopped into the back and began to row.

"I have Brad in the dinghy, Jasper," Heather said into her comm unit. "We need a pickup. Over."

"Walt, you got her?" Jasper said in her ear.

"Coming to you. Tell me when you see my boat. Over." Walter's voice was barely audible over the noise of his motors.

"We can't leave!" Brad objected to Heather. "Horatio—he saved me! He saved Uncle Albert and Lacy, too. He's the one who bulldozed the rehab center!"

"Brad's right," Walter said in her ear. "Albert told me he promised a guard named Horatio a ride off the island. Over."

"This is Dirk. Bruce, Cliff, and I are in Sankaddan. We'll look into it. If everyone's safe, we need to get our hands on Niles if possible. He's a wanted man. But with or without him, we need to be gone by dawn. Over."

"Jasper here. Meet you in Sankaddan. Out."

Heather nodded at Brad

"You've got a covert kind of future for you, kid. We're almost done with this operation, but I'd say you're just getting started."

"Something for me to pray about," he said, then looked out to sea.

In her heart, Heather said her own prayer—for Bruce. He'd be going in without her.

...✝...

"Seems this is pretty extreme for a fella we're not even sure is alive."

Glancing at Clifford Lavers, Nathan paid his mouthiness little mind. Clifford's skills as a Christian operative were known around the world, regardless of his loose tongue. Bruce, who knelt with them behind a sea wall on the edge of Sankaddan, shrugged in the fading darkness. Like his brother, Bruce had a reputation among COIL field agents as a selfless and committed man—and he had scars to prove his dedication.

"If Brad and the Jamisons say this guy helped them," Nathan said quietly over the waves at their back, "then we can't leave him behind."

"If he's still alive." Clifford shook his head. "Brad did say Horatio was shot."

"Why don't you shut your mouth?" Bruce finally told his brother. "You know you're going with us no matter what."

Nathan didn't mind the brothers' banter. Actually, he didn't mind their company at all. Since leaving COIL's primary infiltration team to operate underground, he was usually alone—and more often than not, he was lonely. For this reason, he anticipated contact with Chen Li. What mission was she on? Would she be free to meet in person? He had to see her again!

"Four soldiers." Nathan pointed at a cement building and a Jeep parked in front. "According to our intel, that's Sankaddan's only clinic. If Horatio's alive, he'd be in there."

"Yeah, but there's still four soldiers!" Clifford looked to his brother. "Tell him, Bruce!"

"Tell me what?" Nathan kept his eyes on the clinic. The sun was nearly peeking over the horizon. Jasper was down the shore three hundred yards at the main pier, probably still arguing with customs officers since he didn't have the right shore papers. The team was running out of time if they were to catch a ride with Jasper on the sailboat off the island. "See that Jeep? That's Fredrick's Jeep. That means Fredrick is inside. You two approach from the east. I'll take them on the west."

"Wait." Clifford set a firm hand on Nathan's forearm, stopping Nathan as he started to rise over the sea wall. "What do you expect us to do exactly?"

"You have tranqs, don't you?" Nathan held up his own pen tranquilizer device. "Use them."

"Seriously, Dirk . . ." This time, Bruce objected with pleading eyes. Nathan was certain the brothers knew he was really Nathan Isaacson, but they were still respecting his cover as Dirk Salverskein. "We're used to team coverage."

Instantly, Nathan understood. The Lavers brothers were prime operatives, but they were team operators, not solo agents, as Nathan had become. They were familiar with NL weaponry and tranq guns that could disable the enemy from a safe distance.

"Nothing to it." Nathan forced a smile. "East side. Distract them. Don't worry; God's with us!"

Before they could object, Nathan leaped over the low wall and crouched as he ran for cover behind a single olive tree that grew at the edge of the clinic parking lot.

Once behind the olive tree, he looked back to see the brothers were on the move. The four soldiers near the entrance of the clinic were heavily armed with rifles and sidearms—perhaps a sign of their two fruitless days and nights of manhunts all over the island.

The volcano belched fire and rumbled, welcoming the dawn as the sun shined on the upper section of the cone. A shimmering lava flow appeared on the deserted western slope. If the island weren't about to be consumed by the volcano, Nathan might've entertained the idea of returning after the rescue operation to help the peasants set up a new government in place of General Yousef's. However, the increased activity of the violent eruptions signaled the end of the Republic of Zalzuna.

The Lavers brothers were in full sight of the four soldiers now, and Nathan tensed his weary and bruised body for one more conflict. His knee brace joint needed some attention, and he could've used a twelve-hour snooze, but lives were in the balance. People came first.

The soldiers spotted Clifford and Bruce. Nathan started across the gravel lot a heartbeat later. The brothers were mock arguing as they approached the clinic—pushing, shoving, and yelling threats at one another. Nathan hoped it was enough of a distraction as he dashed toward the Jeep.

By the time Nathan reached the Jeep, the soldiers had passed the front bumper of the vehicle. Clifford and Bruce were so vocal that Nathan's footsteps weren't heard on his intersecting path. He planted his left foot on the Jeep's right front tire, and sprang over the hood, his arms reaching out for maximum effect.

Though the soldiers were grouped tightly, tackling four at once was a stretch, but Nathan only realized this in midflight. Though his wingspan was over six feet wide, he collided with only two of the soldiers. The impact of his body against his targets was enough to startle the other two soldiers, but Nathan had his hands full with the first two. He hoped the Lavers brothers were close enough to deal with the others.

Rolling in the gravel, Nathan recovered and faced his foes. Instead of rising to his feet, he dove from his knees at both men. He grasped one by the ankle and stabbed the other in the arm with the tranq. The one whose ankle he held raised a handgun. Nathan thought more in that instant about the noise a gunshot would make rather than about getting shot. With more speed than he thought he had left, he threw his braced leg at the man's gun hand. The handgun clattered on the ground and slid under the Jeep.

Desperately, the soldier clawed for the lost gun, but Nathan was stronger, his grip firmly on the man's ankle. He tranqed him in the thigh, then turned to face the two other soldiers.

The brothers stood over their two motionless, sleeping islanders. Bruce extended his hand to Nathan and jerked him to his feet.

"Remind me to bring you with us next time we have a church rugby game," Clifford said. "That was some tackle!"

Nathan strode to the clinic double doors. It was dark inside, a long hallway before them.

"Remember," Nathan whispered over his shoulder, "Horatio may not be the only friendly in here. And leave Fredrick to me."

Leading the way down the hallway, Nathan's slightly squeaky knee brace sounded louder against the plain walls and closed doors. The clinic seemed to be abandoned—as much of the island would be if the volcano had its way.

Turning a corner, Nathan came upon a nurse's station where a middle-aged woman looked up from where she was pilfering medical supplies from a drawer. Stopping in front of her, Nathan blocked her escape. Caught in her looting, guilt flashed across her face, but Nathan reached out and lifted her chin.

"Where is he?" Nathan felt his fury building. "Where is Fredrick?"

She jutted her chin to indicate a secondary wing, then Nathan moved aside so she could scuttle toward the exit.

As Nathan walked down the other hallway, he heard voices ahead. He recognized Fredrick's voice right away, but the other one . . . It was Trevor Niles! Nathan stopped a short distance from a door that was open a few inches. After so long, Niles was about to collide with justice.

"Change of plans," Nathan whispered to the brothers. He clenched his right hand around a tranq pen. "I hear Trevor Niles' voice. Let me take him. You two get Fredrick."

Moving in front of the door, Nathan gestured to the

brothers to crowd close. Still, he waited as he peeked through the gap.

A man, presumably Horatio, lay in a hospital bed, a tube protruding from his bandaged chest. As Nathan watched the young man sleep, Fredrick leaned over Horatio and jostled the wounded man. Groaning, Horatio woke and gasped at the pain and the sight of Fredrick.

"I'm glad you're alive, Horatio." Fredrick squeezed Horatio's wound. "Thanks to you, your cult friends got away. They used you and left you behind. See how they are? I tried to help you, to teach you. Now, you'll learn the hard way, the worst way."

Clifford impatiently pointed at the door, urging Nathan to barge into the room and interrupt the torment of the young man, but Nathan wasn't so sure. Who exactly was this man, Horatio? Would he cave under the pressure of his ruthless enemies?

A second figure came into view on the other side of Horatio's bed. The treachery of Trevor Niles, Nathan knew well. The villain of Gilgal smiled down at the wounded man.

"Look at me, Horatio," the assistant governor said. "You fooled even me, and that's not easy to do. There will be consequences, of course."

"Imagine," Fredrick continued, "everything we would've done to the cultists you helped, you'll bear it all now. And since I don't have an assistant any longer, I'll do it all myself. So, rest up, soldier. You'll get what you wanted—attention from me."

"I'll never . . ." Horatio lifted his head with a wince, tears in his eyes. "I'll never regret helping them!"

"Oh, you will, you little—!" Niles lifted a fist, but Fredrick grabbed the smaller man's wrist.

"Not yet." Fredrick smiled. "Wait until he regains his strength. Isn't that right, Horatio? We always let our subjects rest before their questioning begins."

Nathan had heard enough. How Horatio had managed a change of heart under the dominion of such evil had to be an act of God alone! His few words spoke volumes. Brad had been right to send them back; Horatio couldn't be left behind.

Horatio shuddered under the glares of the two men, then seemed to fall asleep. Nathan stepped through the door, the Lavers brothers right behind him.

Niles looked over his shoulder first.

"Patrick!" the man gasped, as if the name were a curse word. He backed away from the bed.

"How's your jaw, Niles?" Nathan asked as he moved close to Niles in case he tried an offensive move against Horatio. Niles seemed to be unarmed. "When you baited Christians to your little island, you didn't guess you'd get the likes of me, did you? Still trying to make up for Gilgal, huh?"

Fredrick grasped for his sidearm. He cleared the holster, but managed nothing else before Bruce wrapped a burly fist around the bald man's thick wrist, and forced the gun to the floor. With his chin trembling, Fredrick looked up at Bruce, as if Fredrick had never had to face anyone larger than himself before.

"Seems a shame we don't have time to enjoy your company." Nathan was ready to block a punch if Niles threw one. He fingered the tranq pen. "The island's going down, Niles, and after what I've seen, Interpol will be hunting you wherever you run. But I intend to make sure you don't run."

"I know you won't hurt us." Niles lifted his chin defiantly. Nathan prayed for restraint right then. God and the authorities would deal with such wickedness; revenge wasn't his to take. "You're Christians. You're weak. You can't even fathom hurting your enemies!"

"Fathom?" Clifford laughed as he checked Horatio's vitals. "Oh, we can fathom it, I assure you. The way we see it, though, now that we know how easily you two geniuses can be out-maneuvered, we don't see you as much of a threat."

"You'll never get off Zalzuna." Fredrick's face was inches from Bruce's wide jaw. "My men are everywhere!"

"But I think your men must have abandoned you, Fredrick," Nathan stated. "I didn't see any men, did you guys?"

"Nobody." Clifford chuckled. "How else could we walk in here unarmed?"

"Clifford," Nathan said, "get Horatio out of here while we clean up this mess."

"What?" Fredrick's face twisted. "Horatio? You came for *him*?" The bald man shoved Bruce aside to stop Clifford from taking Horatio. "No! You can't! He's my soldier!"

Clutching Fredrick by the throat, Bruce held him back. Fredrick punched Bruce twice on the side of the head, but Bruce seemed unfazed. He calmly jammed his tranq into Fredrick's shoulder. The bald man gurgled a scream then relaxed, and Bruce lowered him to sleep on the floor.

"Once in a while, you might get God's children," Nathan said softly as he inched closer to Niles, "but if you'd read just one of those Bibles you hate so much, you'd know Jesus Christ wins in the end. You can't beat your Creator, Niles.

You should've learned that in the Coral Sea. Now you'll answer for your crimes."

Niles chose that instant to attack, or perhaps Nathan's words were enough to throw him into a fit of rage. He swung at Nathan, who backed away. Then the man tried to claw at Nathan's eyes, with a cry like an angry cat. Nathan swatted his hands aside. When Niles gathered himself and charged, Nathan was ready. Stepping past Niles, Nathan pushed the man against the wall, then tranquilized him in the back of the neck. The man slumped to the floor.

For a moment, Nathan stared at the deceptively peaceful men who'd caused so much evil, and Nathan felt a strange remorse now that it was over. Soon, Corban Dowler would give him a new mission, and he'd be alone again, isolated from the people he cared about—to wage war against evils that threatened the advocates of the gospel of Jesus Christ. Was Chen Li as weary as he was?

"So, what about us?" Bruce shrugged. "Will we be working together again someday? Heather Kooper says she really likes your style."

"To be honest with you, Bruce, it's important no one includes me in any mission report. You understand?"

"I get it. You don't exist."

Nathan touched the comm in his ear, then knelt next to Niles.

"Jasper, this is Dirk. We're on our way, but we have only a few minutes head start before more trouble arrives, so get the motors running. Over."

†

CHAPTER THIRTY-TWO

Chen Li stood in the semi-open cockpit of her fifty-foot Neptunus Express speedboat. She drifted one mile off the southern shore of the Republic of Zalzuna, but with the powerful binoculars to her eyes, she felt only two hundred yards away.

Her cockpit radio crackled as it broadcasted urgent voices from shore. After eavesdropping on several frequencies for the last three days and nights, she knew most of the voices by now, even the handles they went by. And she recognized the Predator speedboat back from Mykonos—idling a quarter-mile west of her. According to the COIL rescue team on the island, the Predator was to be a backup getaway vessel if the team's slower moving sailboat was inadequate, piloted by Jasper.

Dawn broke across the sky, and the volcano spewed more fire and ash. But Chen Li kept her gaze fixed on the Sankaddan clinic wherein the three operatives had entered to rescue one last victim of the Zalzunian regime.

Corban Dowler had sent Li to Zalzuna four days earlier, and she understood why—not only was she to keep secret watch over the team and report back to Corban, she was also there to confirm if Trevor Niles was on the island. Li hadn't lived a day since her Gilgal mission without wondering what

Niles was up to—what evils he was inflicting upon innocent people. And Li hadn't been on site long, pretending to fish from her boat stern, when Niles' name was transmitted by the team.

Within minutes, Li had texted Corban to confirm the murderer and persecutor of God's people was indeed there. Waiting for Interpol to show up was another story. The international police force would take Niles into custody, they promised, but they wouldn't sanction an all-out operation—or risk lives—to nab him inside a sovereign nation. That left Li to pray for the COIL team to get him so it didn't fall on her shoulders. But she'd get him if she had to. The fear she'd once had of him was gone. And Corban had sent her with enough COIL weaponry to take on an army.

Though it was standard protocol to recall COIL agents every few months to debrief or train, Li had remained in the field. Over the last two years since Gilgal, Li had weathered a couple dozen missions across Eastern Asia, some with other COIL agents and some as a solo operative. Briefly and rarely, she made face-to-face contact with a COIL superior, like Corban. Such was the demand for dedicated men and women of God.

Receiving messages from Patrick Gibson from time to time—that handsome operative with the leg brace—had been a selfish delight she craved even now. Twice, he'd saved her life in the Coral Sea, and she'd dreamed of a moment when, if God willed it, Patrick could see what a strong woman she'd become.

But Corban had been less than helpful to connect her with Patrick Gibson—or whatever his real name was. If ever there were a time for her and Patrick to reunite, it was now—for the capture of Niles, who'd left scars on them both. Yet once again, she was alone. This time, her orders were to wait offshore of a communist country, anchored far enough away to seem disconnected but close enough to respond—if the team had no other option. She'd remained silent, so no one but Corban knew she'd been there for several days.

Finally, the team of three emerged from the clinic. The sea was relatively calm, but her vision was still interrupted by the rolling of the boat on the surface. However, she glimpsed two of the COIL men each carrying a body. One was in the arms of Bruce, the larger of the Lavers brothers she'd heard about, and over the shoulder of the third was another person. Li looked at the ink she'd written on her wrist to remind herself of the radio transmission. They'd called this newcomer Dirk. If he were indeed a COIL operative, as far as she knew, he was no one Li had worked with—someone with a handlebar mustache, the radio had mentioned.

The team moved down to the shoreline and into the surf to avoid confrontation with Sankaddan troops, but from Li's vantage point, their situation was hopeless—more so now in the daylight. A truckload of armed troops was driving up the road toward the clinic, and those soldiers would pass within sight of the COIL team hustling up the beach toward the sailboat.

"Dirk, stop moving!" a young man's voice warned over the radio. Li guessed it came from the other speedboat, which had the same view as she did. "You can't reach the boat! There are gunmen above you! Over."

The warning came too late. Li grit her teeth as she prayed

for the safety of the team and the two men they carried. The soldiers spotted them on the shoreline. The truck halted for them to pile out and give chase. Li breathed with relief that the soldiers didn't open fire; rather, the Zalzunian troops seemed intent on taking prisoners. A prisoner in Zalzuna? According to reports she'd heard, death would be better than facing Niles in an interrogation room.

In the confusion, Li couldn't see who was who right away from her distance, but she could see that the three COIL men were forced to split up. Two continued toward the sailboat, but the one with a man over his shoulder turned and hurried down the coast, east toward the cliffs in the opposite direction. If he reached the cliffs, he'd be boxed in, and unlike most COIL infiltration teams, these didn't seem to have any NL-series weapons to tranquilize the enemy.

The Predator speedboat engines rumbled to life and sped toward the sailboat and the two men on foot. They were moving fast enough that they could actually escape the soldiers—if the speedboat made it there in time. Those two looked like the Lavers brothers. Which meant the third was the one called Dirk.

Li hit redial on her sat-phone and Corban picked up on the first ring.

"You wanted me to call you if I felt I needed to make contact, Boss." Her finger hovered over the boat's starter. "One of our own, a guy they call Dirk, is about to get cornered by Zalzunian troops. He has a man over his shoulder, and everyone else is preoccupied for evac."

"Dirk, you say?" Corban cleared his throat. "Okay, that'd be . . . Dirk Salverskein. Yes, he's one of ours. If you think you have to, make contact, Li. I don't know who Dirk has over his shoulder, but if Dirk has him, he's someone important. Do what you have to. Dirk mustn't be captured. Make your move, Li."

"I'm on it."

"And Li?"

"Yeah, Boss?"

"This Dirk is an old friend of yours. Stay safe!"

Hanging up the phone, Li pushed the starter. Twin engines vibrated the small speedboat. Thrusting the throttle forward, and with a whip of the wheel, she pointed the bow at the island where she planned to intercept Dirk and his burden. Before the boat was up to full speed, she turned on the autopilot and lunged into the cabin where she'd arranged several non-lethal COIL carbines for such an emergency. By the dimness of the cabin's tinted windows, she strapped on a bulletproof vest. With trembling hands, she checked the two magazines, then slung a rifle over each shoulder.

When she reached the cockpit and stepped to the helm, she resumed manual control. Turning east a little, she circled around until she could put a small peninsula between her and the soldiers. For a moment, she couldn't see Dirk. The cliffs spanned high on her right as she raced through the surf parallel to the shoreline. As long as the other speedboat was doing its job . . .

Suddenly, Li remembered what Corban had said—that Dirk was an old friend. That was an oddly distracting piece of information. And it had sounded almost like a warning. Who in her past could he be? Perhaps one of the COIL agents who'd trained her in the early years in Hong Kong? That was unlikely. Most of those men were Chinese. Dirk, at least from this distance, seemed to be European, and quite tall.

She emerged from around the peninsula the instant Dirk and his load reached the end of their path along the shore. Li acknowledged him out of the corner of her eye, then flipped the throttle down. The boat lurched as it slowed drastically, and it would've thrown her forward if she hadn't been expecting the momentum shift. The shore was only twenty feet away, and the surf was bound to wash her into the rocks if she stayed there too long.

Climbing from the cockpit, she bounded onto the bow as it rocked.

"Swim for it!" she yelled at Dirk, close enough now to see the man's overgrown mustache. "Come on! You've got sixty seconds!"

Before she finished speaking, he splashed into the water toward her. Li didn't have a chance to watch or help him as five soldiers onshore opened fire seventy yards away. They obviously planned to kill whomever they couldn't capture.

The zip of assault rifle rounds made Li crouch on the bow to make herself a smaller target, but she found herself standing again an instant later, her own NL rifles firing tranquilizer pellets at a rate of six hundred rounds per minute. With a five-hundred-round magazine in each carbine, she had the enemy outgunned as they ran toward her and fired with thirty-round AK-47s.

But they had live ammunition, a fact that Li was forced to remember as two rounds thumped into the fiberglass hull at her feet.

Continuing to fire in short bursts as she'd been trained to

do, she saw two of the enemy go down, tranquilized for twenty minutes by the pellets' toxic vapor. Splashing against the hull told her Dirk was nearly aboard, but she couldn't help him while she was laying down cover fire.

The remaining soldiers backed down the shoreline, away from her and their own fallen comrades. Another fell, and the final two turned and ran away.

"Hang on!" a man's voice warned. Li glanced back at the man Dirk now at the helm. "I'm getting us out of here!"

"Punch it!" she screamed, her mouth going dry at the sight of an RPG launcher in the hands of the soldiers onshore. Kneeling on the bow, she welcomed the feel of the horsepower whisking them back out to sea. A grenade exploded in their wake, but the boat was quickly out of range.

To the west, the Predator speedboat glided across the surface on a southern heading. Li counted the people on deck and guessed they'd taken on the Lavers brothers, Horatio, and the one called Jasper, who'd evidently abandoned his sailboat altogether.

A small fleet of Greek navy ships appeared on the horizon to the northwest, which gave Li satisfaction. That was her doing through Corban. The citizens of Zalzuna would have immense need of humanitarian aid when the volcano soon erupted and overwhelmed the three cities on the island. No doubt, Interpol agents were coming as well, intent on arresting Niles. Li hoped he didn't escape by blending in with the islanders. She'd search the refugee ships herself if no word of his arrest came soon. The Zalzunian troops would have questions to answer themselves as they raced about with loaded weapons instead of aiding their own people.

"Seems like every time we meet," the man said at the helm behind her, "I'm reminded of how God's timing is meant to make me trust Him more."

That voice!

Li turned slowly and stared at the mustached man in the cockpit. He smiled as he leaned into the bumps of waves against the hull. She had to look down at his left leg to see the brace before she believed it was really him.

"*Patrick!*" Her breath caught and she sat down on the bow to keep from falling over—instead of rushing into his arms like she wanted to, like she'd dreamt of doing. "You're . . . *here!*"

"You came for me." He kept grinning. "That's just what a real partner would do!"

"It was the least I could do after all you did for me." Li looked down at her legs, not trusting them yet. "I've never been in a firefight like that before. I'm still shaking."

"Well, I couldn't have done better myself. Come on." Nathan gestured to her. "Did you see who I found onshore? He was up to his old tricks."

Crawling off the bow, she stood when she reached the cockpit. Someone lay on the floor. The familiar face belonged to Trevor Niles. He stirred as if waking from a tranquilizer.

"You know, Patrick, this isn't the first time you've caught Niles."

"All the more reason for you to help me secure him. Do you have any—"

Raising an NL-3 muzzle, Li fired a few pellets at Niles' chest. The man settled back into a deep sleep.

"That'll hold him until you get some flex-cuffs on him."

"Right." He sighed, his eyes on her face. "It's good to see you, Li. This is long overdue."

"I'm not . . ." Li felt a sob in her throat. "I'm not going to let you just walk out of my life again. It's been *two years!*"

"We'll work something out." He winked, that same confidence in his eyes she remembered so well. "Corban'll just have to understand."

She went to him and he wrapped his arms around her.

Two months later . . .

Like a statue, Brad Alden stood on the pitcher's mound. The stadium was packed. They were there for him—the nineteen-year-old pitcher in the Major League game.

He glanced at third base. That runner would never get home. Brad shook his head at the runner on first base. That one would never touch second. Then he focused on the batter, a professional of thirteen years. But Brad already knew the man couldn't handle a change-up pitch.

"Strike 'em out, Brad!" a woman yelled.

Brad knew that voice. It was Lacy. And Walter sat beside her. He'd flown out for the game, bringing Horatio with him. Though Brad's mother was there, too, his dad was preparing a sermon for the Sunday service. That's what really mattered, and Brad was proud to know his father knew his priorities— and that he'd taught them to his son.

Far in the back of the stands, a tall man stood near the top. Brad could see only his silhouette, but he knew who it was, and he knew the man had a handlebar mustache. He knew why he was there, too. It wasn't to watch Brad pitch; Brad hadn't signed any lengthy ball contracts for a reason.

His baseball career was already over, though not because of lack of skill. It was a matter of priorities. Brad had seen the suffering. He'd waded through a part of humanity that much of the world turned a blind eye toward.

For Brad, a lifestyle that pleased only himself would never suffice again. He was joining Dirk's side—or whatever the operative's real name was. And somewhere out there, the Lavers brothers, Heather, and Jasper were also serving God to the utmost.

Just one more pitch.

Brad cracked his neck to the left, then to the right . . . the wind-up . . . and . . . the pitch!

As with all of my novels, I desire to draw attention to the Persecuted Church worldwide, and the ministries that serve them. We are thankful to be able to donate a portion from the sale of *The COIL Series* books to these ministries. May God be glorified.

In this book, I wish to introduce you to Vision Beyond Borders. The following info is excerpted from the Vision Beyond Borders (VBB) website. Visit them at https://visionbeyondborders.org/ to read testimonies and more information about their many ministries.

VBB has been committed to meeting needs of hurting people for over 20 years. In 1984 at the age of 21, Patrick Klein…began a ministry…taking Bibles into China and other parts of Asia. The ministry gradually grew and began work in other countries outside of Asia. In 2001, the name was changed to Vision Beyond Borders, better describing the work it does throughout the world.

The goal of the ministry is to serve the worldwide church by providing necessary tools and training for the local people to fulfill Christ's "Great Commission" in their own countries. This is done by supplying them with native language Bibles, training materials, seeds, clothing, medical supplies, prayer teams, and evangelism to children. Last year alone, VBB helped to ship and deliver over 96,000 Bibles to numerous countries in all types of languages.

~~*~*~*~*~*

You can find a copy of *By Faith Alone: Confessions of a Bible Smuggler*, by Patrick Klein, Founder of Vision Beyond Borders, at: http://charitylafountain.wix.com/by-faith-alone.

~

God's Word for God's People – Bible Delivery Ministry

Since its establishment, Vision Beyond Borders has helped distribute over 1 million Bibles worldwide. There is truly no greater gift we can give to people than the gift of God's Word in their own language. For many people, however, the hope of owning their own Bible seems impossible.

In China, believers often share one copy of the Bible. Each person receives a page, memorizes that page, then gathers together again to exchange their Bible portions. In most Muslim countries, Christians risk imprisonment and/or death for sharing copies of God's Word.

We believe it is <u>imperative to share the message of hope and love</u> with the world! Where Bibles are illegal, this means "smuggling" them into these countries to deliver them to the local Christians. We do so <u>with short-term mission teams who volunteer</u> to go with a team leader. We then carry the Bibles through customs.

We believe we have a responsibility, a command to take the Gospel to the whole world. How can we do that without the authority of the Scriptures? <u>Where God's law and man's law conflict, we will follow God's law.</u> Jesus himself was often commanded to stop preaching. The disciples were often jailed for their preaching. They chose to follow God's laws.

<u>William Tyndale smuggled out pages of the Bibles</u> in bales of cotton, translating them into <u>the first, English-language Bibles.</u>

Tyndale's work of translating Scripture so that we may now read it freely was all done "illegally." Tyndale learned the Hebrew language and <u>translated the entire Bible while in hiding</u>. When he was finished, <u>he was arrested, imprisoned, tried, and convicted.</u> He was strangled and then burnt at the stake in the prison yard on October 6, 1536. <u>His last words were, *"Lord, open the king of England's eyes."* This prayer was answered</u> three years later when King Henry VIII published the English "Great Bible" in 1539.

We must be willing to submit to every authority in our lives, as the Word asks; but also to submit to God when God's law and man's law contradict, remaining obedient to Him alone.

Short Term Missions Trips

VBB organizes <u>year-round short term missions trips</u> for different purposes, including: Bible Delivery, Refugee Camp visits, Vision for Women trips, and Vision for Children, which include visits to orphanages. For more information or to sign up for a trip, see the schedule at <u>https://visionbeyondborders.org/trips/</u>.

Other ministries of Vision Beyond Borders

*The Word in Pictures – Flannel Graph Ministry Flannel graphs were created to communicate the Gospel and history of the Bible. Over 2,000 children's workers have been trained in Vietnam; many of the trained workers use these tools to reach children with the Gospel. In one area of Vietnam there are over 90,000 Christian children. The flannels are used to help instruct them. Get the free flyer: https://visionbeyondborders.org/ministries/flannel-graphs/.

*Tape Players Over the past 14 years, VBB has delivered over 10,000 hand-wind tape players around the world to help reach remote villages with the Gospel. Since these players are hand-wound and don't need batteries or electricity, they are especially useful in villages where people are illiterate.

We are currently in need of 8,000-10,000 additional players for use in Nepal, East India, Vietnam, Laos, and Burma.

One report said over 1,500 people had come to Christ through 16 hand-wind tape players in central Nepal. There've been reports of whole villages becoming Christians from one player.

VBB has partnered with Global Recordings to bring the Gospel on tape to many people who have never heard of Jesus Christ and His gift of salvation in their native language. For more info about the hand-wind tape players, email info@visionbeyondborders.org.

*Vision for Children seeks to match poverty-stricken, orphaned children with sponsors to meet each child's physical, medical, educational, and spiritual needs.

Over the years, the program has grown tremendously, extending the Lord's hand of love and provision to some of the poorest countries in Southeast Asia. We are now working to find sponsors for children in 6 areas of Nepal and throughout India and Burma.

Many children we serve have been found on the streets after being abandoned or were left at the orphanages because their parents were too poor to feed them. To read more or to sponsor a child: https://visionbeyondborders.org/ministries/vision-for-children/.

*Rescuing Women from Slavery and Sex Trafficking - Vision for Women is working in some of the world's poorest countries to meet the spiritual and physical needs of our sisters in Christ.

Little value is placed on women and girls in these countries where they are sold into sex-slavery by members of their own families. In Nepal alone, an estimated 500,000 women and girls have been sold into sex-slavery to work in the brothels of India.

Please commit to praying with us that God will continue to show us how to effectively reach the women in these and other countries with His love and to share the saving knowledge of Jesus Christ as we work to meet their needs. Download a free prayer guide at https://visionbeyondborders.org/ministries/vision-for-women/.

*The Karen – The Karen, the largest and oldest indigenous tribe in Burma (Myanmar), and other ethnic tribes are being systematically exterminated by a ruthless military dictatorship. Many of the ethnic minorities in Burma are Christian, in a predominantly Buddhist society, and are oppressed and persecuted for their faith. Watch this video documentary about The Karen people at: https://visionbeyondborders.org/ministries/the-karen/.

*Seed Ministry – VBB purchased and distributed over 30 milli on packs of seeds around the world since 2000. We have had the opportunity to empower orphans, widows, and poor villagers to feed themselves; provide for basic necessities; and become self-supporting. This vision to plant food crops has decreased opium production as vegetable crops replace them in the fields. Visit https://visionbeyondborders.org/ministries/seeds/ for more info.

*Vision for Pastors - The Vision for Pastors program provides an opportunity to support a pastor for as little as $25.00 per month. https://visionbeyondborders.org/ministries/vision-for-pastors/

*Medical Funds Ministry - If we can take care of physical needs in people's lives, doors open for us to meet their spiritual needs as well. Visit https://visionbeyondborders.org/ministries/medical-funds/.

VBB Special Ministries

*VBB <u>delivers medicine and medical supplies and sponsors medical teams who provide free treatment</u> in remote villages, schools, and orphanages.

*VBB <u>partners with other ministries to improve living conditions</u> by projects including: drilling wells, constructing toilets, building schools, churches, and orphanages, helping Christians start small businesses to become self-sufficient.

*<u>Clothe the Naked</u> – Each year, VBB <u>volunteers carry tens of thousands of pounds of clothing</u> to children and families in more than 20 countries. VBB has also shipped over 200,000 pounds of clothing around the world.

*<u>Give Rest to the Weary</u> – In many countries, extreme poverty drives parents to leave their children in the streets to face sickness, prostitution, and possible death. There are kind-hearted adults with a mission to make a difference. They provide a safe place for these children. VBB <u>finds sponsors to help these children's homes</u>.

*VBB <u>sponsored two rickshaws</u> to be used in S. Nepal. The rickshaws provided work for families. Now 15 families are using additional rickshaws. Change is taking place.

<u>https://visionbeyondborders.org/ministries/special-ministry/</u>

~

Note from the Author

To learn more about <u>Vision Beyond Borders</u>, to <u>watch a short video</u>, to <u>see current project needs</u>, or to <u>schedule a trip to deliver Bibles or serve the needy</u>, visit: <u>https://visionbeyondborders.org/</u>. Follow them on Twitter @VBB__. May the Lord bless each of us with His wisdom and direction in how we can be part of this God-honoring ministry. Thank you for reading.

Acknowledgements

My thanks to Dee, Jamie, and Ed
for their help in the lengthy
editing and proofreading process—
an adventure all its own!
And to my reviewers,
who help so much to get the word out!

ABOUT THE AUTHOR

D.I. Telbat desires to honor the Lord with his life and writing. Many of his books focus on persecuted Christians worldwide—their sacrifice, their suffering, and their rescues.

After studying writing in school, David worked for a time in the newspaper field, but he is now doing what he loves most: writing and Christian ministry.

On his Telbat's Tablet website/blog, David Telbat offers FREE, clean, weekly Christian adventure and suspense short stories, or related posts, which include his novel news, author reflections, book reviews, recent research, and occasional challenges to today's Christian. You'll also find links to his Paperbacks, eBooks, Audiobooks, and his complete bio. Subscribe to his blog at ditelbat.com to receive his posts in your inbox (1ce/week), as well as exclusive gifts & discounts.

Visit D.I. Telbat's Amazon Author Central page at http://viewAuthor.at/AmazonAuthorPg, and his *COIL Series* page at https://www.smashwords.com/books/byseries/5645. You can also follow him on Twitter, @DITelbat.

Please leave your comments wherever you bought this book. Reviews tremendously help authors, and David Telbat would love to hear your thoughts. He takes reader reviews into consideration as he makes his future publishing plans.

Discounts are available to place paperback copies of D.I. Telbat books in church or prison/jail libraries. Contact Dee at ditelbat@gmail.com.